RUNNING DOWNWIND

ENDORSEMENTS

Running Downwind is an eloquently written story of love and loss that transports the reader back to the 1960s, an era marred by two heartbreaking tragic events. Personally wounded, two of Lewis's characters embark on a quest for healing and are providentially united as they search for answers to deep-rooted questions of faith. Readers will be both surprised and intrigued by the unexpected sequence of events that leads to the thrilling culmination of this beautiful novel.
—Taylor Moore, author of *Firestorm*

Excellent Christian romance for the lactose intolerant! Timothy Lewis charms with witty prose, unique and deeply relatable characters, and a rich Texas backdrop. Flee reality for a while with Running Downwind. It's a breath of fresh air.
—Leona Worcestor, award-winning screenwriter & actress

Talk about a GIFT! Tim truly has the knack of forcing readers to turn to the next chapter. Real life, relational characters inhabit every page of this intense story. Discover meaning, love, and dreams at the end of the rainbow. Tim puts you front and center of the JFK Assassination and UT Tower Shooting. Great people can be molded from the dark-

closet skeletons of their past. Life may be short, ending suddenly, so GO FOR IT! Make your dreams a reality. *Running Downwind* will encourage you to complete yourself!
—**Shannon Brooks**, Insurance Investments—Ranching, Life Coach, Volunteer Minister for Christ

Set in the 1960s, *Running Downwind* is a story of a man and a woman who experience heartbreak amid two national tragedies and still find a way to turn to God in their pain, find healing, and find one another. Tim Lewis shows us people can experience hope, forgiveness, and love in spite of the brokenness that comes from life circumstances and our own choices. This love story will draw you in with wit and humor and leave you grateful for how God can redeem each of our stories and bring people into our lives who help us heal and love us through the journey.
—**Emily Wood**, Director of Women's Ministry at First Presbyterian Church of Amarillo

It was an ordinary Monday on the University of Texas campus, when I suddenly heard gunshots and watched the glass door explode in front of me. I can still hear the bullets. Still see people rushing to find cover. The Tower shooting remains embedded in my mind to this very day. Tim Lewis weaves this tragic event with the earlier killing of JFK to tell the story of two people forever changed by these happenings. Brought together amidst sorrow and pain, their healing and redemption provide a beautiful story. Tim captures the essence of the 1960s in his remarkable new novel.
—**Carolyn Hinton Canon,** eyewitness to the University of Texas shooting.

Bestselling author Timothy Lewis brings us another spellbinding love story in the spirit of his debut novel *Forever Friday*. *Running Downwind* transports us to the

tumultuous 1960s with plot twists that will keep the reader turning pages to see what happens next. Lewis writes like some of the best romance novelists of our time but with an intriguing spiritual dimension.
—**Will Vaus**, author of *My Journey with C. S. Lewis & Other Companions*

RUNNING DOWNWIND

TIMOTHY LEWIS

A Christian Company
ElkLakePublishingInc.com

COPYRIGHT NOTICE

Running Downwind

First edition. Copyright © 2022 by Timothy Lewis. The information contained in this book is the intellectual property of Timothy Lewis and is governed by United States and International copyright laws. All rights reserved. No part of this publication, either text or image, may be used for any purpose other than personal use. Therefore, reproduction, modification, storage in a retrieval system, or retransmission, in any form or by any means, electronic, mechanical, or otherwise, for reasons other than personal use, except for brief quotations for reviews or articles and promotions, is strictly prohibited without prior written permission by the publisher.

This is a work of fiction. Apart from well-known people, events, and locales that figure into the narrative, all names, characters, places, and incidents are products of the author's imagination or are used fictitiously.

Cover and Interior Design: Lana Ziegler, Derinda Babcock, Deb Haggerty

Editor(s): Cristel Phelps, Deb Haggerty

PUBLISHED BY: Elk Lake Publishing, Inc., 35 Dogwood Drive, Plymouth, MA 02360, 2022

Library Cataloging Data

Names: Lewis, Timothy (Timothy Lewis)

Running Downwind / Timothy Lewis

384 p. 23cm × 15cm (9in × 6 in.)

ISBN-13: 978-1-64949-756-7 (paperback) | 978-1-64949-758-1 (trade hardcover) | 978-1-64949-759-8 (trade paperback) | 978-1-64949-760-4 (e-book)

Key Words: 1960s; JFK Assassination; Questions of Faith; Romance; Loss, University of Texas Tower Shooting; Hope

Library of Congress Control Number: 2022948784

DEDICATION

To my mother,
Who loved the seashore.

To my father,
Who followed her there.

And to the Reverend Billy Graham,
Whom I'll one day meet atop the streets of gold!

ACKNOWLEDGMENTS

As a child of the 1960s, the historical events herein became the early spiritual and social bookmarks of my own life story. However, retelling the period in a unique way required the help of not only a few fictional characters, but real folks too.

Without a great publishing team, *Running Downwind* would continue to languish inside my laptop. A huge thank you to publisher, Deb Haggerty, who initially read the manuscript and then believed in the story. And to the Managing Editor for Fiction, Cristel Phelps, who with much expertise and good humor, took my prose and polished it to a high sheen. Finally, I can't forget Derinda Babcock and Lana Ziegler, cover designers and graphic artists extraordinaire.

Along the way, my beta readers kept my writing sharp with knowledgeable hearts and fresh eyes. Special thanks to the Kathryn Circle of the Claude, Texas, Methodist Church, John Clark, Steve Kersh, Mike Nichols, Natalie Nichols, Chris Ferguson, Millie Otwell, Susie Culver, Rick Culver, Sally Kinsey, Ned Jacklin, Deb Jacklin, Peggy Pollard, Jo Cooper, Dwaina Pitts, Claire Longstreth, Ann Root, and Terry Beasley.

To be honest, without the love and support of my wife, Dinah, I'd still be stuck on chapter one. She's my

TIMOTHY LEWIS first editor, toughest reader, brightest "laugher," and best listener—not always in that particular order.

Most of all I thank God, the author, editor, designer, and publisher of the pages we turn into ...

Life!

It is easy to acknowledge, but almost impossible to realize for long, that we are mirrors whose brightness, if we are bright, is wholly derived from the sun that shines upon us.

C.S. Lewis, *The Four Loves*

PROLOGUE

OCTOBER 1967

Every day, just before sunrise, he watched for the Lady Who Walked on the Sea.

Mick McFarland sat up on the side of his bed. The clammy, predawn darkness argued he'd earned the right to hide beneath the sheets until noon, especially since most celebrities were allergic to morning. But sleep was no longer his friend, his pillow a sweaty stranger. So, after slipping on a pair of cutoffs, he exited his small bungalow and padded between the rippled sand dunes onto the wide beach.

Yesterday, Mick thought he'd glimpsed the Lady's shadowy form hovering atop the distant waves, her head down, eyes in frantic search for the crude mirror she'd lost over five hundred years ago—bits of polished iron pyrite attached in mosaic fashion to heavy slate. Legend promised that whoever found a piece of the mirror discovered love that very hour. Yet nothing shimmered amongst the ribbon of washed-up shells, not even a barnacled glass shard.

Today, as first-light's delicate fingers reached over the horizon, the cavern that had replaced his heart screamed the truth: *The Lady's merely a seabird in search of breakfast. Or mist mixed with imagination.*

He dug his toes into the sand.

You know what's real, the cavern scolded. *The legend's a fairy tale, especially the love part. Any mirror made with iron rusts away. Stop lying to yourself.*

Why?

Mick shoved his hands into his pockets. He *loved* a good lie—had even lived a better one. Actors made the best liars. Everyone knew that.

A tear escaped down his cheek, even though no audience saw it.

After the nightmare you've experienced, there are no real tears left. You know how you are and will always be.

Mick sighed, then spoke in surrendered agreement. "I'm a gullible man plagued with emotion. My condition is a disease, embarrassing and incurable."

Which is exactly why Julia loved you, though she should've known better.

"Loved?"

Cherie too.

Stepping into ankle deep surf, Mick swallowed hard, fighting off a thousand unborn echoes of what could've been. "I will always love you," Cherie had said over and over, her voice fading into silence beneath a blazing August sky.

He studied the pallid horizon, his words a salty whisper. "If only I could've felt the same toward her. If only God had—"

Saved you from yourself?

Mick gazed heavenward, the brightest stars still visible. Ten weeks ago, he'd arrived uninvited on this lonely strip of sand called Padre. As beautiful and unforgiving as the surrounding Gulf of Mexico, this barrier island just off the southern Texas shore was the site of hundreds of shipwrecks ... including his own.

RUNNING DOWNWIND

Insistent, the cavern mocked how he'd lost both women in scarcely over a year. Refusing to listen, he pressed all thoughts toward finding the Lady.

His final hope.

A wavelet slapped Mick's bare ankles, turning his attention toward the incoming tide.

No Lady this morning. No connection. Told you.

Before the hurricane, he would've delivered a witty comeback. Even after Cherie's death, he offered a few clever outbursts of wry humor. Julia would roll her eyes and smile. Once, she accused him of "selective buffoonery." They'd both laughed out loud.

Now the smiles were gone. The laughter too.

Turning to leave, something caught his eye. Shiny. Tumbling in the surf. The wavelet retreated, leaving an egg-sized piece of brilliant mosaic dots.

Could it be?

"Julia." Fresh tears wet his face. "Can you ever forgive me?"

As if stumbling upon timeless treasure, Mick picked up the mirror-like piece and nestled it within the cup of his palms. He examined each reflective facet, then fixed his eyes upon the glowing horizon ...

And waited.

CHAPTER 1

Fifteen months earlier

August 1, 1966

The University of Texas

"There's a sniper on top of the Tower!"

The frantic scream burst outside an open window, reverberating through the vacant concert hall. Mick slid off the piano bench and stood.

What are you doing? You promised yourself this wouldn't happen.

"Relax." Ramona remained seated. "A student in guerilla theater is protesting the Vietnam War. Yesterday, the undergrad drama majors joined the fray."

Mick raised on tiptoes, peering over the edge of the orchestra pit. "Guess everyone's gone to lunch."

"The perfect time to finish my audition." She patted the empty side of the bench. "You play. I sing. You recommend me to your agent."

"But the scream sounded so ... so real. I was up there several hours ago."

"The tower?"

"That view of the city is one of the few things I'll get up early to see when I come home. Helps me stay sane when I'm away."

Ramona laughed. "Tony Award winner, Mick McFarland, was fooled by a squealing freshman. Has a week back in Austin made you naïve?"

Thinking he'd heard a distant commotion, Mick didn't reply. But now ...

Silence.

He sat next to Ramona.

You know why you agreed to meet with her.

Mick regretted his fascination with alluring women. The fragrant perfume combined with subtle scents of hairspray and makeup. Before rediscovering Cherie, he'd helplessly fall under their siren song, convincing himself they cared about—

Distinction and dollar signs. Walk out of the hall. Cherie will never know.

Ramona nudged closer. "About my voice?" She touched his hand, outlining the finger that would wear a wedding band by Christmas. "Should I move to New York?"

Mick edged sideways.

Remind this woman you're engaged.

Every newspaper in the country carried the story. During Mick's performance here two nights ago, he'd called his fiancée on stage to join him singing *People Will Say We're in Love*. Cherie felt ill, yet sang anyway, the entire house jumping to their feet.

"We could be Manhattan neighbors." Ramona stroked Mick's wrist.

"Nope. She'll borrow way too much sugar."

He wished Cherie had stayed for the after-show autograph party, when he was coerced into the current session at Hogg Auditorium.

You should've politely declined.

Except Ramona was the daughter of Senator Al Montgomery, Mick's lawyer-father's wealthiest client.

RUNNING DOWNWIND

Beauty, politics, and money. A dangerous combination.

Ramona continued. "What about Midtown apartments near the theater district. Are they expensive?"

"What Kind of Fool Am I," punched Mick's thoughts, another show tune from his latest repertoire, the parody comical. He scooted to the far edge of the bench.

She followed and grabbed his arm, repositioning herself more dangerously than before. "Mickey. Don't you think I'm ready for Broadway? I'm sure there's room for another big star. Don't you, Mickey?"

He didn't answer. Didn't appreciate her calling him Mickey, the endearment belonging exclusively to Cherie.

Ask her to sing, "The Lady Is a Tramp."

"Now that's funny," Mick blurted.

"Funny?" Ramona released his arm. "You think my career's a joke?"

Outside, what sounded like engine backfire recoiled into a sharp rifle crack, followed by glass shattering, then more rounds. Gunfire mixed with screams.

"Hey," shouted a male voice. "Just been ankle-shot. Gal over there's been hit too. She's down. Somebody help."

"Stay here." Mick leaped out of the orchestra pit and raced up the aisle to the lobby. The madness was real, transpiring during wasted moments when ego dulled his senses with selfish pleasure. The guilt he'd feel would ensue soon enough, but he must help whoever was in trouble.

More shots echoed beyond the front entrance, followed by the piercing ricochet of lead blasting limestone. He dropped to the floor, his eardrums playing ping-pong with his pulse.

"Don't go out there," said a shaky female voice. "That man up there will shoot you."

Mick crawled toward the voice. Two coeds huddled behind a freestanding marquee advertising his benefit show from the previous night, as if a life-sized, cardboard cutout of *Mick McFarland* protected them from a madman. One of the girls began to cry.

Creeping closer, Mick wondered if they recognized him. The situation was dire, yet nothing made sense. A dream was the logical answer, the kind twisting normalcy into bizarre, familiar into frightening. When Mick experienced nightmares, his subconscious battled the inexplicable, forcing him awake. Yet ...

He'd not been asleep.

Staccato gunfire.

Another scream.

Reality squeezed Mick's guts, reality wrapped in foreboding, a sickening premonition of evil dancing with innocence.

Calm down. Pretend you're acting.

"A guy called for help," Mick heard himself say. "A girl's injured too."

"Please don't go out there." The student's plea was barely audible above the whimpers of her friend. "We'd just left acting class when a man on top of the tower leaned over the edge and ... he ... we ..." She swallowed hard. "We ran back here."

"Hey?" called the male voice. "Can anybody hear? Gunman's moved to the other side of the tower. Gal's still down. I can't stand. Call an ambulance."

"There's a phone in the box office." Mick fixed his eyes on the calmer student. "I need you to dial zero and ask for help. The campus operator knows what to do."

Her jaw dropped.

"Swallow your fear and make-believe you're acting. You can do it." Mick inched forward. "Stay close to the floor, below knee level." He'd heard the same *below knee level* direction during a staged gun fight. Surely the director researched bona fide survival tactics and knew his stuff. If this were a musical, the actors would sing and dance about the mayhem, then retreat to the safety of the green room for matinee munchies. "On hands and knees," Mick repeated for emphasis.

Since the building's front entrance was in the direct line of fire, he sprinted back through the hall. Ramona was gone. After spending his college years performing in the Hogg, Mick knew the rear exit was partially hidden from the tower's view. His routine back then was to step outside between scenes for a little fresh air that uncluttered his thoughts and helped him remember lines. He'd breathe deeply while gazing up toward the tower's west side. There was something majestic about bone-white stone against the clear Texas sky.

Need enough time to dash around the Hogg's far corner.

Mick habitually glanced skyward before bolting out the door. Maybe the maniac wouldn't notice.

A bullet whizzed past.

"Got something against red hair and freckles?" Mick hoped the joke would keep him from losing the caffeine he'd swallowed for breakfast.

He dove around the corner.

"Missed me, you moron."

Dropping to a knee, he tossed everything north of his toenails. Fear had strange side effects, especially on an overactive gag reflex, but humor made anything bearable. His mistake was pausing to look up when he should've been running.

Running like the halfback-hero his father wanted in a son.

Running away from temptation like a faithful fiancé.

Instead, he wiped coffee-flavored bile on his shirt sleeve and wondered if he had the guts to do the right thing.

Make your father proud.

"There's a second time for everything."

Leaning against the Hogg, Mick sucked in a lungful of hill country heat. His father, Ed McFarland, was a former All-American athlete who mastered any challenge. As a star Longhorn fullback, his stocky, muscular legs relentlessly pounded at the opposing team's defense, wearing them down until he ran at will. He now applied the same technique to his law practice, gradually breaking apart the strategy and nerve of opposing council. When Mick won the Tony, his old man's pride seemed genuine ... for a week. He'd popped no more buttons since.

An ambulance siren wailed several blocks away.

Good girls. They'd located the phone.

"Fella's gone again," the male voice shouted. "He'll be back soon. Can't tell if the gal's alive. If she moves, he'll finish her."

Mick crept around the front of the Hogg and hid behind a low-hanging cedar. The hollering man managed to drag himself behind a fat live oak, his blood smeared snaillike across the hot sidewalk.

"Help's on the way," Mick called, still considering his options. When playing little league baseball, he'd been a poor batter. To compensate, he learned to bunt. Mick was swift enough to make it to first base in time to toe the bag. The distance from the cedar to the oak was similar.

Bottom of the ninth. Two outs. Your turn at the plate.

Right.

With a little luck, he'd reach the oak without the sniper ending his game.

Mick lunged forward, but Lady Luck had a different strategy. Perhaps she didn't appreciate the skill involved in successful bunting. Upon reaching the oak, he felt as if he'd grabbed a live wire. Electric fire seared the length of his left arm, ascending into his shoulder. He winced and tumbled to the ground, retching up his final sip of breakfast. The thought of seeing his own blood made him dizzy, though there was only a trickle. The bullet grazed a path just above his elbow.

"Nicked your funny bone, did he?"

Mick nodded. The injured man looked as though he'd stepped out of a Saturday afternoon western, complete with spurs and a sweat-stained hat. Drugstore cowboys in Austin were as common as pretty girls. This fellow could've ridden in off the Chisholm Trail.

"Lowlife shot me in the ankle." The cowboy held up a bloody leather boot, poking his index finger through the bullet hole. "Ruined a fine pair of handmades. Can't hang on 'til the buzzer with a busted ankle."

"You ride the rodeo circuit?" Mick tried to ignore his throbbing arm.

"Bulls."

"Are they as mean as they look?" An absurd question, but asking it somehow bolstered Mick's courage.

"Let's just say I live eight seconds at a time."

Mick eyed a bloody bandana wrapped around the man's ankle, wondering if the tower shooter had one tied over his nose and mouth like an outlaw in a movie. "Guess that's why they're red," he muttered.

"Whad'ya say?" The cowboy dug a snuff tin from his shirt pocket.

"Nothing important." Mick rubbed his elbow and cringed.

"Hurts, don't it?"

"The pain's tolerable," he lied, thinking he might pass out. "I just need to sit here a minute."

The man grunted, then took a large pinch and packed his lower lip. "Minute's about up. Not much time before the shooter makes it back to this side of the tower. Somebody needs to return fire, send him on through the wide gate."

"Gate?"

"Hell's gate. Ain't that the wide one?"

"I wouldn't know."

"Since this fellow's keen on murdering innocent folks, Jesus won't be lifting the latch."

Mick cringed. The last thing he needed was some folksy bull rider spouting simplistic religious views during the onslaught of a madman. Mick believed in God's existence. Beyond that, a person's degree of faith was complicated and a sore subject, one he and Cherie fiercely argued.

More shots echoed in the distance.

The cowboy cocked his hat. "Give me a 30-30 with a scope, and I'd be honored to send the gutless coward to his final destination. First, we need to help that gal over yonder."

The girl!

During the fog of survival, Mick shifted focus to himself. He stood and wobbled, still dizzy from the pain.

"Hold on there, pard. Wait 'til you're ready. A dead man can't save nobody."

"I'm fine."

The man spat again and pointed. "Best bet is to drag her into the flowerbed yonder, behind that hedge. Get you both outta sight." He glanced at Mick. "Gal's a good fifty yards, then another ten to the hedge. You still okay?"

"Better than her."

"Yeah, sidewalk's a real britches burner, and that dress ain't very thick." He spewed a dark stream of tobacco juice toward the tower. "I'll holler when I see the shooter."

Third spat's the charm.

Mick rushed toward the fallen coed, who lay with her back toward him. Plaid summer dress, bare arms and legs sprawled into a lifeless clump. Blood seeped from underneath her left shoulder combining with a tangle of strawberry blonde hair.

Hair—same color and length as Cherie's.

Dress—same color and length as—

No.

Oh, God, please—

No!

Without warning, foreboding burst into unfathomable. Fighting off more dizziness, Mick's ears rang.

"Hey, pard. Crazy fool's coming back."

Mick scooped Cherie into his arms and headed for the hedge, the front of her dress drenched in blood.

Crack!

A bullet whizzed past.

Ten feet until safety.

You'll never make it.

Three feet.

Another shot.

"Aaugh!"

Ducking behind the dense hedge, horrendous pain pierced Mick's right leg. Easing Cherie onto soft earth, he again battled dizziness. This time he didn't wretch. His brain ordered him to press an ear against Cherie's chest, listen for a heartbeat. However, the ringing made it impossible to hear. He gently blew the hair out of her face. Her eyes remained closed.

"Hey?" the cowboy called. "You two all right? Anybody hit?"

Mick didn't shout a reply in case the madman could hear. They were hidden from view, however manicured leaves wouldn't stop a BB, much less a high-powered bullet. Placing his cheek against Cherie's mouth and nose, he detected a slight breath, a murmur perhaps. "Cherie. Please wake up."

A sudden volley of gunfire echoed from every direction, followed by off-key choruses of nearby ambulance sirens.

"Woo-hoo. Hey? Folks are firing back. Must've gone home and fetched their deer rifles."

The shooting lasted a few minutes, ending in an abrupt calm. Only the sirens resumed.

"Cherie. Can you hear me? The ambulance will be here soon."

She released a breathy moan, her eyes still closed. "There's something ..." Her voice trailed off.

"What? Something you need?"

She shook her head. "Something ... you should ... know."

"Please don't talk," Mick replied, relieved she was alive. "Just breathe."

Struggling for air, she tried to say more.

"Save your strength." He stroked her cheek.

Cherie opened her mouth. "That night in New York ... when ... we—"

Mick placed a gentle finger over her lips.

She pushed his hand away.

"That's all in the past," he pleaded. "Port wine is strong stuff."

Cherie frowned.

"And I'm a weak man."

Her frown melted into a faint smile. "I'm ... weaker ... woman."

"Not true." Mick forearmed his sweaty brow and swallowed. Cherie was the strongest woman he knew. He swallowed again, then continued. "You said God forgave us."

She nodded.

"Then no more worries. Right?"

"Mickey?"

RUNNING DOWNWIND

"Yes?"

"We're—"

"Gonna be fine. I promise."

Cherie moved her lips. No words came.

"Tell me later." Mick spoke tenderly. "Wait until then."

"No, Mickey. We're …" She coughed.

"Please, Cherie. When you're better. Don't talk until you're—"

"We're pregnant."

"What?" Sweat scalded Mick's eyes. His and Cherie's moment of reckless passion occurred two months prior on the night of their engagement. Since they weren't yet married, she suffered enormous guilt. Blaming herself, she'd almost ended their relationship the following day.

"Mickey?" Blood trickled out a corner of her mouth, her voice barely audible.

"Right here."

Cherie opened her eyes, her gaze penetrating deeper than any bullet.

"Mickey?"

"Yes."

"Never forget—"

"Don't talk that way. You'll be fine.

She coughed again, gasped for breath. More blood oozed from her mouth.

He wiped it with his shirttail.

"Never forget … your child." Cherie closed her eyes.

Instead of acting …

Mick McFarland cried.

CHAPTER 2

They remained hidden behind the hedge as more shooting erupted from both camps amidst the cowboy's warnings and cheers.

Minutes?

Hours?

Mick wasn't sure. Though Cherie kept slipping in and out of consciousness, he was positive she'd seen him cry. "I will ... always ... love you," she repeated in broken whispers until the ambulance arrived.

The bullet had passed through Mick's upper thigh without hitting bone. While the driver and an orderly attended to Cherie, Mick tied his shirt in tourniquet fashion. After placing Cherie onto a stretcher, they sped across campus to the frenzied emergency room at Brackenridge Hospital.

People crying.

Trails of red footprints.

Nurses and doctors slip-sliding through the melee.

"Room three," a commanding triage doctor stated behind a grim expression. Mick tried to stay at Cherie's side, but the doctor refused.

"I should be with her," Mick argued. He watched the stretcher disappear between double metal doors. "Please. I need to—"

"You *need* treatment. She needs surgery." The doctor ordered an intern to hand Mick a sterile gauze pad.

"Hold it against your wound." The intern pointed toward a congested hallway. "Wait over there."

Instead, Mick crept behind a large planter. When the intern disappeared into a crowd of newly wounded, Mick limped through the double doors to room three. A young nurse frantically changed the bedding.

"Have they taken her to surgery?" Mick asked.

The nurse extended a pale glance. "Sir ... you shouldn't be in here."

"I'm looking for the woman they just brought to this room."

"You must return to the lobby."

Mick stepped toward the nurse. "Her name is Cherie."

"I said you must—"

"Cherie Dennis."

The nurse paused and faced him. "You should check with the front desk."

"Is she in surgery?"

"I'm not sure."

"But you can find out."

"Today, that's impossible."

"Please try. I'm her fiancé."

Turning to leave, the nurse hesitated in mid-step, then spun back. "Sir ... she was already ... I'm so sorry."

"No!" Mick wagged his head. "That was someone else."

"There was nothing the doctor could do."

"Please listen. Cherie Dennis is her name." Mick felt woozy. "We're getting married."

The nurse placed her hand on his arm. "Sir ... you're bleeding onto the floor."

Mick's sterile pad resembled a soggy slice of red velvet cake. The ringing in his ears returned, evolving into a whishing roar. He watched the fluorescent-lit ER spin into patchy blackness, then shoot skyward, flinging him into a dizzied descent. Fear stairstepped his spine, squeezing his brain amidst flashes of dimming light.

Spinning.

Falling.

He was dying, spiraling helplessly in the wrong direction.

A fate he deserved.

"I should've told Cherie I loved her," he tried to scream. "Loved her as much as she did me." But he couldn't force the words from his lips, his breath sucked into a dark vacuum leaving only muted echoes.

And then, he heard his mom crying uncontrollably, his dad bullying some poor soul. Perhaps the cowboy was right, and they'd all passed through the wide gate. Mick's father, Ed McFarland, was no surprise, spouting Hades-related expletives in most every conversation.

But why his mother?

Besides raising Mick and younger twin girls, Fran McFarland spent her life aiding the less fortunate, establishing an annual citywide shoe drive for needy schoolchildren. Her life's sweetest icing was sitting in church with her family on Christmas Eve and Easter, the only services Ed attended.

A doctor raised his voice above the ER's din, his tone bleak. The next thing Mick knew, he was in an air-conditioned Cadillac, whisked by police escort to Houston's Hermann Hospital.

Emergency surgery kept him alive, while heavy pain meds and strict hospital regulations hindered him from attending Cherie's funeral in Austin. Her parents phoned Mick after the service, but he'd been asleep. Therefore, they'd left a message at the nurses' station wishing him a speedy recovery. They owned a business in Arizona and needed to rush back.

Just as well.

Considering Mick's tabloid past, they acted politely guarded around him. And now, how could he face them again, considering his role in the death of their only daughter—the couples' single chance at having grandchildren.

After endless hours of daily blood transfusions, horrific nightmares, and two weeks at Hermann, Mick felt the news reporters closing in, a learned sixth sense of survival for any celebrity. So, he devised a plan and phoned an old high school drama friend—Freddy Blalock—who lived nearby. Freddy had a peculiar sense of humor and comedic timing, bolstered by a boisterous laugh. Deciphering if he were serious or joking proved impossible, except for the laugh. But he could keep a secret and wouldn't ask questions.

The next morning, Freddy arrived on schedule, wheeling Mick outside through a rear entrance before his bland breakfast tray cooled. No one offered them a second glance. Mick didn't ask where his friend hijacked the scrubs and lab coat yet had a strong inkling. A local thespian group was doing a musical spoof of *Dr. Kildare*. Even though Freddy ran a busy Houston mortuary, he remained active in community productions. Theater people might be quirky but stuck together, a code they'd adopted as teenagers.

"I'd just as soon act as embalm," Freddy stated as they sped away from the hospital in a black Shelby Mustang. "Both are rewarding professions, however, one requires a lot more makeup."

Mick waited for, at least, a precursory cackle, but Freddy remained deadpan.

RUNNING DOWNWIND

They stopped at a gas station where Mick changed into fresh street clothes, then pushed on to Union Station. Freddy pulled up in front and shifted into neutral, speaking as the engine idled.

"How do the duds fit? They look a little big."

"They'll do fine. I'll replace them one day."

"Forget it." Freddy passed him an envelope. "Here's your cash and train ticket. A private compartment to New Orleans isn't cheap."

Mick produced a personal check. "This should cover it."

"I said forget it."

"Can't. Already made out. I carry a blank in my shirt pocket for emergencies." Mick handed him the check. "Sorry, it's a little creased."

"Less likely to bounce." Freddy remained straight-faced.

"Did you bring the cap and shades?"

Reaching into the back seat, Freddy grabbed a St. Louis Cardinals baseball cap and pair of dark sunglasses.

"I thought you were an Astros fan?"

"I am." He gunned the engine. "Those belonged to a client."

Mick exited the car, choosing not to inquire about the clothes.

The signature laugh peeled into traffic.

Thirty minutes later, Mick boarded a streamlined Pullman and located his compartment. If the conductor recognized him, he didn't let on. Nor did the porter when Mick ordered stationery and stamps, plus two aspirins with a triple whisky chaser. His bullet wound was still tender, so he couldn't sit without something strong to dull the pain. The ten-hour trip to New Orleans would be too long to bear.

Mick swallowed the aspirin with a drop of whisky and paced the small compartment, his thoughts continually returning to Cherie. When the train jerked to a start, he braced his knees against the base of the sofa-seat, peering out the thick, tinted window through a blur of regret. He blindly watched the city slide by.

She's dead; you're alive.

He sipped his drink. Guilt and shame had branded him—each word acrid, each letter hot.

Cherie loved you more than you deserved.

"Always," he whispered, the thought instantly wetting his eyes.

They'd known each other forever, being first introduced at Mick's fifth grade Halloween party, the year Cherie's family moved to Austin from Philadelphia. Vince Beasley, his best buddy—they wore matching devil costumes—poked him in the side with his pitchfork as the boys waited in line to bob for apples. Vince grinned through the mouth hole of his rubber mask. "That girl at the punch bowl likes you." He pulled the tight-fitting mask above his forehead and twisted an eyelid inside out.

"Which girl?" Mick returned the jab but left his face covered, never having mastered the impressive ocular talent.

"Witch hat, glasses, blondish hair. The new chick."

"So? I don't like *her*." Earlier, she'd grabbed Mick's hand in the dimly lit spook house. Terrified as to why, he'd jerked it back. His history with blondes of any shade was a one-sided longing. A platinum goddess he'd worshiped since first grade barely knew his name. He was scrawny and unpopular. Any female who didn't claim him as kin wouldn't purposely hold his hand.

Glancing over at the newbie, Mick thought she might be cute.

"Then why are you gawking at her?" Now both of Vince's eyelids were everted.

"Because *you're* so ugly." The reply was a standard comeback line, earning a guffaw from a weird kid dressed as Howdy Doody.

During Mick's turn at the apple tub, he attempted to redeem personal dignity by attacking a large Delicious, plunging his head beneath the icy water. The problem—he'd neglected to remove the rubber mask, which filled instantly, nearly drowning him. Cherie was the only classmate who didn't double up with laughter when he spewed liquid all over his costume.

She scampered to the girls' bathroom and returned with wad of paper towels.

"We'll always be friends, Mickey."

When the train cleared Houston and reached open track, Mick balanced the drink atop a small tray table, then collected his writing supplies. He sat gently on the sofa-seat. Cold fire seared up his right thigh. He'd been shot with something akin to a 30 carbine, probably because he was at close range. Victims farther away suffered the results of a more powerful rifle, the rounds completely disintegrating flesh and bone, even textbooks.

Enduring the pain, he penned his parents a sketchy note, then wrote a similar message to his agent, Tinker

Wellman. Mick assured everyone he was fine but had some "issues" to work through. Above all, they shouldn't worry nor try to find him. He'd contact them every few weeks and eventually reveal his whereabouts.

He took a healthy swig and considered his plan. Most people thought the mighty Mississippi ended in New Orleans.

The river didn't.

Its massive waterway coursed a hundred more miles, the final seventy through Plaquemines Parish before extending tea-stained digits into the salty Gulf of Mexico. Along the way, the current dumped tons of nutrients into adjacent bays, bayous, and estuaries, making the Mississippi Delta the richest fishing grounds in the world. Highway 23 paralleled the river, passing through various townships, including the small village of Persimmon. At a population of less than a hundred, Persimmon, Louisiana, was the last place anyone would consider searching for Mick McFarland ...

Who had an open invitation.

From the train station's Western Union office, he'd rushed a telegram to his buddy, Bret Babineaux. "Babin" was Mick's closest ally at the University of Texas, majoring in accounting. After earning his CPA and working four years for a prestigious accounting firm in Baton Rouge, Babin cleared his adding machine, moved to Persimmon, and became a licensed fishing guide.

"Captain Bret Babineaux," Mick announced above the Pullman's steady metallic hum. He'd not seen "Cap'n Babin" in a couple of years, but the short pact they'd made as fraternity brothers remained.

Whatever you need. Whenever you need it.

Two simple phrases Mick *needed* desperately. If Babin wasn't chasing redfish and speckled trout through the maze of inland lakes and marshes or trolling offshore for tuna in the Gulf's bottomless blue, he'd be waiting at the train station in New Orleans. Once the telegram was delivered, he'd get there as soon as humanly possible.

Mick studied his half-empty glass, then downed a huge gulp in Babin's honor. The last time they'd been together was at a frat brother's wedding. Babin preferred beer, dancing the two-step while hugging a bottle *and* a woman.

What was her name?

Hmmm. The question lingered a moment in Mick's mind before drifting into space. He peered into the glass and focused on the whisky's comforting warmth. Other than wine with dinner, he rarely indulged in anything stronger than iced tea.

Until today.

"Today's different." Mick spoke with blurry confidence. "My current situation requires something stronger, at least a finger or *two, to* forget what's *too* painful *to* remember."

He grinned.

Only a seasoned actor could pull off delivering a line with more than *two to's*. Otherwise, his brilliant word combination was *too* confusing *to* remember.

The grin expanded into a satisfied chuckle as the frat brother's wedding floated back across his cranial border. Yes, Babin was indeed with a woman, a striking redhead named Sally.

"But spelled with an E," Mick announced to the tiny compartment, then raised his glass. "S-A-L-L-Y-E." He toasted each letter, contemplating how Babin and Sallye were engaged or at least considering the prospect. Mick attended the same wedding with Cherie, but they weren't ... yet ...

His eyes drooped, too heavy for his brain to complete the thought. He was numb from the neck down and wondered if he might drop the glass, so gripped it between his palms.

"A real man doesn't feel his liquor," his father advised, "he holds it. A challenge you need to master."

"Done." Mick raised his arms. "I'm *holding* my booze with both hands ... and ... don't *feel* ..."

He slugged down the remaining contents and fell asleep.

Long after the sun disappeared into the Delta, Plaquemines Parish exuded a level of late summer humidity Mick had never experienced.

"Are you sure this pickup doesn't have air-conditioning?" He massaged his temples. For the last hour, he and Babin journeyed south out of New Orleans. They were still thirty miles from Persimmon, the windows rolled down, the damp heat thick with night.

Babin laughed. "That's what the cold beer's for, in that bottle you've not touched."

"Sorry. I drank something on the train that went to sleep a lot friendlier than it woke up."

"That's what you get for nursing the hard stuff." Babin effortlessly flipped his empty out the window and into the pickup's bed. He reached into the ice chest positioned between them and grabbed another brew. Holding it out the same window, he pried off the cap with the door handle. "Air's muggy all right. At least we're outrunning the skeeters—the small ones anyway."

Mick nodded, focusing on the headlights' leading edge. Before explaining why he'd come, Babin offered his place instead of a hotel. Mick could stay as long as necessary.

RUNNING DOWNWIND

He'd not revealed Cherie's pregnancy, only that she was murdered by the tower shooter. He was hit as well, thus needed a secluded environment to escape the press.

"I'd like to cut up that sorry sniper for fish bait." Babin pounded his fist on the steering wheel. "Better yet, feed him to the sharks."

"You, me, and a cowboy." Mick hadn't seen the bull rider again, nor read anything about him in the newspaper. Hopefully he was still living eight seconds at a time.

The farther south they traveled, the more the air condensed, clotted with brackish river odors and gelled with the deep, gentle rhythms of the marsh. Mick's head throbbed in unison with his leg, yet inwardly he felt better than since the entire ordeal began. This was a place where he'd not be bothered.

"They're never any news reporters snooping around Persimmon." Babin spoke above the wind noise, as if he could read Mick's thoughts. "As far as fishing towns go, we have a gas station, marina, and barber shop. Not much else. Best place to find a hotel, buy groceries, or get a soda is up in Port Sulphur. Or down where the highway ends in Venice. When we *do* get reporters around here, that's where they congregate."

"Great to hear. Does Persimmon have a drug store?"

"Why?"

"I need some aspirin."

"Closest thing is a bar called Feltons, which doubles as a café. They stock every known and unknown brand of legal headache killer."

"For hangovers?"

"And the occasional good-natured brawl. Earns them a tidy sum. When Hurricane Betsy blasted through here 'bout a year ago, her backside destroyed their building, but not the fancy electric sign—'cept for busting out the 't.' The owner kept it like that as a good luck omen to ward off future storms. Now it spells Felons."

Mick chuckled. "Probably a more accurate name."

"'Specially since you're here." Babin drained his bottle and flipped it into the bed. "Remember Sallye?"

"The tall redhead with you at the wedding?"

"Yep. Her folks are loaded, but she wanted to earn her own way. So, she's a waitress at Felons ... also the bouncer—a judo expert. Many a disorderly drunk never knew what hit him."

"Then the *beauty* is the *beast*."

"My Sallye could've been an Olympic gold medalist."

Unsure how to respond, Mick sat silent. Not because of her physical prowess, but because Babin called her *My Sallye*. The endearment meant he'd finally allowed a woman to penetrate his life.

They passed a sign announcing Persimmon in one mile.

"Sallye's smart," Babin continued. "Thrives on the art of surprise."

"Is that a warning?"

"Sort of." He grinned. "'Cause she gets in these moods."

"Moods?"

"Uh-huh. But first, she's a big fan of yours."

"What's second?"

"Prides herself in keeping secrets. Knows dirt on folks she won't even tell me."

"That's a relief. Is there a third?"

"She's writing her doctoral thesis in cognitive psychology."

"Sounds uninteresting." Mick stretched his legs and yawned.

"Her emphasis is on mental perception."

Mick shook off the yawn. "Does she want to be a shrink?"

"Hardly. Research is her deal." Babin slowed for an intersection. "She also has a passion for helping screwed-up people."

"Like me," Mick said.

"Just letting you know what to expect."

An amber caution light blinked a few blocks ahead. Mick sat up straight, glad to finally be *somewhere*. "I guess you and Sallye are engaged?"

"Yeah, though we haven't set a date. She finishes her degree next May. We'll decide after that."

Mick's head still pounded. "Would you mind stopping at Felons, or is Sallye in one of her *moods*?"

"Whatever you need, whenever you need it."

"That's what I'm afraid of."

The car hit a bump, and Mick grimaced.

"I think gettin' shot has made you soft," Babin said.

CHAPTER 3

By mid-autumn, Persimmon's persistent summer swelter diminished into decent stretches of pleasant weather. Scores of eager fishermen rocked Babin's boats every weekend, packing ice chests full of fish demanding to be cleaned. Mick volunteered for the messy job because it kept him busy and in the background. In addition, working with his hands was cathartic, enabling him to sometimes force the tower shooter into the far reaches of his psyche.

Sometimes.

His bullet wound had healed nicely into a bright pink scar, yet his soul ached constantly over Cherie's final words:

I will always love you.

To ease the discomfort, he spent weekdays helping Babin refurbish an eighteen-foot sailboat washed up during Hurricane Betsy. The owner, a Midwestern banker, christened the single-masted sloop *No Qualms*, mooring her across Bastian Bay in the beach community of Grand Isle. During the storm, she broke loose and was heavily damaged but didn't sink. After Babin rescued her from the marsh, the owner collected the insurance, selling her for pennies.

Mick loved sailboats, having sailed numerous times off the Galveston coast during his childhood. His father's law firm sponsored the trips, encouraging overworked associates to spend time with their families. The sailing vacations remained some of Mick's favorite memories, even though the name *No Qualms* was sadly laughable, reminding him of his former self. Now both he and the boat were wrecked by disaster. If he could repair *No Qualms*, perhaps he could one day fix himself.

Carpentry was a skill he'd mastered while building theater sets. Babin was impressed, so handed off much of the basic work to spend more time with Sallye. They insisted Mick join them for supper and drinks each evening at Felons, even when Sallye was working. Mick didn't have much appetite, yet obliged, knowing he'd starve if left to his own cooking. While he ate to survive, he sipped a little brew to be sociable, introducing himself to the locals as "Michael." His fair complexion soon reddened in the Louisiana sun. Shaving daily wasn't a priority nor were regular haircuts. Broadway's gleaming lights lured the interest of few fishermen, so no one recognized him. Moreover, Sallye hadn't asked a single personal question.

"It's the calm before the storm," Babin warned one overcast morning. He punctuated the cliché with a major grin.

Mick studied the sky. "It doesn't look ominous to me."

"I'm referring to Hurricane Sallye. You think Betsy was bad, wait 'til Sallye makes landfall."

"I wasn't around here for Betsy." Mick waved a hand. "Wouldn't know."

"You'll know. Sallye'll strike when you least expect it."

Several weeks passed with Mick *expecting* an encounter each time he saw Sallye. However, she focused upon her own issues, most often the complexities of her dissertation or some humorous tale about a drunk she'd booted from the bar.

RUNNING DOWNWIND

When Mick wasn't cleaning fish or working on *No Qualms*, he and Babin "rig" fished offshore for red snapper and amberjack. Mick looked forward to their trips, the ocean's endless horizon loosening the knots in his stomach, easing his nightmares. They'd pack a hearty lunch, then board Babin's largest boat and motor down the Mississippi to South Pass, one of three channels splaying fingerlike into the open Gulf of Mexico. Positioned in deep water near the continental shelf stood a cluster of offshore oil rigs, where they'd drop anchor before dropping their hooks. Many of the rigs damaged by past storms remained abandoned, making perfect manmade reefs. Sometimes Sallye joined the fun, out fishing them both.

"Not fair," Sallye pronounced in late November. They'd just arrived at a rig, positioning the boat beneath a thin column of shade. Before eating her lunch, she peered into the translucent Gulf, while a cloudless sky mirrored the water's sheer depths.

Babin spoke. "I'm gonna fry a turkey tomorrow for Thanksgiving."

"Don't you always?" Sallye broke off a piece of her sandwich and plunked it into the water. "Reminds me of hunting defenseless deer at a feeder."

Mick dug in an ice chest for a cola. "Frying a turkey?"

"Of course not." She pointed her finger pistol like, leaned over the boat's edge and pretended to shoot. "Not fair."

"What?" Using the lid on his tackle box, Mick tried to pry the bottle's cap. "What's not fair?"

Sallye dipped her finger into the water. "We know exactly where the fish are."

Before Mick could respond, Babin loudly cleared his throat. "I guess you Texans either roast your turkeys in the oven or smoke 'em ... right?"

"We'd rather smoke cigars."

"Right." Babin raised his eyebrows. "We fry our birds around here, usually outside, submerge 'em in a vat of peanut oil." He cocked his head toward Sallye. "Though I wouldn't try it in a *hurricane*."

"Uh-right." Mick returned a knowing nod. "Would you pitch me the opener?"

Sallye leaned closer to the water. "We're outsmarting these poor fish, and—"

"They don't know and don't care." Babin frowned, then reached into a utensil box and pitched Mick the opener. "Right, Mick?"

"Don't you dare agree with him." Sallye sat upright, facing Mick. "Fish are living creatures. Wouldn't they have feelings?"

"I don't know how anyone would ... um ... know for sure." Mick shrugged. "I mean with a fish."

"Nonsense. When you gaze into their eyes you can see joy, hurt, and other crucial emotional signals. Just like people."

Mick studied the soda's label.

"Just like you."

Babin handed her a pole. "It's time to stop gazing and start fishing.

RUNNING DOWNWIND

Thanksgiving passed, complete with deep fried turkey, cornbread/oyster dressing, and a mayhaw jelly cake. Sallye hadn't mentioned anything further about eyes—Mick's in particular—which made him wonder exactly what she'd seen. He still suffered an occasional nightmare concerning the tower shooter—the worst episode happening shortly after Sallye's offshore decree. Positioned atop an abandoned oil rig, the sniper fired at a school of enormous yellowfin tuna. Mick shouted for him to stop. The iridescent fish morphed into people. When he saw Cherie's lifeless body suspended just beneath the surface, he'd awakened in a river of sweat, followed by cold chills.

To lessen future nightmares, he continued suppressing his past through a rigorous daily routine. The last thing he needed was Sallye preaching to him about what he already knew. With any luck, her rushed holiday schedule would cancel any future *moods*, at least where he was the target.

On Christmas afternoon, Mick phoned his parents, who asked more questions than he answered. Fran became weepy, anxious about her son's health. Ed—well-mellowed on Scotch—orated the metaphorical career merits of abandoning the sideline for the goal line. Mick promised to take care of himself, stating he wouldn't be absent much longer.

The next morning, he called his agent. Tinker ranted nonstop about shaky future contracts. To complicate matters, an army of Broadway gossip publications and tabloids demanded information on Mick's whereabouts, some willing to pay big money. He finally calmed Tinker's nerves, assuring him everything was better.

Everything wasn't.

Cherie's final words haunted Mick more each day. Not only was December her favorite month, they'd spent last

Christmas together in Brazil, which proved pivotal to their relationship.

Each time Mick envisioned Sallye, he shivered. Were his eyes relaying silent signals?

The New Year arrived with no emotionally taxing fireworks. Then February paraded into the Delta with the lively excitement of Mardi Gras celebrations, ending with Fat Tuesday.

Still, nothing.

Mick felt relieved. Even lucky. Perhaps Sallye offered up her *moods* for Lent. Then on Valentine's Day, his luck ran cold.

An uncharacteristic arctic front crept slowly out of Canada, the frigid air sliding as far south as Plaquemines Parish. Moisture was predicted to move in from the Gulf, making an ice storm imminent. Light frozen rain wouldn't develop into heavy sleet until after midnight, but the roads were already slippery, travel discouraged. Undaunted, Babin and Sallye drove up to New Orleans for a romantic dinner in the French Quarter, with arrangements to stay put if they couldn't return. The plan required Mick to eat solo at Felons. It was within walking distance, plus he preferred spending the evening alone. Cherie never required over-the-top romance, but they'd both enjoyed the holiday, so he fought off a few more resurrected regrets. Deep in thought, Mick barely noticed Sallye standing on the opposite side of his table.

Staring.

"I've finally got you figured out."

Mick set aside his cheeseburger. "Oh ... Sallye. I thought you and Babin were—"

"Smart?" She laughed. "Traveling over slick roads in a pickup with no weight in the back is dumb. We finally turned around or rather, slid into a perilous one-eighty."

"Are you both okay?"

RUNNING DOWNWIND

"Of course. An updated forecast reports the possibility of dense, frozen fog later tonight. Babin's over at the marina tending to his boats. He'll return shortly and honk. I'm to meet him out front."

Mick shoved back his plate. "I should help."

"Relax. He can handle things." Keeping her eyes fixed on Mick's, she pulled out a chair and sat, but didn't remove her jacket. "I'm more concerned about you."

"Because of what I *can't* handle?"

"I won't disagree."

"Is this where you tell me I'm nuts?" Mick cocked his head to one side.

Silence.

She leaned forward. "Hardly."

He straightened. "Then ... what?"

"I think you're stifled by fear. Without going into all the *clinical folderol* as Babin declares, I detect you're afraid of ... something."

A shiver swept the length of Mick's spine.

Sallye continued. "A childhood event is a common catalyst."

"Childhood?"

"Naturally. A troubling incident gaining traction over time, culminating with the tower shooter."

"Lots of my past was a little disturbing, not just when I was a kid. How do I choose?"

"Only you can answer."

He waited for her to continue.

She didn't.

"Okay." Mick scratched his head. "The catalyst was my birth. I wasn't ready to face a world outside the womb."

"Be serious."

"Which also means I hate my parents, or at least one of them. Isn't that the standard diagnosis?"

"I'm a friend, Mick, not a psychiatrist." Sallye frowned. "And your life isn't a movie."

"That's a relief. I'm tired of being the star."

"Which is a great place to start."

"The star thing?"

She nodded. "Isn't that why you're here?"

A honk sounded from out front.

"Wait! Let's say I locate the catalyst. What next? And I can't answer *that* question."

Sallye stood. "Determine how the catalyst affected you, which takes time. A true understanding may not happen overnight."

"How about a fortnight?"

She replied with a playful smirk.

Another honk.

"Sorry I interrupted your dinner." Starting for the door, Sallye paused and spun an about face. "Everybody's got something rotten poisoning their plate, much harder to swallow than a cheeseburger."

He watched her disappear, then paid for his meal and left, ignoring the cold. Hurricane Sallye wasn't as severe as Babin predicted. Clinical folderal aside, Mick suspected she was correct. What he'd not anticipated was the affection he now felt for her. They hadn't known each other long, but she'd cared enough to be concerned. Babin had latched on to a fine woman. Mick vowed to make sure his friend knew.

Around three o'clock the next morning, Mick awakened restless. At least he'd not encountered another nightmare. Wrapped in a blanket, he peered out the bedroom window. The expected frozen fog had rolled in off the marsh, eerily clinging to every bushy twig and bare tree branch. Soon, the windows would glaze over. He trudged to the kitchen and brewed a cup of hot tea, then sat at the table and stared outside. The weather reminded him of growing up in Austin, where frozen precipitation was as much of an anomaly as in Persimmon.

He considered Sallye's catalyst concept, vividly recalling the tower shooter and the events following. When the recollections became too painful, he reversed his thoughts, working backward through his professional career and into his college and high school years. Mick carefully scanned his memory, unraveling the cobwebs for every possible silk attached to fear. Two cups later he was about to drift off empty, when an event as sharp as well-honed steel sliced through his sleepiness.

The setting—junior high school. Sullied by a name that still disgusted him.

Max Darnell.

No one knew how many grades Max Darnell flunked. Rumor decreed he was raised rich but ran away from home and lived in a cave near Town Lake. Each morning before school, he'd eat a live rattlesnake for breakfast, then shave with a switchblade stolen off the corpse of a *dead* hobo. The first time Mick heard the tale he laughed, explaining to his buddies that the caves around Austin were full of bats, a live snake would bite back, and a corpse—by redundant definition—was already dead. They responded with the same dull expressions he'd noticed in fifth period American History when Mrs. Morton read a chapter aloud from the novel, *Johnny Tremain*. His friends' sleepy disinterest in Bostonian Tories and Whigs was the result of ingesting as many corndogs and ice cream sandwiches as humanly possible during a twenty-minute lunch.

Mick didn't care what extracurricular activities involved Darnell if they didn't include him. He'd feared the bully since he could remember, exercising great pains to avoid him.

Then one Friday, a Darnell minion overheard Mick's disgust concerning his master's habit of breaking into the front of the lunch line. After school, during Mick's walk to his weekly piano lesson, Darnell came calling, shouting Mick's dreaded nickname.

"Hey ... Mickey McMouse."

Mick didn't need to glance behind. He knew the definition of trouble—Darnell and his slimy sidekick. If ignored, maybe they'd terrorize a more deserving opponent. An evil dictator perhaps?

"McMouse. I'm talking to you."

Due to the weekend, the entire eighth grade was saddled with extra homework. Under one arm, Mick balanced a three-ring notebook and a stack of texts. Under the other, half a dozen spiral folders, plus his jacket. Even though the calendar touted late autumn, afternoons in Austin remained warm.

"Teach him a lesson," the minion chided.

Mick kept walking.

Darnell moved in close, matching Mick's stride. "Can't you hear with them giant floppy ears?"

The bully stank with the acrid ammonia of bat guano.

"Let's cut off his left ear and use it for a kite," the minion suggested.

"Shut up and hold this." Darnell removed his sweater and shoved it toward his little friend. "My momma give it to me. Don't want McMouse blood spattered on the sleeves." They laughed.

Darnell continued. "Ain't your momma the lady who gives shoes to poor kids?"

RUNNING DOWNWIND

Mick nodded, unsurprised at Darnell's grammar, yet amazed he knew anything about the needs of others.

"Your momma can't never give you no shoes, 'cause you got big 'ole fish flippers instead of feet. That's why I'm gonna toss your sissy butt into Town Lake."

The minion hee-hawed and slapped his mentor on the back, who returned the slap with a powerful pop. "Hey man, that hurts."

Darnell extended no sympathy. "Know what I heard, McMouse?"

"Um," Mick stalled, acting as though he could remember. There was a fire station in the next block, which might delay trouble. On pleasant afternoons the firemen worked outside on their equipment.

"Answer me, McMouse."

"About what?" Mick's voice trembled.

"You been badmouthing me in the lunch line, ain't 'ya."

"Maybe."

Smashes of light flashed across Mick's left eye an instant before the pain exploded. He dropped his load and connected a wild swing, bloodying the Minion's nose.

The minion screamed. "Cut him."

Boom! More pain. Darnell's second punch blinded Mick's right eye. He sat hard as the world spun into a salty blur. The minion picked up Mick's heaviest book to heave like a small boulder. Mick rotated instinctively and kicked, his feet tangling with Darnell's knees. Just as Darnell fell, the minion launched the book, hitting the bully in the crotch.

"Aww." Darnell rolled, scooped up the book one-handed and thrust it into the minion's groin, who crumpled to the ground.

Mick stood, but was immediately tackled from behind, the force of the blow knocking out his wind. He gasped for air.

Darnell dug his knees into Mick's back, then ground his face into someone's lush lawn. "Eat grass, you flipper-footed baby." He jerked Mick's head up by the hair. The rasp and click of slick steel announced the older boy's intentions. Putrid breath burned Mick's neck.

"I'm gonna slit your red-headed throat," Darnell whispered, "then cut off your peanuts and feed'em to—"

A screech of heavy tires interrupted the melee's gruesome climax.

Darnell flung the switchblade into an azalea bush and ran, his friend limping in the opposite direction. A fireman returning a ladder truck to the station witnessed the knife pull. After making sure Mick wasn't seriously hurt, he radioed the cops, who arrested Darnell a few blocks away.

The piano lesson was forgotten.

From his law office, Ed phoned the school superintendent and demanded immediate justice. Fran, the fireman, and the cops met with the principal, who expelled the bully and his cohort.

A week passed before the minion returned to campus. Darnell didn't.

His family moved to California. Whispers later surfaced about the dad serving time in Alcatraz for tax fraud, which explained a lot.

When the fragrance of spring's first wildflowers sweetened the Mississippi Delta, Babin and Sallye set July thirtieth as their wedding date. The official nuptials were scheduled in Sallye's childhood church up in Baton Rouge, with a reception following at her family's farm.

The couple announced the news locally over evening drinks at Felons. On a whim, Mick stood and delivered a toast, then clinked champagne glasses with the majority of Persimmon's population, celebrating well into the wee hours. The following week, Sallye returned home for graduation and wedding preparations.

She'd not mentioned another word about Mick's *catalyst*, nor had he breathed a syllable concerning Max Darnell. But Mick occasionally caught Sallye's clinical gaze, wondering what she saw ... if anything.

All he could detect was his own confusion.

Hence, Darnell remained a possible catalyst. Because Mick fought back that day, his courage gradually matured until he was able to conquer his fear of bullies, the tower shooter included. However, the name, Max Darnell, still grated on Mick's nerves like an irritating jingle. Which meant there was another connection, something much deeper.

He just couldn't find it.

Equally troubling was the wedding. Both Babin and Sallye understood Mick was in hiding and couldn't attend. Otherwise, he'd have been best man. The main reason—which he kept to himself—was the date: the one-year anniversary weekend of his benefit performance at Hogg Auditorium.

Since Christmas, Mick phoned his parents weekly. He considered confiding in them, but the moment never seemed right. On the surface, the calls delighted his mom and calmed his dad. Still, Mick detected anxious undertones. Adding to the tension, the tabloids and major newspapers pestered them.

"Son, tell your agent to make these reporters back off," Ed cautioned, "or I'll pound the jerks with a two-fisted lawsuit. And speaking of your agent, why would a grown man keep the name, Tinker?"

Letting his father ponder the dilemma, Mick said a quick goodbye and rung his agent. "Sorry I bothered your folks, but the press smells a story. There's also been a private investigator sniffing around. Somebody—not I—leaked confidential information about your AWOL status from Hermann Hospital. Their whiff of interest has intensified into an all-out stink. Before long, they'll know why you were admitted, and then *dig up dirt* on Cherie ... pun intended."

"Not funny." Mick scowled. "I should come out of hiding and slug you."

"I'm glad I command your attention. Why don't you tell me what you're really running from?"

Mick slammed down the phone. "I would ... if I knew."

By May, the dense heat conquered the marsh. Mick had wrestled a lifetime's worth of fish, not caring if he ever caught or cleaned another. However, refurbishing *No Qualms* was a different matter. Complete with two bunk beds, an adequate galley, and functioning head, she was beautifully restored and refitted from bow to stern. As added pluses, he and Babin installed a state-of-the-art two-way radio, new engine, and retractable keel that adjusted to the water's depth. When everything was shipshape, they motored through the marsh, cut power, and caught the breeze.

During the initial outings, they remained close to shore, silently navigating the deeper ponds and waterways. However, in early summer, they ventured down to the mouth of the wide Mississippi, sailing amongst the long steel ribbons of commercial barges. Soon, both men acquired billowing sea legs, voyaging miles from land for days at a stretch, enjoying the windswept freedom of the open Gulf.

RUNNING DOWNWIND

Upon the completion of *No Qualms*, all refurbishing efforts transferred to remodeling Babin's house. He and Sallye would soon live there. Mick insisted on moving out, but no rental property was available.

Babin grinned. "You may have to sleep with the bullfrogs."

A week before the wedding, Mick was at the marina swabbing one of the inland fishing boats. He'd grown accustomed to physical labor within the sauna climate, his arms and legs more bronzed and muscular than ever. But the stronger his body became during daylight hours, the weaker his mind seemed after sunset. A crazy paradox. Perhaps he'd tried too hard to connect the Darnell catalyst with Cherie and blown a few million brain cells. Mick wasn't certain anymore if just her final words haunted his soul, or something else she'd said. To compensate, he blended a little whisky into every evening, constantly assuring himself he'd never rely on the hard stuff—like his father.

As Mick worked, he mulled over the need to stay on in Persimmon, at least until he reconciled his thoughts. "I can live right *here*," he stated, then emptied a pail of dirty mop water over the side." Looking up, he saw Babin standing on the dock, expressionless, holding two colas.

"Only if the marina had a room to rent, which it doesn't."

Mick climbed out of the boat. His buddy handed him a cold bottle. They sat, dangling their feet above the murky water.

"I mean live on *No Qualms*. Rent her from you."

"Nothing doing." Babin dug an opener from his shirt pocket. "Friends stay free 'cause I tend to work 'em to death." He pried the cap off his bottle and pitched the tool to Mick.

"Then sell her to me." Mick followed suit, his drink releasing a fizzy spurt. "Thanks for giving me the spirited one."

"Anytime."

Mick took a sip. "I want to pay for my own place."

"Why?"

"I hear marriage is expensive."

"Only if you're poor. Sallye and me ain't." Babin pressed the cool bottle against his cheek. "Got a better reason?"

"There'll be a decent place for you to stay when she's in one of her moods."

"Hmm ... maybe I'll consider the offer."

"Good, 'cause I *ain't* poor either. Broadway issues fat paychecks."

"If you're around to collect 'em."

"I've still got a little cash on hand. My agent could wire the rest."

"Which means he'd know where to find you, unless ..."

"What?"

Babin swished a mouthful of cola and swallowed. "When I was at the gas station a minute ago, a guy pulled up in a fancy Cadillac with Florida plates. He shouted for the attendant to fill the tank, dropped a ten on the trunk and rushed over to the pay phone. Since the booth's door won't close all the way, I heard a portion of his conversation, along with a name."

"Mine?"

"Yeah ... unless there's another Mick McFarland in town."

RUNNING DOWNWIND

"What else?"

"Got the impression that the person on the other end of the line was supposed to meet him and didn't show. Caddy-Boy wasn't pleased."

"His kind never are."

"The more he talked, the louder his volume. He finally went to cussing about *not losing to the competition*, hung up and stomped back to the Caddy. Didn't even wait for his change."

Mick frowned. "Somebody's recognized me."

"Yep."

"Got any ideas?"

"Maybe." Babin thought for a moment. "When you toasted Sallye and me at Felons, there were a couple of fancy dressers drift in. Strangers. Think it was one of them?"

"Probably. They first tipped off whoever hired them. Then to double profits, leaked my location to a bunch of sleazy tabloids."

"Figures."

"Now there's a contest to see who can locate me first. Caddy-Boy's probably meeting up with a photographer."

"So, he'll be back."

"Soon. With an ally."

"Then what?"

Mick blew a long sigh. "The *competition* won't lag far behind. News-rags will wave twenty-dollar bills around Persimmon, along with my photo. Folks will trip over each other to talk."

"Like you're a wanted criminal." Babin leaned over to one side and dug a key from his pocket. "Why don't you hightail this place for a day or two. Take my pickup."

"Thanks, but there's already a feeding frenzy for a bite of the big money. Once this crew detects my scent, they won't give up. They'll join forces, fan out, and find me ... unless I leave the country."

"And go where?"

"The Yucatan. I've got show-biz friends down in that part of Mexico."

"Mighty tough career." Babin swished and swallowed another mouthful of cola. "How do you get there from here without being seen?"

"Won't be easy."

"I reckon they're already watching the New Orleans airport."

"And train depot." Mick wagged his head. "Plus, all roads within a hundred miles are paved with twenties."

"You shouldn't be such a popular guy. Face it. Every way out's blocked."

Mick focused his gaze a few slips over on *No Qualms*. "Not the Gulf."

Babin studied the sailboat and scowled. "Bad idea."

"Why? We know she's seaworthy."

"I mean sailing alone."

They finished their colas in silence. Images of the tabloids resurrecting Cherie's death in supermarket checkout lines flashed before Mick's eyes. For her sake, he had to find the courage to leave.

And then the bull rider's voice broke through the periphery of Mick's thoughts.

Let's just say I live eight seconds at a time.

Mick stood and successfully launched his empty bottle into a trash barrel twenty feet away. "*No Qualms* is worth the risk. I need to move on." He offered his friend a hand up. "You'd do the same."

Babin's bottle hit the mark. "Then we best quit lollygagging and stock some supplies. Mexico ain't no afternoon voyage."

"You're selling her to me?"

"Nope. She already belongs to you."

RUNNING DOWNWIND

"Look, I insist on paying—"

Babin cut him off. "Since you did the grunt work, you've earned her. Sallye and I may get wiped out in the next hurricane and need a little fast cash—or a lot. Means you better stay alive and in touch."

A sizable lump formed in Mick's throat. "Whatever you need," he said finally, "whenever you need it."

"By the time you're sipping margaritas, the tabloids will be hounding somebody else," Babin joked early the next morning. He stood on the dock, helping *No Qualms* get underway. "You'll eventually land somewhere, sometime."

"I appreciate the encouragement." Mick positioned himself in the cockpit. After a night of careful consideration, they'd agreed upon a leisurely route. *No Qualms* carried more than two months' worth of supplies, which was beyond enough. "Anything else?"

"Remember to conserve radio power." Babin raised his eyebrows. "That fancy piece of electronics ain't for entertainment."

"If I get bored, I'll fire the emergency flares."

"And stay within sight of the shipping lanes."

"No worries. I've memorized their coordinates."

"I suppose an actor would, though it might be best to post them on the fridge, double check for accuracy."

"Don't need to. I've got an excellent memory." Mick cranked the engine as Babin cast off the bow line.

"I never drop important *lines*," Mick shouted, unsure if his friend heard the pun.

Maneuvering *No Qualms* out of the slip, he motored through the marina, then glanced back at the dock.

Babin still held the thick rope in his hand.

CHAPTER 4

The heavy boom swung from port to starboard with a generous creak, startling Mick out of a dreamless sleep. He opened one eye. Patches of drippy storm clouds swirled high above the taut mainsail. A hazy setting sun peeked at intervals at a choppy sea, white capped and menacing.

A smart man would reef the sail, not take a nap.

"Please. One complaint at a time." Mick knew a brief comment spoken aloud to oneself was normal behavior, but in the past two weeks, he'd enjoyed lengthy conversations.

You're not crazy, just lonely.

"Stop reminding me."

He checked the binnacle compass and reset the autopilot, adjusting course a little west of south to circumvent the worst of the storm. Babin was correct, the Yucatan Peninsula was hard to miss, a straight diagonal across the Gulf of Mexico from Louisiana to Campeche. However, his friend's navigational charts were mainly limited to U.S. waters, so Mick relied on the compass.

His stomach growled informing him of suppertime. He'd been at sea for over a month and hadn't seen a ship for the past three days. The lack of sightings meant he was off course, which could be corrected if not for the storm. Knowing he should eat something, he went down to the galley, though couldn't decide what. On most nights, he'd not slept for more than four hours at a stretch, the mounting fatigue taxing even small decisions.

"So much for leisure."

After digging through a trunk of foodstuffs, he finally smeared peanut butter on half a dozen stale saltines, washed down a few bites with warmed-over coffee, then climbed topside. In the deepening dusk, the storm appeared to sidestep his position, so he released a little more sail and retreated to the cockpit. Soon, a small glow appeared several miles astern, the running lights of a passing freighter. Mick watched until certain the boat was heading in an alternate direction.

The shipping lanes.

He was on course. After a lengthy yawn, he stretched out beneath the awning to finish his nap, hoping to rest easy.

Instead, he experienced a hard dream.

Mick was back at Felons on Valentine's Day, but Sallye wasn't who sat across the table eyeing him.

"Cherie?"

"Expecting someone else?"

"I don't remember you having *moods*." He chuckled. "When did that start?"

"Please listen." She leaned forward. "You've evaded your own conclusions."

"I have?"

"When haven't you?" Cherie smiled. "Max Darnell *is* the catalyst, but as you already know, there's a much deeper connection."

Mick frowned. "I can't find it."

"Oh Mickey. Don't you remember the power struggles?"

"Power struggles?"

"With your father, Darnell, me."

RUNNING DOWNWIND

"You?"

Cherie giggled. "Ours started innocently enough when I grabbed your hand in the haunted house."

"You were kind to me, the only one who didn't laugh when I nearly drowned. That was no power struggle."

"Not at first. But think back, Mickey."

"What do you mean?"

"You wrestled with your dad over self-esteem."

"Granted, Dad's hard to please."

"And fought with Darnell over fear of bullies."

"I was never *really* afraid of him."

Cherie crinkled her forehead. "You're not a very good liar. Until facing him, you crossed to the other side of the street."

Mick had never seen Cherie more beautiful. "What about you?" he asked softly. "What did we struggle about?"

"Mickey ... never forget your child."

"I haven't." Mick realized he was crying. He wiped away a handful of tears.

She didn't respond, but stared so deeply into his burning eyes, he'd awakened.

Trembling.

Calling her name.

His voice muted beneath a heavy blanket of darkness.

The low clouds returned, along with a stiff breeze. Mick's head felt harpooned, so he rummaged through the aft supply locker and found the flask of whisky he'd packed. Sailing solo, he'd vowed to consume just a *tad* for medicinal purposes only—physical or mental. Between his headache and his dream, this was a medical emergency.

The sailboat pitched, as a cold rain spattered across the deck, blowing underneath the awning. Even though the whisky warmed his throat, he shivered. Goose bumps peppered his bare arms and legs, as images of the tower massacre returned. On that horrific day, Cherie's arms and legs were bare, singed with burns from the scalding concrete.

Mickey ... never forget your child.

The rain increased as the sailboat climbed the crest of a steep wave, allowing it to slide underneath. Mick downed more whisky as lightening crackled, followed by extended thunder. And then a sudden change in wind direction signaled the storm altered course. He knew the mainsail needed attention, but a fresh recollection of Cherie's pregnancy paralyzed him.

Shortly after they'd arrived in Austin for Mick's benefit performance, she'd had a routine checkup with Doc Price, the McFarland family physician. He was her childhood doctor, and the MD for most of their classmates. The walls of his exam rooms were plastered with their annual school portraits. Cherie felt comfortable with him. Knew she could reveal anything without fear of betrayal.

Mick had no clue she was as fertile as the Nile. Thinking back, the appropriate symptoms were there. Morning nausea, an odd craving.

Was Doc Price sure?

Wasn't there a rabbit involved?

Old Doc never touched a drop.

Mick raised his bottle to the wind, then allowed himself a final tad.

He chuckled.

Doc Price was privy to enough toxic information to publish an Austin tabloid. He even knew about Mick's *first* alcohol extravaganza during his senior year of high school.

RUNNING DOWNWIND

He'd traveled to El Paso over Christmas break to work a month's construction for his Uncle Harley, earn a little spending money. Mick recently turned eighteen so was sure his dad convinced Harley that Mick needed to become a real man. The task was assigned to an older cousin, Leonard, who drove Mick and a stack of American greenbacks across the Rio Grande to a nightclub in Juarez. After swallowing enough tequila to covet who ate the worm, a beautiful girl latched on to Mick and asked him to dance. The mariachi band played two tunes. Before striking up a third, dizzying nausea made him bolt for the men's room. The next thing Mick knew, the cousins were inside Leonard's car, speeding through the darkness.

"Where are we?" The dashboard lights hurt Mick's eyes.

"Crossed back into Texas about thirty minutes ago." Leonard glanced in Mick's direction. "You, okay?"

"My head hurts."

"Too much tequila is the worst culprit."

"There's more than one?"

"If you consider the senorita."

"A girl?"

"Plus, count the gash on your forehead."

Mick felt for his wound. "She hit me?"

"Not for the amount she hoped. After a couple of dances, you threw up in the john and passed out. Banged your head on a rusty washbasin."

"Great. Where'd I get the bandage?"

"The bartender's a family friend, so we got outta there without much trouble. When you get home to Austin tomorrow, get a tetanus shot."

Mick frowned.

"And smile. You're *almost* a real man now."

"Almost?"

His cousin laughed. "Learn to hold your liquor and you'll discover what other intoxicating pleasures money can buy."

"I don't—"

"Grow up, Cuz." Leonard winked. "That pretty senorita never intended to entertain you for free."

Mick felt nauseous again, this time for what his cousin *almost* bought.

Back in Austin, Doc Price administered the tetanus shot while lecturing upon the merits of sobriety and chastity. Mick mentioned neither the tequila nor the girl. Maybe Doc Price could read minds.

Too bad you didn't follow the good doctor's regimen.

Mick nodded, his thoughts briefly returning shipboard. The storm hadn't strengthened, so he pressed the flask to his lips for an additional, final sip. Whereas Juarez awakened his principled sensibilities, fame dulled them into a looser moral prescription.

Except when he was with Cherie.

She'd refused to go any farther than kissing. The only time he'd forced the issue wasn't successful.

"You know how I *feel*." Cherie fought back tears.

"Not yet." Mick stroked her forearm. "But I'd like to."

She pulled away. "Not funny. You should be pleased I'm saving myself for my future husband."

He frowned. "Because of the *God* thing?"

"Christ lives in my heart. You know that too."

"Can't he take a sabbatical?"

"Still not funny." She sniffed. "I want to be obedient to him, no matter what. Don't you?"

Mick didn't answer. From the beginning, he'd admired Cherie's spunk, even her cheerful outspokenness. Yet somewhere along the way she'd found *religion*, making the whole God experience personal. Her resoluteness

RUNNING DOWNWIND

frustrated him. To suppress physical desire, he'd attended a few worship services with her, hoping she'd view him as a good person.

On the night of their engagement, Mick received the surprise of his lifetime. He'd just returned from Brazil after starring in the movie version of the hit Broadway musical, *Rain in Rio*. To celebrate the film—his cover for a surprise proposal—he booked rooms in a ritzy Manhattan hotel housing an exclusive, yet private dinner club for celebs. After a gossip columnist leaked the plans, Mick was barely on one knee before reporters leapt out of the shadows with bulb-popping cameras. When Mick presented the three-carat diamond, the entire room burst into applause. Cherie acted surprised, though Mick knew she'd been expecting the ring for weeks. So, they ate, drank, and danced themselves silly.

During the second bottle of Cherie's favorite port, she grabbed Mick's hand and led them up to her room. "We will always be friends," she said before turning back the bedcovers. It was the last time she spoke the phrase. "I will always love you," became her mantra from that moment forward.

The next morning they'd awakened to the headlines, *Matrimony Muzzles Mick*, and *Will Wedding Bells Rein-in Rio?*

Crash! The sailboat's bow plummeted from atop a liquid cliff in response to what he hoped was a rogue wave.

It wasn't.

Foam-crested giants charged out of the darkness, pounding the hull. Careless self-pity had tossed his life into the middle of a fist fight between Poseidon and Oceanus. Or was it creeping callousness?

"She was drunk," Mick shouted into the darkness. "I could've stopped her that night but didn't. *I* wanted what

I wanted. Maybe I'm supposed to die." However, more than his own selfishness, he feared the truth. Cherie had said *your* child, not *our* child.

She knew how selfish he'd become.

Guessed he'd forget the "our."

Hoped he'd remember the "your."

The devil's mask was ripped from his face, with no more paper towels.

Mickey ... never forget your child.

As much as the shooter wanted Mick dead, Cherie's honor demanded he stay alive. Demanded he keep the pregnancy secret.

Demanded he remember.

Which meant lowering the mainsail.

And the power struggle. Overcoming the painful ghosts of what would've been.

Was that the missing connection?

Mick stood, wobbled, held firm. If only his head would catch up to the rest of him. Then as on a stage manager's cue, a wall of wind driven rain blew him backward into the cockpit. He bumped his leg. Pain seared from his still sensitive scar. A terrific gust fanned the boom across the deck at rocket speed.

Crack!

He'd read about storms ripping masts from the decks of ships, but never thought he'd witness the event. Black water poured in from every direction. The boat rolled onto its side.

Mickey ... never forget your child.

As a former Boy Scout, he'd conquered the mile swim with ease, yet could scarcely hold his breath *beneath* the water for one pool length. Actors in musical theater enjoyed a love affair with air. Of all the tragic ways one might die, Mick feared drowning most.

RUNNING DOWNWIND

Mickey ... never forget your child.

Grabbing a floating cushion, Mick coughed up saltwater while fighting for life amongst the tangle of lines and shredded sail. The boat capsized. He managed to hang on to the slimy keel. Inching aft toward the upended stern, he determined to keep his head above the mess that defined his life.

Mickey ... never forget your child.

He grabbed the rudder and held on. Locked both arms and rode the inverted hull throughout the night like the tough bull rider would've done.

And Mick McFarland remembered his child ...

Eight seconds at a time.

CHAPTER 5

Julia Lawrence stood knee deep in dark surf and studied the breaking waves. The moment just before the sun popped above the Gulf of Mexico was her favorite time of day. Unless overcast, a starlit sky gave way to a symphony of light. Soft woodwinds of pink and purple appeared on the horizon, accompanied by crimson bowstrings before bursting into brassy orange and yellow. She never knew precisely when the moment began, nor how long it lasted. Seconds? Minutes?

An exact measurement didn't matter. It was when she watched for the Lady Who Walked on the Sea ... a time when Julia tried to forget what haunted her soul and remembered to dream.

She examined the watery line of unlit sky. No colored motifs yet, nor even a fading yellow moon. The Conductor must still be tuning his orchestra.

The previous night had proven anxious, crowded with uncomfortable premonitions. Thunder and lightning blew in from the Gulf around midnight, pounding Padre with high wind and rain, then marched across the bay toward Port Isabel. She'd noticed more wet weather than usual, but after growing up on the Texas high plains, most coastal downpours were tame. This storm must have been trying to impress its Panhandle cousins.

She sighed. Her history of jumping off one teetering precipice only to crash upon another had finally ended ... at least that was her prayer. What bubbled in her gut was an intense anticipation.

Of fear?

Excitement?

Perhaps a mixture of both.

Her habit each day for the past four years was to exit her bungalow a little before dawn. She'd crank her pickup, then drive along the soft beach to an inlet guarded by an abandoned lighthouse. If the surf wasn't cold, she'd wade out far enough to feel the pull of the mighty undertow. The sensation of sand sliding beneath her feet and tugging her toes was addictive. This morning the Gulf maintained the temperature of bath water, the norm for late summer.

"On Padre Island, a lighthouse shines for the Lady," Julia whispered, "its white fire illuminating the predawn darkness." The words composed the opening sentence to her childhood nanny's favorite legend. Until Julia ran away to Dallas at age seventeen, she'd heard countless renditions, told in tempo to the comforting clicks of Carmen's knitting needles.

A wave slapped the hem of Julia's shorts, pitting her nanny's tale of the Lady against historical fact.

Did saltwater have memories?

Could those memories discern truth?

Backing up a step, Julia steadied her stance. In 1554, three Spanish galleons loaded with conquistadores, treasure, and slaves sank off the island. The ships were on route from the New World back to Spain. Most of those who swam to the beach were killed by the Karankawas. A handful of the more fortunate survivors escaped to points south. According to Carmen, the Lady—named Chimala—

was held captive aboard the ill-fated ship, *Espiritu Santo*. Chimala purposely drowned.

Julia smiled at the recollection. She could repeat the entire tale verbatim. When her mother's wrath grew unbearable during winter months, she'd spend frosty evenings in a clapboard shack with Carmen and her ranch hand husband, Paco. Julia's final visit with the couple remained etched in her memory. Outside, a bitter mixture of sleet and windblown snow. Inside, the only warmth she knew.

"That lighthouse is nothing but a rusted ruin." Paco poked a mesquite log into a potbellied stove. "And *banditos* stole the giant lamp."

"Then may the crooks be roasted and eaten by cannibals." Carmen jabbed a needle into a ball of yarn, as if skewering meat. Paco argued that ritual cannibalism was extinct along the Texas coast, as well as the tribes who'd practiced it. Still, his wife refused to travel any closer to the ocean than San Antonio.

Carmen's eyes bulged. "Chimala was a beautiful Mayan princess who'd been given a powerful, visionary mirror. Just minutes—"

"A visionary mirror?" Paco winked at Julia, then banged the bowl of his hand carved pipe against the stove to dislodge a fat cone of ash. "What happened to the seven little *hombres* and the wicked queen? Didn't Walt Disney make this tale into a movie?"

Carmen ignored the interruption. "Just minutes before Chimala's capture, Naiya—her brave warrior and daring lover—broke his protective mirror in two, instructing Chimala to selflessly gaze into her half each morning as the sun's first rays reached over the edge of the earth."

"Only a vain fool would wear a mirror for armor." Paco packed the bowl with fresh tobacco.

Unabated, Carmen continued. "Since Dominican priests had converted Chimala and Naiya to Christianity, the couple prayed to the one true God, asking him to allow love's pure reflection to bond their souls." Carmen's bottom lip quivered, enhanced by a well-timed tear. "Yet while struggling in the storm, Chimala lost her precious mirror, her only link to Naiya."

After a strategic pause, Carmen laid aside her knitting, then thrust her arms forward, wriggling her fingers in a watery, come-hither motion. "No longer wishing to live, the princess opened her mouth, inviting the angry waves to fill her lungs and sting her nose."

Paco calmly lit his pipe. "The sea doesn't need an invitation." He chuckled. "This Chimala must be *un poco loca*."

Carmen stood. "You're the one who's crazy, and more than just a little." She faced Julia. "Death was Chimala's only hope. Before her spirit journeyed to heaven, perhaps the angels would let her search for the mirror, connect with Naiya one last time." Carmen clenched her fists, raising them toward the ceiling. "Naiya, her brave warrior and daring lover—now on a slave ship bound for Spain."

"You should go to confession for dragging the Almighty and his messengers into your fables." Paco sucked the pipe's stem making the ash glow.

"And the Lady still searches?" Julia asked on cue.

"Yes, but by the grace of God, which is *muy bueno*. And why is it very good?"

Julia knew better than to answer aloud this time, stealing her nanny's fervor. Paco said nothing, puffing silent smoke.

Lowering her hands, Carmen clasped them over her heart. "Then I'll tell you why, *mi niña dulce*. Whoever finds even a small piece of the mirror will discover love that very hour."

When it came time for Julia to leave, Paco handed her a small package wrapped in brown paper. "Don't open until tomorrow."

Carmen smiled. *"El Dia de Reyes."*

"Three Kings Day," Julia whispered, then hugged them both before hurrying out the door. She fought the urge to cry, wondering if she'd ever be their *sweet girl* again.

At a quarter past midnight, Julia escaped into frozen darkness aboard a northbound train. She'd forgotten about the special holiday. Inside the package was a little mother-of-pearl Bible. As much as she would miss her visits with Carmen and Paco, the cheerful potbellied stove no longer warmed the chill inhabiting her soul.

Forcing her mind out of the past, Julia turned toward the lighthouse, its shadowy form barely visible against a scud of low clouds.

Paco was correct.

The towering structure existed as a rusty iron shell, the lens hijacked by vandals of a previous generation.

She stepped forward, then stopped, gazing up at the lamp room. The flame was snuffed long ago. Yet could a spark remain for those believing life held hands with mystery. For those who understood fact intertwined with faith.

She'd not heard anyone besides Carmen mention the Lady.

"Even a legend can carry a grain of truth," Julia mouthed. "At least I hope."

Was she superstitious?

No.

Did she believe in miracles?

Perhaps.

In Christ?

Absolutely.

What about genuine love between a man and a woman?

Except for Carmen and Paco, Julia wasn't sure.

Her fiery mother, Oklahoma Hale Lawrence, sought prestige through the power gained from sleeping with money. Known simply as "Lahoma," she was the only child of May Hale, a destitute, yet kind-hearted, girl from Tulsa who fell into prostitution during the 1920s Texas Panhandle oil boom. Hours before Lahoma's birth, May was mortally wounded in a shootout between bootleggers and Texas Rangers.

"Is not *su madre's* fault she's mean," Paco expressed to Julia on occasion. "Lahoma shared the womb for five hours with an angry bullet."

Even though the Gulf was warm, Julia shivered at the memory of the distant, striking beauty who'd refused to be called *mama*. Therefore, Julia called her mother *Lahoma*, as did everyone else.

"Lahoma should've never have survived her own birth," Julia announced to the vacant lighthouse, "much less childhood." She knew her mother was raised in more than a dozen foster homes, some forcing her into slave labor while trying to survive the ravages of the Great Depression.

"About the time I'd feel I'd earned my keep," Lahoma admitted during a rare reflective minute, "the *man* would stuff his wife and brats into a Model T and head west. Escaping the Dust Bowl was reserved for blood kin. An orphan became used baggage, cast out the rear window as roadside litter."

RUNNING DOWNWIND

"Trash begets trash." Julia mouthed self-pity into the salty breeze, though she knew differently. Paco and Carmen treasured her, making sure she attended weekly mass and knew right from wrong.

They also showed respect to Lahoma.

She'd met them years earlier during a cattle buying trip to Matamoros. Paco saved her from getting swindled, while Carmen helped Lahoma survive a surprise, but serious, bout of morning sickness. A novice at ranching and pregnancy, Lahoma needed the couple's knowledge and skills, thus hired them for a wage they couldn't refuse.

A flock of seagulls floated overhead in search of breakfast. Julia waded a few more steps toward the beach, then paused. Why was Lahoma haunting her head? The fact her mother despised men was no secret, blaming their ilk for May's death as well. "A man's sensual desire is like a stray dog's appetite," Lahoma often bemoaned. "Let 'em have his fill and five minutes later he's still hungry, this time begging morsels from the neighbor's pantry." Lahoma never admitted the reason outright, but as a teenager suffered from more than hard work and abandonment. That's why she used men for revenge and financial gain. That's why at sixteen, Lahoma married Valton Lawrence, a lanky young rancher dying of cancer in a nearby hospital.

A shy cowboy, Valton was the last surviving member of the struggling Lawrence clan. Faced with land foreclosure, he sold his cattle and gambled the revenue on finding oil. After two dry holes and a cancer diagnosis, a major gusher erupted into riches, his story headlining the local paper.

A week before his death, Lahoma wiggled into her tightest dress and visited the lonely bachelor. According to Carmen—whose information was gleaned from an orderly, who'd heard it from the nurse who'd walked in on the pair—Lahoma lied about her age, enticing Valton to do some extracurricular drilling on the sixth day. To avoid scandal, the hospital chaplain performed an immediate wedding ceremony, allowing Lahoma permission to stay the night. The following morning Valton passed. Eight and a half months later Julia was born. To Lahoma's embarrassment, Valton's last well was anything but dry.

Wading ashore, Julia plopped upon a mound of sand and hugged her bare knees. She and her mother shared the same shimmering black hair and pale gray eyes, though males didn't instantly melt in Julia's presence. She was too plain, too honest with her feelings. Lahoma sported a lifestyle more defiant than death and just as deceitful. Mature men who knew better found the woman mysterious, fascinating. Men too young or wild to care simply *found* her. Because she'd let them.

Men like Ray Hendrix.

A hint of light teased the horizon. During low tide, shallow pools dotted the beach. When the sun rose high enough to freshen the breeze, the pools rippled silver. Perhaps this would be the morning Julia would see the Lady and find a mirror piece.

Julia pressed her toes into the cool sand. Instead of watching the waves, she remembered a seasonal cowboy who'd roared his shiny Ford pickup down from Montana ... and into her dreams.

When Julia met Ray Hendrix that blustery spring, his tanned face and Colgate smile promised endless highways of adventure. However, by midsummer, there were only dusty back roads and a hard, half-ton bed—secluded

RUNNING DOWNWIND

spots where a young cowhand enjoyed every pleasure a freedom-starved girl offered. Then one day Ray and his pickup hightailed it north without warning. While Julia waited through the autumn for his return, Carmen treated her *niña dulce* for morning sickness.

At suppertime on Christmas Eve, Ray returned, drunk. Hearing his pickup, Julia waddled out the front door, bursting with thirty-six weeks of hope and misery. Visibly stunned, Ray climbed out holding a six pack of Lone Star but left the engine running. After chugging three cans, he sidestepped responsibility and retreated behind a scraggly mesquite to empty his bladder.

Julia only drove the Ford a short distance. Her plan was to make Ray think she was enraged enough to crash, forcing him to his senses. When she accidently rolled the vehicle on loose gravel, her unborn baby screamed for birth. Throughout the night, Julia faded in and out of consciousness, laboring in her own room under the care of a money-hushed midwife.

"You've killed *it*," Lahoma said the next morning. She stood in front of the window opposite Julia's bed. "God's punishment for recklessness. And on a day we celebrate the birth of his Son."

Julia refused to discuss her faith or cry. In years past, she'd done both in the presence of her mother and suffered the consequences. Tears followed numbness soon enough. Hopefully, God would forgive her.

"Boy or girl?" Julia tried to remain calm.

"Does the sex matter?"

"Please. I need to know."

Lahoma sat at the foot of the bed. "Girl."

"Was she pretty?"

"Makes no difference. She died."

Julia swallowed hard. "Do you think my baby suffered?"

"You don't remember?"

"Only the endless pushing."

"No. The child didn't suffer. Juanita's a good midwife. One who'll hold her tongue for an extra dollar."

"What happens next?"

"I've made arrangements for a private Christian burial."

For another dollar, Julia thought. "Thank you."

"Don't bother." Lahoma stood. "At least the blameless spend eternity in heaven."

Julia stared out the window.

"You, however, must pay for your sins." Lahoma paused. "There's a military school for young women in Biloxi, Mississippi. They won't put up with your ridiculous fantasies, nor your insolence."

"When?"

"Spring term begins in two weeks. I've made all the arrangements."

"Of course."

"Don't you dare sass me."

"I'm sorry, Lahoma." Julia faced her mother. "What about Ray?"

Lahoma smiled. "Long gone."

Julia thrust her thoughts out of the past and focused on the expanding dawn. Like Gulf waves in a storm, hard memories refused retreat. Shortly after losing her baby, she'd learned Lahoma'd slept with Ray that same spring. He'd secretly romanced the daughter beneath a rising moon, then finished the night with the mother. Lahoma discovered the betrayal and introduced him to her twelve-gauge, double-barreled bodyguard, which was why he'd fled back to Montana. Likewise, the truth of the whole twisted affair—along with military school—had forced Julia to flee as well.

But why Ray had returned that tragic Christmas Eve remained a mystery, except he carried a payload of Lone Star. The dolt could write a Pulitzer about alcohol impairing one's judgment.

Julia laughed out loud.

She knew when her mother's loaded *bodyguard* meant business.

The reason why Ray Hendrix was *long gone*.

A dolphin's laugh followed Julia's, echoed by a chorus of joyful Bottlenose chatter announcing the floating ball of sun. She'd never seen the Lady, but often witnessed families of these magnificent sea mammals welcoming the sun. This morning they seemed more excited than usual, as if trying to communicate something.

She stood and studied the horizon.

Nothing.

The fireball floated higher, a blending of misty beams and emerald sea.

Still, nothing.

And then *something* appeared in the distance.

Was it a large piece of driftwood?

Or human-like?

Julia rushed toward the form, her heart beating double-time.

Could the legend be true?

Entering the water, she splashed closer.

A tumble of arms and legs topped a wave, then disappeared.

She stopped.

What was that?

Where was that?

"There," she screamed.

"Right there!"

The form emerged but was again pounded by the rolling water. A massive wave rose over the spot and crested, spitting a tangle of human flesh into the shallows.

Julia stared, stunned beyond expectancy.

Floating in the surf was no Lady ...

But a lifeless man.

CHAPTER 6

Hugh Ryder believed when a man reached his fifties, life became too comfortable and way too predictable. That's why he was partial to a healthy tropical squall, especially one that rocked Padre hard enough to forewarn an active hurricane season. Last night's thunder fest made him feel alive.

The person who stressed *experience* as the best teacher was correct. Too little could get a guy into trouble, whereas too much made him overly cautious. Paranoid. Finding the right balance of knowhow was necessary for a man's imminent success.

For Ryder, the feat meant purchasing an Amphicar, a sporty amphibious vehicle he'd dubbed "Frog." He borrowed the idea from Ila Loetscher, an adventurous and kind-hearted local woman intent upon saving the endangered Kemp's ridley sea turtles. He'd accompanied Ila and other do-gooders down to Mexico to dig turtle eggs before poachers sold them as a delicacy.

Wouldn't that make 'em *poached eggs*?

He chuckled.

Before the unborn critters lay sunny side up on a rich man's plate, Ila and company reburied hundreds of Kemp's ridley eggs on secluded Padre beaches, hoping they'd hatch. With any luck, the female turtles returned as adults to establish nesting areas. He respected Ila because she left him alone. Watching for hatchlings everyday fit perfectly into his plans.

Last night's storm pitched him out of bed earlier than usual. So, he climbed in Frog and headed up the beach past the old lighthouse while the stars still twinkled. Wherever he went, his water-defying car was a novelty, helping business and adding to his cover. Frog was also an interesting sideshow for rubberneckers atop the two-mile-long Queen Isabella causeway to the mainland. Looked as if a lunatic had driven a bright green convertible into the Laguna Madre. The Germans who'd designed Frog were geniuses, probably sons of decent men and women forced to waste their engineering talents on that maniac, Hitler. Ryder would've gladly served America during WWII, then fought in Korea. Instead, he'd served *time* elsewhere.

"Due to my own stupidity." Ryder's words blended with the predawn breeze. "If I were a generation younger, I'd be hopping out of Hueys in Viet Nam."

He hit loose sand and downshifted Frog into second gear. The day he needed such a vehicle soon approached, at least that's what the retired shrimpers over at the donut shop predicted. That's why Ryder also ordered a heavy-duty battery and extra strong ragtop, one that withstood torrential rain and high wind. As a final precaution, he purchased aggressive tires.

"Been stuck more than once."

He frowned.

Embarrassing.

Made him look like a helpless tourist.

To Ryder's knowledge *and* relief, no one had ever seen him bog down while driving out to check for turtle hatchlings.

RUNNING DOWNWIND

The sand ahead was deeper. He punched in the clutch and dropped Frog into first. The less others knew about his background, the better. Raised in eastern New Mexico, the shrimpers forgot Ryder was a *foreigner*, their standard slang for someone not born in Texas. To them, he was a circuit farrier who'd grown weary of shoeing horses for a living and opened Ryder's Roughshod Gourmet.

"Any tradesman who thinks he can cook gourmet food must be arrogant," Ryder often joked, even though "Roughshods" was the most popular beachside eatery on the island. Since he preferred working his own schedule, a sign on the door read:

Open, Unless Closed

When a handful of haughty tourists insisted Ryder be more specific, he added:

Closed, Unless Open

In his opinion, they could either loosen up and live, or take their life-strangling ideology and grumble someplace else. Irritating the complainers made him chuckle, that's why the sign. Spoiled folks initiated the reason he rented a couple of private bungalows—to quiet men hard on their luck.

Or women.

Young gals like Julia Lawrence, who'd occupied the fancier one going on four years. He'd passed her pickup a minute ago, parked near the surf. A clean '56 Chevy he'd noted for sale during his daily post office run. She needed trustworthy transportation, so he'd stopped and made a deal.

Ryder grinned, remembering how she'd bonded to the truck like a barrel racer to her horse. Julia first refused financial help, then relented, paying Ryder a little each month. He'd lied about the cost, charging her much less than the seller asked.

"Of what she ain't aware, ain't nobody's business ... especially hers." Ryder loved repeating the phrase, knowing his slight untruth helped her. He also knew her habit of sitting cross legged on the beach in front of the lighthouse, beneath starlight's final dregs. Why she watched the sunrise every morning remained a mystery.

Removing a hand from the steering wheel, he gestured to the approaching dawn. "A female's entitled to secrets ... same as a male." Ryder's best deduction was Julia had trouble sleeping, though she never looked tired. Like him, the gal probably wasn't afraid of a little rough weather.

Maybe looked forward to it.

They'd met the Saturday she climbed atop Roughshods's pitched tin roof during a sopping November squall. President John F. Kennedy had been assassinated less than twenty-four hours prior, the whole country was floundering in shock. Ryder stood on the narrow crest—for the third time that day—punching down the plastic billow of his oversized poncho, while trying to adjust the TV antenna. His first two attempts to pick up Walter Cronkite's nonstop news ended with fuzzy, rolling zigzags instead of a clear, steady screen. Crazy gal must've seen the ladder and guessed Ryder's plan. Nearly startled him into an early grave. Wet tin is slicker than oil on ice.

"Got bailing wire?" Julia shouted.

"What? Who are—?" Ryder wheeled around, nearly losing balance.

"Increases the reception."

"Whoa."

Julia grabbed his arm. "Careful." Cold rain plastered her blouse to her chest. "Bailing wire," she shouted again. "Long strands."

RUNNING DOWNWIND

"Basement." Ryder pointed to the ladder.

Julia followed.

He'd never seen this gal but might as well take a breather. Ten minutes before she'd thrown him off kilter, some daredevil in a small plane buzzed overhead, low enough to scratch his back with the propeller.

Stepping off the bottom rung, he ducked through a narrow opening underneath Roughshods into an enclosed section supported by concrete stilts. Located on ground level, the "basement" provided convenient, cost-free storage for beach homes and businesses. Ryder's basement smelled of leather, newsprint, and automotive grease.

The odors of freedom.

He slipped out of his poncho and plugged an extension cord into a nearby outlet. A fluorescent lamp blinked to life, exposing everything from car parts to plumbing fixtures. Broken furniture, empty soft-drink bottles, and worn-out western boots crowded the top of a green work bench. A dozen wall mounts boasted an assortment of electrical supplies, tools, and horse tack. Stacks of old newspapers occupied one corner, while a couple of expensive bookcases competed for footage with a crate of wholesale hospital garb. An aluminum canoe dangled by chains from an overhead crossbeam, the boat's belly overflowing with grocery sacks—all sizes.

The space was a testament to the Great Depression's foremost lesson.

Keep today what tomorrow may require.

"Are you a restaurant owner or a junk collector?" Julia rubbed her bare arms and shivered.

"You're soaked. Where's your raincoat, Miss ...?"

"Julia Lawrence. I didn't have time to pack." She swallowed. "I need a room and a job."

Instinct cautioned him not to be nosey, at least about the raincoat. He liked the name Julia. A gal of similar age could've been his daughter—if he'd been careful. Instead, he was careless and lost out on love, which negated the whole parenting scenario from the get-go.

Ryder refused to look at Julia's wet blouse, even though he'd noticed a considerable spatter of dried blood on the left sleeve. "Done much waitressing?"

"More than I cared to."

"Where?"

"Dallas."

"Is that where you're from?"

"Just where I've been."

"What's your age?"

"I ..." She took a deep breath. "I turned twenty-one yesterday."

Ryder scratched his chin. It didn't itch, but he needed a moment to think. "Why should I hire you?"

"Because I know about bailing wire."

He chuckled to himself, stepped to the crate, and dug out a long-sleeved nurses uniform. "This'll do for now. I have extra aprons upstairs."

"Then you'll hire me?"

"Wouldn't have mentioned the apron."

"Thanks."

"Gotta spare bungalow upstairs too. You can stay there."

"How much?"

"With meals ... a little less than your paycheck."

"I don't know what to say."

He cleared his throat. "Tell me more about bailing wire."

RUNNING DOWNWIND

Unless cooking, Ryder spent the remainder of Saturday glued to Cronkite. Julia took orders, bussed tables, and rang the cash register, proving herself to be smart and efficient.

The next day, when Jack Ruby gut-shot Lee Harvey Oswald on live television, she trembled for hours, barely able to speak and pour iced tea for the Sunday lunch crowd. At first, Ryder thought her reaction uncharacteristic for such a tough, headstrong gal, one who'd survived the human wolves who preyed on pretty young waitresses in a major city ...

Until he recalled her statement: *I didn't have time to pack.*

Ryder stroked the stubble on his chin.

He could only imagine why.

Braking Frog to a stop, he killed the engine, then opened his pocketknife and pried the cap off a warm grape soda, one-handed. He took a swig. Tastier wake-up juice than coffee. He'd drunk 'em room temperature in prison, learning to like 'em that way. The beverage produced more sweet fizz and didn't chill his bottom teeth.

Ryder wriggled lower into the driver's seat and propped a foot on the dashboard. He'd ascertained more behind bars than an appreciation for lukewarm soda pop. The slammer was where he'd finally been knocked onto his knees—so to speak—long enough to crawl into the outstretched arms of his Savior. No preacher on the outside could ever convince him to journey salvation's road. Why? 'Cause most churchgoing folks were a fraudulent flock, full of hypocrites, snitches, and gossips.

Add *judgmental* to the congregational mix and they were worse than inmates.

Ryder took another sip. His sentence of hell on earth was what saved his soul from eternal damnation. He chuckled at the paradox, remembering a few valuable survival lessons acquired while serving time. The most important:

Stay alert.

The second most important:

Don't ignore your God-given talents. After scrubbing pots for six months in the warden's private kitchen, then working as the cook's assistant for another six, Ryder discovered a culinary knack.

He gulped down the rest of the soda and grinned. The warden loved fancy eats and ordered Ryder a gourmet cookbook, which he'd worn out. The day his incarceration ended, he headed to the nearest bookstore and bought Julia Child's *Mastering the Art of French Cooking*.

Even watched her on television.

And after learning the receptive merits of bailing wire from "the other Julia," he never missed an episode. Mrs. Child was a big-boned, horsey sorta gal, but he liked a woman who could handle herself in a man's world. If she weren't already married, he'd consider looking her up when the time was right. Drive Frog to New York City and ask her to dinner.

"Think I'll do it anyway," he muttered, "and invite hubby to come along. He's probably all right."

Reaching into Frog's backseat, Ryder grabbed a flannel shirt he kept on hand for cool mornings. The only time he bothered wearing a shirt in hot weather was for trips into town, or when he knew the Department of Health was dropping by Roughshods for a fun-filled visit. They didn't take kindly to a bare-chested cook, even though he wore boots, jeans, and a full apron. Customers didn't care, joking about him looking sexier than a movie star. Most folks wore their bathing suits for lunch—except on Sunday—and casual attire for breakfast and supper. On weekends, he donned a western shirt. Seemed proper, though he left the top three or four snaps undone. A man's chest needed room to breathe. The hair on his had been silver as long as he could recall. Matched what sprouted around the perimeter of his scalp and bunched into a ponytail. Silver was a color he loved about as much as gold.

He slipped into the flannel and chugged the remaining two fingers of soda. Horace "Dipp" Dipple—his cellmate for seven of the fifteen years he endured at The Walls Unit in Huntsville—believed the bottom inch of any beverage was backwash. Spit. He'd bought the idea from his zany, junior high science teacher. Ryder explained to delirium if the theory held true, the dregs belonged to the drinker, who wouldn't taste the difference anyway. Yet, Dipp refused all final sips. The man hid a ruler beneath his prison garb, so he'd not miss a single, saliva-less drop. Since Dipp quit school after the fifth grade, he wasn't known for packing an arsenal of intelligence. Instead, he'd packed a revolver. He served a life sentence for *accidently* murdering his wife. In Ryder's opinion, every inmate was there ... *accidently*.

Ryder snapped the flannel up to his neck. Within thirty minutes the sun would transform the rain-cooled breeze into steam. At The Walls, he'd coveted all brands of outdoor air—scorched, frozen, anything in-between. The lack of it was the hardest part of being locked up. No balmy gusts massaging his back or caressing his face. No smoky winters and sage scented summers. On his parents' ranch near Nara Visa, NM, he'd lived for the comforting squeak of saddle leather, accompanied by the lonely wail of Mother Nature's breath. If it screamed down off the Great Plains, the pitch was shrill, the temperature cold. Roared up from Texas, baritone hot. A whirlwind might snake out of the sky with the destructive power of a thousand runaway locomotives, then unwind to creep silent as fog.

"Here," Ryder whispered. Just saying the word made his insides tingle. He scanned the dunes in both directions, then checked his wristwatch. Night was already bleaching into day. He sucked in a deep draught of free oxygen and released it out both nostrils, slowly. After spending nearly a third of his life in a stinking cell, air on the outside always smelled sweet, sea breeze the most fragrant.

"Here," he repeated. "Right here for over a hundred years. Can't be anywhere else." He only talked out loud to himself about truth, facts worthy of the confidence born from proper research. After studying beach erosion and tidal currents for a decade, he was certain the Singer treasure lay within his grasp. *Money Hill* he'd heard in prison. A stockpile of silver bars, jewelry, and Spanish coins belonging to pioneer rancher, John Singer.

Ryder grinned. When John and his wife, Johanna, established their spread on the island around 1851, they soon discovered significant treasure washed up from sunken Spanish galleons. Ten years later, Texas joined the Confederacy. As Union sympathizers, the Singers were ordered off Padre, but buried their wealth before leaving. Their plan was to return after the War Between the States and reclaim their riches ... except for an unforeseen complication. A barrage of wind and waves demolished familiar landmarks, their fortune lost.

Interesting.

As soon as the next major hurricane accomplished its counterclockwise dirt work, the Singers' mislaid treasure would be Hugh Ryder's find of a lifetime. He couldn't rent

RUNNING DOWNWIND

a bulldozer and start moving mountains of sand. Folks would become suspicious. Some might unravel his plan. So he'd wait until a strong enough storm made landfall, providing a brief window of exploration during the eye, or immediately afterward.

Ryder stroked Frog's dashboard. No heavy equipment required. Just a vehicle able to transport the cache on either land, or water, back to the safety of Roughshods. Constructed primarily of steel and concrete, the building was designed by an eccentric architect as a hurricane proof beach house. The place looked more like a business than a summer home yet survived countless storms. He needed the structure to outlast one more.

"Ryder. Help!"

"Julia?"

She stood fifty yards away.

Ryder sat up straight and cranked Frog. "Where's your pickup?"

She was too far away to hear.

"Wonder if her pickup won't start," he muttered. The battery was old and probably needed recharging. She'd borrowed his booster cables several times in the past few months. Yet while most women worked themselves into a lather over such things, Julia didn't. Her alarm must be about something else. A man could use her nerves for welding rods.

He stomped the gas in her direction. Julia looked as if she'd been swimming, then rolled in the sand like a sweaty mare. Why was she was running back toward the lighthouse?

"Hey?" Ryder pulled alongside. "Where's your truck?"

"Near the lighthouse."

"What's the emergency?"

Julia hopped over Frog's passenger door without breaking stride. "Tide's coming in."

"Usually does 'bout this—"
"Pickup's in the surf. Won't start."
"In the surf? Why'd you park—?"
"There's a man ... " She paused to catch her breath.
"Where?"
"In the back."
"Didn't let him ride up front?"
"Please listen."
"Tell me."
"Ryder ... I think I've killed him."

CHAPTER 7

"Killed him?"

Julia nodded. Trouble was her ever-present stalker. Foul weather from the previous night produced more than a wishy-washy premonition. The storm churned up a man. Spit him out of the deep like the whale did Jonah.

Ryder clutched Frog into high gear, shouting above the engine's whine. "Killed him? Why?"

"Accident."

"How?"

"My pickup."

"Ran him down?"

"His head hit the tailgate."

"Backed over him?"

"No."

"Was he trying to hurt you?"

"No. I pulled him out of the water."

"You're sure he's dead?"

"Maybe."

"Maybe? So, you don't know."

"I couldn't find a pulse."

Julia swallowed hard, hoping Ryder wouldn't ask more questions. She wasn't certain of anything, except that the man wore battered cut-offs, had red hair, and hung precariously off her pickup's tailgate in a foot of rising water.

When she'd dragged him onto the beach, he briefly opened his eyes, gasped for breath and then lost consciousness. He needed immediate medical attention, which meant transporting him to the hospital in Port Isabel. Except hoisting him into the cab was impossible. Her only choice was to somehow inch him up into the bed. She'd read accounts of people in dire circumstances acquiring Herculean strength.

Not her.

Not now.

His limp body was buoyant at knee deep. If she backed her pickup out far enough into the surf—the tailgate partially submerged when a wave rushed in—floating him into the bed might work.

After positioning her truck, she tugged him back into the sea, waited for a large wave, then thrust him forward at the height of the swell. The man's head hit the steel tailgate with a crack. If he didn't drown, he'd die from a fractured skull.

Julia watched helplessly as the undertow rolled him over, face down. She climbed into the bed, grabbed his arms and pulled him onto the tailgate as far as his waist. His legs caught on the edge, so she tugged harder.

No progress.

Planted her feet and jerked.

Still stuck.

Leaping back into the water, she started to push against his legs, then gasped. A fresh, smile-shaped scar occupied the back of his right thigh.

RUNNING DOWNWIND

She froze.

Cowboys called the scar *the guilty grin*, but it was never connected to happiness. That's when she noticed the man wasn't breathing, so scrambled forward to check for a pulse. Seconds later, when the pickup wouldn't start, she ran to find Ryder.

As Ryder and Julia neared her pickup, she watched water slap the front bumper. Before long, the rising tide would sweep her only vehicle out to sea. Worse, her little mother-of-pearl Bible was stored in the glove box, in case she needed to flee from another life-threatening situation.

Wheeling Frog to the Chevy's rear, Ryder braked hard. "Didn't tell me the poor fellow lost his shirt." Ryder removed his boots, then unbuttoned his flannel. "He ain't dead, least not from this angle."

"How do you know?"

"Wrong color. Skin's pink as a healthy newborn's." Ryder chuckled and stepped down into the water. "I'll drape my shirt around his shoulders before the sun rises any higher and boils him into a lobster." He approached the man and paused. "Now would 'ya look at that." Ryder leaned closer. "He's been shot."

"We should carry him to a doctor. Now."

"No need. Scar's been there a while. And saltwater's a natural healer."

"Ryder. Please."

"He's alive all right. I just saw his foot move. Hop up there and put your ear close to his mouth. I'll bet he'll whisper something sweet, or at least raise an eyelid."

"I'll pass." Julia climbed out of Frog and waded around to the front of her truck. Leaning against the grill, she smeared a rogue tear. She'd not let a man see her cry since Ray Hendrix and wasn't about to start now. As a child, she'd seen an occasional gunshot scar on shirtless cowboys—the curved mattress stitch with the unmistakable dimpled center. Thank goodness this redheaded stranger was alive. The last thing she needed was a link to another mysterious death.

"Whew. Talk about booze breath." Ryder's voice carried atop the uncomfortable breeze. "Fellow ain't full of saltwater, he's full of whisky. Probably saved his life. Guess he was too drunk to drown."

As much as Julia liked Ryder, he could be a stubborn know-it-all. She'd never heard of anyone being too drunk to drown and, under less trying circumstances, would've argued the opposite. But since the man was alive, she'd keep her mouth shut. Too bad things hadn't ended as well for her in Dallas.

"Now that he's dressed for dinner," Ryder continued, "let's prop the spare tire against the cab and lean him on it. I reckon if he's busted any bones we'll know soon enough."

After maneuvering the heavy spare, they worked in tandem, gently rolling the man onto his back, while inching him into a reclined position. Other than a host of bruises and scrapes, he appeared normal, inhaling and exhaling with silent ease.

Ryder groaned. "My knees ain't as flexible as they used to be." He peered out over the water. "The boy's dehydrated too. Booze will do that to a person. Kind of a paradox, ain't it?"

Julia chose not to answer.

"Bet a sip or two of a grape soda will open his eyes. But first, let's tow your rig to the lighthouse before we gotta swim."

RUNNING DOWNWIND

After connecting the vehicles with a chain, Ryder eased Frog forward. Julia steered her pickup, glancing periodically into the rearview mirror. Refusing the stranger medical help made no sense. Ryder wasn't a doctor, and the man could have internal injuries. At least his color was good and skin warm, which ruled out hypothermia. She wasn't familiar with the term until coming to Padre, but on occasion, the newspaper reported someone dying in the Gulf due to prolonged exposure, which drops body temperature to dangerous levels, summertime included.

So, how long had he been in the water? What happened to his boat?

Except for a shaggy beard, the man's face was smooth, with a smattering of tan freckles, not weathered into splotched leather like the locals. He appeared close to her age, mid-to-late-twenties. Probably one of those spoiled young oil company execs who believed God created women for male pleasure.

She shivered, realizing how much the thought mimicked Lahoma's mindset. "I refuse to become my mother," Julia whispered. Perhaps he was a decent guy who'd simply been deep-sea fishing with his buddies, had too much to drink and stumbled overboard. But if that were true, why hadn't anyone noticed and sent a search party?

Located at the edge of the dunes, the lighthouse cast a column of morning shade wide enough to park both vehicles. After Ryder unhitched the tow chain, she felt the pickup bobble when he climbed into the back.

"Brought three grape sodas," he yelled. "Fellow might not appreciate drinking alone."

Julia had no intention of further ignoring the man's medical needs. As soon as Ryder dribbled a little liquid into the poor guy's mouth, she'd jump-start her battery, then insist they all head to the emergency room. If Ryder objected, she'd hop back into the cab and drive away. No matter how much he complained, she wouldn't stop. Unless he wanted to leap off the causeway into the bay, he'd better bail out before they reached the blacktop.

She opened the glove box to grab a brush. Lahoma had constantly chided her daughter about appearance, so the act became a forced habit. Julia paused, then slammed the lid. Windblown hair didn't matter. She had no desire to impress anyone.

Placing her hand on the door handle, she paused again. Hot breeze gusted through the cab carrying distant cries, most likely the yearnings of hungry seagulls. A wispy hiss signaled Ryder prying the cap off a grape soda. He mumbled something and pried off another. She wanted to open the door, but her arms were heavy.

Why did this mysterious man bother her?

Interest her?

When she'd pulled him from the water, she'd felt nothing but the panicked rush of adrenaline. A job needed doing, which she'd faced. But when his eyes blinked open before he lost consciousness, Julia found herself looking down at the scene from an invisible pinnacle. She'd heard of people having out of body experiences caused by near-death trauma. However, her summit view didn't make sense. He was the person who'd nearly drowned.

She gathered her emotions, opened the door and stepped out. "Ryder?"

"Yeah?" He sat on the rim of the bed, blocking her view of the man.

"I need your booster cables."

"Not yet necessary." He pried the cap off a third bottle.

"I think it is."

"Hope you drink 'em warm."

She waved the soda away. "He's going to the hospital whether you like it or not."

RUNNING DOWNWIND

"Shouldn't we let Mr. Leonard decide?"

"Who?"

Ryder scooted against the cab's rear window and grinned. The man looked at Julia with tired eyes.

"Leonard, Mick Leonard." His voice was barely audible. "Thanks for saving my life."

Julia only stared, knowing what her subconscious communicated.

She'd seen this man before.

CHAPTER 8

Distorted strains of the hit single, "Monday, Monday," blared from a car parked outside Mick's bungalow. He sat up in bed and groaned, not so much from the mottled bruises that stained his body, but from a desperate tiredness gripping every joint and muscle. A dull ache orbited a lump on his scalp the size of a small planet.

He'd have to rally to die.

Moreover, he was totally dependent upon the kindness of two strangers who'd asked no questions. Surely, they'd noticed his telltale scar.

Reaching to the bedside table for an aspirin, he remembered how Ryder retrieved the bottle from his unusual car immediately following the rescue, now three days past. Ryder insisted Mick swallow a couple of the pills with a sip of grape soda. Julia nodded in agreement, yet a look of apprehension squeezed her oval face. Mick expected her to continue making pleas for medical help on his behalf, but she hadn't. He was relieved.

And strangely disappointed.

"Monday, Monday" continued as more cars parked outside Mick's screened window. The Mamas and the Papas wouldn't appreciate having their tight harmony fractured into earsplitting decibels, but anyone in showbiz learned success arrived with a public price, where fans left the bill.

He gazed at the door. The daily noon concert announced Roughshods was open for lunch, which also meant Julia brought him a tray. He considered getting dressed and raising the blinds but didn't, preferring the dimness. Fortunately, the extra-large scrub pants he wore as pajamas didn't irritate his bruises.

Made him wonder if Ryder had worked in a hospital? Or Julia?

Perhaps her husband was an orderly. She wore no diamond, no wedding band, though bare fingers indicated nothing. Rings were easily lost.

Mick stroked his chin, still surprised at the smoothness. The beard he'd grown at sea disappeared down the drain at Julia's insistence, who encouraged the feelgood merits of being cleanshaven.

He whispered her name.

"Julia."

Mick wasn't sure why. Maybe because she'd saved his life. Today, he hoped she'd bring coffee, which tasted better after an aspirin appetizer than water.

"Julia," he repeated slowly. Were there two syllables or three? Resting his chin lightly atop his fingers, he spoke her name a third time.

"Julia."

His chin dipped twice, indicating two syllables, a trick learned at West Avenue Elementary.

Mick sighed.

West Avenue Elementary was the birthplace of trouble. On the first day of first grade, he'd *stumbled* into love with a petite blonde wearing a yellow dress.

Literally.

Tripped over a rogue shoelace and fell heart first into the sweet giggle of Deanna Jessalynn Merroney—nine beautiful syllables that rarely recognized his existence until much later. For the next five years, he'd secretly recited her entire name during recess ... while swinging. After grasping both chains, he'd pump his legs until climbing high enough to kick a wall cloud. Then hanging on with his right hand, he'd carefully pronounce her name, his chin bouncing in glorious triplicates above the fingers of his left. A self-fabricated rumor boasted he'd orbited a complete revolution, which required traveling upside down at the perilous apex. Mick suspected his closest friends knew he wasn't courageous enough to attempt such a feat. As for the rest of his classmates? Perhaps a molecule of his suspected daring still rested within their latent memories, even inside the mind of Deanna Jessalynn Merroney.

At least you were brave enough to write her initials in your spelling book.

Beginning about the third or fourth grade, a girl would write her boyfriend's name multiple times on the protective manila covers of her textbooks. By May, the covers had disintegrated into inked blue fuzz. A guy wouldn't dare post his feelings publicly toward the opposite sex. He'd be labeled a sissy, a lover-boy-pansy. So in microscopic script, he'd carefully pen the name of his ladylove—once—on the inside bottom flap adjacent to the binding. The act was heady, the secret scribble ... pure enchantment. Naturally, Deanna's name held Mick's place of honor.

In the fifth grade, he risked a much bolder step. On page 163 of *The Wonder of Words*, he wrote DJM beside a printed love poem, which was more of a mushy limerick. Then after his devil mask fiasco at the Halloween party, he erased her name *and* initials because she'd giggled into candied ecstasy. He should've replaced Deanna's initials with Cherie's, at least on the cover, but never did. So, for the remainder of Mick's public-school education, his textbooks were nameless wannabees. Sterile consequences of a fickle boy-heart.

After punching his pillow into a lump, Mick lay back and waited for Julia. He'd never met a woman with slate-colored eyes. Eyes which bore compassion yet seemed layered with distant secrets. If she'd mentioned her last name, Mick couldn't recall. He'd known her—what—all of seventy-something hours since she'd hauled him from the waves.

Only to lie about his name.

"Leonard, Mick Leonard."

He'd almost said, Mick *Mc*-Leonard, but didn't. It was too similar to McFarland, plus the same number of syllables. He could've feigned confusion and told the truth. Instead, he sipped a small swallow of grape soda and repeated the alias.

"Leonard, Mick Leonard."

Thanks, Cuz. Payback time for the night in Mexico. Mick couldn't take a chance on the press, nor his parents locating him, so borrowed Leonard's *first* name to use as his *last*.

"Monday, Monday" ended with the DJ babbling about an active Atlantic hurricane season, with a new tropical storm named Beulah lurking somewhere out in the Gulf. He wished everyone a safe and fun filled Wednesday and broke to a commercial.

"Wednesday, Wednesday," Mick repeated, wondering if he could compose the Mamas and the Papas—a hit about the trials of hump day?

Probably not. Way too depressing.

He and Cherie had met the famous folk group when she accompanied him on a *working vacation* to England. One night at Dolly's, a private London rock club, the Mamas and the Papas strolled in and gave an impromptu performance. Afterward, Cherie procured each of their autographs on four separate bar napkins.

Selfless Cherie, so unassuming and naïve. The image of her lying in her own blood was forever tattooed on Mick's memory. "I should've drowned when I had the chance," he announced to the gloomy room, "like a real man. My death would've improved the quality of my life." He knew how ridiculous the logic sounded, his face hot with sudden tears.

A rap on his door.

"Just a minute." Mick wiped his eyes with the bed sheet. "Come in."

Julia entered carrying a tray. "It's dark in here." She switched on the top light. "Talking to yourself, Leonard, Mick Leonard?"

"Just Mick. Okay?"

"We'll see."

He hated the harsh glare of an overhead light, but there was no lamp, no phone either. Moreover, it wasn't the gentle feminine reply he'd expected, which made him wonder if Julia questioned his identity. Due to her hundred-watt curtness and his recent blubbering, Mick avoided direct eye contact as she set the tray on his bedside table.

She continued. "The way you kept introducing yourself the other day reminded me of Bond, James Bond."

"How so?" Mick faked a careless yawn, followed by a nonchalant eye swipe.

"Leonard, Mick Leonard," she repeated, this time with a proper English accent.

He nodded. One of his favorite actors was Sean Connery, who portrayed the fictional British spy, James Bond, introducing himself in every film as "Bond, James Bond." Glancing her way, Mick offered a wry grin. Julia possessed a sense of humor as subtle as his own.

"Well, *Just Mick*. Eat every bite, including the fruit, and drink the water."

"No coffee?"

"Nope. Way too warm outside. Dehydration doesn't agree with you."

"Half a cup?"

"Maybe you'll feel like getting dressed and coming over to the restaurant for a little supper. Afterward, there should be a cool breeze blowing off the water. As soon as the last customers leave, I'll brew a fresh pot."

"I'd like that." Mick's answer seemed as much a surprise to her, as it sounded to him. "I hope the coffee's not too much trouble."

"Me too ... I mean ... I pour coffee all day."

"Unless you're closed."

"Ryder never locks the place." She opened the door.

"Wait." Midday coastal brightness poured into the bungalow. "There's one condition before you go."

She spun and faced him, her eyes now like polished silver.

"You know my last name. Tell me yours."

"It's ..." Julia paused, emitting a silent sentence seasoned with indecision, punctuated by her smile. "Lawrence, Julia Lawrence."

He watched her leave, suspecting she still didn't buy the Mick Leonard routine, even though only a small percentage of the population had seen him on stage. Never mind he looked different in costume and makeup. Fortunately, the film version of *Rain in Rio* wouldn't be released until next year.

Mick wasn't hungry so forced a few labored calisthenics, mostly stretches. Too exhausted to dress, he lay back down, annoyed by the top light Julia neglected to switch off. He considered throwing something and smashing the bulb, but the act would require physical effort. Instead, he studied the wardrobe Ryder'd loaned him—a pair of rubber flip-flops, two pair of faded cutoffs—Mick's were too tattered to keep—and a loud, long-sleeved, western plaid shirt with pearl snaps. Besides being too large, the entire outfit was an oxymoron, as was Mick's life.

More than anything, he'd wanted to be popular. Run with the "in" crowd, a beautiful girl hanging on each arm and his every word. Sage advice recommended weaving wisdom into one's dreams because they might come true, which was akin to the trite phrase, "never say never." Mick's problem: *Never* eventually happened but forgot to include *wisdom*.

In junior high—the years when sweaty male puberty produced *matter* over *mind*—he'd remained the smallest boy in his class, which posed a significant problem when trying to make the football team. Fran kept promising he'd grow as tall as the males on her side of the family and fill out like the males on Ed's. The torture of waiting would've been bearable if Mick's ears and feet had grown in concert with the rest of him. But for reasons of genetic insanity, they suddenly sprouted into awkward adolescence. He couldn't recall who'd coined the nickname, "Mickey McMouse," but what began as a mere eighth grade whisper soon erupted into Max Darnell's battle cry on that fateful Friday afternoon. Mick suffered a bloody nose and two black eyes, but he'd stood up to the bully, and everyone knew.

On the following Monday, he'd experienced a brief bout of notoriety, which only heightened his desire to run with the popular crowd. When a couple of acclaimed athletes invited him to join them at lunch, his hopes rose, then skyrocketed as Deanna waved and smiled from across the cafeteria. After school, Mick told his buddy, Vince, who attributed the miracle smile to gas. Since they'd both grown up around babies and were privy to why newborns grin, Mick knew Vince was mostly joking.

Mostly.

Deanna *had* waved.

But Vince's comment forewarned of the brutal obscurity Mick was forced to acknowledge on Tuesday and for the remainder of his eighth-grade year.

With junior high finally over, high school loomed large. However, the summer's anticipated growth spurt amounted to nothing more than an increased shoe size. Mick dreamed of ordering Joe Weider's bodybuilding course but was too embarrassed to ask his parents for the money. Weider, a famous strongman, had been a scrawny teenager, yet changed his physique with homemade barbells and healthy eating. Therefore, Mick downed spinach until his teeth turned green—Popeye's never did—and lifted anything heavy he could find. Every morning, he'd lock the bathroom door and weigh. By Labor Day, he'd dropped six pounds.

Texas boys *not* involved in high school football were prone to ridicule, where those stuck in PE were immediately labeled as outcasts. Therefore, Mick joined the band at the beginning of his freshman year. The school board considered marching as exercise, which exempted band members from suffering the mindless drudgery of jumping jacks and dodge ball. Since piano was Mick's only instrument, the band director, Mr. Gar—short for Garcia—suggested Mick join the rhythm section and wield a pair of cymbals. Due to Mick's summer workouts, he crashed and twirled the heavy, brass disks with ease. By the first halftime show, he'd mastered the intricate military footwork of "six to five," while keeping razor straight diagonals amidst pointing his feet through millions of countermarches. Band members rarely held the elite social station of athletes and cheerleaders, but most horn-blowers couldn't have cared less. They exercised their own strict pecking order, governed by a unique set of values and acceptance standards.

Cherie, who'd played clarinet since seventh grade, was thrilled when Mick joined the musical ranks. She also tooted a mean alto saxophone, earning a coveted spot in the award-winning jazz band. Moreover, she convinced Mr. Gar to give Mick a piano audition.

"At least tryout." Cherie punched Mick's arm as they hid in the band hall before first period. A practice room was the perfect place to avoid upperclassmen intent on hazing freshmen. Vince had been forced to roll a marble across the floor of the boys' bathroom with his nose.

"Tryout for what?" Mick tried to open a package of peanut butter crackers without the cellophane making a crinkly noise.

She disregarded the question. "I've cleared it with Mr. Gar. Don't disappoint me." Cherie frowned.

"Sorry. I already have a class during second period."

"Study hall's not a credited class. It's easy to drop." She reached for the crackers, but Mick was too quick. "And," she continued, "study hall's bor-ing."

"Jazz is diff-i-cult," he replied in a similar singsong fashion.

"Listen. I believe in you. You can do it."

"I hate the piano."

"Wrong." Cherie grabbed the crackers. "Snacks in here will get us both into trouble." She crammed them into her purse. "What you hate is practice."

"Same thing."

"Not with the right music."

Mick's stomach growled. He'd skipped breakfast but would starve to be a member of the jazz band. Those kids were cool. Almost popular. "Explain."

"Look. You dislike piano because you can't stand Bach and Mozart."

"Beethoven's okay."

"Yeah, but his stuff's still way too structured. Too many exact notes. Jazz is freeform, the melody more of a suggestion built on chords."

Mick nodded. "I like that. I hate chaining my fingers to the little black dots."

She grinned. "You'll love playing chords."

He did. To his surprise, his piano teacher adored them too, eagerly instilling the basic chordal tools of the jazz pianist's trade—ninths, thirteenths, diminished, augmented. So throughout marching season, Mick memorized chords in various keys. In less than a month, he played the underlying progressions with his left hand, while improvising a melody with his right.

After the audition, Mr. Gar welcomed Mick into the *Class of Cool*. His parents seemed pleased, even Ed, who'd only watched Mick march in one halftime. Fran attended every game, yet centered attention upon the cheerleaders and twirlers, the details of their routines touted vigorously each week to her twin daughters. When Mick broke the jazz sound barrier after Christmas, the joyful sonic boom was from Cherie.

His sophomore year dittoed the stunted physicality of his freshman, except he no longer hid in the band hall before school. Cherie continued her role as a loyal female ally, advising him about girls he thought were cute. Since neither of them had a date to the After-Finals Formal, they sat with each other most of the night. Cherie

RUNNING DOWNWIND

wasn't as talkative as usual, studying Mick with a pained expression. He assumed it was because while out on the dance floor, she'd caught him sneaking peeks at Deanna. Then in the midst of Doris Day's hit, "Secret Love," Cherie stopped dancing and began to cry. Surely her tears weren't about Mick watching Deanna. They'd discussed his meaningless infatuation on a regular basis. However, he'd accidently trounced Cherie's feet a couple of times during the previous song, pretty hard, which would make any girl cry.

"I'm sorry I hurt you," he whispered.

Pushing out of Mick's grasp, Cherie buried her face in her hands.

"I'll be more careful. Promise."

Except for the tremulous rise and fall of her shoulders, Cherie remained frozen. The song ended. People stared. Mick tried escorting her from the dance floor. She wouldn't budge.

"Cherie? What's the matter? What'd I do?"

She pushed away again, turned on her heel and stopped.

Mick crept forward. "We'll always be friends," he said softly, remembering Cherie's cheerful mantra.

Her muted sobs exploded into heaving wails. Helpless, he ran to the boys' bathroom for a wad of paper towels. When he returned, she was nowhere in sight. To worsen the situation, her friends refused to divulge what happened, or where she'd gone.

The next morning Mick discovered a note taped inside his locker.

Bye, Mickey,
We're moving back to Philadelphia today because of my dad's job. Sorry I didn't tell you sooner. Also, sorry I cried last night. It's nothing you did—just everything involved

with leaving. I've kept in contact with some former classmates in Philly, so the rest of my life should be okay. A few of them dance on a local television show—American Bandstand. Mom says I can tryout. I'll write if I have time. Promise!
We'll always be friends,
Cherie

Mick awoke in a pool of sweat, his mind taking a moment to remember the year was 1967, and he was in a bungalow on Padre Island. The lunch Julia delivered sat untouched, spoiling atop the bedside table. A couple of giant green houseflies buzzed busily above the fruit.

Sitting up, he faced the window. Darkness outlined the blinds, signaling what he already knew. He'd slept through the afternoon and into the night. His slumber wasn't restful, but hard, filled with cliffhanging chapters of unfinished dreams. He remembered struggling to get somewhere, or to find something, a frantic journey of grasping at places and objects forever out of reach.

He'd also dreamt of Cherie—not unusual—and the note he'd discovered the final day of their sophomore year. She was moving far away. They'd been friends since the fifth grade, and her leaving wasn't fair. He'd still needed a girl he could talk to. At first Mick wrestled emptiness, missing Cherie more in June than he'd admit. However, by mid-July, he'd slipped into the haze of summer's carefree humdrum. When school resumed for the fall semester, he registered as an upperclassman. That's when everything changed.

Everything.

He grew so fast his arms and legs ached, shot up six inches, gained thirty pounds. His airy tenor voice evolved into a rich, smooth baritone. Becoming a high school junior was the beginning of his ending.

Whenever Mick thought back to those awkward, adolescent years, there was much he knew, yet didn't know. Saw, yet couldn't see. His eyes kept flinging open and slamming shut at the same time. What he'd *not* seen the night of After-Finals Formal was the depth of Cherie's love for him. What he saw was her deep, constant gaze, which embarrassed him.

Frightened him.

She'd promised to write.

Yet never had.

When *American Bandstand* made it to national television, he'd watched it often, hoping to see her.

Yet never had.

Years later—after they'd rediscovered each other—she gazed much deeper than before. Could almost read his mind. If he'd given permission, she'd have gladly sprinted through his fickle man-heart's door to live deep within his soul.

But he never had, so she never could.

And now she was dead.

The door forever bolted shut.

CHAPTER 9

Julia poured herself a well-deserved mug of coffee and eased open the rusty screened door leading to Roughshods's outside dining area. The screen complained with a springy whine. Careful not to let it slam, she located a corner chair, kicked off her sandals, and propped her feet against the wooden deck railing. A steady Gulf breeze encircled her toes and cooled her legs. She was glad when the wind blew off the water instead of the land. After sunset, squadrons of mosquitoes buzzed out of the bayside marshes, the direction of their bloodsucking attack contingent upon Mother Nature's breath.

Inside, she could hear Ryder barking orders to his dishwashers, a couple of pimply teenage boys who spent more time popping each other with wet rags and staring at her than scrubbing pots. Wednesday evenings were hectic. That's when Ryder cooked buffalo bourguignon, substituting bison and beer for the traditional beef and burgundy. She imagined the nasal disgust the French would voice over Ryder's rustic interpretation of their beloved dish, deemed a southern Texas favorite.

And it wasn't even seafood.

Folks from as far away as Corpus Christi and Laredo drove to Roughshods for the popular fishless fare.

She laced her fingers around the mug as a thumbnail moon rose over the darkening water. Mick had missed supper and now coffee. He wasn't coming, but that didn't surprise her, not really. Down deep it pleased her. Intuitive skills dulled in Dallas had finally regained an edge.

Skills she'd spent a lifetime honing.

Survival skills.

If only she could remember where she'd seen him. She'd tried to match his face with each letter of the alphabet hoping to recall a specific event or location, but each time came up empty. Mick Leonard probably wasn't even his real name, yet she'd eagerly told him hers. She should've walked away. Handing out personal information was another example of the ease in which certain men could enter her life, then control her.

Not this time. Not this man. She wouldn't grant permission. That part of her life was over.

Drawing the mug to her mouth, she took a tasteless sip. She'd brewed a full pot just in case, now feeling foolish. Except Paco, every man she'd allowed breathing room eventually disappeared. As badly as she hated to admit Lahoma's truth, men would ultimately disappoint, the letters *m-e-n* integral to the spelling of the word, disappoint*men*t.

An echo of cash register rings signaled Ryder's final tallying of the day's receipts. At first, she'd thought him trustworthy and almost lowered her guard, but something held her at bay. Nothing menacing. She didn't feel unsafe in his presence. He obviously liked her and commanded an almost fatherly interest. But buried beneath his good-old-boy exterior was a layer of intolerance not exclusive to her intuitive powers. Customers guilty of using too much salt, not enough appropriate language, or wearing a hat during Sunday dinner were fined a quarter per offense, the hat-wearing rule applying only to men. Most patrons thought it funny, some even made a show of paying in advance. A few grumbled while dropping coins into a #10 can labeled, *The Sin Tin*. After a disgruntled patron raised a stink because it was unclear exactly when the rules were, Ryder posted a sign above the chiming Jax Beer clock.

[sign block starts here]

Attention customers! Today only:
It's time to respect the food, the ladies, and the Lord.

[Sign block ends here]

Julia smiled. She didn't know if a man wearing his hat during Sunday dinner was any more disrespectful than Ryder cooking the same food while shirtless. God was probably more concerned with a grateful heart on both sides of the plate. Whereas a customer's excessive use of salt simply annoyed Ryder's culinary pride, a surplus of briny oaths in the presence of females disturbed him deeply.

But how much was too much?

On some days, a single infraction pushed him to the brink of madness. On others, he'd pass the salt while swapping ribald tales with hardboiled fishermen's wives. Ryder appeared bound by religious and ethical oddities as sporadic as the wind-driven waves.

The screen whined and slammed. "Hope you're not planning on another cup of joe." Ryder's apron was slung across a bare shoulder. He cocked a boot heel over the bottom rail and pried open a grape soda. "When the puberty patrol thought I wasn't looking, they helped themselves to the rest of the pot."

"So?"

"Heard 'em whispering last week about mixing coffee with beer."

"Why?"

"Why not when you're sixteen?"

Julia could've offered a host of reasons—underage foremost—but raised an eyebrow instead. "Where'd they get the beer?"

"Poured whatever the customers left in their bottles into an empty gallon pickle jar. Thought I didn't see that either. Took 'em all summer to fill it." He chuckled. "They'll get crocked and then be too wired to sleep it off."

She cringed. "You should've put a stop to it. What if they get sick?"

Ryder shrugged.

"Or arrested?"

He peered out over the water. "Stubborn ignorance breeds hard consequences."

She responded with silence. Stubborn ignorance had been her harshest teacher.

After a moment, Ryder spoke. "Didn't you say Mick would make an appearance?"

"Guess not."

"Ain't he 'bout recuperated?"

"Guess not." Julia wished she'd never mentioned Mick Leonard's health status. The sooner he exited the island, the better.

"Any signs of turtle hatchlings?" She hoped to change the subject.

"Next to last group's about to bust outta their shells. Biggest bunch in years. I'll check on 'em at midnight and then again before first light. Might need your help herding the little critters into the Gulf."

"Might?"

"All them hazy mornings this summer threw 'em off their nighttime break-out schedule. The last group barely made it into the water before becoming creature-breakfast."

"You'll know where to find me." She suppressed a grin. The image of Ryder, jeans rolled high above his boot tops while shooing hundreds of silver dollar sized Kemp's ridley hatchlings toward the ocean was comical. She'd helped him during a few rare dawn events, plucking defenseless baby turtles out of crab holes, while watching for sea gulls and other natural predators. He kept a pistol handy to scare off hungry bands of coyotes, which seemed to know the hatching schedule better than humans.

Ryder cleared his throat. "Found what's left of the boy's sailboat. Ain't much."

"*His* sailboat? Are you sure?"

"Positive. Unless you've run across somebody else wholly washed up and half-dead."

She ignored the remark. "Where?"

"Five miles up the beach from the lighthouse, not far from that big group of hatchlings. The mast was still in one piece. Got ripped clean off. Except for a few splinters, everything else belongs to the fish."

Her stomach tightened. *Hard consequences* still hounded her at every turn, even those she didn't own.

Ryder studied the label on his soda. "Has Mick said where he was headed?"

"Not a word."

"Mexico's my guess, but it's hard to say. And since he's not mentioned anyone else on board, I suspect he was alone."

Julia hadn't considered the possibility of others, imagining a crew of bearded, barely dressed, comatose men piled in the back of her pickup. She shuddered.

"Reckon the boy's guarded about his scar?"

"Wouldn't you be?" The defensive response slipped out before she could stop it.

"Maybe." Ryder swigged his soda, then faced her. "Depends upon what I was running from."

Julia opened her mouth to reply, but the words caught cold in her throat. She knew the horror of fleeing from a life-threatening situation.

Ryder continued. "Only a fool or a desperate man would sail solo this time of year. My guess—the boy needed to get away from outlaws. Or in-laws."

"Funny," she managed. "Maybe the FBI."

"Naw. If he was a wanted criminal, flotillas of feds would storm the beach worse than Normandy."

"Who then?"

"Don't have a clue." Ryder drained the remaining contents before wiping his mouth with the back of his hand. "I reckon we'll know enough when he's ready to tell us."

"Enough? We saved his life and that's all we get?"

Ryder grinned. "I don't harbor fools."

CHAPTER 10

The temperature inside Julia's bungalow was still too hot for sleep. So, she changed into cutoffs with a sleeveless blouse, smoothed her hair back into a ponytail and returned to the chair on Roughshods's deck. The moon had evaporated into a vast ocean sky matted with stars. The scene reminded her of hot August nights on the ranch. Barely a teenager, she'd slept outdoors atop a loaded hay wagon. Holding a flashlight, she drifted off while reading dusty issues of *The Saturday Evening Post,* rescued from one of Lahoma's attic cleaning binges. The weekly novellas were Julia's favorite, particularly "The Quiet Man," an Irish love story by Maurice Walsh. The magazine's cover featured a rugged Coast Guard seaman, standing stalwart atop his ship's pitching deck. An iceberg loomed in the background above windblown waves. She desperately wanted to hop an Atlantic Ocean freighter and sail to exotic places.

Two years later, she'd accompanied her mother to their local movie house to see the film version starring Maureen O'Hara and John Wayne. Lahoma thought it would be set in the American west as a classic shoot-'em-up. During the opening scene, she recognized the folly in her presumption. Loud enough for all to hear, she labeled the picture unrealistic and sentimentalized.

"Living off the land's not an easy life," Lahoma bemoaned toward the end. "It never breaks into song, nor ends happily. And rue the man who attempts to maneuver me, even John Wayne."

He wouldn't want to. Julia scrunched low into her seat. The truth? Maureen O'Hara portrayed a stunningly strong character, a woman who'd make short work of anything unallowable. Julia had read that the role mirrored Miss O'Hara's real-life constitution—feisty, quick-witted and extremely intelligent. Men played by *her* rules.

When the credits rolled, Lahoma decried director John Ford a charlatan and the entire movie industry a hoax. Instead of exiting through the lobby, she marched upstairs to the manager's office and demanded a refund. Embarrassed, Julia refused to ride home and walked five miles. She pondered over Maureen O'Hara the entire way—a talented woman tough enough to make it in Hollywood yet considered loving and kind. By the time Julia traversed the ranch's main cattle guard, she'd pledged to personally master the same character traits.

She worked hard at her promise, not surprised when Lahoma grew even more intolerable. So the hay wagon remained Julia's fair-weather bedroom.

The summer before her junior year in high school, she'd awakened to rumbles of thunder, the wagon surrounded by wild Mustangs. She'd heard reports of renegade bands still roaming at will across the southern plains but had never seen any. As the horses nipped for the best position to crunch alfalfa stalks, she envisioned a life free from the ranch. Lightning penciled the edge of the prairie, and then a sudden cool wind whipped the Mustangs back into the night. While the storm passed in the distance, Julia vowed escape *as soon as possible.* If not to Ireland, another scenic location far from her mother's tightening reins.

RUNNING DOWNWIND

The following Saturday, she traveled to Amarillo with Paco to sell steers. After sweltering all morning at the stockyards, they spent a cool afternoon inside a downtown theater at Julia's request. This time she viewed *The Quiet Man* without interruption. When "The End" scrolled across the screen, she augmented her vow to include meeting her own "quiet man."

As soon as ...

Wistful disappointment drew her mind back to Roughshods's deck. Sucking in a long breath, she slowly released it. Padre Island was better than she'd hoped, but not part of her original design. The stupidity of pregnancy at seventeen, then losing her baby, had detoured freedom's journey. On the night Julia ran, she'd not intended Dallas as a final destination—her train ticket was punched from Amarillo to Kansas City. Then on to Chicago, New York, and the Canadian side of Niagara Falls. (From there, she'd decide whether Ireland was real or merely a schoolgirl's dream.) But a paralyzing snowstorm blanketed the Midwest, rerouting all northbound passenger traffic south to Dallas's Union Station.

Indefinitely.

It was her reaction to the conductor's emphasis on the word "indefinitely" that attracted trouble. Each time he repeated the disappointing announcement, the derailing of her plans made her cry. In defiance, she'd laughed out loud. A flashy young businessman across the aisle moved to an adjacent seat.

"Ah, such a misty-eyed beauty," the man whispered, "with such a curious cackle."

Before she could protest, Dario Rossi's smooth Italian accent had diverted her plans.

Indefinitely.

A swoop of headlights, followed by a dozen Jax Beer chimes signaled Ryder's midnight run to check for hatchlings. As with Lahoma, he required little sleep, becoming much more animated after the sun set. Julia purposely yawned, hoping to dissuade thoughts of her mother and attract fatigue. Instead, her mind returned to Dario.

He'd lived for the night as well, his downtown Dallas supper club, The Scarlett Stallion, open until four a.m. Upon closing, he rewarded himself with a Churchill cigar and a petite glass of rare sherry, while offering his *amici* the run of the bar. They'd play cards, sing Verdi arias, and discuss business until the coffee shop opened at the nearby Blackland Hotel. At six o'clock sharp, he'd escort his pals to breakfast unless the law intervened. Belligerence might land an inebriated hothead in the drunk tank, but never Dario, who answered every question with sober patience. Rumors circulated about his connection to illegal gaming and prostitution; however, none were proven. Gambling at The Scarlet Stallion was strictly prohibited, as was the hiring of underage girls for waitressing or entertainment. All female employees were held to a strict moral code they dared not break.

Several of the downtown clubs attracted rowdy fraternities or blue-collar audiences with cheap booze, low class strippers, and raunchy comedians. Dario took pride in hosting the white-collar and political elite, men who expected fine dining amidst the sophisticated charms of Las Vegas-style show girls. "My club is an establishment where a man feels comfortable taking his wife," Dario boasted, "or another man's bride."

An insightful chill ran the length of Julia's spine. Dario had used her from the beginning. Citing safety concerns, he insisted upon providing Julia a suite at the multistoried

RUNNING DOWNWIND

Blackland until she could afford a decent apartment. And since she was still a few months shy of her eighteenth birthday, he'd arranged a job for her at the hotel's street level coffee shop, early shift.

"What could be more perfect," he'd announced on the cusp of a broad smile. "We'll be together every morning."

Julia soon realized *togetherness* meant serving him and his pals breakfast at a large, circular booth reserved just for them, but they were generous tippers. After Dario paid the tab, each man tossed a dollar onto the center of the table, except Sal Angioli, Dario's eldest and closest friend. Sal would place a meaty hand over his heart and blurt: "*Julia, tu sei la mia rosa!*" then add at least five dollars to the top of the pile.

"Did Sal call me his rose?" Julia asked Dario after the initial exclamation.

He nodded. "You remind him of his Jewish wife who survived Auschwitz but died later from the effects of cruel Nazi experiments."

"Is that why he's such a generous tipper?"

Dario laughed. "Yes, and because he's the wealthiest jeweler in the state."

Occasionally, Dario's contribution to the gratuity pile was a two-dollar bill. "Any time you find President Jefferson lying on the table," he'd instructed her early on, "never unfold him. Without delay, hand him back in change to the booth nearest the exit."

"Why?" Julia remembered the rough, sour-faced trio who sat there each morning.

"Just business." Dario caressed her face with the back of his hand.

"Those men scare me. They never smile."

"Humorless but harmless."

She wrinkled her forehead. "So why the two-dollar bill?"

"Bitter men work cheap."

"But—"

Dario gently pinched her lips. "Hush now, my Julia. No more questions. You must always do what I ask because I've been good to you."

"More hard consequences," Julia mouthed into the salty Gulf breeze. In the beginning, Dario had been too good, too patient, too tender, his dark curls and dimpled smile gradually deepening her desire to please. After losing her baby, she'd begged God's forgiveness for having unwed sex, vowing eternal celibacy. Then fear and loneliness crept in, forcing buried passions to the surface. Passions begging surrender at any cost.

Except weekends and holidays, she'd work at the Blackland Hotel's coffee shop until noon, then run errands while the rest of the city crowded into noisy lunch counters. She'd often return to her suite to find Dario sleeping in her bed. After a warm bath, she'd curl up beside him until he awakened. He rarely sought physical pleasures—none until she turned eighteen. Instead, he arose to smoke unfiltered *sigarettas* out on the balcony while reading both Dallas dailies, until long shadows crisscrossed the busy streets below.

For supper they'd dine at the club. The first time she was allowed to stay for the floorshow, scantily clad showgirls pranced across the stage. Julia covered her eyes. Chuckles rattled around the table as embarrassment heated her cheeks.

RUNNING DOWNWIND

"Don't listen to the riff-raff," Dario whispered. "Modesty becomes you."

Feeling prudish, the following afternoon she purchased the most revealing evening gown she could find. It was Valentine's Day, and she wanted to surprise him.

It was also the first time Dario slapped her.

"From now on, I'll furnish your wardrobe." He marched to her closet for another dress, then flung it in her direction. "You're not a prostitute, even though you've birthed a child out of wedlock."

"What?" Julia's legs grew weak. "No. I've never—"

"You're lying." Dario's face reddened. "A woman's body is a window, revealing the secrets of her soul." He turned to leave, then stopped. "On matters of female purity, my Julia, I forgive only once."

She didn't cry until the suite's door clicked shut. Tears of bewilderment streamed into hurt and anger. How dare he have his way with her, then judge her *impure* because she was a woman.

It wasn't fair.

She'd heard a woman's body changed after having a baby, but had no idea hers had, nor how a man who wasn't a doctor could tell. And now she was considered *dirty* because her womb had carried a child.

A dead child.

If Dario had known the tragic ending, he would've never charmed her into a new beginning. Perhaps Lahoma was right—Julia deserved scorn. And now she'd broken her celibacy vow.

Julia cried until each tear crusted dry and her face muscles ached. Overcome with hunger, she ordered a two-pound box of the Blackland's signature pecan pralines, instead of joining Dario for supper. By midnight, she'd consumed the entire box, plus a generous glass of his expensive sherry.

The next day was Saturday, so she slept in. At noon, a bellman knocked on her door delivering dozens of yellow roses plus a note from Dario.

> My Julia,
> May a thousand bright petals heal the crimson of my caring.
> Yours,
> Dario

Julia tapped her cheek, still ruby-raw from the slap. The apology was semisweet. She wanted to hate him, but no one had ever sent her flowers, and the symbolism of his words touched her deeply. That afternoon, an exquisite evening gown arrived from Neiman Marcus.

The first of many.

Six months later, when she couldn't stuff another dress into her closet, Dario moved her into the spacious penthouse suite. She'd long resigned the thought of having her own apartment, the subject moot after her insistence instigated another slap, succeeded by more yellow roses, more beautiful words.

The fiercer second slap had left an unsightly bruise. As before, flowers arrived the following day while Dario was at the club. She'd cooled somewhat but was bent on leaving him this time. However, at her earlier request, he'd snagged a pair of impossible-to-get tickets to *West Side Story*, the most popular Broadway musical touring event of the year. The tickets were clipped to the flowers and the curtain was at eight.

"Why cheat myself?" she argued aloud. "Besides suffering Dario's nonsense, I've worked hard." She entered her closet and studied the striking new cocktail dress she'd anticipated wearing. "Leaving *him* will be on *my* time schedule," she whispered to the matching shoes and purse.

Hours later when the conductor raised his baton for the overture, her swollen face bore a layer of makeup as heavy as any actress. And by the time the hero kissed the heroine, Julia's burgeoning wardrobe and glamorous nightlife had convinced her to forgive.

Again.

When the next Valentine's Day appeared on Julia's calendar, Dario was out of town on business. The months had passed without incident, although she'd learned his apathy for all holidays. Battling a winter cold, she ordered room service for supper, then slipped into a warm robe and flipped on the mahogany, console television. *A Tour of the White House with Mrs. John F. Kennedy* was just beginning. Julia watched with interest.

Upon Dario's return, she mentioned the fascinating documentary. Instantly, his face contorted with anger, his mouth bellowing rapid Italian she couldn't interpret. He raised his hands as if to choke her, but instead, picked up a heavy brass vase and swung it at the rounded picture tube. The glass shattered with a loud pop.

Neither spoke for a moment. Dario relaxed his shoulders and eased the vase to the floor. He studied the damage, then slowly spoke. "Before departing for the club this evening, call down to the front desk and apologize for my clumsiness. Insist they charge the breakage to me." He yanked the console's plug from the wall.

"The TV show was harmless," Julia whispered, "about the home of our President."

"His home?" Dario spun an about face. "Or his palace?"

"What's the difference?"

Dario raised his chin, his neck flush. "Our Chief Executive either serves or rules. Democracy or tyranny. If he considers himself a king, he must face the consequences."

"Meaning in the next election, the people will decide."

"Oh, my naïve little Julia." Dario wagged his head, punctuated with a smirk. "The *people* are nothing but weary, constipated sheep in need of the proper stimulation."

He stepped across the room and peered out the window. "Do you understand, my lamb?"

Julia didn't respond. He'd never called her *lamb*, the inference an insult.

"Answer me." His voice rattled the glass. "Do you understand?"

"Y ... yes." She was too frightened to argue.

"Good." He faced her and smiled. "Our greatest president said, 'The tree of liberty must from time to time be refreshed with the blood of patriots and tyrants. It's as natural as manure.'"

After Dario left, no delicate petals ensued, no beautiful words. His political reasoning was difficult to follow, although she suspected he'd taken the *manure* quote out of context—if it was a quote. Mentioning Jackie and JFK was a mistake, one Julia wouldn't repeat in Dario's presence. Even so, she was afraid to stay with him for another minute.

Yet terrified to leave.

For the next year and a half, Julia treaded the dark waters of indecision, while Dario acted as if nothing had happened. Since she was expected to dine most nights at The Scarlet Stallion, she did, but left before the floorshow.

RUNNING DOWNWIND

Dario didn't seem to care. Then in early autumn, he announced an overnight business trip to Los Angeles, insisting she accompany him.

"Pack your most expensive gown." He flashed a satisfied smile. "We've got a suite at the Rosewall Hotel. Presidents have stayed there. And we'll dine with some of the biggest names in the entertainment industry."

"Movie stars?" Julia's fear of Dario's violent outbursts still held her captive, but a trip to Hollywood glowed with glints of much needed freedom. Besides, he was in a rare good mood. She might as well take advantage.

"Stars?" Dario laughed. "You still have much to learn. Your so-called *celebrities* owe their careers to these men. Those whom you consider famous are merely puppets of the powerful."

The flight to LA proved uneventful, with Dario napping the entire way. Julia hoped some of the good-natured *amici* and their wives or girlfriends would be on board. But first class belonged exclusively to Dario and Julia.

Not even Sal made an appearance. She'd grown fond of being called his rose. Due to his steady kindness, she trusted him almost as much as Paco. Sal seemed to know when she felt the most vulnerable to Dario's public embarrassments. More than once, Sal redirected an uncomfortable dinner conversation.

At the busy Los Angeles airport, Dario received an overhead page and was pointed to a private phone booth near the main entrance. After an animated conversation, he emerged red-faced. "There's been a change of plan regarding the Rosewall."

"Is there a problem?"

"Not anymore." He motioned for Julia to follow him outside.

The automatic doors opened with a blast of heat. "I thought LA would be cooler than Dallas." Julia turned her back to the sun. "It must be a hundred degrees."

Dario glanced at his watch and frowned. "A limo will deliver you and your luggage to a different hotel. You will return here in the morning."

"A different hotel? But I ... " She carefully selected her words. "I don't understand."

"You're not meant to. Just know everything's been arranged."

Or rearranged, Julia thought, feeling blood rush to her cheeks. They'd been together almost three years and she'd earned the right to at least be treated as an adult. "I thought we were—"

"You were mistaken." He leaned close, lowering his voice to a whisper. "These things happen in business. You will accept them without hesitation."

Before Julia could protest further, a tall man in a crisp chauffer's uniform stepped out of the passing crowd. "This way, madam." He gently ushered her into the rear of his waiting limo. She glanced back at Dario, who'd already disappeared into the terminal.

"Would madam like me to raise the air-conditioning?"

"I'm okay."

The chauffer merged into traffic. "How about the privacy partition?"

"What about it?"

"Does madam prefer up or down?"

"It makes no difference."

"Oh, but it does." He glanced at her in the rearview mirror and grinned. "I'd enjoy a bit of kind conversation."

Julia nodded, even though she didn't feel like talking. His mild demeanor reminded her of Sal. Except for his slimmer build and slight British accent, the two men could've been brothers.

"The name's Calvin." He tapped the shiny black visor of his cap with a gloved finger. "How about we navigate the less traveled route to your hotel? Freeways give me ghastly heartburn, especially in this horrid heat wave."

"Fine," she replied, her mind questioning why Dario's plans were altered, which obviously upset him. But now that she'd had a moment to ponder the situation was relieved to stay somewhere else.

"There's not a vacant room in the city." Calvin motored along palm lined boulevards. "One would think the Trojans were hosting an enormous match."

"Excuse me?"

"The Trojan is our local college mascot." His grin spread the width of the mirror. "Has madam ever heard of USC?"

"The University of Southern California." She remembered it as one of the colleges she'd considered attending before her life changed. "And please call me Julia."

"Right you are, Julia. Are you a sports connoisseur?"

"Should I be?"

He laughed. "There's nothing like a riveting afternoon of American football at the Coliseum. The contest is so, shall I say, satisfyingly barbaric."

"If there's no game, then why are the hotels full?" She wondered how Dario managed landing an additional room.

"Billy Graham's in town," Calvin said matter-of-factly. "The stadium will be packed tighter than a large family's insufficient luggage, even in this weather. Are you a Graham enthusiast?"

"Should I be?" Julia didn't mean to repeat herself but had heard or seen the name Billy Graham somewhere.

The chauffer shrugged. "Graham's been attracting larger crowds than Elvis. Why don't you go hear him and make your own determination."

"A puppet of the powerful," she muttered.

"Pardon?"

"Never mind." She cleared her throat." I'd love to go. What's the ticket price?"

"Ticket?" Calvin seemed taken aback.

"How much does it cost to get in?"

"Oh ... there's never an admission charge. Mr. Graham wouldn't permit that sort of rubbish." Calvin cocked his head in her direction. "Since the Coliseum's only a few blocks from your hotel, I suggest you walk. The evening may be hot at first but should cool off nicely after the sun sets."

Since the opportunity to dine with celebrities was squelched, she could at least view one from a distance. Dario would never know. "What time does everything start?"

"The preliminaries begin at seven thirty. I'd get there at least an hour early, or you'll sit in the stratosphere." Calvin wheeled the limo onto a private concrete drive. "And here we are."

Her hotel, The Cassy House, looked more like a quaint country inn. It was situated amongst a cluster of newer, low-rise apartments with a sprinkling of historic residences, art deco ornate. As they pulled beneath the arched stone portico, the chauffer explained how the lobby contained an inconspicuous portrait of the mythological soothsayer, Cassandra, a raven-haired beauty who'd predicted the fall of ancient Troy.

"I adore the hotel's subtle comedic irony," he added, "and I'm a Trojan fan." Calvin switched off the ignition, then stepped out and unloaded Julia's suitcase before opening her door. "The owner graduated from USC's archrival, UCLA."

RUNNING DOWNWIND

"So what about Cassandra?" Julia felt eerily empathetic. "Did anyone believe her prophecy?"

"Sadly, no. Epidemic skepticism is what set the stage for the clandestine Trojan Horse." He signaled to the doorman, who carried Julia's case inside.

"Why wouldn't they take Cassandra seriously?" She stepped toward Calvin. "Why wouldn't they believe?"

"Hmm." He folded his arms, leaned against the limo and thought for a moment. "No one really knows. Legend states the god, Apollo, was so captivated by her mortal beauty, he granted her the gift of prophecy. Then later added a curse of disbelief."

"Because?"

"Some mythologists say Cassandra cheated. With *whom*, or concerning *what*, is unclear. Others maintain she simply rebuffed Apollo's advances, therefore the god sought revenge.

"He should've taken her seriously." Julia furrowed her brow. "He should've believed in Cassandra."

"Interesting." Calvin bent Julia's direction. "You and Cassandra could've been sisters, same facial structure, hair and eyes. Hmmm ..." He rubbed his chin. "Does anyone believe in *you*?"

For such a nice man, he posed the oddest questions. "I don't know."

"Most people don't." He straightened. "A different chauffer will collect you in the morning, ten o'clock sharp."

"I'll be ready."

Calvin returned to the driver-side door and opened it a crack. "By the by, Ozzie is the jolly chap manning the concierge desk, not at all stuffy. Let him know if you need anything."

"Thank you."

"And don't forget about tonight. Drink lots of water."

"Will you be there?"

"Of course." Calvin adjusted his cap. "I'm in the choir. Lead tenor."

She watched him climb back behind the wheel and drive away. The chauffer's answers were more peculiar than his questions.

Two hours later, Julia exited her room in the casual skirt and blouse she'd arranged to wear on the flight home—so much for the carefully selected evening gown. Whenever she and Dario went out, he only allowed her to carry a small purse for tissue, a comb, and a lipstick. Anything larger was an insult, making him appear a cheapskate to other men. *He'd* provide whatever she needed. She'd considered reminding him how most of the *amici's* wives and girlfriends carted what amounted to small suitcases, but then thought better.

"Tonight, I refuse to think about any of *that*," Julia said aloud. The purse she'd packed was much too formal, so she stuffed a few dollars into the top of her left sock ... just in case. The tissue, lipstick and comb fit neatly into a skirt pocket. In addition, she'd pushed a dime into the coin slot of each penny loafer, enough to use a pay phone and buy a soft drink.

She made her way to the lobby, recalling her conversation with Calvin. He'd spoken in riddles, unaware how questionable her life was. He'd also mentioned the Coliseum was within walking distance from Cassy House, but since she was a stranger to LA, she stopped at the concierge desk for directions.

RUNNING DOWNWIND

"Coliseum's less than a quarter mile." Ozzie grinned. "When you walk out the hotel's front entrance, follow the drive to the street, turn right, go a block, then turn right again."

"O-kay." She rolled her eyes.

"It's LA. There'll be searchlights scanning the sky. Just follow the crowd." He looked at her thoughtfully. "Ever seen a big stadium up close?"

"The Cotton Bowl." Her first year in Dallas, Sal had insisted taking her there for the New Year's Day football classic. Dario hadn't joined them but granted his permission.

"Then you know what to look for." Ozzie pointed to the television in the lobby. "Maybe I'll see you on the tube."

"On TV?"

"Coast to coast. Hard to believe."

Julia nodded. "I hear Billy Graham's as popular as Elvis."

"Yeah, but without the pelvis." Ozzie glanced about before dancing in a circular motion, his hips swaying side to side. "You didn't see me do that," he whispered.

"Never." Julia smiled and stepped away, then stopped. Hanging in a shallow alcove was what had to be Cassandra's portrait—a dead ringer for Lahoma.

Feeling unsteady, Julia leaned on an adjacent table. Atop was a flourish of freshly cut, pale purple roses, complementing the lobby's sophisticated theme.

"Our long stem, local beauties," Ozzie said. "Yesterday's were pink. Tomorrow, who knows. When you get back, I'll hijack several for your room."

She gazed at the roses, glad they weren't yellow. Trying to better understand Dario, she'd asked a florist what the various colors meant. Yellow symbolized *friendship* and *caring*. But in the Victorian era ... *jealousy*.

He'd exhibited all three.

"Ever seen lilac ones?"

Julia shook her head no, remembering the color meant *love at first sight*. She'd once dreamed of the wonderful concept, now a greater myth than Cassandra.

"I'll snip off the thorns, so you won't get stuck. Hurts like the mischief."

"Roses will be lovely, thank you." She paused. "I'm used to the thorns."

Julia exited through the main entrance, passing beneath the arched portico. At the end of the concrete drive, she turned right. She'd intended leaving the hotel much earlier but was delayed by a nap and a ravenous snack. Then spent longer than planned soaking in a luxurious marble bathtub.

And now, the sun was setting.

In less than a block, the sidewalk flooded with people of all ages, street traffic slowing to a standstill.

I'm not the only one running late.

She hurried her pace.

After a block, Julia made another right, then passed a group of teenagers who sang as they walked, one strumming a guitar. The song was the same tune as a popular folk hit, but with different words.

Words about God's love.

Though peculiar, Julia listened until the thickening crowd pushed her out of earshot toward the towering Coliseum. She crossed an ocean-sized parking lot, then merged into a current of people carrying—of all things—Bibles.

How strange.

Julia treasured her little mother-of-pearl Bible because it was a gift from Carmen and Paco, but never read it. Out here people lugged them to a concert. Either Los Angeles was the most religious city in the nation, or some of the inhabitants were confused.

RUNNING DOWNWIND

The entire throng climbed stairs leading to a side entrance. Once inside, they passed through a tunnel and trudged up a series of switchback ramps. With each higher level, more and more people crowded in. Most of them carried Bibles too.

Was this some sort of religious show?

The thought made her uncomfortable. She considered returning to Cassy House, but moving against the flow was difficult, if not impossible.

When they could go no higher, smartly dressed ushers directed everyone through an opening to the nearest vacant seats. Julia's legs felt weak as the massive green playing field stretched far below. A full moon rose in the cloudless night sky, hanging level with her gaze. She squeezed into a seat in the topmost section as an amplified organ echoed hymn-like strains. Upon viewing the distant speakers' platform, her memory kicked in.

Billy Graham was no common celebrity.

She'd recently scanned an article in the *Dallas Morning News* about a courageous evangelist from North Carolina and the successful gospel meetings he called crusades. After she'd mentioned the story to Dario, he'd scoffed, labeling Graham as nothing more than a glorified carnival barker who duped simpletons. Julia knew better than to openly disagree. However, this preacher from modest beginnings not only dined with movie stars and world leaders, he'd golfed with them, spent time in their homes.

She shivered at the memory. Graham's picture was what had caught her attention. He wasn't bad looking, plus was as influential as any powerful politician, if not more so. And now, there he was in person, seated on the platform.

A famous, human-shaped dot.

"I shouldn't be here," she muttered, then stood to make a quick exit, but her legs felt weaker than before.

Sweat beaded across her brow. The upper section seemed even higher with everyone seated. Suddenly queasy, she plopped back down. Closing her eyes, she tried to ignore the voices below breaking into song. Hundreds of them. Calvin's choir.

They sang for what seemed an eternity, mainly hymns she'd never heard. And when the music swelled into *Amazing Grace*, the people around her stood and joined in. Hundreds multiplied into thousands.

Julia remained seated, trapped inside herself. This event wasn't a concert, but a gigantic worship service, the last place she deserved to be.

Her eyes filled with tears.

Sleeping with Ray was bad enough. On top of that, she'd pulled an idiotic stunt and lost her baby.

Her child.

Rolling his pickup was an accident, yet she felt like a murderer. To earn God's forgiveness, she'd vowed a lifetime of celibacy. In less than a year, she'd broken her promise.

Broken it.

How could she ever face God again?

She was more spineless than Ray *and* a pathetic liar.

When the song ended, the crowd sat silent. A woman handed Julia a tissue, so she purposely coughed before wiping her eyes and nose, faking allergies. Then Billy Graham strode to the microphone. His pleasant southern accent caught her off guard, making him instantly personable and more real than she'd expected. The man *was* handsome, even from a distance.

Still, she had no right to listen, though couldn't help herself. Graham spoke with bold confidence undergirded by an innate honesty. Carefully chosen phrases expanded into sentences overflowing with wisdom and authoritative truth, not only from the Bible he held, but resonating from the recesses of his soul. He recited powerful passages about love, patience, and God's endless grace. She'd heard many of the Scripture verses before, but never really listened, nor cared. Suddenly, the words possessed new meaning.

They became personal.

He explained how Jesus, God's only Son—his baby—became a man and willingly suffered unimaginable torture then faced brutal execution to forever reconcile the evil imbedded into all humanity.

Why?

To pay sin's exorbitant price.

"My evil," Julia whispered, "my sin." Her own words startled her, forming unexpectedly atop her tongue before falling from her mouth. Embarrassed, Julia clamped her lips together to avoid further slips.

Graham shared a funny story about his own imperfect past. Julia couldn't help but giggle. When he spoke of another personal incident, she laughed out loud. A third reminiscence segued into the broken life-stories of others, each person pardoned by God through a humble confession of wrongs, and a sincere belief in Christ.

Again, Julia's eyes filled with tears. This time she didn't try to hide her feelings because she wanted that same forgiveness.

Wanted it desperately.

Desired it for eternity.

Lahoma had refused her daughter a grain of mercy. Dario, only once. Perhaps genuine and lasting forgiveness wasn't *humanly* possible.

Julia wasn't sure she could forgive herself.

And then Calvin's odd question popped into her head: "Does anyone believe in *you*?"

"Yes," she whispered. "Jesus does. And I believe in Him."

The organ played as Graham explained how Christ longed to live in the heart of anyone willing to accept Him as Lord and Savior. But the decision must be sincere, personal, and when possible, made public.

Unashamed, Julia stood and joined the multitude already descending toward the speaker's platform. She'd always believed Christ existed, but until tonight, that belief only occupied her intellect, hovering far above her heart.

Now her belief was deep.

Now her belief was Divine.

For the first time, she understood Jesus died to live again.

To become a living part of *her*.

And God had forgiven ... *her*.

When she reached the field, a woman handed Julia a pamphlet and shared a short prayer. Graham spoke parting words of encouragement to all those gathered and voiced a benediction.

The service ended.

On the way back to Cassy House, Julia followed the crowd until realizing she'd taken a wrong turn. She retraced her steps and soon spied a quaint, curbside park, complete with benches, a fountain, soft drink machine, and an enclosed phone booth.

She glanced back at the Coliseum. From this distance, the search lights reminded her of long, white soda straws. Feeling thirsty, she approached the machine. When every compartment proved empty, she crossed to the fountain and sat on a bench. Traffic on the street had thinned with only a few strolling passersby—mostly couples.

Julia shivered. Even though the air was warm, goosebumps peppered her arms. Who knew the night would prove so ... lifechanging.

Plus make her feet hurt.

Not that she could she ever tell Dario.

A small car puttered to the curb and parked near the telephone booth. An inside light blinked on. The driver—a young woman—was the lone occupant. With the motor still running, she dug through her purse, then stepped out and approached Julia.

The woman smiled. "Can you change a dollar?"

"Your door's still open." Julia returned the smile.

"It's okay. I'll only be a minute."

"And your engine's—"

"I know. Earlier, it barely started. The battery's ancient."

Julia nodded. Paco's truck suffered similar age-related issues. He could've penned a treatise on the value of carrying jumper cables and more than one spare tire.

"I need to make a quick call before leaving town and can't find a dime." The woman held up a dollar bill.

"You're welcome to my twenty cents. Please keep your dollar."

"No, I insist." She dropped the bill on the bench.

Removing a loafer, Julia dug a dime from the slot, then reached for her other shoe.

"One coin is all I need, thanks. Save the rest for someone else." She scampered into the phone booth and closed the door.

Julia noticed how stylishly the woman dressed. However, the little car, an older model Volkswagen, displayed more rust than paint. In the moonlight, the vehicle looked like a monster June bug. Before escaping to

Dallas, Julia longed to own anything motorized attached to wheels. But after her pickup accident—

The phone booth opened with a squeak.

"That was fast," Julia said.

"My friend was *out* somewhere—no surprise—so I left a message with the hotel's front desk." She stepped closer and lowered her voice. "I'm going to help him remember."

"Remember?"

"How much we mean to one another." The woman peeked up at the moon and giggled. "Love at first sight." Without another word, she hopped in her car and drove away.

The lilac rose.

A shudder traced Julia's spine. Another odd happenstance that some—like Carmen—considered a sign.

Love at first sight.

What exactly did the axiom mean for Julia?

For the young woman?

Julia gazed heavenward. The moon floated pearl-high above the Coliseum, recalling bright nights atop the hay wagon. More than Ray, Lahoma, and even Dario, she'd held herself captive. Julia Lawrence was her own cruel jailer.

She pressed her lips together.

Graham's message was unlike any speech she'd ever heard. And she still had questions.

However, one thing was clear.

The freedom she'd sought all along was well within reach. Finding that freedom simply meant knowing ... the One to grasp.

RUNNING DOWNWIND

Upon returning to Texas, summer's white heat eventually cooled into autumn's pleasant amber, lasting well into November. Julia hadn't breathed a word about her Coliseum experience to Dario, who seemed more preoccupied than before. Even so, he might soar into a tirade, meaning she had to be careful. Her birthday was less than a week away, a milestone she'd planned to celebrate in her own way. Hopefully Dario wouldn't remember nor care.

The morning she turned twenty-one, Dallas buzzed with excitement. President John F. Kennedy would visit the city later that day, his motorcade passing only a block from the Blackland. Rumors of Secret Service agents staying at the hotel ran rampant, although she'd seen no James Bond lookalikes lurking about the hallways, lobby, or coffee shop.

The press was a different matter. Since Texans voiced strong and diverse opinions about the young president's reelection bid, an army of reporters had interviewed Dallasites all week. Yesterday, a reporter cornered Julia at work, following her into the kitchen. She held no interest in politics, but the man was insistent. To get rid of him, she mentioned Jackie Kennedy's fascinating televised tour of the White House. The reporter scribbled a short note and scurried away, his expression lukewarm.

Fearful of another outburst from Dario, Julia gave the reporter a false name in case he quoted her directly. She'd planned to find an out-of-the-way spot along the motorcade route and catch a glimpse of the First Lady. For days, the other waitresses talked nonstop about Jackie and how she rarely traveled with her husband.

Air Force One wasn't expected to land at Love Field until noon, so the coffee shop was crazy crowded for breakfast. An hour passed. Dario and his gang were seldom late, but their booth remained empty, as did the one nearest the exit. Julia assumed both groups were delayed by thousands of well-wishers already elbowing onto the downtown sidewalks.

"Serves Dario right," she mouthed while filling saltshakers during a brief lull. "I just hope he's not following JFK supporters back to their hotel rooms and destroying *their* televisions." She punctuated the remark with a frown. Instead of replacing the TV in her suite, Dario purchased a thick, scholarly volume on Thomas Jefferson and ordered her to read it. The prose proved painstakingly dull, until Julia remembered Dario's quote and thought it might belong to Jefferson. But there was no *manure* in the index, so she'd only covered a few pages when Dario grew frustrated and demanded the book back.

Fine by her.

Julia poured more salt. Today was her legal birthday into adulthood. She sighed, still hoping Dario wouldn't remember. After their September trip to Los Angeles, he'd worked constantly, napping only once at her penthouse suite. He'd made sexual advances, but his sleepy intentions slipped into loud snoring before anything happened, which was a relief.

Or a miracle.

She'd privately read her little Bible and prayed, asking God's protection. Prayer still felt foreign—she stumbled with her words—but Dario's need for rest squelched his desire for her.

Miracle or not, the result was a definite answered prayer.

She finished filling the remaining shakers, wondering if Dario's admiration for Jefferson had any connection with the two-dollar bills. The mysterious gratuity game had developed into an obsession. Since the beginning of November, she'd handed one back in change every morning.

RUNNING DOWNWIND

And now it was the 22nd.

Yesterday, she'd accidently dropped the bill in transit, briefly exposing the inside of the fold after it fluttered to the floor. A crude map was drawn in red ink. A slender, well-dressed man quickly rose out of the exit booth and covered the map with his spit polished shoe. He was new to the group, however, looked vaguely familiar. She'd probably seen him at the club.

"Allow me." He retrieved the bill and offered a pleasant nod.

She knew Dario witnessed the event, thus feared negative consequences.

Eight o'clock. Another hour had ticked by, both booths still empty.

Then Sal burst through the door, exclaiming how Dario was hit by a bus while crossing Commerce Street. Julia bolted outside, only to find him down on one knee holding a diamond ring as large and brilliant as his smile. Confused relief blurred her vision. Before she could speak, he slipped the ring onto her finger and carried her inside.

"My Julia's work here has ended," Dario announced, kissing her ring. He lifted her hand high enough for all to see. "Let us celebrate this extraordinary day." The entire room cheered over the pop and pour of champagne, while the cook served platters of eggs Benedict amidst the *amici's* off-key arias.

CHAPTER 11

The Jax Beer clock chimed six o'clock. Julia opened her eyes. Light hugged the rim of the eastern horizon, battling a thick swath of low haze. The steady Gulf breeze blew her thoughts well past the wee hours and into the dawn.

Where had the night gone?

Not only had she slept through Ryder's return from checking hatchlings, she'd dreamed about Dario, the nightmare's wake leaving a stiff neck, drippy nose, and tangled hair.

She glanced out over the water. This was probably the morning she'd have seen the Lady and discovered a mirror piece.

While redoing her ponytail, she wished the outgoing tide would sweep the guilt of her naïveté out to sea. Dario Rossi's jubilance had nothing to do with their "phony" engagement, nor her twenty-first birthday, but what would happen at exactly 12:30 p.m. when the motorcade reached Dallas's Dealey Plaza.

The assassination of the President of The United States.

"Guess I'm too late for coffee?"

Julia leaped to her feet, seeing Mick Leonard out of the corner of her right eye. Instead of turning his direction, she rubbed her neck.

"You're early," she said flatly, glad she'd fixed her hair. "Breakfast is at seven. Come back then if it's not too much trouble."

"I need to apologize."

"For what?" she lied.

"Everything."

She faced him. "Everything?"

"First, startling you into a near heart attack." He smiled sheepishly. "Second, wearing a long-sleeved western shirt with cutoffs ... in public."

"Don't forget the flip-flops."

He studied his feet and nodded. "That would be third." Meeting her eyes, he smiled again. "Fourth, missing last night's dinner and coffee."

"Ryder's teenagers drank it, the coffee, that is." Unsure of what to say next, she surrendered a nervous giggle. Mick Leonard did look ridiculous, except for the dimples she'd not noticed until now.

"Ryder's got kids?"

"Sort of." She intended to explain, but giggled again, forgetting how lack of sleep made her giddy.

Mick raised an eyebrow. "Are they funny-looking?"

"Green by now." The teens' nightlong date with the spiked pickle jar flashed across her memory. She laughed out loud.

"Martians?"

"No*p*e," she replied, overemphasizing the *p*. "Spaced-out gawkers." She laughed hysterically.

"You're right. I should come back later." He turned to leave.

"Wait." She'd probably regret stopping him, but her sleep deprived inhibitions weren't ready for Mick to go. Not yet. Not until he and his dimples apologized for complicating her life. "Is there a fifth?"

RUNNING DOWNWIND

He spun an about-face. "Aren't you afraid I'll drink it?"

Julia gasped. "The day we found you, then you heard—"

"A little. I was too drunk to drown, remember?"

She nodded.

"Still, I owe you my life. And I'm thinking ... umm ... I need to explain my ... situation."

His lifeless body tumbled into her memory. The smile-shaped scar. She nodded again, slowly, hoping to suppress the embarrassment that painted her cheeks.

He inched forward. "Ryder wasn't right about everything."

"He wasn't?"

Mick Leonard's eyes matched the awakening indigo sea.

"No*pe*," he mimicked. "I'm way too shy to whisper in your ear."

An engine roared from below as Frog skidded to a stop. "Finally," Ryder shouted. "Hop in you two. We're on the verge of a turtle stampede."

"Did he say turtle stampede?" Mick peered over the rail at Ryder, then back at Julia who was already scampering down the stairs. A key lesson he'd learned as an actor was that real life rarely made sense. There was no script created for a director to recreate—or *regurgitate* as the joke went—into two acts of clear, well-paced scenes. Real life unfolded at the confusing velocity of its own absurdity.

"Get a move on, son." Ryder gunned the engine. "Before a herd of hatchlings claw their way topside into a frenzy."

Julia leaped into the back of the odd-looking convertible called Frog, leaving the passenger side vacant. Ryder tromped the accelerator the instant Mick swung his second leg over the door. He slammed the seat. Hard.

"Hey." Julia raised her voice above the wind noise. "He's got an injury."

"I'm fine."

"Liar." She bumped the back of Mick's seat.

"Until now."

Ryder double-clutched into high gear. "Probably not the first time a shot man rode shotgun." He chuckled.

"Cute. Glad you're so subtle this morning."

"It's a long story," Mick said, more surprised at Ryder's casual candor than his driving.

"Usually is." Ryder tilted his head toward Julia. "You promised to be at the lighthouse."

"*You* didn't listen. I said you'd know where to find me."

"Finally." Ryder shook his head and chuckled. "Never debate the female brain."

"How's that?" Mick was relieved the conversation had shifted focus.

Ryder cocked a thumb back toward Julia. "The gal's been camped out at that old lighthouse every morning for the past four years. Until today, which proves my theory—A man's wrong even when he's right."

"Or thinks he's right, when he's dead wrong," she countered.

"Might as well eat both halves of the apple, son. You're gonna choke anyway. Life ain't no Garden of Eden."

Mick laughed for the first time since leaving Persimmon, the easy humor and clean ocean air invigorating every exhausted pore in his body. "So what's all this about stampeding turtles?"

"Newsflash." Julia leaned forward. "Ryder's famous for stretching both truth and untruth."

"Then, no frenzy?"

Ryder grunted. "You wait. Them hatchlings will swarm up out of the ground like bees from a hive, then make a mad dash for the water."

RUNNING DOWNWIND

"Especially if the sun comes out and they warm up a little." Julia sat back. "Mass chaos, but with slow forward progress. Picture several hundred children ice skating for the first time."

Growing up in a city where a hard freeze was a major headline, Mick had never ice skated. Though, his kindergarten class learning to roller-skate was an overabundance of nervous energy, producing more spills than speed.

After passing the lighthouse, the beach road disappeared into deep sand. A wispy mist fell at intervals. Ryder downshifted, keeping a steady pace while explaining Padre Island's role in the plight of the endangered Kemp's ridley. "Besides being the smallest sea turtles in the Gulf, they're the most endangered."

"How come?" Mick asked.

"Poachers. They kill 'em for food, boots, jewelry, you name it."

"Even the eggs are a delicacy," Julia added.

As Ryder explained further about his turtle adventures, Mick grew more intrigued with the complicated woman who'd pulled him from the sea. She seemed timid one moment, bold the next. He'd intended meeting her for dinner and coffee until his good intentions faded into troubled dreams.

Mick refocused his thoughts. "Who'd you say drove across the border into Mexico to collect turtle eggs?"

"A bunch of us coldblooded-critter-lovers." Ryder grinned. "Then we raced back here and buried 'em along the Gulf side of the island."

"How deep?"

"Couple of feet. About a hundred eggs per manmade nest."

"I never realized turtles dug nests."

"Only the females," Julia said. "Their nests are called clutches."

"I keep an eye on the ones closest to Roughshods." Ryder dodged a snarl of beached seaweed. "It takes ten or more years to know if any of our hatchlings survived into returning mamas."

"What about the papas?" Yesterday's song still lingered in Mick's memory.

"Nope," Julia answered, then bluntly, "Men want women, but run the other way whenever things get tough."

"Guess we're not good in a *clutch*," Mick added.

No response.

He glanced at the others, regretting the pun. Ryder fiddled with the switch to the windshield wipers, while Julia stared blankly at a band of dark clouds still hovering above the water. Mick fingered the snaps on his shirt. He'd meant the male *turtles* chose to run from responsibility.

Not all males.

Not him.

Not anymore.

His stomach tightened. How much did his new friends know?

Ryder maneuvered Frog between a couple of fat sand dunes carpeted with a tangled mix of sea oats and flowering vines. He braked to a stop. "Good. We're not too late." He pointed to a flat area free of vegetation. "That's where we buried 'em, at the base of that taller dune. See the bowl-shaped indentions in the sand?"

Mick counted a dozen or so nesting cavities.

"When the eggs hatch," Ryder continued, "sand on top of the nest sinks, filling in the space below. Takes the little critters up to three days to climb to the surface. Cracks appear when they're close to wiggling out."

"Are there cracks now?" Mick asked.

Ryder killed the engine and propped a boot on the dash, beside the steering wheel. "Cracks are what half this fuss is about." Reaching forward, he carefully rolled his jeans above one hairy knee, then repeated the process with the other.

"What's the remaining half?"

"Coyotes." Ryder frowned. "Them mangy scoundrels keep sniffing around and licking their worthless chops." He eased his foot back onto the floorboard and pulled a small caliber pistol from the glove box. "I've got tracks to follow." Ryder opened his door and stepped out. "Don't forget to clear the seaweed on the beach between the nests to the water. Holler if you gotta wrestle something meaner than a ghost."

"He means ghost crab." Julia watched Ryder disappear behind a dune. "They're the same color as the sand and hard to see."

"Do they eat hatchlings?"

"With gusto. Like warm sugar cookies." She climbed out of the back seat. "Ever plucked a baby turtle from a crab hole?"

"Not that I remember."

She grinned. "It's a painful kindness you'll never forget."

"That's what worries me."

Upon viewing the clutches up close, Mick noticed the cracks. Julia explained how each egg was the size of a ping pong ball, with a soft, leathery shell the hatchling sliced apart with an "egg tooth" located on the end of its nose.

"Like a little fang?" he asked.

"Not at all. More like a petrified booger."

Mick chuckled, thinking how Broadway bluenoses would gag on their caviar at such a description. Julia's earthiness was refreshing.

"How do coyotes know where the nests are?"

"By smell." She walked toward the water.

He followed. "Coyotes can smell the eggs?"

"Right after they're laid, and again when they begin to hatch. So can skunks."

"I don't smell anything."

"You're not a coyote." A playful grin punctuated her obvious "skunk" implication.

"Think Ryder will shoot a coyote?" Mick inwardly cringed. The thought of hearing gunfire was troubling, a newfound worry that never bothered him prior to the tower shooter. Mick wasn't an avid hunter. Though as an adolescent, tromped across acres of dove and deer leases to prove his skill with a shotgun and a rifle, his worth as a native Texas son.

"Don't worry." Julia scooped up a clump of seaweed. "Ryder's all yip and no bite."

"The stretching of another untruth?" Mick was amazed at Julia's quick perception.

She shrugged. "Newsflash number two. The man's not fired a shot when I've been with him."

They spent the next half-hour clearing seaweed and other debris from the hatchling's path to the sea—a reptile's sand dollar roadway sixty feet wide and fifty yards from dune to water. The continual stooping winded Mick, who'd sell his birthright for breakfast and coffee. Muscles he'd not used in a month begged for rest, while the camaraderie of cause renewed his energy.

When they reached the surf's edge, Julia scampered back to Frog. She returned carrying two aluminum pails.

"Collecting shells?"

"Seawater." She handed Mick a pail. "For pouring over hatchlings that bog down in loose sand and lose traction. Their flippers are paper thin."

He splashed out to ankle depth and filled it to the brim. "Will this do, or shall I keep searching for a more perfect gallon?"

She made a face. "Too much foam. Keep looking."

RUNNING DOWNWIND

Wading out knee deep he tried again. She shook her head, smiled, and motioned to continue their game. Akin to a schoolboy bobbing for apples, Mick dipped his pail a third time, wondering when she'd peek underneath his devil's mask. Would she laugh with the crowd or run solo for a wad of paper towels.

And then the mist cleared, revealing a golden ball of sun.

"Don't go any deeper," she shouted.

"Why?"

"We've got turtles."

Mick bolted for the beach as hundreds of charcoal-colored hatchlings emerged from their nests like college football fans pouring onto the field after the final second.

"You cover half and I'll watch the other." Julia was already positioned on the opposite side of the hatchlings' path. "Instinct will lead them to the ocean but won't protect them from danger."

"Chocolate cookies," Mick called, wondering how many he'd have to pluck from crab holes.

"What?"

"They look like chocolate cookies, not sugar."

She didn't answer but dropped to a knee and gently poured water over three babies stuck in the same spot. He followed suit and freed a couple of stragglers, remembering also to watch for predators. As the group continued to grow in number and march toward the sea, Mick felt enormous and miniscule at the same time, the audience and the actor. For on this stage of sand and saltwater played out nature's drama of beauty and birth, a story pushing his buried tensions to the surface.

A freeing, of sorts.

Perhaps an initial cleansing of his troubled soul.

He held back a frenzy of tears.

"Ghosts," Julia yelled. "Twelve o'clock."

At midpoint, the front line of hatchlings encountered an onslaught of ghost crabs. Where he'd noticed no holes before, dozens of golf ball sized openings appeared. With the sun positioned just above the horizon, distinguishing the clawed scavengers was difficult as they darted spiderlike across the sand. Mick repositioned himself closer to Julia.

"Ouch." She plucked a hatchling from a crab hole.

"Are you all right?"

"Just nipped my little finger. Oops, there goes another."

She'd no sooner rescued a second doomed hatchling, when a ghost the size of Mick's palm pulled a defenseless baby into a nearby hole.

"Your turn. Now."

Mick plunged his hand into the opening until he felt a wiggle, followed by a hard pinch. "Yow!" His fingers held the hatchling, but the crab held him. "It's got my thumb."

"Don't crush the baby."

"I won't." He released the hatchling, who immediately rejoined the parade as if nothing had happened. Mick waved his hand, but the beady eyed monster held firm. If crustaceans received joy from clamping onto humans, this little guy was in ecstasy. "How do I get it off my—?"

Julia reached over and jerked the ghost from Mick's thumb.

"Yow!"

She laughed. "Pretend I'm removing a bandage."

"Yeah, one welded on with evil hospital tape."

"You'd be upset if someone confiscated *your* breakfast."

"Thanks. Next time *I* get to track coyotes."

When the ghosts retreated, Mick returned to his post on the opposite side. He'd suffered only the one hard pinch—which left an angry blood blister—and snatched as many hatchlings to safety as Julia. The crabs reminded him of sun-bleached mice, not scurrying after chocolate cookies, but wriggly blobs of dark, Scandinavian cheese.

"Hooray." Julia waved her arms. "We have babies in the water."

He turned toward the surf as scores of hatchlings propelled themselves forward in the way nature intended—swimming. Minutes before, the babies were bashful landlubbers. Now they confronted the waves with a miniature might, dipping and diving into a freeform aquatic flipper-dance. As more pushed offshore, the initial swimmers disappeared, drawn into the watery depths of time and distance by the same invisible instinct of their ancestors.

"Frenzy's over." Julia moved back and forth behind the final group with the skill and cunning of a champion boxer, daring any predator to strike within spitting distance. "Don't let your guard down."

Mick watched in amazement until the last straggler paddled into the head-bobbing surf. He gazed skyward, expecting gulls and other predatory birds, but saw only a few remaining clouds. Facing the sun, he reveled in the warmth of new life. The possibilities of regeneration.

Of second chances and fresh starts.

Boom!

A distant gunshot.

"Julia?"

At first, he couldn't find her, his panicked thoughts whirling out of control, spiraling downward into a personalized Pandora's Box of fear and regret.

Boom!

Another shot.

Closer.

Much more powerful.

An aimed explosion echoing death.

"Julia!"

The dread of remembrance stair-stepped from stomach to throat. By the time he realized she'd run up the beach toward Frog, there stood Ryder.

Holding his pistol.

Eyes wild.

Mick ran to meet his new friends.

"Dead coyote. Back there in the brush." Ryder climbed into Frog and started the engine. "We could flip for who gets to bury the scalawag, but we'd best hightail it back to Roughshods."

Julia hopped into the back seat without protest. Mick swung into the front as Ryder pressed on the gas. This time he knew what to expect.

"All the hatchlings make it?" Ryder shifted into second gear.

Julia's voice trembled. "As far as I could tell."

"One coyote." Mick paused to gather his wits. "Two shots."

Ryder peered into the rearview mirror. "First bullet was only meant to scare him. Second blew out his heart."

"You're still holding your gun." Mick faced Ryder. "Why?"

Ryder frowned.

"The second shot wasn't mine."

CHAPTER 12

At breakfast, Julia poured an endless stream of black coffee while Mick rustled through newspaper pages at a corner table.

"Are you okay?" he whispered each time she refilled his cup.

"I'm fine."

"Sure?"

"Positive." She really wasn't *fine*. The powerful gunshot unearthed a horrible memory, so she'd refused Ryder's kind offer to handle the meal without her. Working helped calm her battered nerves. "Ready to order?"

"I still need another minute."

When *another minute* swelled into forty-five, Ryder grew impatient and fried Mick a generous platter of eggs and chorizo, laced with potatoes, onions, and jalapeños.

"Wrap the food in foil," Ryder instructed when Julia returned Mick's uneaten order to the kitchen. "The boy may be famished in thirty minutes."

"He just walked out the door."

"Ryder peered into the dining room and grabbed a grape soda. "This will fix his appetite. I ain't wasting good cooking, even for the likes of him."

"The likes of *him*?"

"Anyone who'll sidestep that breakfast is bound to be bloated." Ryder pried off the cap. "Nothing like a little sweet carbonation to dispel what ails you."

Julia glared. "Don't *sidestep* my question. Do you know something about Mick I don't?"

"Only that the boy ain't gone yet. Not completely."

"What do you mean?"

Ryder removed his apron. "He's parked himself on the deck."

"What's that for?" Mick scrunched his brow. At Ryder's insistence, he'd followed the cook downstairs to the parking lot.

Instead of answering, Ryder handed over an opened soda with a rolled up twenty stuffed into the bottle's mouth. "Works best if you chug the entire contents."

Mick pointed to the bill. "I mean ... that."

"It ain't no fancy green soda straw."

"Why?" He removed the twenty, which hadn't touched the liquid.

"Appetite enhancer. Down it before it goes flat."

"I mean the money."

"New duds." Ryder cocked his head. "Shy away from anything cowboy. The style don't suit your personality."

"Thanks ... I think. I'll repay you."

"No need." Ryder grinned. "Found the money in a coyote track."

Julia was serving lunch when Mick returned a few hours later, freshly showered and in stylish clothes that fit. After

RUNNING DOWNWIND

locating the paper he'd been reading at breakfast, he sat at the same table and requested a cheeseburger, which Ryder prepared beneath a satisfied smirk.

"Is this the only newspaper?" Mick watched Julia clear away his lunch plate.

"You must be housebreaking a hound." She'd intended asking how he felt, but flustered by his new wardrobe, uttered a wisecrack she'd heard Ryder spout to a customer.

Mick thought for a moment. "An Alaskan Malamute. Pantomimes when he needs to go outside, then begs to read the editorials."

"Wouldn't a sled dog prefer the travel section?"

Mick grinned. "How do you know about—?"

"Sled dogs?"

His grin widened. "Malamutes aren't common this far south."

"I used to read *National Geographic*." She leaned against another table. His dimples made her kneecaps vibrate.

"Used to?"

"I moved on." She pointed to the paper. "Ryder's too cheap to subscribe to more than one daily."

"Does he look at it?"

"First thing each morning before anyone else, but only his favorite parts. Swears customers smear jelly on the front page, and ketchup on the classifieds."

"Is he interested in the sports section?"

"When the Astros win."

"Entertainment?"

Julia wagged her head.

"Could I see yesterday's edition, or even the day before?"

"Too late. Ryder might clip an interesting recipe, but all newspapers are sentenced to the dungeon."

"Dungeon?"

"Roughshods's basement." She pointed to the floor. "Beneath us lies a mountain of junk held hostage. He never throws anything away." She cocked her head to one side. Mick's interest in journalism surpassed Dario's—and heaven help her—Lahoma's. Except for an occasional glance at the Sunday comics, reading a daily paper was a time-consuming habit of no interest to Julia. Any pertinent news broadcast via television or over her pickup's radio. "Are you a detective?"

"Not hardly."

"A reporter?"

"Never." Mick's grin dissipated. "Thanks for the lunch. I should get back to my bungalow."

"Wait." She was weary of their game. Her lack of sleep forced boldness front and center. "Who are you?"

He sat back. "I'm Leonard, Mick Leonard. Remember?"

"Oh, I remember." She paused, deciding to play her trump card. "I saved your life, and you *owe* me. So, Mr. Mick Leonard ...

"Who are you?

"Exactly?"

He stood and faced her, his blue eyes gentle.

"I'm not sure I know."

During the afternoon lull, Ryder strode about with a pencil stub behind his ear, humming over a list he'd concocted on the back of a legal-sized envelope. When Julia suffered a vicious attack of the yawns, Ryder decreed she return to her bungalow for a nap.

No longer antsy about being alone, she was still plagued by questions and couldn't sleep. Playing her trump card hadn't helped. Unless Mick was mentally unstable—or had amnesia—why would he question his own identity? Plus, a man whom the waves spit up penniless now wore expensive Bermuda shorts, a mod blue and white striped polo shirt and canvas sneakers. Half a mile up the beach was a seasonal clothing store/souvenir shop. Mick had obviously gone there.

Where did he get the money?

For supper, Mick returned to his table and ordered crab cakes with remoulade sauce, plus a large shrimp cocktail. Instead of dessert, he asked to scrub pots. Julia communicated the generous offer to Ryder, who declined. He'd prepared a lemon icebox pie.

After the final meals were served, they all ate a piece at Mick's table, while Ryder announced how tropical storm Beulah was upgraded to a hurricane. He discussed appropriate preparations for a possible direct hit, including what he'd planned to purchase on the mainland. When Mick stood to leave, Ryder began a lengthy description of the last group of hatchlings, finally requesting Mick to accompany Julia that evening to check on them.

"Um ... sure." Mick offered a pleasant smile before heading out the door.

Julia watched him leave, then stood and crossed to the cash register to tally the day's receipts.

Ryder followed.

"Gotta make a run over to the mainland." He cleared his throat. "For supplies."

"I know."

"Because of Beulah."

"Ditto."

"The reason we're closing early."

She glanced up from her work. "Why wouldn't you let Mick scrub pots?"

"He's a guest, for now."

"For now? Is he staying on?"

Ryder shrugged. "I ain't holding no guarantees."

"Is that why you loaned him money to buy clothes?"

"Didn't need to. Found a twenty on the beach close to his boat's severed mast. Figured the bill was his."

She nodded. At least one troubling question was answered.

"The boy may be on the run, but he ain't no freeloader."

Julia nodded again.

Or thief.

She'd learned Ryder either liked someone or didn't, no middle ground. For now, and for whatever odd reason, Mick garnered Ryder's good graces.

He continued. "I expect this last group of hatchlings to appear any day. The nests ain't far beyond the lighthouse. Shouldn't be any poachers this close by."

"I heard you tell Mick, remember?"

"Right."

"Just *checking* doesn't take two people."

"Safety reasons."

"I can take care of myself."

Ryder ignored her remark. "Have you seen my wallet?" He patted his back pocket.

Julia's heart sank. Maybe her concern about Mick's finances had merit. She punched open the cash drawer. "It's where you always keep it."

After grabbing his wallet, Ryder wiped his face with his forearm. "Been a rough day but ended smooth."

He stepped toward the door.

"Yessir. Started out rough but ended smooth."

Ryder chuckled as the screen banged behind.

CHAPTER 13

Ryder cranked his car and headed toward the hardware store in Port Isabel. He preferred splashing Frog across the bay but chose the speedier causeway. The store closed at eight o'clock in the evening, and he wanted to peruse the aisles. Savor this stage of his plan.

He also needed to check his post office box, having made a habit of doing so when there weren't a bunch of busybodies snooping around. Most folks posting or retrieving mail were locals who'd eaten at Roughshods. Not only did they expect Ryder to remember what they'd ordered, but the names of distant kin who'd visited Padre five years ago from Kalamazoo. Retired men were the worst, shaking his hand or slapping him on the back while launching into worn-out repartees. The problem was most of them couldn't keep their protruding nose hairs out of Ryder's personal business. They'd glance at his mail, then ask if he'd received anything "interesting."

What was that supposed to mean?

If bills and junk catalogs sparked interest, Hugh Ryder hit the daily fascination jackpot. He frowned, aware of his own paranoia and released an unsatisfying belch. His customers' irksome curiosity was *primarily* courteous banter. Innate expressions of a Texan's social graces.

Taking a hand off the wheel, he dug a handkerchief from his pocket and daubed his eyes. Late season sea breezes mingled with lush coastal vegetation and swirled with pollen made his eyes itch, then water. They'd been leaking on and off all day. Driving Frog at fifty miles per hour with the top down didn't help matters, but it was way too hot to ride covered. The thick heat made him crazy. Even though the sun was low, a higher than usual humidity wrapped its sweaty arms around temperatures challenging the century mark. The clear ocean view from atop the bridge usually cooled his nerves; however, a white haze blurred the lines between sea, sky, and sanity.

He belched again for good measure, knowing his anxiety was more than curious customers or heat driven haze. The coyote-killing gunshot still rang in his ears, the powerful blast reverberating off the dunes like cannon fire.

Ryder breathed deeply, attempting to calm his nerves. The dead animal wasn't what bugged him. More than enough worthless coyotes slinked through the brush. At issue was the crude boldness of the incident.

The fatal round was most likely fired from a .357 Magnum, a booming "life-ender" which made his little .22 sound like a cap pistol. Mick heard the difference. But the boy played it cool, which wasn't surprising.

And Julia?

Trembled like she did the day Ruby shot Oswald. However, the girl was sharp, aware the coyote situation was peculiar. Given enough time, she and the boy might start to figure things out.

"Poachers," Ryder said aloud, regretting having mentioned the excuse that morning. Turtle poachers sought undeveloped eggs and adult turtles, not hatchlings. Wouldn't waste a bullet on a coyote. That's why Ryder rushed everybody outta there. The mysterious, trigger-happy shooter couldn't be trusted.

Ryder pressed on the gas, wagging his head in disbelief of his own shallow thinking. Reckless compassion for the safety of others was as potent as truth serum and could spoil everything.

Everything.

From now on, he'd be more cautious with his explanations.

He'd been a convincing liar in prison, at first relishing the challenge. A smart man behind bars cogitated every conceivable rationale for his actions, keeping a spit-load of believable answers within tongue's reach. Then during his fifth year of incarceration, a link in his chain of elaborate falsehoods broke, slamming him into the dark hole of solitary confinement for a week. Seven days was enough hell for any man, so the moment he glimpsed daylight, he staggered into the prison chapel and grasped Christ's nail-scarred hands. Suddenly, outright lying was no longer an appropriate avocation. Some loudmouthed radio preacher admonished believers to be serpent-wise yet dove-innocent. Since the occasional small fib was necessary for survival, Ryder labeled an untruth as *snaky shrewdness.*

He smiled. *Snaky shrewdness* was also the reason he'd kept abreast of inmate goings-on. Critical information cost a few packs of cigarettes each month, which wasn't a huge sacrifice since he didn't smoke. The advantage of knowing when to keep silent far exceeded the price of tobacco and the painful complications of being labeled a snitch.

"Poachers," he repeated. Either he'd select his words more carefully or say nothing. Somebody was up to no good and Ryder needed time to consider the situation.

Switching on Frog's radio, he turned the volume high enough to hear above the wind and road noise. His favorite DJ, Bear Bradford, was finishing a storm update with his comical spin. "No kidding folks. The boys over at the weather station swear on Jean Lafitte's skull and crossbones it's too early to predict where the eye will slam ashore. That's why a hurricane *watch* will soon be issued for the entire Texas coast. But believe me, my country music mateys, don't let your guard down 'cause this *watch* ain't no tame Timex. It's a stinker of a ticker attached to the twisted bands of a tropical time bomb. Bottom line? Beulah's big and mean. And means business. Big mean business. So stay off the water and stay tuned. The Bear'll keep you informed."

Bear's witty doubletalk lightened Ryder's mood. He wished he'd heard the full report, though unnecessary. Throughout the day he'd caught snippets of excited customer buzz about tropical storm Beulah now upgraded to a hurricane. That's why he'd asked Mick and Julia to drive out and check on the final group of hatchlings. They'd be safe enough for another forty-eight hours. But turtles or not, he'd make sure those kids were off the island before wind and high water tumbled his patient plans into a dangerous frenzy.

"Toe the line, do the time," Ryder whispered, recalling the mantra he'd adopted while on the inside. He rubbed the stubble on his chin beneath a faint smile. That same infant truth benefited him on the outside as well, finally coming of age as a Caribbean-born temptress named Beulah. Due to his astute observational skills and meteorological record keeping, the news wasn't a surprise. In addition, he'd spent untold hours in the county library studying ships' logs, tidal currents, and weather charts.

The old timers predicted a major blow too, something folkloric about large numbers of seagulls squatting on the beach all summer rather than on the water. Yet Ryder considered himself a connoisseur of science. A fancier of fact. In the end, barometric pressure didn't lie. It had ridden the rollercoaster of deception since June and was about to descend the final terrifying drop. Hence, the reason for his well-timed trip to the hardware store. As soon as Bear announced what Ryder already knew, the beaches would empty. Then barelegged hysteria would storm the aisles with a vengeance worse than any hurricane.

As Frog neared the causeway's halfway point, Bear played a Hank William's tune. Ryder considered himself a fan of any music not involving amplified screaming, so he boosted the volume. The third time Hank lamented losing beer due to a hole in his bucket, Ryder realized he'd left his supply list back at Roughshods. He pounded the steering wheel with his right palm.

"Sell saddles to seahorses."

The list—fine-tuned for months—brimmed with specific last-minute items, including a sieve-type bucket he'd special ordered. Recalling everything might be possible if he could relax his mind. Once he reached the mainland, he'd find a quiet bayside parking spot, then dredge the details of recent memory in a logical sequence.

Bear thanked the music world for the genius of Hank Williams and moved to country crooner, Jim Reeves, spinning up his latest hit, "Blue Side of Lonesome." It was Ryder's new favorite. Fretting the list was pointless while driving, so he upped the volume even more.

Odd.

Jim died two years ago, the result of a tragic plane crash, though his label still released tunes.

Reaching behind the passenger seat, Ryder fingered a grape soda, then thumbed open his pocketknife and pried off the cap. He'd only heard the song a few times. Had a catchy melody. But what intrigued him most were the lyrics. Nice to know some other guy regretted dumping the gal he'd loved, even though Jim's deserved it. Too bad ole Jimmy wasn't around anymore. They could sip grape sodas and discuss the women they'd each loved and lost. Or in Ryder's case, the woman.

Jayne Hansen.

During the height of the Great Depression, she'd traveled all the way from Great Britain to study oil painting at the burgeoning artist colony on the outskirts of Santa Fe, New Mexico. Jayne soon fell in love with piñon smoke, thick brown adobe, and the crisp Sangre de Cristo Mountains. She also fell desperately for Hugh Ryder. Barely twenty, he vacationed *between successes* in a casita on Canyon Road, his thick dark hair and rugged complexion making him look more Spanish than Anglo. The truth? Ryder was on the lam from his brief, but brilliant, summer kidnapping campaign against heartless bankers. Evil men in eastern New Mexico and the Texas Panhandle who'd swindled his parents and countless other decent folks out of their ranches.

Newspapers headlined Ryder as either *The Masked Outhouse Bandit*, or *The Sunday Outhouse Bandit*. Both versions were correct. He'd park his vehicle in an ambiguous location near the rear of a bank president's home, then pull a bandana over his nose and nab the man in the midst of his pre-church jaunt to the john. Coffee proved a great colon kicker, instantly moving hubby and the dense Sunday edition from the breakfast table and out the back door. While the banker attended to his "reading," the harried wife washed the dishes, woke the brats, put on the noon pot roast, and got everyone dressed for worship. No one dared interrupt an important man's solitude.

"Of which the greedy gut was ... privy."

RUNNING DOWNWIND

Ryder sipped his soda. The pun pleased him immensely, so he repeated the phrase again before recalling what happened next.

"Of which the greedy gut was ... privy."

After sneaking up to the outhouse, he'd wait for the newspaper to rustle at least twice, then throw open the door and stick a pistol in the president's face. Convincing a man in such a vulnerable position to ride over to the bank and open the vault was easy. Ryder bagged the loot, preached a short sermon on "loving thy neighbor," then locked the man in the vault. If anything unusual occurred, Ryder bid a pleasant good day and aborted the plan. It happened only once, the banker clutching his chest after handing over the cash. Ryder feared the man suffered a heart attack, so dumped him at a doctor's residence and sped away unnoticed. Ranching communities balanced atop the rim of the Dust Bowl contained more tumbleweeds than citizenry or cops.

Ryder grinned at the memory, his thoughts blending with an oncoming spurt of island bound tourist traffic. His misdeeds never hurt anyone, the kidnapped bankers were always rescued within a few hours.

As Bear continued to spin up songs, Ryder eyed the end of the bridge up ahead. A tugboat pushing a barge released a steam-generated warning blast. Identical to the work whistle at The Walls, the sound unnerved him. He'd spent fifteen years behind the impenetrable red bricks laboring for his crimes, yet still didn't see them as such. The bankers who'd foreclosed on hardworking families were the real criminals. That's why Ryder's scheme included mailing *most* of the cash to folks who'd been swindled.

Most.

Not all.

He'd buried the rest in obscure places on ranches where he'd worked as a farrier, in case someone needed future help. Except for minimum expenses, the money no longer belonged to Ryder. He'd located his own source of wealth. Even built a safe place to keep it.

Taking his foot off the gas, he slowed Frog to thirty mph.

Ryder chuckled.

Who knew the slammer would provide his claim ticket to the Singer fortune. *Life* had an odd way of evening the score.

Or perhaps ... *God*.

Shortly after Ryder's kidnapping crusade made the papers, a banker in Dalhart, Texas, figured he might be next. Instead of the Sunday edition, he toted his twelve gauge into the outhouse. Glancing through a peephole, the banker eyed Ryder's distant approach and hastily fired, blowing off the door. The ill-timed blast missed its mark but caused a neighborhood uprising. Ryder barely escaped. Suddenly, freedom trumped social justice, so he clung to the baked August back roads, never landing anywhere for more than a few hours. Exhausted, he finally headed for Santa Fe, leaving false clues he'd hightailed it to California.

In the 1930s, Santa Fe's unusual valley of *avant-garde* artists and Old-World farmers asked few questions and expected fewer answers, making the place a fine hideout from the law's strangling fingers.

An unhurried community of unbridled creativity and fresh produce.

The uncommon and the commonplace.

If things got dicey, a resourceful young man with a surefooted mule could lose himself up in the mountains for days on end. Or an entire season.

RUNNING DOWNWIND

Unless he became careless.

Bear broke to a commercial as Ryder exited the causeway onto the mainland. He clicked off the radio and steered Frog into the parking lot of a fishing pier. A few vehicles sat scattered about, but no one was in sight. After stopping near the water, he chugged the rest of his grape soda and uncapped another.

"Dang that Bear for playing 'Blue Side of Lonesome.'"

Ryder spoke softly. Since he had important business, he'd not counted on the song riling up his thoughts. He should've kept tending his fret.

Punching open the glove box, he grabbed a pencil and a small spiral notebook, then wrote *HOMEMADE ICE CREAM*.

The item wasn't on his original list.

He frowned.

What forced his kooky uppercase scribble wasn't a hankering for vanilla, nor the urge to crank a freezer full.

The sweet culprit was Jayne Hansen.

Her soft English giggle.

Her smooth, diamond-shaped face.

Instead of rethinking the list, his heart was suddenly haunted with regret.

Making his eyes leak worse.

He'd met Jayne at the Crow's Nest Café, located on a winding Santa Fe backstreet. The place wasn't much more than a crumbling adobe shack supported by a warped-plank door, yet served the tastiest coffee, hot roast beef sandwiches, fried pies, and homemade ice cream in the city. Only two customers ordered pie and ice cream every day that autumn. Ryder, beginning in September—Jayne, adding her taste buds in October. Their attraction to each other was instant, escalating into a closeness Ryder never dreamed existed.

The café's owner, Merly Pruitt, took a shine to Ryder and told him her life's story, pouting whenever his boots didn't cross her threshold. "Surly Merly" he called her, a tough, wafer of a middle-aged woman with considerable bosoms and a hacking cough. Ten years prior—on the respiratory advice of her Boston doctors and urgings of her husband—she'd made the trip west by train, alone. Smoking three packs a day for as many decades seared her lungs into leather. So, the moment the Boston depot disappeared from view, she switched to a healthier vice, one she rarely inhaled.

Cigars.

Even out west they weren't considered ladylike, but Merly didn't care. Her tomboyish ways had never garnered approval from her condescending in-laws, nor the champagne crowd they strove to impress. And Merly was no stranger to expensive tobacco. Her flamboyant husband, an East Coast shipbuilding magnate, kept his entire humidor stocked with Cuba's finest. His monthly allowance check would not only cover her expenses but her smoking needs as well. She'd been in Santa Fe less than a year when the stock market crashed on Black Friday. Boston hubby leaped to his death from the top of a sparkling new ocean liner—at least that was Merly's original story. After their estate was sold to pay off stockholders, she was left with a severe case of survival and the contents of the humidor.

"Outside with that filthy cigarette," she ranted to any customer who didn't know better. "You're killing me." If the customer argued or delayed even for a second, she'd stuff her cigar in deep cleavage and work herself into a coughing fit that would scare a medic.

"You think her husband jumped from the crow's nest?" Jayne whispered to Ryder one snowy December afternoon. "Hence the name of this place?" They sat at a window booth drinking coffee and sharing a fried pie. Behind the counter, Merly cranked a freezer of cinnamon-vanilla-bean ice cream.

Ryder shushed her with a finger to his lips, then took a sip and peered outside. An uneasiness rumbled in the pit of his stomach. For a day that dawned sunny, this one sure clouded over in a hurry. Snowflakes the size of sourdough biscuits fell amidst the plummeting temperature. In another few hours, darkness would destroy a man's opportunity to run.

"Merly can't hear us." Jayne reached across the table and squeezed Ryder's hand. "Tell me before I dash off to my four o'clock painting session."

Instead of answering, he studied the sky. That morning, iron clouds mushroomed behind the mountains, the sign of an imminent blizzard. So, he'd chopped Merly a cord of wood and set a nice fire in the café's kiva fireplace. He'd also bought Jayne an engagement ring, a brilliant fire-opal in a setting of silver and turquoise. The ring—which he'd planned to give her that very night—proved his downfall.

"I won't let on." Jayne giggled. "Trust me."

"Always." He couldn't look at her, so stood and carried their empty cups behind the counter to the coffee pot. Jayne's fierce loyalty punched holes in his guts, which meant he could never reveal his outlaw truth. She'd protect him like a mother grizzly, making her an accomplice.

Ryder gathered his wits, refilled the cups and returned to the booth. "I asked Merly that same question about her husband's death," he said casually.

"About the crow's nest?"

He managed a slight grin. "She puffed on her cigar, said nothing. Stared at me like I was some meddlesome stranger."

"Too personal?"

"I reckon." Ryder fingered the ring in his pocket. He'd no sooner purchased the opal, when he noticed a 200-dollar reward poster taped to the jewelry store's cash register. At the top of the poster was a man's picture.

His.

The banker back in Dalhart saw Ryder's uncovered face. The sketch was only a composite, but the likeness ... startling. Ryder wasn't sure but thought he saw a hint of recognition in the jeweler's eyes.

"Well?" Jayne leaned forward. "Did you ever ask her again?"

"About what?"

"The crow's nest." She wrinkled her nose. "Aren't you listening, darling?"

Ryder nodded. Except for buying the ring, he'd avoided Santa Fe's more populated areas. However, his most foolish mistake was becoming a fixture at the Crow's Nest. Even if he made a run for the mountains, he'd have to come down for supplies. Someone would eventually recognize him. The reward was more than a year's wages for most folks.

He grabbed Jayne's hand, stroking the delicate finger destined to remain ringless. "A few days after I asked Merly about her husband's death, we sat out back watching the sunset. She'd just relit her stogie when a bunch of baby birds near the top of a tall spruce started fussing. 'Stray cat,' Merly said. I'd noticed a grey tom slinking around. He was crouched near the trunk, hoping one of the little ones might fall. Then a big mama bird, a shiny black one, dive-bombed the poor critter. He tried to run, but more birds appeared and pecked the tom until his backbone bled. With each escape attempt, the numbers of birds increased, and the attack intensified. When the massacre ended, the tom lay dead. The mama landed in the spruce and cawed to her babies. Merly pointed her cigar toward the top of the tree and mumbled, 'Crow's Nest.'"

Jayne furrowed her brow. "Did you concoct that story? Your eyes are bright."

Before Ryder answered, Merly strode over to the booth carrying two bowls of ice cream. "My husband was a lyin' cheat who got pushed off the crow's nest of his own yacht." The comment made her cigar bob, dropping a cone of ash into one of the bowls.

"Pushed?" Ryder elbowed Jayne.

Merly set the bowls on the table and thumped his ear. "Had you going about Black Friday, not that you ain't tried selling me a whopper or two." She rolled her eyes. "That tall tale about the crow and the tom was pitiful."

Jayne leaned forward. "Then who pushed him?"

"A jealous woman." Merly smiled. "She got the slammer. I got his Cubans."

After Jayne kissed Ryder goodbye, he brought in more firewood, the snow feathered up to his boot tops. Merly handed him a plate of hot sandwiches.

"Making amends?" Ryder set the plate on the counter.

"No. Roast beef sandwiches." She snickered, then poured fresh coffee.

"Only half a cup."

"Which half?"

Ryder grunted. The joke was Merly's favorite.

She filled the cup to the brim. "I s'pose you're wanting me to tell Jayne you didn't concoct that story about the crow and the tom?"

"We both saw it happen."

"So quit your bellyaching and eat. I'll square things with her tomorrow."

"I'm having supper later ... with Jayne."

"Hope you're a better liar in jail." Merly scooted him the plate and the cup. "These sandwiches are your last decent meal for a while. Fried pies don't exist on the inside." She slid him a warm pie wrapped in wax paper. "Go easy on the prison coffee. The stuff will rot your gizzard."

Ryder slowly removed his coat and sat on a bar stool. "*You're* who pushed the lying cheat."

"And got ten years for my trouble."

"Figures. How'd you avoid a life sentence?" He stuffed half a sandwich in his mouth.

Merly cackled. "Made a deal. Prohibition judges don't take kindly to bootleggers, even dead ones from rich families. Guess you could call me the company namedropper." She faced Ryder. "At first I ran too, but it nearly killed me."

He swallowed. "How long have you known?"

"Long enough to see your backbone bleed."

By the time the snow was over a foot deep, Ryder had pawned the ring and sat in the county sheriff's office under his own admission. The sheriff knew Merly and agreed to secretly slip the 200-dollar reward—plus the ring money—into her cash box when she wasn't looking. And since a cousin had lost his ranch due to a questionable bank foreclosure, the sheriff personally escorted Ryder back to Texas to stand trial, promising he'd put in a good word.

"Fifteen years," Ryder muttered as he watched the sun dip below the bay. Thirty was what the newspapers predicted. His young, court-appointed lawyer—whose voice cracked when he was nervous—squeaked with glee at the lesser sentence. Even so, Ryder shuffled into his cell with a broken heart. He knew Jayne read the papers and would insist on seeing him during the trial.

She never showed.

Nor did he hear from her again, although the hope of contact kept him sane for the first five years. But prison life had a way of whittling a man's expectations, sometimes for the good. After God got Ryder's attention, he tried forgetting about Jayne, though couldn't. Perhaps the Almighty had something further in mind.

Ryder read his Bible daily, hoping to find the answer. The result—Jayne remained in his thoughts, while the revenge he'd sought against greedy bankers evaporated. He was still determined to help folks in need. The money he'd buried wouldn't last forever. That's why he kept the Singer Fortune in his sites. After his release, he'd spent an additional fifteen years in planning and research.

"The wait was worth it." Ryder loved hearing the enthusiasm of his own voice. Riches beyond imagination lay within his grasp.

With his thoughts now centered upon the job at hand, Ryder completed his list, fired up Frog and headed to the hardware store. If he missed an item or two, so be it. He'd remembered the most important things, and still had time to enjoy the aisles.

He punched the accelerator and chuckled, satisfied at the genius of his plan. At times, he was even a bit mystified at his own logical thought processes, knowing better than to think too highly of himself. Men at The Walls who'd forced their egos atop tall pedestals were usually the first to fall, sometimes fifty feet. The same was true on the outside, falling being more of an expression.

As Frog motored into the parking lot, Ryder glimpsed a muscular, bald man loading supplies into the back of a late model pickup. Ryder slammed to a stop. His fists shook, but not from fear.

From anger.

The anger of his own stupidity.

The man loading supplies was none other than his old cell mate, Horace Dipple. Since he was serving a life sentence, Dipp either managed parole, or escaped. How he eluded the authorities was of no consequence. He'd come to steal Ryder's dream.

He pounded the steering wheel. That's what he got for confiding in a killer, for trusting trash. Fifteen lonely years of mindless boredom had seduced Ryder's common sense to reveal far too much. And once again, a loose tongue proved his own worst enemy.

Dipp climbed into his vehicle and drove out of the opposite side of the parking lot. Ryder sat frozen in the tropical heat. He didn't know if Dipp had seen him, or exactly how to proceed. However, one thing was clear:

A powerful message was sent to Ryder from his old cellmate.

A death warning.

Delivered by a mangy coyote.

CHAPTER 14

Julia yawned as she doublechecked Roughshods's inventory for the next day's menu. She'd already sent the ogling dishwashers home, so scrubbed and dried the few remaining dishes herself, then plopped into a chair beneath the comforting whirr of a ceiling fan. People who ordered steaming bowls of crab gumbo for supper in this weather were insane, even though Ryder prepared the best she'd ever tasted.

Unrolling a clean cloth napkin, she daubed the thriving colony of sweat beads inhabiting her face and neck. She'd rarely perspired this much since coming to the island. The day's heat was tolerable, until Ryder asked Mick—in her presence—to help check on the final group of hatchlings.

Did Ryder think the job was too dangerous for her to go alone? "Help" meant Mick accompanying her.

Fine.

When Mick startled her at dawn, he'd said he owed her his life, needed to explain his situation. Dragging him to safety was what any caring person would do.

His *situation* wasn't her affair.

Then during the morning's turtle ordeal, she was drawn into his boyish wonder, their shared delight softening her fears. When she yanked the ghost crab from his finger, his pitiful yell instigated laughter and a rash of corny comebacks from them both. She loved volleying wit, learning the technique from wisecracking cowboys. Due to her James Bond quip about Mick stating his name, lighthearted banter progressed into their private game.

Until the coyote was mysteriously shot.

Afterward, Mick grew distant, yet seemed more worried about her safety than his, a peculiar, aloof concern lasting throughout the morning. His reaction made no sense.

She frowned.

Instead of his life, Mick Leonard owed her the truth, not that she wanted to hear it.

Or perhaps she did ...

Desperately.

That's why her sweat glands went berserk.

"Ryder should mind his own business," Julia blurted, wishing she could've accepted his offer to feed the breakfast crowd without her. She might've ended the workday with more energy. After her restless night on Roughshods's deck, plus chasing hatchlings, she was covered with a layer of salty grit. Normally, she'd enjoy a long and relaxing soak but felt anxious about being alone. Instead, she'd rinsed her face and arms in Roughshods's utility sink, then waitressed all three meals.

Staring at the ceiling fan, she propped her feet on an adjacent chair and kicked off her sandals. The rogue gunshot rattled her nerves, recalling the horror witnessed during her final day in Dallas, a gruesome scene she'd never told anyone.

Julia shuddered.

Even the turtle hatching frenzy seemed a lifetime ago. She was relieved Mick wasn't a thief, but her confused feelings about him troubled her as much as the approaching hurricane and the rogue bullet.

Perhaps more.

RUNNING DOWNWIND

On top of that, her nightlong remembrance of Dario reignited fears of the handsome man who'd so easily enslaved her soul—a possessive narcissist who thought nothing of trampling a young girl's dreams. Shoving Mick into the same, self-serving slot was easy during the wee hours, giving her reason to shun him at first light. However, as the sun brightened, so had her outlook.

The fan wobbled slightly, making an annoying click. Standing, she yanked the cord to the off position. The click stopped. Too bad she couldn't control her life as easily. At first, Dario's words and actions delightfully deceived her, then later diminished her from the inside out.

Was Mick deceiving her as well?

He often acted detached yet possessed a generous interest in her wellbeing. She'd heard concern in the soft timbre of his voice, seen caring in his eyes. Still, how many times had her emotions convinced her to follow disaster? When Julia connected with others, she was far too trusting.

The Jax Beer clock chimed eight. She'd agreed to meet Mick in twenty minutes, so she surveyed the room. Everything was ready for tomorrow's hungry customers. Then while walking toward the door, an idea breeched her thoughts.

I'll ask Mick to drive.

With no power steering and a difficult clutch, her old pickup was like handling a testy steer. If he drove, she'd be less occupied and could better guard her end of their conversation. Satisfied with her plan, she reached to push open the screen, then stopped. A bald man stood at the top of the stairs, staring at her.

"Oh," she said through the wire mesh. "I didn't hear you drive up."

"Where's Ryder?"

"I'm sorry, sir. We're closed. There's another restaurant down the beach at—"

"Simple question, girly." He leaned forward. "Where's Ryder?"

"Around." Julia tagged her reply with a belligerent smirk. She'd known a brilliant nurse named *Gurlie*—a different spelling that made his remark an unintended compliment.

The stranger crossed his powerful arms and scowled. "Around where?"

"How should I know?" She'd never seen this man. Ryder's whereabouts were none of his business.

The man's eyes narrowed. "Ain't that his piece-of-crap pickup I parked next to?" He turned toward the parking lot.

She silently latched the screen. "Nope."

"Don't screw with me." He spun back toward Julia and inched closer. "When do you expect him?"

"I don't." Her terse reply reddened his scalp. She considered trying to slip past and make a mad dash for Mick's bungalow but had spent enough time running from unpleasant men. "Anything else before you leave?"

"Tell him an old roommate stopped by."

"Do you have a name?"

The man formed a thin smile. "John Singer will do for now." He descended the stairs and sped away in a shiny new truck.

For now?

His arrogance incensed her. At least a portion of Lahoma's toughness still flowed through Julia's veins. The name John Singer was vaguely familiar, probably a customer, or an acquaintance in Dallas.

Not my worry.

RUNNING DOWNWIND

She breathed a sigh of relief. The outcome could've been different. Ryder's so-called roommate was more than a little frightening. She'd let her boss know.

Unlatching the door, Julia pushed it open. Approximately an hour of daylight remained. If she hurried, there was enough time to change clothes and run a brush through her hair before meeting Mick.

CHAPTER 15

Hearing Roughshods's screen door bang, Mick sprinted underneath the restaurant and watched Julia return to her bungalow. After exiting his own, he'd purposely waited out of sight until the last customer drove away, thinking she'd be a few minutes.

She wasn't.

He inhaled deeply, trying to slow his rapid breathing. Julia almost caught him sneaking into Ryder's basement, not that he was doing anything wrong. Was borrowing a few old newspapers a crime?

I'm not sure I know.

"Don't mock me." Mick ordered his thoughts to stand down. Ever since he'd uttered the same foolish phrase to Julia, his head ridiculed his heart. He was supposed to meet her in fifteen minutes to check on hatchlings, and the grey matter poised beneath his skull wouldn't relent.

"I don't know *me*," Mick added. "Not anymore."

From his rise to stardom until Cherie's death, he'd viewed life as an entertaining poker game, making calculated bluffs, or folding when necessary. Luck played a part but was easily beguiled by emotion, thus couldn't always be trusted. Logic, however, was reliable because it was based upon reason. That's why he preferred to bet within the safe boundaries of his own capabilities.

Except when he gazed into his psyche, a confused stranger resided, roaming rampant and rent free. Mick had no idea whether he liked the stranger, how long he'd stay, or if they could coexist. And those were the facts.

Facts.

The building blocks of honesty. The currency of our legal system. He'd learned too early from his lawyer father that facts could be rearranged, twisted, molded into mirror images of the truth.

"I'm not Ed McFarland. And never will be."

A good actor reads faces. Julia's was a neon novel with an unresolved ending. The gun blast triggered something painful in her past, a hidden darkness that might forever haunt her soul.

Who are you, exactly?

When she'd asked the question a few hours earlier, he knew he still owed her his life, but explaining his situation needed time. His strategy focused on keeping the Mick Leonard facade until he was strong enough to face the public, strong enough to protect his vow to Cherie. Coming clean with Julia wasn't foremost, because he had no choice than to abandon Padre and never see her again.

Until the coyote was shot.

For the first time since losing Cherie, Mick glimpsed beyond the borders of grief and self-pity. She'd sacrificed two lives while trying to free his. Julia had risked hers to release him from the suffocating sea. He might never be rid of the guilt deserved for abandoning Cherie, but Mick refused to make the same mistake twice. He'd not anticipated expending energy—emotional or otherwise— toward anything but leaving.

Until this morning.

Reaching the Yucatan before he was discovered remained paramount.

RUNNING DOWNWIND

Until this morning.

To complicate matters, he needed money. The cash he'd carried from Persimmon lay scattered about the ocean floor.

So, Mick developed a strategy.

Call and awaken his agent when the man was too groggy to ask questions. Plant a bogus story about a plan to drive through Mexico and Central America down to Rio. Instruct Tinker to wire five thousand dollars to the Western Union office in nearby Brownsville, Texas, released on a prearranged password. If Tinker kept his mouth shut for a couple of months, he'd receive a bonus in the same amount. Six a.m. on Padre Island was in the middle of the night out in Los Angeles. Even though the bungalow didn't have a phone, Roughshods did. And Ryder would be out checking for hatchlings.

Mick sighed.

He'd not counted on stumbling into Julia at dawn.

Not counted on caring.

Until this morning.

Reaching into his shirt pocket, he retrieved a matchbook and thumbed open the cover. There was probably an overhead basement light, but he didn't want to draw unnecessary attention.

A flashlight would be nice.

Mick tore off a match and struck it. When he'd walked down the beach after breakfast to the little shop, he'd only purchased some much-needed clothes. Ryder's "coyote track" money wasn't enough for extras.

The match burned down to Mick's thumb and forefinger, so he lit another, recalling his parents' similar response when he'd begged for something they felt was a foolish extravagance. "When we find the money in a pig track," they'd reply. The elder McFarlands were wealthy, not wasteful.

Mick crept forward, eyeing piles of junk as far as the tiny glow allowed. If basements were supposed to be dry and cool, this one failed miserably. Ryder should invest in oversized towels, add a few redwood benches, and remodel the space into a sauna. The increased revenue might offset the need for finding funds in creature footprints.

Cents in centipede tracks.

He imagined sharing the play on words with Julia. Throughout the day, his thoughts circled back to *her*. She was pleasant during their hatchling adventure, even friendly. And when the ghost crab latched onto his finger, they enjoyed the common denominator of subtle wit laced with good-natured sarcasm. Cherie was the smartest girl he'd ever known, however, in the race of repartee, she rarely left the starting gate.

Who are you, exactly?

"If I admit my guilt, will you stop asking?"

No response.

"Okay then." He blew out the match, as if whispering truth in darkness whitewashed the severity. "I'm the Tony Award winning loser who selfishly held an audition when he should've been with his pregnant fiancée. The result? A madman blasted life out of her and our baby. Didn't you read about it? The story made all the papers."

Mick palmed a sudden sweaty tear. He never knew which nagging fact would bubble to the surface then pop, leaving heartache. Today the word *pregnant* augmented his pain, making him slightly dizzy.

He steadied himself against a support pillar, lit another match and waited for his head to unwind.

The newspaper he'd grabbed at breakfast was the first he'd seen since leaving Persimmon. In the months immediately following the UT tower massacre, headlines concerning the victims appeared regularly, eventually surrendering to more current events. He'd combed every section, reading and rereading the names of those caught in the crosshairs of the sniper, the ones who'd not survived, as well as horrific testimonies of those who had.

Neither Mick's nor Cherie's names were ever listed, probably due to Ed's influence with the press. But that didn't mean they'd been expunged from hospital records. Hopefully, Cherie's pregnancy wasn't advanced enough for anyone at Brackenridge to notice. Doc Price knew, yet never betrayed a doctor/patient confidence.

What if she'd told someone else before telling you?

It was a new and terrifying thought, one Mick refused to consider.

"Impossible," he whispered. "She wanted me to know first."

With a freshly lit match, he proceeded with his mission. After the close call with Caddy-Boy, some overzealous reporter would soon uncover the location of Mick's yearlong sabbatical. His picture would follow. If the story had already broken, there was a fair chance Ryder missed it. To be safe, Mick needed to scan the past month of newspapers.

When Mick lit match number three, he spied a green work bench piled with several cases of empty grape soda bottles, a dozen or so pairs of worn-out leather boots, and a wooden wash tub. To his scorched-fingered delight, the tub held hundreds of candles, a vast assortment from tiny votives and fat waxy pillars, to long, refined tapers. He grabbed a two-foot taper, jammed it into a bottle and lit the wick.

His inner actor-clock warned time was short before he must meet Julia.

Twelve minutes until curtain.

Holding his homemade candelabra, Mick dodged an air compressor, only to stumble over a backless chair.

With his free hand he reached for a heavy oak bookcase, identical to the ones in Ed's law office. Those were stationary, however this one rolled, revealing a cache of newspapers stacked floor to ceiling.

Voilà.

Mick retained balance, as well as the flame. He released a slight chuckle. Julia was correct. Ryder saved everything. The man wasn't a mad scientist trying to destroy civilization, however, Mick felt slightly James Bond'ish. If the papers were stacked in order, he could grab what was necessary and make it back to his bungalow before Julia was the wiser.

Ten minutes.

The papers were in order, just not how he'd anticipated. Instead of organized by days, they'd been dismantled and sorted into subjects. News concerning local weather comprised the larger, foremost stack. Beside it were smaller sized groupings about sea turtles and local treasure hunters. Other piles dealt with the history of the island, restaurant reviews, crime reports, and even the JFK assassination.

"President Kennedy was killed almost three years ago." Mick frowned. Was Ryder some sort of oddball historian?

Perhaps.

But any man interested enough to still be collecting stories about JFK might also keep info about the UT shooting.

Five minutes.

The newspapers located behind the subject stacks comprised haphazard piles of what Ryder probably considered junk—classifieds, comics, want ads. Mick didn't dare risk starting a fire, so parked the candle on the chair, then moved closer, scanning what he could see without digging.

RUNNING DOWNWIND

Three minutes.

Nothing significant.

A shadow hid the rearmost pile. Mick lit another match, hoping something might catch his attention. Staring into the dimness, he noticed the letters *UT*. The remainder of the headline was covered by a furniture ad, so he carefully navigated between the piles.

Two minutes.

The headline read, *UTOPIA ENDS*.

"It never began." Frustrated, Mick kicked at the pile, his foot brushing against something hard. Squeezing between the remaining mounds, he discovered another empty bookcase on wheels. Behind that, a red brick wall.

One minute. Places everybody.

Mick lit the final match. In the middle of the wall hung a rusted steel door with a sign stating: *Private Property. Keep Out. This means you.*

He jiggled the handle.

Locked.

Break a leg. It's showtime!

CHAPTER 16

As Julia exited her bungalow, she hoped the lavender sundress she'd chosen wasn't too dressy. The soft seersucker didn't cling to her body, so it was cooler than shorts and a blouse. She'd previously backed her pickup into a nearby parking spot and left the tailgate down. Mick sat on it, swinging his legs like a toddler on a church pew. She'd not noticed before, but his knees were as freckled as his face.

"Wow." His legs stilled. "You look—"

"Exhausted?" She pitched him the keys. "You drive."

"Great." He scooted to the edge. "I mean, you *look* great."

"Thanks." While getting ready, she'd tried to force the bald stranger from her mind, but he still troubled her.

Mick studied the keys. "Um ... wouldn't you rather?"

"What?"

"Drive?"

"Not really." She swallowed. Maybe she should tell Mick about her frightening encounter with the man who called himself, John Singer.

Mick gestured toward the pickup. "I don't mind riding shotgun."

Julia forced a half smile. "I've been on my feet all day. The clutch is a bit hard."

"Hard?"

"Yeah, it's old and cranky, a cable or something needs to be adjusted so that—" She paused in mid-sentence, shifting her thoughts. Mick's face was a forlorn question mark. "Have you ever driven a standard transmission?"

"Kind of."

"Kind of?"

"I know the gear pattern, and ...."

"Yes?"

He stood and grinned. "And ... I also know the gear pattern."

"Good." His dimples made her kneecaps vibrate. "That's doubly crucial." She'd worry about the stranger later, or not at all. "Hop in, it's simple." Julia climbed into the passenger's side. "Easy as sailing," she hollered.

Mick opened his door and slid behind the wheel. "Thanks for the encouragement."

"Just being honest." After dealing with Ryder's surly former roommate, Mick Leonard's agreeable demeanor was refreshing. Energizing.

"An honest woman, every shipwrecked sailor's dream." He peered at his feet. "Which pedal's which?"

"You really don't know."

"Do I hear enthusiastic empathy, or joyful pity?"

She giggled. "The accelerator's on the right, same as an automatic."

"Check."

"Brake pedal's in the middle, clutch is the one farthest to your left.

"Got it."

"With your left foot, push the clutch pedal all the way to the floor."

"Done." He glanced her direction. "Thought you said it was hard?"

RUNNING DOWNWIND

She raised her eyebrows. "Just don't release it 'til I tell you."

"Yes, ma'am."

"Now, left hand on the wheel, right hand on the stick."

Mick grinned. "This part I know." He shifted through all three gears and even found neutral. But after several attempts, couldn't locate reverse.

"Press the stick inward, like pushing a stake into the ground. Then move it up and to the left." Julia placed her hand over his. The spontaneous act made her mouth go dry. The back of Mick's hand wasn't smooth—like Dario's—and Mick's fingers were longer. "Did you feel reverse click into place?"

He nodded.

Julia removed her hand, hoping he hadn't noticed her sweaty palm. "O-kay." A cool shiver snaked between her shoulder blades. "Move the stick back into first, making sure the clutch is depressed."

"I didn't know clutches suffered from depression."

"You're as unfunny as Ryder."

"I prefer to call it pitiful joy."

"An accurate description." She smiled. "Put your right foot on the accelerator. Turn the key and give the truck a little gas."

The pickup roared to life. Mick gunned the engine. "That clutch is happy now."

"When I say go, release it slowly." Julia braced her hands against the dash. "Slow-ly."

"No need to hold on. This crotchety clutch and I have become fast friends. We understand each other." He gunned the engine again.

"Easy on the gas until we move forward."

"Will do."

"Okay. Go. And don't worry yet about shifting up into second g—"

With a powerful lunge, the pickup bolted forward two feet into a dead stop.

The engine died.

"You pals have a speedy misunderstanding?" Julia cackled.

"That evil clutch popped back at me with a vengeance."

"I'd call it beginner's *hard* luck."

"Guess I deserved that remark." He depressed the clutch and turned on the ignition. "Let's go again."

On Mick's next attempt, they made it out of the parking lot onto a shell-topped road, the pickup surging numerous times before sputtering into silence.

"Reminds me of a popular dance." He glanced her direction. "Know which one?"

"Hmm, let me see. How 'bout ...?" She faced him. "*The Jerk*?"

Mick cleared his throat. "Good try, but newer."

"I haven't really kept up in the last few years." She thought for a moment. "Not *The Swim*, I hope?"

He shook his head and grinned, his dimples even more pronounced in the slanting sunlight. "It's a step I just invented—*The Klutz*."

"And destined to become a fad."

"Naturally." He restarted the engine.

"This time, lead with a little more gas."

He shifted into first. "When we wreck, remember more gas was your idea."

"Oh, I'll remember."

Mick's takeoff was flawless, so he punched in the clutch and shifted into second.

"Not too fast," she warned.

"Don't worry. I've got it. How 'bout we drive to the beach, then on toward the lighthouse?"

RUNNING DOWNWIND

She pointed to a sandy road winding between the dunes. "Head that way. We'll see if your dancing has improved."

He shifted into third, leaned back and stuck his elbow out the window. "It's all about rhythm and control."

"Right, but you need to downshift."

"Why? I like this speed."

"'Cause this close to the beach, the sand becomes ..."

They hit soft roadway. The engine chugged and died.

"Deep," Julia finished. She opened her door and peered at a rear tire. "Try backing out."

Mick restarted the engine, jammed it into gear and spun the tires.

"No, that's first gear. Put it in reverse."

"I'm trying." He fiddled with the stick. "Where is first, exactly?"

"Exactly?" Julia folded her arms. "I'm not sure I know." She'd intended to playfully mimic Mick's earlier remark concerning his identity, surprised at the curtness in her tone.

"Guess I deserved that too." He located reverse but didn't elaborate further.

Mick had no trouble backing out and took additional runs at the same soft spot to practice downshifting. She complimented his quick mastery, while he praised her thorough instruction. However, as they proceeded toward the final group of hatchlings, uneasiness filled the space between each congenial sentence.

Julia stared out the window. She should've kept her mouth shut. The way men bottled their secrets was frustrating—and if totally honest—women too. Secrets aged for too many years fermented into poison.

Unless they were already deadly.

While driving past the lighthouse, an image of the Lady rimmed Julia's thoughts. Ryder was aware of her daily habit of watching the sunrise, though never asked for an explanation. Still, she wished he'd not blurted her dawn whereabouts to Mick. The legend of the Lady was private, as if belonging only to her. Carmen's frequent telling was one of Julia's few pleasant childhood memories. Most important, sunrise was a time when heavenly fingers of light massaged hope into her heart. Her search for the mirror piece was nobody else's business.

"Beautiful old structure, though a little ominous." Mick slowed their speed. "How tall?"

"Over a hundred feet. It's been here since before the Civil War."

"What happened to the lamp?"

"Vandals."

"I wonder how many ships were saved from running aground?"

"Hundreds, maybe thousands." She had no clue but hoped Mick's interest in the lighthouse might override any curiosity concerning her morning ritual. "We could take a closer look on the way back."

"I'd like that."

The solid beach soon disappeared into crescent ridges of deep, windblown sand. He downshifted.

"We're close enough," Julia said. "Let's walk the rest of the way."

"How come?" He braked to a stop.

"The hatchlings are located about a hundred yards ahead, six nests just off the water. I don't want to risk running over them."

"Ryder wasn't concerned when we plowed through here this morning."

"We had plenty of room because the tide was out. Now it's in."

RUNNING DOWNWIND

"Oh, right. Just testing your knowledge." Mick killed the engine. "Why weren't the eggs buried up by the dunes?"

"I asked the same question. According to Ryder, the spot where these eggs were originally laid was close to the water."

When they reached the nesting cavities, there were no warning cracks, so they checked the area for signs of coyotes and other predators. Other than a handful of expectant ghost crabs scattering back into their holes, the beach remained empty.

"No overabundance of critter interest in this bunch of babies," Mick said, as they ambled back to the pickup.

"Not yet." The breeze off the water stiffened, cooling Julia's legs. Except for pressing Mick about his identity, letting him drive was a good idea.

She relaxed.

He continued. "I've decided the ghosts would rather chomp fingers than hatchlings."

"Your fingers." She couldn't help but giggle, then recalled how strong his had felt beneath hers. "Mine are too quick."

A sudden gust billowed Julia sundress almost to her waist. She squealed and clamped her fingers to her sides.

"Not quick enough." He jogged ahead and opened her door.

"You're just hoping for an encore." She climbed inside.

"Most encores are overrated."

"Most?"

He grinned and closed her door, then hopped in the other side. "Promise me something?"

"What?"

"That you'll wear this same dress during the hurricane." He restarted the pickup.

She smoothed her skirt beneath a smirk. "I refuse to make false promises."

"I'll remember that." Mick made a U-turn and headed back toward the lighthouse. "Ryder's convinced that Beulah will make a direct hit on this end of the island."

Julia nodded.

Do you agree?"

"I have no choice."

"How so?"

"The man's rarely wrong." She sighed. "Sometimes he makes me want to rip the hair from my scalp."

"When you do, leave enough sprouting around the edges for a ponytail."

"Whatever for?"

"Then you two can be twins."

She reached across the seat, delivering a playful punch. Mick swerved, pretending pain. The tension they'd felt earlier was history.

"Do you own a pair of scuffed boots and faded jeans?" he continued. "How 'bout a seafood-crusted apron?"

Crinkling her nose, she hit him again.

As they neared the lighthouse, Mick coasted to a stop, but left the engine running. The sun had dipped behind the dunes, leaving the top of the rusty iron structure bathed in orange light. "Too bad it's been neglected," he said softly. "Ever been inside and climbed to the top?"

"Customers report the place is dark. The stairs are steep and narrow."

"I'll assume that's a no."

"Some swear there are bats."

"Ah, the unsavory aroma of bat guano. Reminds me of a kid I knew who lived in a cave."

"And he convinced you to be a vampire for Halloween?" She laughed.

"I was a devil and …." He paused. "I don't do well with blood."

"The same with me."

Neither spoke for a moment.

"Lighthouse climbing has to be safer than sailing." Mick switched off the ignition. "Is that opening at the bottom, the entrance?"

"Another test?"

"Hmm. Guess that's the only way inside. And look, only four tiny windows up the tower. No wonder it's dark."

"Started answering your own questions?"

"Only on occasion." Mick's face shaped another question mark. "What happened to the door?"

"Vanished about a year ago. Was welded shut when I moved here."

"To keep out more vandals?"

"I suppose." Julia paused. "There was a sign on the door."

"For sale?"

"No, something about *private property*, *keeping out*, and—"

"*This means you*," Mick finished.

"Why, yes." She tilted her head to one side. "Do you read minds?"

"Only the pretty ones."

She rubbed her kneecaps. "Too bad this lighthouse isn't being refurbished like the one across the bay."

Mick agreed, then pushed open the driver's side door and slid out. Reaching across the seat, he offered his hand. She grabbed it and followed suit.

"You say there's another lighthouse?"

"In Port Isabel," Julia explained as they walked toward the entryway. "You can't miss the white tower when you cross over the causeway. A third lighthouse was located just offshore, where the southern tip of the island meets the bay."

"Was?"

"Built out of wood and burned in 1940."

He wrinkled his forehead. "Do you study lighthouses?"

"Nope. I attend a daily lecture of Ryder-babble. Comes with my job."

When they reached the opening, Mick peered inside. "Whew. I'll bet the temp's ten degrees hotter in there. Wanna climb to the top?"

"Maybe. If you promise to go first."

"I don't make false promises."

Julia tried to punch his arm, but he darted inside. She followed him into the stuffy darkness.

"Whoa." Mick's voice was an amplified echo. "I can't see a thing."

"Maybe we should wait and bring a flashlight."

"Just need to let our eyes adjust." He clapped his hands. "Great acoustical bounce. If this were a theater, actors could whisper their lines."

She didn't reply. Something about his statement struck her as oddly familiar.

"I see stairs." He moved forward, stumbling over an empty gallon jar, which clinked into several more.

Julia remained close to the opening. "Careful. Give your eyes another minute."

"That's a curious odor." He picked up one of the jars and sniffed. "Somebody left their ...." Mick paused, grabbed another jar and sniffed again. "How strange."

"What?"

"The first one smelled like coffee. The second more like ... pickles, or bad beer."

"Ryder's two dishwashers."

"The infamous green teens."

She laughed. "And Ryder thought they'd only filled one jar."

RUNNING DOWNWIND

"Guess the man doesn't know everything."

"Nope." Julia felt renewed energy. If those two kids weren't afraid of an old lighthouse, she wouldn't be either. "Let's climb up and see the view."

Mick led them carefully up the winding staircase. They encountered no bats, but the metal steps squeaked and groaned with the crippling arthritis of forgotten time.

When they reached the top, the sun's final rays lengthened into dusk. Mick explored the airy lamp room, while Julia stepped outside onto the catwalk. Breathing deeply, she grasped the protective railing. After living most of her life atop the open plains, she hated confined spaces. And now, as far as she could see, the beach stretched wide its sandy arms, holding back the endless sea.

Mick joined her. "Look what I found?" He raised an unopened grape soda bottle. "I discovered at least thirty more hidden beneath some rubble."

Julia rolled her eyes. "I guess those boys will confiscate anything not tied down."

"Maybe it's not the hung-over dishwashers." Mick paused. "Why sneak all the way up here to drink boring—

"Soda?"

"Exactly." He scooted closer, his voice a whisper. "Does Ryder ever—"

At that moment, a Bottlenose dolphin leaped out beyond the breakers, then briefly danced beneath a smattering of evening stars.

"Did you see that?" Mick pointed a finger as the dolphin jumped and danced again. "I wonder if he sees us?"

"*She*." Julia faced him and smiled. "She's female."

"I didn't know you could tell by ... um ... looking from a distance."

Julia giggled. "I missed seeing her this morning. We were chasing turtles."

"Wow. Was that today?"

"I've been watching her all week. Rather, she's been showing herself to me."

"Ryder mentioned your daily dawn appointment with this section of beach. Is that why?"

She suddenly wanted to tell him everything about the Lady. But the Bottlenose jumped again, tugging Julia's emotions in a different direction.

"I don't mean to pry. I just think it's interesting that you—"

"I found the dolphin's calf lying in the surf last summer."

"Calf?"

"Her baby. Probably a couple of years old. Attacked by a shark."

"Were the injuries serious?"

"I attempted to save the calf, but ...." She felt a rush of tears, so turned away.

"I'm sure the mother knew you tried."

"I hope. She didn't want to leave her baby, but another dolphin appeared and led her out to deep water."

"And now mom's returned to thank you."

"Maybe." Julia faced him with wet eyes. "Or she's trying to tell me something important."

"What?" Mick's voice was gentle.

"That she's pregnant."

"P-Pregnant?"

Julia nodded, then watched Mick's eyes mist hollow. He placed a hand on the rail and pivoted toward the sea.

Mick cleared his throat. "The light's almost gone. We'd better get back down."

Before she could protest, they descended the stairs in a careful, awkward silence. Except for a few vanilla pleasantries about the sultry evening, Mick said nothing on the drive back, focusing on the road ahead. At Roughshods, he located neutral and switched off the ignition. "See you tomorrow." He set the parking brake and handed her the keys.

"Tomorrow?" She wondered what had just happened, hoping he'd at least meet her gaze.

He didn't.

"I'll get your door." Mick stepped out.

"Please don't bother." She exited the pickup, not knowing if he'd heard her reply. When she reached her bungalow, she glanced back. He'd not followed, but stood in the parking lot, his distant stare lost above a pasted smile.

"Tomorrow," he repeated.

Instead of answering, she scampered inside.

Julia waited until she was sure Mick had gone to bed before returning to the beach, this time on foot.

This time, running.

Anger propelled her out the door, while a mixture of disappointment and confusion provoked each step. Their pleasant evening had soured without warning.

Partly because she'd cried.

She'd known better, making the mistake of trusting him, opening the clouded window of her soul.

But the man couldn't handle her tears.

The thin, moon-blanched path between Roughshods and the Gulf snaked between a briar-covered fortress of darkened dunes, the parched sand fisting the arches of her bare feet. Julia slowed her pace. Obviously, Mick's terseness was the result of more than female emotion, having to do with what she'd said, one word in particular:

Pregnant.

Even though the condition had nothing to do with her, she'd watched the energy drain from his face.

Pregnant.

A powerful word, one some men feared more than a nuclear bomb.

She reached the hem of the beach, padded across an expanse of packed sand and stepped into the shallow surf. The tide was going out. When would she learn that men and babies never mixed.

Dolphin babies included … which made no sense.

The fact Mick wanted nothing more to do with her was clear, even though he stated he'd see her *tomorrow*. He'd simply humored her and would be gone when the sun rose. Most likely, the man never intended upon staying and considered their time together a joke.

Thus, the counterfeit smile in the parking lot.

Wading out farther, a hot wave slapped her knees, drenching the bottom of her sundress. In the past week the water temperature rose higher than usual, even for late summer. If she could morph into a turtle hatchling, she'd paddle out until the scalloped sea swept her far away from Mick Leonard, plus others who'd plagued her life. And to think she'd almost shared her most precious secret with someone as deceitful as Dario.

She plopped down into the water, dress and all, the only one she owned. Dario bought her a hundred beautiful gowns, but she'd been the owner of none. Julia drew in a heavy breath and slowly released it. "Dario Rossi," she said aloud, glad that after almost three years there were no tears left to waste on him.

Her thoughts reeled backward to that horrible November day in Dallas—her twenty-first birthday—when she'd waited eagerly beside a crowded downtown street to view President Kennedy's motorcade.

RUNNING DOWNWIND

To see Jackie.

Hours before, Dario proposed with the big diamond, the event nothing but a sham. Then later that afternoon leaped to his own death from atop the Blackland Hotel. At least, that's what the newspapers reported.

Except Julia knew differently.

Knew he was too cowardly to commit suicide.

Knew he was pushed, or more likely *thrust*.

And now, after finally piecing together the remnants of their relationship, Julia was convinced he was somehow connected to JFK's assassination. She'd erased the smooth sound of Dario's lies from her memory. However, her ears were unable to mute the rifle shots that echoed across Dealey Plaza, nor the terror of her own shrill scream. For when the President's motorcade passed only yards from where Julia stood, she'd gazed in awe at the elegant First Lady ....

Who'd watched her husband's head explode.

CHAPTER 17

NOVEMBER 22, 1963

DALLAS, TEXAS

Upon exiting her suite at the Blackland Hotel, Julia made certain Dario was at the club. To avoid further nosy reporters or being caught on camera, her plan was to locate an inconspicuous, yet clear, vantage point to see Jackie. However, lining both sides of Main Street were hordes of onlookers, at least a dozen deep. Others crowded onto balconies and rooftops, some craning dangerously out of multi-storied windows. Tickertape anticipation paraded amongst the eager masses as red, white, and blue patriotic banners fluttered in a spring-like breeze.

Julia pushed through the crowd for blocks, the broad spectator pathway eventually flowing in a right angle from Main onto Houston Street, then winding left from Houston onto Elm. Directly in her path lay Dealey Plaza. Dario called it *Dallas's pitiful little Central Park,* but it was one of her favorite spots in the city. Uncluttered and triangle shaped, the lawn areas contained four large pergolas, reminding her of ancient gardens where Greek gods and goddesses played hide-and-seek amongst the marble colonnades.

She breathed deeply, gazing at the Hertz time and temperature sign atop the Texas School Book Depository.

It announced 12:28 p.m. and sixty-six degrees. A booming nighttime thunderstorm had rattled her suite's large picture windows, leaving behind a damp, granite sky. But by midmorning, the steel haze evaporated into royal blue. Being late autumn, she'd intended wearing a sweater over her white cotton blouse, then reconsidered. She'd be warm in the sun. Besides, the minute Dario had slipped the big diamond on her finger just before breakfast, a hope of better days diminished the chill she'd fought for months.

This was the motorcade's final leg before Elm Street disappeared beneath railroad tracks atop a triple underpass, so the crowd had drastically thinned. Men and women in business attire clustered in small groups beside workers wearing coveralls and service industry uniforms, all having walked from nearby office buildings and warehouses. Farther down, a clean, grassy area in front of one of the pergolas descended gently to a sidewalk at street level. Julia claimed sidewalk space only a few feet from the curb, a perfect location. Nearby, a family with school-age children shared a picnic lunch, while a girl in yellow-ribboned pigtails skipped past, followed by a woman pushing a stroller.

Julia couldn't see the motorcade but could hear distant cheers as four police motorcycles and the lead car rounded the corner onto Elm.

"Here they come," someone yelled. "The President's limo is the second car."

"He and the First Lady are riding in the back seat," shouted a reply.

Then JFK's midnight-blue convertible motored into view, proudly brandishing the Stars and Stripes with the Presidential Flag. Everyone cheered and applauded. A group of women standing behind Julia shouted, "Jackie! Jackie!" and "We love you, Jack!"

RUNNING DOWNWIND

As the limo passed in front of the School Book Depository, Julia noticed Jackie's pink pillbox hat and her white-gloved wave.

I'm standing on the side of the street opposite the First Lady.

Julia lunged forward a half step, then stopped, letting the advance motorcycles and lead car pass. Her next glance caught Jackie's matching pink suit. Julia pictured herself dashing across Elm, but four additional motorcycles flanked the limo's rear, followed by a carload of secret service agents. Someone might get mad, snap her picture, or recognize her and tattle to Dario. In disappointed defiance, Julia balanced atop the curb's rim, leaning forward on the balls of her feet.

A loud pop echoed from the direction of the School Book Depository. This close to the holidays, probably a firecracker. But before the explanation gelled, she heard a hollow click from the same direction, a virtually silent, yet unsettling sound more distinct than before. More pointed.

The President grabbed his throat with both hands.

Followed by a sharp rifle crack.

And a bystander's scream.

And Jackie's stunned expression.

"No!" Julia's mind refused what her heart recognized. The limo, only yards away, seemed to travel in slow motion.

Now feet away.

Jackie's smooth face wrapped in terror.

Jackie reaching for her husband across a scatter of long stem roses.

A terrific boom.

From somewhere near the pergola.

From the top of the grass.

An explosion of hair, skull, deep flesh.

Julia, spattered with red mist.

Jackie, pink suited and blood-soaked.
Crying for help.
Crawling onto the speeding limo's trunk.
White gloves grasping for life.
A secret service agent.
Leaping.
Covering the First Lady with his body.
The limo a blur of blue.
Now beneath the triple underpass.
And now ....
Gone.

Julia didn't know how long she'd stood on the curb. Nor when she'd lain on the grass, or when Sal appeared. She'd been aware of people running, but they'd scurried past in deafening silence. For until Sal spoke, she'd heard nothing after the final shot but the echoes of her own hysteria, and Jackie's pleading wail of, "Oh no!"

"Sal ...." Julia's voice choked into a sob.

"You fainted, *mia rosa*." Down on one knee, he daubed her face with his handkerchief. "Good thing you landed on the grass."

"Why?"

"It's softer than concrete." He smiled.

"No. Why the President? Why would—?"

"Can you sit?"

"I think so." With Sal's help, she rose to an upright position, turned her head and vomited.

"Good thing I brought an extra handkerchief." He wiped her mouth. "Any more where that came from?"

She shook her head. "Sal, I'm so sorry."

Reaching inside his suit coat, he pulled a thin metal flask from a zippered pocket. He unscrewed the top. "Swish and spit a mouthful. Then take a healthy gulp to settle your stomach."

RUNNING DOWNWIND

"Whisky will make me worse." She pushed the container away.

Sal chuckled. "It's seltzer. My ulcer's giving me fits."

Julia obeyed and handed back the flask.

"We need to get you outta here."

"We? Is Dario—"

"Back at the club."

"Does he know I came to see Jackie?"

"No. He's extremely busy today."

"Then how did you?"

"I've been entrusted with your safety."

"Dario had you follow me?"

"Not exactly."

"Please explain."

Instead, Sal stood and glanced up Elm toward the School Book Depository. "Ori ran to get my car."

"Ori?"

"My son. His dear mother named him. He was her light."

"You've never mentioned a son."

"Why would I? He's a good boy." Sal frowned. "Ori's been in Europe and should've stayed. He didn't need to see this."

A man wearing a "press" badge stopped a few feet away and focused his camera lens on Julia.

Lunging forward, Sal grabbed the camera before the shutter clicked.

"Hey!" The reporter looked dumbfounded.

"Have a little decency, pal. The lady's not well."

"Sorry, miss."

Sal pitched the man his camera and pointed to the triple underpass. "See those railroad tracks?"

"Uh-huh."

"Everybody ran that way. Must've found something newsworthy."

"Thanks for the tip." The man hurried away.

Sal faced Julia. "We gotta get you outta here before the entire area's blocked off."

At that moment, a white Cadillac pulled alongside the curb with the radio blaring. A college-age version of Sal hopped out. "I'm Ori."

"Son, let's put her in the back seat so she can lie down."

Within seconds, Julia lay on the smooth leather interior, her head propped on a rolled-up rain coat. Ori accelerated into traffic. An announcer interrupted with breaking news.

Sal switched off the radio. "Head to the Trailways station. Julia needs to catch the noon bus to Houston."

"What?" She sat up.

Ori checked his watch. "Pop? It's twelve-forty."

"I know. All busses are running an hour late because of the crowds."

Julia kicked the seat. "I'm not going anywhere."

"Head the back way, Son, and don't break any traffic laws. The cops are nervous."

"No. Take me to my suite."

"That's not a good idea, *mia rosa*, not right now." Sal glanced at Ori, then at Julia.

"Why not?"

Sal heaved a sigh. "You know Dario, know how particular he is about business."

"So?"

"Well ...." Sal wiped his forehead with thick fingers. "He's spread his entrepreneurial talents a little too thin this time, which wasn't smart. Complicates the law of supply and demand."

The car turned sharply to the right. "Sorry," Ori said.

Julia held her stomach, feeling as though she might lose the seltzer. "Explain."

RUNNING DOWNWIND

"Dario made bold promises, then changed his mind. Now people are angry—powerful individuals who'll require specific answers to delicate questions." Sal lowered his window a crack. "You'd be followed, *mia rosa*, hounded for information."

"But I don't keep up with Dario's business affairs, nor do I care."

"Doesn't matter."

"Then take me to another hotel, or home with you and Ori."

"We'd like nothing better." Sal retrieved the flask and took a sip. "But after what happened today, everyone's on edge. It's best if you're out of the city."

Fragile emotion whirled into contempt. She'd considered Sal a close friend, almost a father. "And what if I refuse?"

Sal calmly repositioned the rearview mirror over to the passenger's side until he could see her face. "Your life's in danger."

"I don't believe you."

"Would I lie about your safety?"

"No."

"Then it's the truth."

"But all my things are at the Blackland."

Sal held up a sealed envelope. "Here's more than enough cash for anything you'll need—and a bus ticket. From Houston you'll travel on to New Orleans. Dario plans to meet you in the French Quarter for an extended vacation when business cools."

Julia leaned back in the seat and scowled.

"When you arrive at the New Orleans bus terminal, go to the Western Union desk. A message will be waiting for you under the name, Katy Jones, along with a hotel key."

"Attached to roses and a poem?"

"Please don't be bitter, *mia rosa*." Sal reached over the seat and placed the envelope in Julia's lap. "Speak to no one unless it's absolutely necessary. Most important, never mention Dario or any of his associates." He patted her hand. "Ah, such a beautiful diamond. Look at the ring often. Remember how much you're loved."

Julia ignored the envelope. Sal wouldn't reveal specifics but didn't need to. Dario's sword of selfishness and greed had finally pinned him against an impenetrable wall, not only endangering him, but all those he held close.

She peered out her window. The downtown traffic honked and crept with its usual Friday afternoon snarl, while people strolled passed storefronts as if nothing had happened.

Maybe they didn't know.

And maybe she'd awaken in her luxurious suite to sunlight caressing her face, the day no more than a bad dream.

An unfathomable nightmare.

A tear formed, but she was too confused and exhausted to wipe it. Glancing down, she watched it splat onto her blouse, wetting a pinpoint speckle of dried blood.

One of several.

She knew the blood was there, just hadn't wanted to acknowledge its telltale presence.

Julia brushed her fingers over the specks. That's why Sal had daubed her face with his handkerchief.

She shivered.

What she'd witnessed at Dealey Plaza was no dream.

A darkening cloud of despair mushroomed over Dallas as the bus rolled south. They heard the President was pronounced dead minutes after their bus pulled away from the Trailways terminal. Several passengers held transistor radios, the tragic news saturating the airwaves. Rumors of the events at Dealey Plaza crisscrossed most every tongue. Some babbled nonstop, while others whispered, or cried. JFK's limo had sped from the triple underpass to Parkland Hospital in eight minutes, but many speculated he'd died before reaching the emergency room.

Julia kept silent.

She knew.

Each time she glanced at her blouse, she heard the final powerful rifle shot. Saw the horror on Jackie's face. Watched her scramble onto the limo's trunk to retrieve what had to be a piece of her husband's ....

Burying her face in her hands, Julia wept. Thankfully, the nonstop bus to Houston—a Five Star Luxury Coach—wasn't full. She had a pair of seats to herself. Besides providing a sparkling onboard restroom, the service included a hostess who boarded passengers, served food and beverages, and handed out pillows, blankets, and magazines. Even so, Sal insisted on buying her a sandwich and a candy bar at the terminal. She wasn't hungry, so he'd asked Ori to run to an adjacent leather goods shop for an adequate purse.

"To carry your lunch and envelope," Sal said when Ori returned. "And this." He pulled Julia's little mother-of-pearl Bible from his coat pocket.

"Sal? How did you know where to—? When did Dario—?" She turned away, too stunned to continue. Dario knew about her Bible. She'd revealed having it early on. He'd been clearly agitated, calling the book "an ancient collection of meek-minded myths." After Dario smashed the television, she'd hidden the Bible beneath her mattress, fearing he'd disagree with a teaching and toss it off the balcony. He must have rummaged through her personal belongings on a regular basis as a way to control their relationship, revealing the spoils to his buddies.

Sal spoke tenderly. "If Dario thought clearly, he'd want you to keep what's rightfully yours."

"But he's confused." She faced Sal. "You saved my Bible before he could destroy it?"

Sal's eyes grew moist.

"That's what I thought," Julia stepped forward and wrapped her arms around him.

"The hostess is almost ready for you," Ori said.

She released her hug and stepped back. "Will you see Dario again?"

"Of course. And then I'm due some time off. Maybe I'll return to Europe with my son.

Ori smiled. "I'll keep him out of trouble."

"While I vacation with Dario in the French Quarter."

"That's what he says," Sal answered.

"What do *you* say?"

Instead of answering, he retrieved the flask and took a long sip.

"Sal?"

He swallowed. "My opinion is no longer important."

"What do *you* say." Julia widened her stance. "I'm not leaving until you tell me."

Sal raised the flask, then lowered it. "First, Dario must sleep in his own bed. Second, I hope you understand that we …."

"We, what?"

"You'd better board. They're waiting."

RUNNING DOWNWIND

"Not yet." She reached up and cupped his chin between her thumb and forefinger. "I deserve to know the truth. What's second?"

"We were never in agreement." Sal sighed. "Someday, perhaps I can say more."

"Today."

"The climate's much too dangerous. Knowing nothing is better."

"I'm your rose, remember?"

He nodded, then took another sip. "In tug-of-war, a contestant who plays for both teams is a fool, for he must stand in the middle and risk being torn in half."

"Meaning?"

"Always trust your instincts, *mia rosa*." Sal recapped the flask and returned it to his pocket. "Always." He motioned to Ori, and they walked away.

As soon as Julia boarded, the bus eased forward onto the street. She peered out of the window. Sal stood at the curb with both hands over his heart.

"*Julia, tu sei la mia rosa!*"

Four hours later when the coach reached the Houston terminal, the entire world was in mourning. Vice President Lyndon B. Johnson had already been sworn in as Commander In Chief. Julia stepped off the bus into the humid coastal air and entered the main lobby. A voice over the intercom announced that the bus to New Orleans was now boarding.

"Just my luck," she muttered, exhausted. For most of the trip she'd pictured Jackie's desperate reach atop the limo's trunk, or worried about Dario's shenanigans. Had Sal overreacted? Perhaps he'd overdramatized the situation. After what happened in Dealey Plaza, he was probably in shock like everyone else and not thinking rationally.

Thirsty, Julia headed toward the concession area. The envelope in her purse contained ten one-hundred-dollar bills. A thousand dollars was more money than she'd ever seen in one place, much less need. She considered returning to Dallas long enough to grab her things, though feared Sal was partially right. Her life might be in danger by simple association. In the past few weeks, she'd noticed several shady characters hanging around the club and didn't want them harassing her. So before continuing on to New Orleans, she needed to purchase a change of clothes, hairbrush, toothbrush, and a lipstick. The Trailways hostess provided directions to a nearby department store, but now there wasn't time.

Just off the main lobby, a crowd gathered in front of a portable television rigged atop a tall stepladder. News photos snapped earlier in the afternoon showed Jackie standing beside LBJ on Air Force One. She still wore the same blood-spattered suit, but no pillbox hat.

Julia gasped.

Seeing the impeccable First Lady without her hat made her seem exposed. Vulnerable. And especially ....

Real.

The final boarding call to New Orleans blared overhead. Rushing outside, Julia fought back a new round of tears. *A Tour of the White House with Mrs. John F. Kennedy* painted the canvas of its inhabitants with the vibrant colors of a magnificent fairy tale. Not as President and First lady, but Prince Jack and Princess Jackie. Awakening each day in a grand castle. Waltzing in patent and pearls through eloquent state dinners as young and privileged American royalty. Now the beautiful princess stood alone, hopeless and hatless, mourning her prince, their *happily forever after* slain by evil's heartless dragon.

The bus to New Orleans provided an onboard restroom but was no Five Star Luxury Coach. Operated by a smaller, regional carrier, there was no hostess, nor an ounce of refreshment. The driver, a portly man named Ernie, seemed more concerned with stopping at numerous diners along the way for pie and coffee than staying on schedule. Many of the passengers were regulars, obviously knowing what to expect. Julia selected a soft drink at the first stop, provoking questionable looks from the cashier when she tried paying with a hundred-dollar bill.

"Is this C-note genuine?" The cashier sniffed the ink.

"Genuine?"

"Got anything smaller?"

Julia shook her head.

"She's good." Ernie winked from a nearby barstool. "Ain't any counterfeiters on my bus."

"Don't make no difference if the Pope's on your bus." The cashier scowled. "Not handing out all my change. Bank's closed 'til Monday."

"Thanks anyway." Julia set the drink on the counter.

"Aw, just put it on my tab." Ernie waved Julia out the door and grinned. "How 'bout another wedge of that chocolate pie?"

Later, when Julia realized the trip would stretch into a nightlong journey, she complained to an elderly woman seated across the aisle.

"Now don't you worry, honey. Ernie will get us there in time for breakfast." She held up a silver handled cane. "I'll tap your armrest if you're asleep."

Hugging her purse as a pillow, Julia reclined the seat and closed her eyes. The day began in so much promise yet ended in despair. She squeezed her purse tighter, feeling the comforting outline of her Bible, thankful Sal had brought it. Once, he'd stopped by her suite while she'd been reading Psalms. He made no comment but chuckled when he saw the book lying open on the couch. After he left, she didn't know if he was showing approval or condescension.

Now she knew.

Julia peered out the window into the passing darkness. What kind of vicious tug-of-war match was Dario playing? And why would he stand in the midst of two opposing forces and risk being torn—? She bit her lip, refusing to complete the thought. Surely Sal was waxing figuratively. He'd mentioned Dario reneged on some promises and upset powerful people.

But who?

Rumor stated that other Dallas nightclubs were jealous of Dario's success, but the owners usually slapped each other's backs and got along, even sharing acts on occasion.

Julia turned onto her side and closed her eyes. Dario was famous for not keeping his word when it came to her but had no clue he followed the same deceitful pattern in business. His timing was terrible.

Of all days to be selfish.

Of all days to upset powerful people.

As the bus lumbered through the muggy wee hours, Julia drifted in and out of sleep. Occasionally, she'd hear Ernie announce the next stop, followed by a shuffle of footsteps mingled with hushed voices, or rouse enough to realize various seats had changed passengers. Pushing her thoughts far away from Dealey Plaza, she dreamed of Lahoma and then Ray, who instantly became Dario. She awoke in a sweat as lightening flashed, punctuated by a

RUNNING DOWNWIND

loud thunderclap. Small hail pelted against her window, melting into hard rain. She shivered, positioning bare arms between her purse and the seatback, praying the nightmare of past and present would end. And then Ernie spoke with an English accent while Calvin drove the bus. The chauffeur led the passengers in *Amazing Grace,* until the LA Coliseum loomed large beneath the high, clear, moon. On the playing field, Billy Graham stood boldly atop the hay wagon platform, surrounded by wild mustangs. Upon his command, the horses leapt over the stadium's topmost section. They landed in thick grass, running downwind until the emerald prairie billowed into ocean waves lapping the Padre Island shore. On the beach stood a lighthouse, its beacon illuminating the Lady Who Walked on the Sea.

"We made it." The elderly woman punched Julia with her cane.

"What?"

"Told 'ya Ernie would get us here on time. He's already gone inside."

"Why?"

"Pancakes for starters. Hope I didn't startle you, honey, but you wouldn't stir."

"Are we in New Orleans?"

"On the outskirts. This is Ernie's favorite breakfast place. Mine too. Ever had scrambled eggs with onions and oysters?"

"With what?" Julia sat up straight and smoothed back her hair.

"I'll save you a chair."

"Where's the bus terminal?"

"Downtown. Now don't you worry, honey. We'll get there directly."

As the woman ambled up the aisle, Julia wished she could return to her dream. She glanced outside. Gray daylight seeped through a layer of mist hanging beneath patchy clouds. Ernie had stopped at yet another diner, the parking lot jammed with pickups, law enforcement vehicles, and work trucks of every description. The hickory lure of sizzling bacon made her stomach rumble. For the first time since leaving Dallas, she was hungry.

When the final passenger exited, Julia stood, rubbing both palms across her wrinkled clothes. "If only I could wash my face," she announced to the empty seats, then remembered the bathroom in the rear. It offered no soap or paper towels—not even a mirror—and the sink's lone faucet emitted a trickle. Julia scrubbed with her hands, using a wad of toilet tissue to pat dry, which kept snagging her engagement ring. She thrust it off her finger, not caring if the symbol of her phony engagement slid down the drain.

The jewelry piece wouldn't fit.

Julia gazed into the sink. The stone's multifaceted brilliance no longer emitted luster, so she considered flinging it down the toilet. Instead, she dropped the ring into her purse, deciding the fate of the big diamond ... later.

Deciding about Dario ... later.

Feeling better, she exited the bathroom and stepped off the bus.

Besides bacon, the aroma of hash browns and fresh brewed coffee drew her toward the door. Just outside, a young man wearing a jumpsuit stenciled with *Caxton's Flying Service,* propped his foot atop the arm of a wooden bench. He didn't look up but pointed to a newspaper balanced over his knee.

"There's the guilty communist. Can't believe they've already nabbed him."

"Pardon me?" Julia paused as the door swung open. Two sheriff deputies exited while tipping their hats.

RUNNING DOWNWIND

"Right here on the front page of today's paper." The young man thumped a photo with his finger. "A mugshot of the scumbag who murdered JFK. See."

Instinctively, Julia stepped closer, then felt her body tremble. The face in the mugshot resembled the man who'd covered the dropped two-dollar bill with his shoe, the sharp dresser who'd smiled at her. The person she'd seen at the club.

"No," she whispered, backing toward the bench. She sat down hard. "Can't be."

"You know him?"

"No. He looks like a guy who ..." Her voice trailed off.

"Paper says the sniper's name is Lee Harvey Oswald. Sound familiar?"

"Absolutely not. I'm thinking of someone I met in passing. He didn't tell me his name."

"Says this Oswald nut acted alone, shooting the President from a sixth-floor window of the Texas School Book Depository." The young man eyed Julia. "You sure he's not—?"

"Positive. That's somebody entirely different."

"Yeah." The young man nodded in agreement. "Scientists say we all have a double out there somewhere." He thumped the photo again. "I'd hate to be his."

A driverless pickup's horn began honking. Painted on the door was the image of a small airplane. "Oops, getting a call on my radio." The young man handed her the paper. "Hold this a minute." He hurried to the pickup.

Julia didn't want to look at the shooter's picture—nor his name—but couldn't help herself. She wasn't *positive* about anything. This Lee Harvey Oswald was unshaven, sporting a large cut above his right eye, so probably wasn't the same person. The man she remembered was meticulous about his appearance, and much more pleasant than the three sour faces occupying the booth every morning. The booth where she'd delivered the two-dollar bills.

Why would an assassin be involved in Dario's ridiculous gratuity game anyway?

Still, the resemblance was uncanny.

She frowned.

Dario wasn't the best judge of character.

The young man stood with his pickup's door open, gesturing with his free hand while talking into a radio microphone. Julia wished he'd come get his paper. Wished he'd never shown her the mug shot.

Why *her* out of all the people who'd stepped off the bus?

Flipping the front page over, she noticed a short news item on the back: *Dallas Nightclub Owner Leaps to His Death*.

Her heart froze.

The brief article confirmed that Dario Rossi, owner of *The Scarlet Stallion*, jumped through a large plate-glass window from a luxury suite atop the Blackland Hotel. Police reported the incident occurred a few hours after JFK was assassinated. Discovered at the scene was a suicide note penned in Rossi's own handwriting. The note explained his deep admiration and love for the President, thus an inability to cope with the tragic loss. However, witnesses both inside and outside the Blackland told a more gruesome story. Inside, they heard shouts, followed by a series of screams. Outside, they discovered Dario's body severed in half, most likely by the razor-sharp window glass. The entire matter was still under investigation.

Lightheaded, Julia dropped the paper and gasped for breath.

She couldn't cry.

Couldn't stand.

RUNNING DOWNWIND

Couldn't run.

Sal's tug-of-war explanation had nothing to do with *business*. Dario's dilemma was a deadly assassination game involving two-dollar-bills, grim men in a booth, a crude map drawn in red ink, a lookalike shooter with a shiny shoe, a pleasant smile ....

And she'd been part of it.

Instantly nauseous, she hugged her purse against her middle, rocking slightly. Sal was correct. Her life *was* in danger.

Dario was murdered.

She might be next.

Sal warned she must always trust her instincts, which now screamed the New Orleans bus terminal wasn't smart. At Dealey Plaza, she'd heard shots fired at the President from opposite directions, meaning there was more than one gunman. Who knew how many others were involved in the slaying on various levels? From this point forward, any form of public transportation was out of the question. They—whoever *they* were—could be waiting for her.

Perspiration beaded across her brow. She felt hot and cold at the same time.

"Ma'am? Are you all right?" The young man picked up his paper. "You look pale."

"Do you run a flying service?" Julia managed.

"Yes ma'am. Mainly crop-dusting. Cotton, soy beans, rice."

"Mainly?"

"Been known to fly a few passengers in the fall and winter when work slows. Gotta little Cessna 210 that'll carry four."

"Are you Caxton?"

The young man grinned. "I'm Bud. Caxton's my old man."

Julia's mind whirled. Growing up, she'd known a handful of crop-dusters, all of them daredevils. A duster's cockpit allowed only enough room for the pilot. However, a flying service near Lahoma's ranch flew landowners over their spreads in a larger plane during the offseason. "Where do you fly?"

"Wherever there's a good paying job," Bud answered casually. "Usually up and down the Mississippi Delta and along the Louisiana coast.

"What about Texas?"

"LSU whipped 'em good in last year's Cotton Bowl." He chuckled.

"What about Padre Island?"

"Didn't know it had a football team." He laughed again. "Good area for deep sea fishing, though. Been several times."

"I'm hiring you to fly me there. Now."

"Padre? Today?"

She nodded.

"Aren't you on Ernie's bus?"

"Not unless he's headed to Padre."

"Lady, that's over 700 miles. And there's no airport on the island."

"There's a beach." Julia stood. "Are you skilled enough to land on sand?"

He bristled. "I can set that single engine Cessna down anywhere—shell topped roads, deep gravel, even plowed dirt."

"Okay. So, what's the problem?"

"The cold front that blew through here a couple of hours ago is headed toward the Texas coast. Flying through its back door could be mighty risky." Bud studied the sky. "Looks like more foul weather's gonna follow." He shook his head. "If it was just me, fine. But Lady, no amount of money could—"

RUNNING DOWNWIND

"A thousand dollars?" Julia opened her purse, pulled out the cash and fanned it like a poker hand.

Bud's chin plummeted. "That's a respectable pile of dough."

"Somewhere on the beach there's a lighthouse. We'll land there."

He grinned. "Got any luggage?"

CHAPTER 18

Mick stood in the pitch-black shadows underneath his bungalow. Twenty minutes earlier he'd watched Julia exit hers, considered trying to stop her but knew where she was headed.

The beach at the lighthouse.

Knew she went there every morning. But why at midnight? And why was she running?

You already know.

He wandered aimlessly across the parking lot, trying to ignore the nagging truth. In the midst of the evening's warmth and beauty, his vocal cords had frozen into an ugly silence.

As he neared Roughshods, he smelled the cigarette before noticing its pinpoint reddish glow.

"You people keep late hours." A bald man stepped out from beneath the steps into tepid moonlight.

"People?" Mick was in no mood to talk to a spying stranger. Especially one who might be a reporter, even though his demeanor seemed coarse for a journalist.

The man released a throaty chuckle. "Lover's quarrel?"

"Excuse me?"

He waved his cigarette toward Julia's bungalow. "That's one angry broad. Bolted outta her place like a wet cat." He eyed Mick. "Hope she ain't Ryder's gal, 'cause he ain't never been keen on sharing nothing."

Mick chuckled silently. Baldy's grammar needed work, but he had a sense of humor. "If you're here for breakfast, you're early."

"Ain't hungry."

"Me neither." Mick didn't inquire further about the man's business because he obviously knew Ryder, probably just a doughnut shop crony. If the glaze-lipped crowd ever assigned each other nicknames, Cue Ball was a good one.

The man studied the cigarette while rolling it between his thumb and forefinger. "Where's Ryder?"

Mick shrugged. He was exhausted, and Cue Ball asked too many questions. "Have a good night." Turning to leave, Mick stopped. The guy might be a private investigator, so he glanced about the parking lot. Nothing but a couple of dented steel trash barrels and Julia's pickup.

"Got time for a smoke?" the man asked.

"Where's your car?"

"Motel just up the beach. Thought I'd stretch my legs."

Mick looked past the stranger toward Julia's bungalow. "You chose a frigid night for it."

The man snorted. "I'm from outta town. Ryder's an old college roommate."

"College?"

"Ain't that what I said?" He tossed his cigarette butt onto the ground and produced a pack of smokes. "My roomy finished a few years ahead of me."

His *roomy*? Mick swallowed a laugh. He wouldn't be surprised if some newspaper hired a PI. But any snoop worth his nameplate would, at least, be a believable liar.

"So how 'bout that smoke?" the man pressed.

"Never took up the habit."

RUNNING DOWNWIND

"Maybe you should reconsider." Cue Ball tapped the bottom of the pack against his palm to free a cigarette.

Mick grimaced. Most people in showbiz smoked because it calmed their nerves. A little tobacco might be just the thing to soften the sting of his blunder with Julia concerning the dolphin's dead calf. 'Cause for a third time on the same day, a common word had left him lightheaded and heavy legged.

Pregnant.

Therefore, he'd not offered Julia his hand when they'd descended the dangerous lighthouse stairs. If he'd fallen, both of them might've been injured—or killed. She deserved neither. Then on the drive back to Roughshods, he could barely speak because Cherie's blood-soaked body kept surfacing his thought-pool without warning.

Pregnant.

The baby growing inside of Cherie couldn't be saved either, a child that was *his too*. Worse, it was *his* fault. As a result, he suffered pain he could never share, a chronic ache debilitating his soul.

"What's the verdict?" Cue Ball raised his chin. "I ain't got all night."

"I'll pass."

The man dug a stainless-steel lighter from his pants pocket. "You and the gal rent from Ryder?"

"Who wants to know?"

"Reunion committee. They're particular about accommodations. Need something nice."

"And you're the chairman?"

He scowled and lit another smoke. "I only see two crummy little bungalows. Where does Ryder stay?"

Mick answered with an irritated silence. The man was no reunion committee chairman. If he'd attended college—which was doubtful—he should've enrolled in some speech and acting classes.

"It ain't no hard question."

"Ryder just bought a place over in Port Isabel," Mick lied. "I hear it's *nice*, a huge mansion."

"Ain't what I was told at the hardware store. Fellow there said he stayed across the bay in this dump."

"Next time try the doughnut shop." Mick eyed Cue Ball. "Their info is more up to date. They fry it up fresh every morning, then sugarcoat it."

"A midnight comedian. Got another joke?"

"Yeah. But I can't recall the punch line."

The stranger leaned forward and blew smoke in Mick's face. "Tell Ryder that John Singer's looking for him."

"If I don't forget."

He thumped the remainder of his cigarette at Mick's feet. "Here's a line you'd best remember. I ain't got the appetite for no funnyman."

Cue Ball turned on his heel and disappeared into the night. If he'd headed toward the lighthouse, Mick would've followed. However, the obnoxious stranger stomped off in the opposite direction.

Probably back to hell.

This time, Mick laughed out loud to a punch line he wouldn't forget.

Instead of returning to his bungalow, he leaned against Julia's pickup.

Bet'cha Cue Ball shaves with a switchblade and eats rattlesnakes. He and Max Darnell should be roomies.

Mick nodded at the thought. "I ain't got the appetite for no *bullies*," he said aloud. The eighth-grade incident with Darnell had bolstered Mick's courage for a weekend, but also planted a troubling seed into his psyche. Then when Cherie was killed, something snapped. Whereas he'd struggled much of his life to suppress the fear of being bullied, he was no longer frightened. Now men like Cue Ball disgusted him.

RUNNING DOWNWIND

Ed would be proud.

Even Mick's fear of death had lessened. When his sailboat sank in the storm, he was more disappointed than afraid. The truth—he'd wanted to die ... until he decided to live.

Hopefully, his decision wasn't a mistake.

He glanced in the direction of the lighthouse. Cue Ball's amateur acting proved him a liar. Clearly, John Singer wasn't his name, nor college reunion plans his business. The man was up to no good and might try and harm Julia.

Mick decided to wait outside her bungalow and keep watch. Tomorrow he'd warn Ryder, even though Roughshods's respected owner was a likely lighthouse door thief. He'd probably lifted the lamp as well.

Guess what's locked behind steel door number one?

At least Mick hadn't discovered any incriminating newspapers in Roughshods's basement, unless they were held hostage in the secreted red brick room. And if the grape sodas atop the lighthouse were purposely stashed, then Ryder wasn't too worried about someone having easy access and finding them. Why he spent time up there was anybody's guess. Maybe he enjoyed the view.

Or observed dolphins.

Or watched over reckless teenagers.

Mick lowered the pickup's tailgate and stretched out on the smooth, plank bed. He stared at the moon. The stranger's late-night encounter stirred kernels imbedded in Mick's memory. Not just a vehement disdain for bullies, but other troubling seeds, some deliberately sown during his own adolescence. When he'd finally joined the select ranks of the popular crowd during the latter part of high school, the seeds sprouted without warning, spreading narcissism's tangled vines throughout his college career, then blooming into a professional garden of selfishness.

The tendrils of trouble, the weeds of the weak, the—

"Enough." Mick ordered his thoughts to stand down. As an actor, he'd worked hard incorporating various figures of speech into witty comebacks, a necessary requirement for any multi-interviewed celebrity. He loved a timely metaphor or an amusing pun. Alliteration was his favorite ... until the skillful usage of repetitive beginning consonants backfired.

Drawing blood.

Slicing him with deep truth.

The clever cleaver.

"I said stop." Mick refocused his attention toward the moon. "That Old Devil Moon," he whispered, recalling the familiar Broadway tune, as well as the first girl he'd ever kissed on stage. And off.

He frowned.

Not Cherie.

Not back then.

She'd innocently pecked his cheek more than once, but he always backed away. And then her family moved to Philly. Besides, Cherie was an angel. The girl he'd kissed—all nine shapely syllables—was three-quarters devil.

Deanna Jessalynn Merroney.

Her lips immediately changed him. The musky sweetness still haunted his conscious.

That Old Devil Moon.

The melody resonated throughout the chambers of his memory. Due to his reputation as an accomplished jazz band pianist, he'd been requested by the high school drama teacher, Miss Kreg, to tackle the difficult Broadway score to *Finian's Rainbow*. He did, learning he possessed a knack for show tunes as well as jazz.

During cast auditions, head-cheerleader Deanna easily won the female lead against a field of twenty or so

RUNNING DOWNWIND

disappointed hopefuls. And since her middle linebacker boyfriend Lance privately threatened each of his challengers, the male lead went uncontested. The problem—Lance could make a defense sing, but not his vocal cords. Mick tried lightly playing the melody underneath the accompaniment whenever Lance sang, but without result. When Miss Kreg suggested extra song rehearsals, Lance reluctantly agreed, then doubled into mock silent laughter when she wasn't looking. The next morning, Lance caught Mick at his locker and doubled his fists.

"More rehearsals weren't my idea," Mick said.

"That's right, music nerd, 'cause I don't need 'em. Old Maid Kreg should clean the wax outta her ears. Right?"

Mick stared at his algebra book. Miss Kreg was barely thirty.

"Right?"

No reply.

"Guess you're deaf too." Lance cracked his knuckles. "I won't break your hands this time." He jammed a steel forefinger into Mick's chest. "'Cause you're gonna play my notes nice and loud. Got it?"

Mick nodded, embarrassed for the cowardice crawling beneath his skin. He'd grown taller, but was still a lightweight, constantly wrestling the fear Darnell planted in the pit of his stomach.

That evening Mick played with gusto, though Lance continued to struggle. Mick pounded the keys louder, but the boy missed every pitch. Midway through *That Old Devil Moon*, Mick's bullied anxiety finally exploded into rebellion. "Can't you hear the melody?" He eyed Lance. "The notes go like this." Mick belted out the entire verse a cappella. A dozen dropped jaws arced into smiles, Deanna's the most profound. By the end of the night, Lance'd lost his girlfriend *and* the male lead.

"That Old Devil Moon," Mick whispered a third time, wishing he could blame his troubled past on a song. Afterward, Lance left him alone, acting like the incident never happened. An unexpected miracle. Rumor avowed the head football coach was sweet on Miss Kreg, which probably had something to do with Lance's amnesia. However, the moon could've played a role. Lunar phases impacted ocean tides, planting crops, and even when babies were born.

Or not born.

Mick shivered.

Kissing Deanna each night of *Finian's Rainbow* released a whirlwind of complicated desires and emotions he'd not previously felt, followed by awkward situations he'd never experienced. Suddenly, popular girls wanted to date him—including Deanna—who telephoned each evening during the McFarland cocktail hour. "I'm sure it's for you, Son," Ed would say, then chuckle his approval from behind the broadsheets of the *Austin American Statesman*. Mick first assumed his father's lighthearted interest doglegged from the evening's apportionment of scotch. But then recalled Ed attending *Finian's* final matinee performance prior to happy hour and instigating a standing ovation.

By Mick's senior year, his muscle mass finally met his height, forming a six-foot, two-inch frame weighing a toned 190 lbs. The adolescent throngs predicted he and Deanna would be chosen *Favorite Couple* for the class of 1956. However, Mick's interest in her waned. Deanna proved to be a controlling tease, more so than girls just as beautiful.

In October, Mick and Deanna commanded the male and female leads in *Brigadoon*, playing each night to a packed house. Before the show closed, Mick succumbed to mounting peer pressure and asked Deanna to go steady. Her manipulative strings soon morphed into jealous chains. Their relationship scarcely lasted through Christmas, ending in a turbulent split as Time Square's bulb-encrusted ball dropped on New Year's Eve. Devastated, Deanna fell into the consoling charms of Lance's older brother, Rich, who was home from college. By spring break, Deanna and Rich were wed. Everyone knew the real reason but acted as if the two were soul mates and their marriage would last forever.

Upon graduation, Mick had been voted most popular, most handsome, and prom king. Then through his dad's University of Texas contacts, secured a four-year theater scholarship. He immediately pledged Ed's old social fraternity, rushing through the oaken hundred-proof-door into the perfumed embrace of college life, enjoying his pick of gorgeous coeds. Even so, academic excellence was required, and Mick studied hard.

His final year at UT proved him an accomplished actor when he earned the lead in *Death of a Salesman*. Ed brought clients to the opening, one being the brother of a legendary Broadway director. The show ran for two weeks. On closing night, the director sat in the audience. Afterward, Ed and Fran hosted the cast party in their spacious home, where the director asked Mick to sing. A month later, he received his theater degree and boarded a flight for a New York audition. Following a series of callbacks, Off-Broadway whispered his name. When the first curtain fell, a dozen Manhattan beauties whispered his name as well.

In less than a year, the whispers rose to standing ovations and public accolades. Mick worked harder, widening his talents with an expedited course in professional dance. He signed with a premier talent agency, tried out for a Broadway touring company, and was offered the male lead in *West Side Story*. The show traveled across the US, playing extended engagements in a myriad of major cities, including Boston, Chicago, Dallas, and San Francisco. What began with energetic clarity soon blurred into monotonous theaters, bland hotels, and incessant fans. Most of them female. Many offering more than quiet conversation after a late supper.

When the tour ended, Mick auditioned for the new musical, *Rain in Rio*, this time landing in Midtown Manhattan's elite theater district as a star.

On Broadway.

Bully for Broadway.

Three months into the sold-out run, he agreed to a lucrative recording contract with a major west coast record label located in Los Angeles. He'd sign autographs on Broadway's famed 42nd Street, then jet first class across the country to the corner of Hollywood and Vine.

Hooray for Hollywood.

A gust of night breeze pushed Mick's thoughts back onto the island. He slid off the tailgate and stood. In retrospect, his fame seemed surreal, especially his ease in front of an audience. Acting was merely pretending, a skill most people enjoyed as children and lost as adults. It's not that when puberty struck their imaginations ceased to function. They simply grew too sophisticated to allow what their heads and hearts conjured as real. Great acting made audiences believe in the unbelievable. The problem was when a life built upon fiction blurred into reality, especially the reality of relationships.

Plopping back down, Mick inched his torso back far enough to sit and let his feet dangle. He knew where his thoughts now headed but didn't stop them. LA was where he'd finally reconnected with Cherie. He'd not seen nor had any contact with her since the After-Finals Formal at the end of their sophomore year in high school.

And then Cherie appeared *out of the blue*.

Literally.

A setting September sun held southern California hostage in the tongs of an unaccustomed heat wave. After an exhausting day of recording, Mick returned to his suite at the Rosewall Hotel, changed into swim trunks and headed upstairs for a cool dip in the spacious rooftop pool. The clientele—celebrities, politicians, and people too wealthy to ask for autographs—occupied every lounger. Mick swam a few laps, then relaxed chest deep on the steps in the shallow end.

A striking blonde in bathing attire entered the pool area, followed by a dark-haired man in an expensive suit. They spoke briefly before she scampered onto the diving board, springing airborne into a perfect jackknife. Then swimming underwater, headed straight for Mick.

Her head surfaced. "We'll always be friends."

"What?" He leaned forward behind a massive grin. "Here?"

"Why not?"

"Cherie? Cherie Dennis?"

She smiled.

"I can't believe ... How did you find—?"

"Your parents."

"They should've warned me."

"I swore them to secrecy."

Mick laughed. "That's a first."

"Ed swears when you win an Emmy, he'll have your name painted on the dome of the Texas State Capitol."

"Right. Dad swears all the time, remember, words no one dare paint." Mick glanced about. The man in the suit was gone. "Who's your well-dressed friend?"

"No friend, just some jerk on the elevator. He tried to impress me, insisting I meet him later for a drink."

"And you declined?"

"That's why he followed me, bragging about a nightclub he owns in Dallas: The Scarlet Stud, or something similar. I told him I'd never heard of the place but would inform my *husband*."

"You're married?"

"Not hardly. I'm still waiting for the right guy." Cherie swam forward and pecked Mick on the cheek.

This time he didn't back away.

They began seeing each other whenever Cherie was in New York or LA but only as close friends. Upon earning a degree in fashion merchandising, she traveled the country as a buyer for a dozen high-end boutiques.

During the nine years they'd been separated, Cherie had—in her words—*discovered Christ*. She wasn't shy about her belief, nor judgmental. Yet where she'd always held Mick in highest esteem, she now embraced her *Lord*.

Did that mean Jesus was a Member of Parliament?

Cherie also adopted a new, personal code. *Live simply so that others may simply live.* As a result, she'd pared down her belongings, moved to an efficiency apartment, and drove a dilapidated Volkswagen.

"To make a bold statement, plus save gas," she'd admitted to Mick early on. "I'd rather my employers book me into less expensive hotels, but I have no say in the matter."

"They just don't want you staying in a hippie commune." He raised his eyebrows. "I hear room service delivers goods and services not on the menu."

Cherie ignored the comment.

RUNNING DOWNWIND

"Meaning that drugs are free, as well as love."

"Then you need to clean out your ears. *Everything* comes with a price tag."

When *Rain in Rio* entered film production, Mick spent a year in Brazil. He tried hard to behave, flying Cherie down for two weeks at Christmas. By February, the tropical heat weakened his resolve, especially during the wild nights of *Festival*. To combat temptation, he telephoned her daily. The long-distance charges were outrageous, but worth it. Cherie was the only woman strong enough to halt his rollercoaster relationships. As soon as he returned to New York, he'd asked her to marry him.

A garbage truck rumbled past Roughshods's parking lot, rousing Mick's attention back to the job at hand. Julia still hadn't returned. He had no clue of the hour, probably around two a.m. At least Cue Ball hadn't resurfaced.

Cherie had.

True.

Mick swallowed.

But her memories didn't require his tears ....

This time.

CHAPTER 19

The night grew eerily dark. Exhausted, Julia trudged back to her bungalow, the trail difficult to see. What began as innocent wisps sliding beneath the moon thickened into ominous pallets of high clouds. She'd learned since coming to Padre how these skittish formations preceded trouble.

When she reached Roughshods's parking lot, moonlight filtered through a gap in the sky. Julia glanced ahead at her pickup and stopped walking.

Mick sat on the tailgate.

"Maybe he's waiting for a ride," she muttered, remembering her prediction about his leaving the island by dawn. Was he mocking her or expecting to talk? She felt suddenly breathless, knowing better than to raise her hopes. Knowing from experience nothing had changed.

She waited for darkness to return before moving silently toward her bungalow. If Mick Leonard was still around in the morning, he'd have to initiate their conversation. Whether he received a response was something she'd have to consider. Gathering what little strength her body held, she opened the door and slipped inside. Hopefully, he hadn't noticed.

Julia switched on a lamp, then plopped onto her bed. She'd returned earlier than planned, not that a wee hour lighthouse excursion was an intended event. Nor had she expected her mind to dredge up Dario. Worse, what happened her final day in Dallas. She hated the memory, yet sometimes its return was unavoidable. The recollection refused to leave until she'd relived every shocking detail.

Realizing he'd dozed, Mick roused with a jerk, then saw a light on in Julia's bungalow. He'd missed her return, as well as the arrival of high clouds darting across the moon. Mick had no clue if she'd noticed him, or if so, cared.

He repositioned himself on the tailgate, pressing his palms against the cool metal. There was something comforting about an old pickup, simple and unfettered. Nicer still was the vehicle's owner. A sensitive and caring woman who'd pulled his lifeless body from the waves.

A girl to whom he'd lied.

A girl who'd later cried.

A girl he didn't deserve.

Who are you anyway?

"I'm the famous Mick McFarland," he said aloud.

And I'm the infamous Mick Leonard."

CHAPTER 20

The next morning, Ryder slapped two dozen sausage patties on the griddle, then mopped the sweat from his brow with the hem of his apron. The air was way too sultry for eight o'clock, the humidity inside Roughshods clung to his skin like an oily mist. Shortly after sunup, a hurricane watch was posted for the lower Texas coast and points inland. Hurricane Beulah's forward movement had slowed, churning some four hundred miles out in the Gulf, strengthening into a major blow. Forecasters predicted a direct hit on the island within the next forty-eight hours.

Peeking through the service window into the dining area, Ryder grinned. Folks loved his generous family-style breakfast platters. The place was packed. Both seasonal and year-round residents savored every bite, knowing from experience that weeks might pass before their favorite restaurants reopened after the storm, if at all. With an approaching gale of this magnitude, even native islanders would board up and retreat across the bay to higher ground.

He watched as Julia hurriedly took orders and served coffee to everyone but Mick. The boy sat at a corner table reading the morning paper, obviously pretending not to care. Her avoidance of him was no surprise. Ryder had spent a portion of the night atop the lighthouse watching for Dipp. Shortly after midnight, he viewed a slender figure scampering between the dunes, knowing instantly it was Julia. He'd downed a few grape sodas while keeping an eye on her, just in case Dipp showed.

The lowlife hadn't.

Why Julia was on the beach at that hour instead of daybreak was anyone's guess, except Ryder wasn't just *anyone*. Prison not only honed his intuitive skills, he'd mastered the art of reading a person's body movements up close or from a distance. Clearly, the girl was upset. Later, he'd returned to Roughshods and noticed Mick sleeping in the bed of Julia's pickup, one leg drooping off the rear like the tail of a guilty puppy. The kids must've had a spat during their evening drive to check for hatchlings, the boy saying or doing something stupid. Probably both.

Ryder retrieved a pound of bacon from the fridge and crossed back to the griddle, performing a little heel-to-toe polka hop. He dumped the pound beside the sausage. As thrilled as he was about the storm, he couldn't afford any setbacks, especially with Dipp snooping around and complicating his plans.

"If you don't take care of business, business will take care of you," Ryder declared to a clump of sizzling hash browns. He couldn't remember where he'd heard the maxim, or if he'd birthed it himself, but its wisdom proved invaluable serving time *and* customers.

Grabbing a spatula, he separated the bacon, flipped over each sausage patty, and scratched his bare scalp with the handle. Mick and Julia needed to be off the island when Beulah hit for more reasons than weather safety. Therefore, he'd close Roughshods after lunch, making sure the pair worked out their differences *together* before nightfall.

"Looks like you're feeding the entire county." Mick stood in the doorway. "Need a hand washing dishes?"

RUNNING DOWNWIND

"I need ten hands and five times as many fingers." Ryder motioned toward a mound of plates stacked beside a large utility sink. "Scrape those and get 'em soaking while I fry some eggs. You'd best eat in here where the forecast is friendlier."

"You've noticed?"

"That, and where you slept."

Mick rubbed his neck. "I guess that's why the back of a pickup's called a *bed*."

"You ain't the first male genius to figure that out." Ryder cracked a dozen eggs onto the griddle. "Guess you'd prefer yours over-easy."

"Or soft-boiled for a hard-head." Mick filled the sink with hot water.

Ryder chuckled. The boy could laugh at himself, which wasn't an inborn trait but a learned skill, one most men were too proud to master.

"Some bald guy stopped by late last night." Mick picked up a table knife and a dirty plate. "He was looking for you. Called himself John Singer."

"Don't believe I know a Singer." Ryder tried to remain calm. He'd barely rubbed the sleep from his eyes when Julia stomped into the kitchen with a similar tale.

Mick scraped the leftovers into a metal pail. "He claimed to be an old college roommate."

"Is that right."

"Said he needed a place to hold a class reunion."

"I never went to college, not that I didn't have aspirations." Ryder reached above the griddle for a clean platter. "This Singer fellow must have me confused with some other egghead."

"Makes sense." Mick slid several plates into the water.

"Did the stranger say where he was staying? I could stop by later and clear up the confusion."

"Some beachfront motel."

"Humph. What was his mood?"

Mick seemed puzzled. "His mood?"

They both glanced up as Julia clipped three orders to a wire strung across the service window. She frowned and walked away.

"Highly irritated." Mick faced Ryder. "Think the man's demeanor will improve?"

"In due time, I reckon. Now come get some grub before it's gone."

The Jax Beer clock chimed twice. Ryder stood behind the cash register and watched the screen door nip the heels of the last lunch customer. Across the room, Julia wiped down tables and filled salt and pepper shakers. He heard water running in the kitchen, meaning Mick was rinsing dishes. The two kids still weren't speaking, but that would change. Ryder had requested they board-up the Gulf-facing windows while he attended to pressing business on the mainland. The job would keep 'em busy for the rest of the afternoon.

After removing his apron, Ryder pushed the screen and stepped out onto the deck to let his chest hairs breathe. He crossed to the rail and surveyed the waves, breaking more forcefully than yesterday, though without much breeze. Overhead, a layer of high haze intensified the sun like a magnifying glass. Beulah's outer rain bands should hold off for a while, giving him time to make last minute preparations without getting wet ... at least from precipitation.

Ryder combed his fingers through damp hair. He'd lied that morning about knowing the man who called himself

RUNNING DOWNWIND

John Singer. Clearly, Mick wasn't fooled and hadn't let on, same as when the coyote was shot. Every man had reasons for his actions or inactions.

Especially Mick.

And Ryder knew why.

Not from intuition, but dogged observation. After Mick washed up on the beach with a gunshot scar, Ryder searched for an answer. There were no wanted posters displayed at the post office, or a passel of lawmen snooping around, so the boy wasn't a criminal. Nor was there news of a missing person. Therefore, he must be running from something.

As it turned out, he was.

Folks in the entertainment industry garnered scant coverage from the local press, but a paper from San Antonio thought the story newsworthy. The owner of the doughnut shop hailed from the Alamo City and subscribed to the morning edition, which arrived by mail the following day. When Ryder made his habitual afternoon stop for a cinnamon-laced bear claw, he scanned every page. Yesterday, he'd discovered the news he'd been waiting to find.

Mick Leonard's picture was on page five of section D. His real name was Mick McFarland, a Broadway star whose fiancé was murdered a little over a year ago by the UT tower sniper. Another photo, taken a few days before the shooting, showed Mick standing on stage next to his bride-to-be, Cherie Dennis.

Ryder swallowed. "Cute little blonde."

Mick was hit as well, then disappeared from the public eye. He was sighted a couple of months back by some folks in southern Louisiana, but no one had seen him since.

"No wonder the boy ran," Ryder whispered.

His thoughts immediately flashed to Jayne Hansen, and the dull years of his own heartache. The boy would eventually recover, but healing took time.

Ryder wagged his head.

Discerning Mick's situation was easy.

Not Julia's.

Three years ago, she'd appeared atop Roughshods's roof extolling the receptive merits of bailing wire. Ryder still knew none of her secrets, though figured she'd run away from a hurtful situation, perhaps dangerous.

He glanced back inside Roughshods. The two kids who'd sprinted the hardest, escaped down the same path and plowed right into each other's pain. His job was to get 'em communicating, move 'em out of harm's way, then spend the rest of the day searching for Dipp.

Maybe he could talk some sense into his former *cellie*.

Maybe he couldn't.

If Dipp really wanted to share the Singer treasure, he'd have shown up for a free breakfast to discuss a deal. The man's preemptive visits were no childish dares, but like the coyote, further bold statements of defiance meant to intimidate.

Ryder slapped the rail with an open palm.

He'd do whatever it took to protect what was rightfully his. And if Dipp got greedy, Ryder would be forced to make his own bold statements.

CHAPTER 21

Frog motored out of sight as Mick stood atop Roughshods's deck gulping iced tea from a quart jar. Earlier, a nearby lumberyard delivered thirty sheets of quarter inch plywood and several pounds of nails. Mick gathered the required tools and a couple of sturdy sawhorses, then hauled the lumber upstairs—two sheets at a time. He'd quickly sweated through his new shirt, so removed it to use as a towel. Now he'd have to wear one of Ryder's loud hand-me-downs.

Even so, performing physical labor felt good again. The last time he'd perspired this much was working with Babin, who probably wondered—along with Sallye—if Mick made it to Campeche. Before too much longer he'd pen the newlyweds a long letter. Or phone them.

Mick downed another gulp. He'd not asked for iced tea. Yet while toting up the last couple of boards, the jar appeared just outside the screen door. The kind act didn't mean Julia was speaking to him. Though while washing lunch dishes, he'd noticed her subtle smirk. He'd added too much soap and was covered in suds up to his armpits.

Glancing at the screen, he chided himself for letting Julia slip past during the night when she'd returned to her bungalow. She must've seen him sitting on her pickup's tailgate.

Dozing.

Thought he was ignoring her—again—so today tortured him with the same treatment.

Can't say you don't deserve it.

"I don't know what *to say*," Mick muttered.

He drained the jar, wishing he could apologize for his inability to handle the word *pregnant*. Except, how could he explain without breaking his vow to Cherie?

After strapping on a leather tool belt, Mick slipped a hammer through a loop, then hooked on a tape measure and chalk line. He filled the pouches with nails. Releasing a pent-up breath, he grabbed the shirt and wiped his face. He'd already told Julia he'd explain his situation. When the time was right, he'd begin by revealing his real name.

Then she'll really hate you.

The screen squeaked open.

Mick spun in Julia's direction. "I ... I didn't realize you were standing there."

"I wasn't."

He grinned sheepishly.

She pitched him a clean dishtowel. "Absorbs sweat much better than a shirt."

"You know from experience?"

She ignored the remark. "A load of kitchen laundry needs washing. I'll throw in your shirt."

"It's pretty sweaty. You may not want to touch it."

"Don't be silly." She stuck out her hand.

"Thanks." He gave her the shirt. "Look. I know Ryder asked us both to board up windows, but ..."

"What?"

"It's really hot out here. Also, I've been thinking—"

"Don't. Talking is better, don't you *think*?" She raised her eyebrows.

"Exactly. That's what I was ... um ... contemplating." He grinned.

RUNNING DOWNWIND

"I'm sure Ryder has another hammer down in the basement. Why don't you contemplate getting it?"

Julia walked back inside, confused at the harshness of her tone. Mick tried to initiate a conversation, and she stopped him. She wanted him to talk, yet at the same time didn't, because that meant letting her guard down a second time. Still, her tacky response was exactly like Lahoma's, and it frightened her.

"I'm better than that," Julia whispered.

The washer and dryer were located inside Ryder's living quarters: a closed-in sleeping porch adjacent to the kitchen. Mounted at the entrance was a wall phone with a receiver cord long enough to stretch through the kitchen into the dining room. Ryder didn't want to waste money on an extension. Whenever a customer needed to make a call, Julia shouted the number to Ryder, who dialed, then lobbed the heavy receiver through the service window to the cash register. Once, when he was seasoning an iron skillet with lard, the receiver was too slick for her to catch, smashing a glass canister of sticky peanut butter logs. So, Ryder switched to penny mints, individually wrapped.

Julia added soap to the washer, pulled the knob and waited for the machine to fill. The load was small—a few soiled dish towels along with Ryder's apron. She dropped in Mick's shirt. A working man's sweat had never bothered her. If Mick only knew how many times she'd helped Carmen with the laundry. Most ranch hands bathed once a week, and Mick ....

She smiled.

He'd practically bathed while washing dishes. His shirt had an outdoorsy odor, like sheets left on the line during an afternoon thunderstorm. The thought made her dizzy, so she sat on a stool beneath the telephone.

"If Mick only knew about *me*," she said aloud. And that was the problem, he didn't. Her night of remembering Dario was a reminder. She knew no more about Mick than he did her.

She stood and checked the water level. Almost full. Mick *was* still on the island, which meant something. Perhaps she'd find the courage to ask a few questions. "He does still owe me," Julia whispered.

Would payback come with a price?

What would he insist knowing in exchange?

The washer filled and the cycle began. She fixed her eyes on the agitator.

Back-and-forth.

Back-and-forth.

Ever since Mick Leonard entered her life, her thoughts about him moved in the same predictable fashion.

Julia closed the lid. She could at least help him board-up windows, then decide how guarded she'd be.

By late afternoon, they'd completed most of the job and downed two pitchers of tea to survive the tropical heat. Their conversation, tentative at first, eased into the rhythm of satisfied teamwork.

"Where did you learn to swing a hammer?" During a break, Mick sat astraddle one of the sawhorses mopping his face.

"What do you mean?"

"You've only bent two nails."

"Compared to your twenty?" She smiled.

"Not fair. I thought I was the only one keeping count."

RUNNING DOWNWIND

Julia picked up the empty tea pitcher and yawned. "I'm worn out. Also starved."

"Me too. How 'bout a sandwich? I make a mean peanut butter and mayo."

"Mayonnaise?" She scrunched her nose. "Too mean a combination for my taste. I'll whip up a nice snack instead, while you bend the last of the nails."

Mick watched her disappear inside Roughshods. Julia looked as lovely in shorts and a T shirt as in a sundress, even more so. Thank goodness her mood lightened, though obviously masked her true feelings. Down deep, she still seemed troubled, which bothered him because he knew why. He'd eventually have to explain his silence concerning the mother and baby dolphin and feared where that would lead.

The final window was in the shade. He measured the perimeter, then selected a board already cut. Holding it in place with a knee, he grabbed several nails. Not only could Julia handle a hammer, she popped an accurate chalk line and mastered a power saw.

An amazing woman.
Who deserved to know the facts.
Yes.
Along with the details.
Naturally.
Mick pounded in a dozen nails, straight and true.
Facts with details.
It's called 'the truth.'
Fingering a final nail from the pouch, he held it in place.
Remember?
"Yeah. Though I may have to bend a few particulars."
So, the truth remains a lie.
Mick reared back and swung the hammer hard ….
Smashing his thumb.

Five minutes later, Julia returned carrying a tray holding a small cantaloupe, a block of hard cheese, and a package of saltines. "I forgot napkins, and a knife to slice the …. What happened?"

Mick sat cross-legged in the shade, his thumb wrapped in the bloodstained dish towel. "Ghost crab. Big one. Don't worry, I got him with the hammer."

She set down the tray and scampered back inside for the first aid kit Ryder stored beneath the cash register. The sight of blood no longer spun her into instant panic, but the thought of Mick pounding his thumb made her cringe.

"I'm okay," he said when she returned, "just a little lightheaded. Probably from the heat."

Julia retrieved the pitcher. "Sip on this. The ice has melted, but the tea's cool."

"Thanks. Growing up, my mom scolded me for not using a glass."

"Better than getting slapped." She knelt beside him, instantly regretting the statement. "Maybe you won't lose your thumbnail."

"Don't make any bets." Mick took a drink and let her unwrap the dishtowel. "The first time I skied downhill, I lost my big toenails."

"Snow crabs?" She laughed.

"My boots were too small. I should've exchanged them for a larger pair but was too involved crashing through fences and sliding off mountains. Some family vacation."

"Sounds like fun." She examined his thumb.

"Which part? The fences or the cliffs?"

"Everything in-between." Julia chose a bottle of hydrogen peroxide and a topical antiseptic. "We never took a family vacation."

RUNNING DOWNWIND

"You're one of the lucky ones." He chuckled.

"I never felt that way." She gazed into the first aid kit. In Lahoma's world, leisure was a synonym for laziness.

"Sorry," Mick said, "I didn't mean that the way it sounded."

"No need to apologize." Julia opened a box of cotton balls. "Besides, few people were interested in skiing where I grew up."

"Which was?"

"Texas."

"Okay. That pinpoints the location."

"We lived a few miles outside of a small town." She gently cleaned the wound, wishing she'd asked Mick about his home ... first.

"Too small for a name?" He raised his eyebrows.

You've never heard of the place."

"Try me."

Instead of answering, she wrapped his thumb in gauze, secured by a strip of tape. "I think you'll survive." She released his hand.

"Thanks. But you never answered my question."

"And you haven't swallowed enough tea." Julia repacked the kit as Mick sipped from the pitcher. "We had snow," she said at last. "A lot some years."

"The temperature rarely dipped below freezing in Austin." He raised his eyebrows. "That's my hometown. Ever heard of it?"

"On occasion." She packed the final item and closed the lid. "I was there once. A school trip to see our state capitol."

"How old were you?"

"Junior high."

"Hmm. A school isn't much of a clue. But measurable snow?" Mick swallowed a final gulp and tapped the empty

255

pitcher. "Means your mystery location is somewhere up in the Panhandle."

Julia shrugged. Her hometown was a place she'd rather not discuss.

"Keeping vital information from the injured is cruel." He studied his bandage.

"I'm sick of tea." She grabbed the pitcher, thinking—in fairness—she should answer his question. "How about lemonade?"

"For a man with a shattered thumb?" He offered a pained expression. "I need something stronger."

"Fine." Julia suppressed a smile. "Gasoline."

"Sure. Um, I'll have ethyl on the rocks. No cheap stuff."

"That's where I'm from."

"A town named Gasoline?"

She nodded. "The businesses are mostly gone."

"Houses?"

"A handful."

"Why the name?"

"Way back, the cotton gin was powered by the only gasoline engine in town. On Saturdays, a sizable crowd gathered to watch it run."

"Was your school mascot a *spark plug*?" He laughed.

"How'd you know?" Julia glanced at Mick's thumb. If it didn't throb, it would. "Is wine, okay?"

"Ryder serves wine?"

"Upon request. The only booze on the menu is beer. Don't know why."

Mick cleared his throat.

"So?" Julia stood.

"Anything but port. Need help opening the bottle?"

"If you promise not to lose a finger."

He raised both hands. "I haven't yet."

RUNNING DOWNWIND

She glanced at the screen door. The wine selection was small, but a glass or two might be what they needed. A tasty addition to the cantaloupe and cheese.

Julia grabbed the first aid kit and headed inside. So, Mick was from Austin. Since he was interested in her past, she'd volunteer a little more information. Perhaps, in turn, he'd relax and reveal a few secrets. "I reckon we'll know enough when he's ready to tell us," Ryder had said.

She smiled.

With the right encouragement, Mick Leonard would be ready.

Was she?

CHAPTER 22

"It's got to be a Pecos cantaloupe." Mick consumed the last slice in a single bite. "I first heard about 'em from my Uncle Harley. Sweetest melons on earth. Only available this time of year."

"You sound like a low budget TV commercial." Julia sipped her wine, then giggled. "I think you've spent too much time with Ryder."

"How so?" Mick hadn't heard her giggle since before the Dolphin fiasco. He still hadn't decided the best way to reveal his true identity, but her improved mood put him at ease.

She nibbled on a saltine. "The man loves late summer for the same reason. Disgusting."

"Summer?"

"No."

"The cracker?"

"Stop." She made a face. "I mean how Ryder knows *everything*."

"True." Mick drained his glass, then leaned over close enough to see beads of perspiration dotting her upper lip. "But does he know where Uncle Harley lives?"

"Pecos?"

"El Paso. About 150 miles from Pecos, not considered far in that part of the state."

"I suspect you've been there?" She took another sip.

"A few times." Mick sat up straight. "My uncle owns a construction company. I spent an entire Christmas break working for him back in high school."

"Is that where you learned to bend nails?"

"How'd you know?"

Since their conversation had drifted west, Mick considered mentioning who he'd worked with that week—his cousin—then gently broach the subject of borrowing Leonard's name. But the embarrassing memory of their trip to Juarez muddied Mick's thoughts. Instead, he encouraged talk in the opposite direction. As the slanting coastal sunlight weakened, so did his resolve to tell Julia the truth.

A little before nightfall, Julia returned to her bungalow for a quick bath and a change of clothes. With Ryder away and the restaurant closed, she'd agreed to meet Mick around eight to prepare supper.

What could she fix?

Both the fridge and freezer had been emptied and not replenished due to the approaching hurricane. Also, they'd eaten the last of the cantaloupe and half the cheese. "There won't be a spark of electricity for days," Ryder previously warned on the heels of a sly grin. "Maybe even weeks. I'm cooking up whatever might spoil." He had, delighting patrons with the varied fare.

After bathing, Julia dressed and brushed her teeth. She ran a comb through her hair, wishing she'd had time to wash it. Grabbing a rubber band, she formed a ponytail while picturing what foodstuffs remained in Roughshods's pantry. Other than standard baking staples were more saltines, a large package of corn chips, and canned items—various meats, soups, and green chilies. Remaining produce included a watermelon, two cucumbers, half a dozen tomatoes, and an onion. "Maybe there's still a lime and a few fresh herbs," she said aloud, remembering Ryder also stocked his favorite fried pies, stashing them out of sight on a top shelf.

Thoughts of the refreshing watermelon made Julia's mouth water. Carmen's cucumber and watermelon salad was a favorite summer treat. Her nanny had a knack for creating delicious meals with whatever ingredients were available. The delicate salad seemed out of character for brawny ranch hands, but the men wolfed down platefuls and asked for more.

Mick might too.

Julia dabbed on perfume she'd purchased, but never used. She applied a hint of lipstick, then laughed. The morning's image of Mick Leonard covered in suds bubbled into her thoughts. He'd probably volunteer to wash the supper dishes, which made her laugh again, so she slapped a hand over her mouth. In the past hour, her sour mood transformed into lightheaded glee. Her plan was to volunteer additional information about *her* past in hopes he would share *his*. Instead, they'd enjoyed an eager, yet trivial conversation concerning everything from books and movies to Ryder's odd habits. Mick's dry wit had lifted her spirits.

For the first time since coming to Padre, she looked forward to sharing a meal.

When Julia climbed Roughshods's steps, dusky stars blinked in-between thickening bands of high clouds. The breeze off the Gulf had strengthened, meaning Beulah was on the move, at least for the time being. Ryder mentioned he might be back about *dark-thirty* to check on the hatchlings, but Julia predicted he wouldn't show his face until breakfast.

Mick leaned against the rail at the top of the stairs. He sniffed. "Somebody smells good. I doubt it's me."

"Probably that clean shirt you're wearing." Julia stepped onto the deck. "Aren't you glad someone washed it?"

"Very." His grin pierced the twilight. "During our snack, didn't you mention a fondness for Marilyn Monroe movies?"

"I did." She noticed Mick's hair was still damp from his shower. He'd donned a pair of Ryder's cutoffs, which didn't look bad with the shirttail out. "Do you know her?"

"Marilyn Monroe?" Mick suppressed a nervous chuckle and pulled open the screen. Julia was obviously joking. But if the starlet were still alive, the odds were good they would've at least met.

He continued. "I was thinking of a film she'd made a while back: *Niagara*."

Julia's stomach tightened as she entered the restaurant. That very movie was the reason she'd chosen Niagara Falls as her final destination the night she'd run away from Lahoma. Like her beloved mustangs, the Falls were free, a timeless blending of beauty and power. "Wasn't it filmed on location?"

Mick nodded. "Have you been?"

"To the movies?"

"Niagara Falls."

She switched on an overhead light and walked toward the kitchen. "I prefer the ocean."

He paused at the register. Since Niagara Falls was only a day's train ride from New York City, he'd visited the area many times. His attempt to admit his real name had failed, so the question was intended as a gentle lead-in about his career. But the location seemed to upset her.

"How about more wine?" Julia twirled to face him, holding the service door halfway open. "This time, you pick."

Mick nodded.

She continued: "Ryder hides the good stuff on a rack beneath the food prep table. I'll grab a couple of clean glasses."

"Let's mix it with coffee." Mick followed her into the kitchen.

"Sorry. All out of empty pickle jars." She handed him the glasses and strode toward the pantry.

"What about a corkscrew?"

"On top of the prep table, next to the knife block."

Mick chose a bottle of Merlot and removed the cork. The wine they'd shared earlier had helped them both relax. He liked that. Even so, he'd make sure they didn't drink too much.

She returned with her arms full.

"Here, let me help," he said. "I've never seen a watermelon that small."

They set what she'd gathered on the prep table.

"It's seedless." Julia smiled and rolled it to the table's center. "Ever had cucumber and watermelon salad?"

"Maybe."

"With lime juice and mint?"

"No, but the combination sounds exotic." He poured both glasses. "Ryder's creation?"

"Carmen's."

Mick furrowed his brow. "Have I met this woman?"

"Nope." Julia took an extended sip. If she expected information from him, she must go first. "She was my nanny."

"You had a nanny?" Mick leaned against the table. "Poor woman."

In response, Julia slid a large knife from the block.

His eyes widened, followed by a purposeful gulp.

She giggled. "I was raised on a ranch. My father died before I was born, and my mother—"

"Built a slaughter house?"

"Good guess." Julia set down her glass and examined the blade. "We only butchered in the winter. Saved on refrigeration."

He nodded and sipped his wine. "And your mom still lives on the ranch?"

"As far as I know." Julia raised the knife and halved the melon in a single stroke.

Mick flinched. "Okay then. Any brothers and sisters?"

She shook her head. "How about you?"

"Two younger sisters. Twins."

"And your mother?"

"Glad she didn't bear triplets."

"Funny. What does she do?"

"Volunteer work for part of the year. Her main job is keeping the family in line, just like any mom I suppose."

"I suppose." Julia set down the knife and peered into her glass. "What about your father?"

"Glad *he* didn't bear triplets. It would have scandalized his law practice."

She laughed. "Can you cube a watermelon?"

"I'll do my best."

As Mick cut the melon into bite size chunks, Julia talked nonstop while seeding and chopping cucumbers. Since leaving home, she'd never told anyone about Carmen and Paco, but decided to mention them, her words flowing with a natural ease.

"They sound like genuine people." Mick's gaze met Julia's. "I'd enjoy getting to know them someday."

RUNNING DOWNWIND

"I'd like that." Julia swallowed. She'd meant to say, "*they'd* like that."

A wordless moment passed.

Mick glanced at his hands. "I'd ... um ... better rinse my fingers." He stepped to the sink.

In a large bowl, she combined the cucumber, watermelon, and some mint leaves. His unexpected comment about Carmen and Paco touched her. Julia halved a lime, squeezed it over the mix, then sprinkled pepper, and a dash of salt. What exactly had Mick meant by *someday*?

He returned from the sink and stood beside her. "As a reward for my expert culinary skills, do I get a taste?"

"A small one," she said softly. "I'll grab a fork."

After a healthy bite, followed by playful attempts for more, Mick launched into a wedding story where he and the other groomsman placed watermelon halves—pulp side up—beneath the rear tires of the newlyweds' getaway car. "In the end, the joke was on us." Mick laughed. "The groom tromped the accelerator and sprayed the entire bridal party with seeds and pink gunk."

Julia smiled and sipped more wine. It *was* a funny story, but she already knew he had a comical side. And now, she was somewhat aware of his family, which meant her plan was working. "Want to chop an onion?"

"For exercise?"

"Our main course—Chicken Casserole."

"I love the fancy French name."

She stuck out her tongue. "While I get what we need, see if you can find a baking dish, a deep one. Ryder stacks them on a shelf above the sink." She set down her glass and started for the pantry. "Can you light a gas oven?"

"Can *you* whack a watermelon?"

Julia glanced over her shoulder with a mischievous grin. "The matches are on top of the stove in an empty baking powder tin. Please set the temp at 350."

The range was similar to Mick's grandmother's, which he'd lit numerous times. He opened the oven door, struck a match and poked it through a small hole next to the bottom burner. Rotating the temperature dial enough to release a little gas, the oven ignited with a familiar whoosh. When the flame was evenly distributed, he turned the dial to 350 and headed to the sink. He hadn't planned on telling Julia about his family—yet—but she'd mentioned hers, the nonchalant comment about her mother's whereabouts screaming truth. Slaughterhouse Mom was probably the reason Julia sat on the beach at dawn.

Perhaps her mother was a female Ed McFarland.

Perhaps worse.

Mick selected a deep baking dish, turned around and almost collided with Julia.

"Whoops." She stepped aside. "I need to rinse my fingers. Something sticky was smeared all over a bag of corn chips."

"Is this dish deep enough?"

"Perfect. Now if I could just rinse—"

"Mmm. Corn chips in a casserole."

"Along with tomatoes, green chilies—"

"And the onion I'll chop. A Carmen creation?"

"May I please rinse my hands?"

"Oh yeah." He set the dish on an adjacent counter, turned on the water and backed out of her way.

"Thanks." She scrubbed for a moment. "Would you hand me a dishtowel? I don't want to drip."

RUNNING DOWNWIND

"Just use your shirt." He grinned.

"I'd rather use yours."

She reached for Mick's shirttail.

He dodged. "Too slow."

The faucet still ran, so Julia cupped her hands beneath the stream, flinging water in Mick direction.

"I barely felt a drop." He moved farther away. "Try and reach me now."

"Not with you watching."

"Planning a sneak attack?" He spun an about face. "I'm not scared. Your hands are too small to hold much."

Julia grabbed the baking dish, filled it to the brim and drenched his shirt.

While the casserole baked, Julia pitched Mick's shirt in the dryer, along with several wet dishtowels. They poured more wine. Then she puttered about the kitchen while Mick sat shirtless atop the work table.

"Come sit." He patted the empty space beside him. "There's plenty of room. Swear I won't throw wine on you."

"Don't make liquid promises."

"You assume I'd waste this expensive, imported Merlot?" He picked up the bottle and read the label. "Maybe you shouldn't get too close."

"I'll keep my distance." Julia stroked her chin. "Took me forever to find paprika that wasn't fossilized. Think I'll rearrange Ryder's spice rack."

"Tonight, I feel like him." Mick grinned.

"Fossilized?"

He glanced down at his bare chest. "All I need is his apron."

"I can fix that." She motioned toward Ryder's quarters. "Washed, dried and ready to wear."

"That's okay. I hear he's not too keen on sharing things."

"Who told you that?"

"Some guy out for a walk."

She bristled slightly. Ryder had his quirks but was one of the most generous men she'd ever met. "The man was probably a wealthy tourist. They're like spoiled children. If it weren't for Ryder, neither one of us would—"

"The guy was a bully. His opinion's not important."

Silence.

"Look," Mick said. "I'll never forget Ryder's kindness." Then tenderly, "Nor yours."

"Thanks."

"Now, intrigue this city boy. Tell him more about ranch life, at least until the shirt dries."

She smiled, scooting atop the work table next to Mick. The freckles on his face and chest sprinkled a boyish innocence. Avoiding any mention of Lahoma, Julia revealed more about Carmen and Paco, plus her love for animals—especially horses—and the windswept prairie spaces. She wanted to express her newfound faith, but Mick inquired further about the horses, so she recalled sleeping atop the hay wagon.

And the wild mustangs.

Twenty minutes later, Julia opened the dryer long enough to retrieved Mick's shirt, then pitched it to him. "Your turn."

"To fold dishtowels?" He slipped the shirt over his head.

She returned to her place beside him. "When they're dry."

RUNNING DOWNWIND

"I could hang them outside. Save on electricity."

She wagged her head. "Tell me about growing up in Austin."

Mick thought for a moment. "I lived there from birth until I finished college."

He shrugged.

"And?"

"Summers were hot."

"Yes."

"Winters mild. Though, once we had snow. It melted."

"An interesting childhood." Julia raised her eyebrows. "Surely you left out a chapter."

"We never owned horses."

"What about smaller pets?"

"When I was ten, I kept a Red-eared Slider."

"A what?"

"A turtle about the size of your palm. Named him Ichabod. And you thought Ryder was the only reptile lover."

She giggled. "Where'd you keep your little friend."

"In a flowerbed outside my bedroom window. Mom wouldn't allow him in the house."

"Really."

"Though when she wasn't home, I'd let Ichabod swim in the kitchen sink. One day during his aquatic session, the phone rang, so I stepped away for a moment. When I returned—"

"Your turtle was gone?"

"Yep. I searched off and on for three days and finally gave up."

"Did you ever find him?"

Mick grinned. "Two weeks later, Ichabod slipped out of hiding and into a bowl of bridge club steak tartare."

Julia burst out laughing. "What happened?"

"A lot of screaming. I was immediately grounded and never saw Ichabod again. Mom didn't host another bridge club until I was in high school."

"Did you like it?" Julia faced him.

"Being grounded?"

"High school."

"Um ... not at first." Mick gazed outside, weary of avoiding the truth. Julia wanted to know more about him. Yet what happened atop the lighthouse—barely twenty-four hours ago—still lurked beneath the surface of their lighthearted conversation, sometimes marching in lockstep with his vow to Cherie. As he'd previously decided, he first needed to reveal his real name, then determine what additional secrets he'd share. Sooner or later, someone would recognize him.

"Before I tell you about high school, there's something else." He gently placed his hand atop hers. "Something I need to—"

Beep!

"The oven timer." He stood, deciding he should silently rehearse his explanation one more time. "Guess our dinner's ready."

"Not quite. You said there's *something else*?"

"Right. I'll tell you later, after we eat."

"Not fair. The casserole will keep."

"Not me." Mick grabbed an oven mitt. "I'm starved."

"This meal sure beats my fried bologna sandwiches." Mick reached for a third helping of salad and casserole. Since the Gulf side windows were covered, they'd dined out on the deck. The cloud bands had dissipated into sparse patches and the breeze softened. A brilliant moon path sparkled atop the waves.

"Bologna? What happened to peanut butter and mayonnaise?"

"*Le luncheon* may be spread from a jar," he said, imitating a French chef. "*Le dîner* demands a more complicated process."

While Mick described how to fry a slice of bologna without the edge curling, Julia stared at her plate, wondering if the hurricane had spun into a different direction, wondering if Mick would ever get to "later" and finish what he'd begun in the kitchen. At one point during the meal, she'd offered a few strong hints. He'd stuttered, his thoughts seeming to be elsewhere. So, she'd backed off, asking him to open a second bottle of Merlot. He had, but the wine remained on the table, untouched, like much of the food on her plate.

"I'm full." Mick scooted back his chair and patted his stomach. "Unless there's dessert. I can be convinced to make room, especially if it's another one of Carmen's recipes. That Paco's a lucky man."

Julia's arms trembled. *Later* had come and gone. Therefore, she'd have to reveal more of herself, something significant. "Remember me saying how Carmen told stories?"

"Are they as good as her cooking?"

Julia laughed to cover her feelings. At breakfast she'd still been hurt over his silence concerning the mother and baby dolphin, so avoided him. By lunch she'd fought a confusing desire to be with him, so privately sputtered an awkward prayer, instantly feeling silly. God was probably too busy with more important issues. And even though there was *something else* Mick needed to say, she was ready for this ride on their emotional rollercoaster to end. Maybe she'd never bolster the courage to admit her greatest mistake—her unborn child. Perhaps Mick's hidden scar hinged upon a secret equally as dark. Yet for this moment—like at the top of the lighthouse—she needed to tell him something meaningful.

Julia faced Mick and swallowed. "On Padre Island, a lighthouse shines for the Lady, its white fire illuminating the predawn darkness."

When Julia finished the legend, she felt better, though wished she could read Mick's mind. She'd shared everything but the ending—*whoever finds a piece of the mirror will discover love that very hour.* That part was much too fragile, much too personal.

Mick studied the water. "Were there really three Spanish galleons full of treasure?"

"The shipwrecks are historical fact. Shortly after I arrived on the island, I spent an afternoon at the library over in Port Isabel."

"The Mayan princess. What was her name?"

"Chimala."

"Find any info on her?"

"No." Julia carefully considered her next sentence. "Nor was there data on her warrior lover, Naiya."

"I thought as much."

Julia studied Mick's profile. Though his remark stung a little, he wasn't making fun or belittling her. She knew the Lady was more fable than truth. Dario would've considered the legend nonsense.

Mick fiddled with his empty wine glass. "Any additional facts?"

RUNNING DOWNWIND

"The Spanish carried Mayan slaves on at least one of the ships that sunk, so that part's accurate. And Naiya would've worn a protective mirror before going into battle."

"Have you told Ryder about The Lady?"

She shook her head. "Nor anyone else."

He faced her and smiled. "I'm glad you told me."

In the distance, headlights appeared along the shell-topped road, swooping between the dunes.

"Ryder's back," Mick said. "Must be checking on hatchlings."

Julia sighed. Leave it to Ryder to return as predicted and spoil things.

"I've never seen the moon brighter." Mick crossed his legs. "If the dunes weren't blocking our view, we could see the nests from here."

"Ready for dessert?" She stood. "There're fried pies in the pantry. Cherry or peach?"

"Peach, please. Unless you have apricot."

"Long gone. Ryder eats those first.

"I would too. Are fried pies on the menu?"

"Never. Ryder's particular about who eats them. Orders from some place in New Mexico."

"Why not local?"

Julia shrugged. "These look homemade. He hides them up in the pantry behind a stack of recipes clipped from the newspaper." She scurried inside.

Mick watched the screen door close. "The legend of the Lady," he muttered, then peered out over the water. No wonder Julia sat at the lighthouse each dawn. The tale was a comforting childhood story, transporting her to a peaceful place where life was predictable and good.

He smiled inside, knowing how she felt. His grandmother's simple home didn't have enough beds for the McFarland clan's visits, so he'd bunked on a pallet in a room adjacent to the kitchen. Before daylight seeped between the blinds, the aromas of coffee and bacon first stirred his consciousness, followed by the sizzle of eggs frying in an iron skillet, the clink of silver on china, breakfast table laughter. Those were the scents and sounds of love and acceptance, the constants of happiness.

The screen swung open with a loud slap, diverting Mick's thoughts.

Julia held a news clipping, her face streaked with tears. "I told you about the Lady because I trusted—" She bit her lip and tossed the clipping on the table.

"You don't understand. I was going to—"

"Tell me everything?"

"Yes."

"Even ... *West Side Story*?"

"There's that?" He leaned forward and reached for the clipping.

"Don't bother. I saw you perform in Dallas."

He froze.

Still standing, she picked up a napkin and wiped her eyes. "Why don't you tell me the rest of *everything* over dessert."

"That'd be great." Mick sat back in his chair. "I knew you'd understand."

She glanced toward the screen, then focused on Mick. "Let's not enjoy our dessert quite yet, *Mister Mick McFarland*. We still have wine, lots of wet, sticky, wine." Julia grabbed the open bottle of Merlot, poured it on his head, then ran down the stairs.

Mick dripped in stunned silence. He unwadded the clipping. The wine stung his eyes, but he didn't wipe them. Beneath his undeniable picture the headline read: *Broadway and Film Celebrity Mick McFarland Still "Mending" His Own Business.*

RUNNING DOWNWIND

Cute. Thanks Tinker, or was Ed the traitor? Lousy agents can be replaced, but not fathers.

Stepping to the rail, Mick watched Julia scamper in the direction of the lighthouse as a thick cloudbank crossed the moon.

Ryder knows. Now Julia.

Boom!

A powerful gunshot blasted from the darkness.

From the direction of the hatchlings.

Followed by the echo of Julia's scream.

Mick leaped down the stairs and hit the parking lot.

Running.

Crossing between the dunes, he remembered the tower shooter.

Sprinting along the beach, remembered Cherie.

"Julia!"

No answer.

The cloudbank passed.

And then he saw her racing toward Ryder.

Who lay motionless in moonlight.

CHAPTER 23

"Jayne?"

"Who?" Julia knelt beside Ryder. "It's me, Julia."

"Right." He raised his head. "Don't hover."

She leaned closer. "Who'd you think I was?"

"Nobody." He noticed Mick standing near, so motioned for them to give him space, then sat upright at the edge of the surf, trying to refocus his thoughts. His left leg hurt, as well as his jaw. "I tangled with a piece of driftwood, that's all."

Mick took a knee. "We heard a gunshot."

"You heard wrong."

"Your jaw's bleeding." Julia said. "The cut looks deep."

Ryder pointed to a barnacled log the size of a railroad tie. "As bright as that moon is shining, you'd think I'd have seen the culprit." He felt his jaw, smearing blood with his fingertips. "A fine time to be caught without a handkerchief."

"Use this." Mick removed his shirt. "It's clean, except for a little wine. Trust me."

"A little?" Ryder cocked his head to one side. "Son, you could wring out a winery."

Julia glared at Mick. "He had an accident. Couldn't be helped."

Noticing her pained expression at Mick's "trust me," Ryder frowned. The climate between those two was still uninhabitable. He ignored Mick's offer. "My jaw's nothing a little saltwater won't fix." Ryder dipped a handful and scrubbed his face. "See. Clean as a new dime."

"You were unconscious." Julia frowned. "You're still bleeding."

"Ain't the first time." Ryder peered up and down the beach.

Nothing.

"If the sound wasn't a gunshot, then what?" Mick stood.

"A cherry bomb. When I drove in from the mainland, figured I'd check on the hatchlings. Saw headlights near the nesting area. Thought it might be poachers. Parked Frog behind a dune and investigated."

Julia scooped a handful of sea and tried to wipe Ryder's jaw.

He waved her away. "I said don't hover."

Mick retreated a step. "I gather you didn't find poachers."

"Naw. Just a dune buggy full of teenagers out for a joyride. Was afraid they'd plow through the clutches, so yelled at 'em. That's when they lit the cherry and I tripped."

"We should call the law before someone else is hurt." Julia stood and glared at Mick. "There's no telling what interesting things the sheriff might find."

Ryder wagged his head. "Waste of time. The adolescent brats would fib their way out." He scanned the beach again. "What I need is a grape soda."

"One of us would be happy to run to the restaurant." Julia continued her glare.

"No need. Got a carton in Frog." He reached a hand toward Mick, who pulled Ryder to his feet. His knee throbbed, but he ignored the pain. Luckily his jeans hid the blood. "Did you kids get the windows boarded?"

"Every last nail." Mick met Julia's glare.

"Good." Ryder examined the sky. "Now run along and gather your belongings before Beulah hits. Both of you."

"What if she changes her mind?" Mick kept his eyes on Julia.

"Not this time," Julia said.

"There could be new information," Mick countered. "Misunderstood facts."

Julia crossed her arms. "It won't alter her course."

"I guarantee, old Beulah's winding up for her knockout blow." Ryder turned to Julia. "Is your pickup healthy?"

She nodded but kept staring at Mick.

"Then I want y'all off the island by noon tomorrow. I'll meet you at the shelter in Port Isabel. Understand?"

"I'd rather take my chances and ride Beulah out." Julia thrust her chin forward.

"Me too." Mick widened his stance.

Stepping back, Ryder studied the pair. "You dueling clowns best dig your graves while there's still time. I'd suggest deep holes on opposite sides of the island. Shovels are in the basement—his and hers."

Ryder left Mick and Julia on the beach and hobbled toward Frog. "Boarding Roughshods's windows must've been more frustrating than building the Tower of Babel," he muttered, then chuckled at the thought, though he didn't feel like laughing. His jaw throbbed in unison with his knee. Both still oozed blood. He'd hated using the poacher excuse a second time.

More bothersome, though, was his cherry bomb tale, especially since the powerful firecracker was recently outlawed. He was confident Mick wasn't fooled by the ruse. But the boy had his own story to cover, the old adage "one drunk won't rat out another" was worth a try. After hearing the kids fuss, Ryder wasn't sure what Julia suspected about Mick's identity, nor what occurred with the wine. For now, those two were locked into a private standoff—which was a good thing—diverting their attention until after the storm.

Then, Ryder's activities wouldn't matter.

The Singer treasure would be safely stored in the brick room he'd built in Roughshods's basement.

Locating Frog, he rummaged through the glove box and found a roll of electrical tape. Then returned to the beach, cleansed the wounds, and applied strips to his knee and chin.

No leaks.

Ryder limped back to Frog, grabbed a grape soda and pried off the cap. Every man's life held a fistful of surprises, both good and bad. Yet few matched the blow of this latest shocker.

He downed the soda and enjoyed a healthy belch. The daylong search for Dipp proved unsuccessful, until Ryder parked near the hatchlings. That's when the convict stepped out of the dunes.

Holding a pistol.

"Now would 'ya look at that, an amphibious car." Dipp tapped the barrel on the passenger side door. "Just like we'd planned."

RUNNING DOWNWIND

"We?" Ryder killed the engine. Show no fear and the idiot could be handled. "We planned nothing."

Moonbeams ricocheted off Dipp's scalp. "Figured you'd forget, so I brought along this handy mind stimulator." He pointed the gun.

"Splattered any more coyotes?"

"Is that how you greet a friend? What about a 'holy kiss?' Ain't you still a *Christian*?"

"You won't see me in hell."

"You're as rude as that girl you hired. The boy ain't no better."

"Leave those kids outta this."

"Your *kids* need to learn manners. After the storm I plan to teach 'em a few. Especially the girl."

"And I'll kill you."

Dipp wagged his head. "Ain't how this poker game ends."

"No?" Ryder chuckled. "You still got nothing but bluff. In case you don't remember, I hold the final card, *roomie*."

Dipp aimed the pistol at Ryder's head.

"Pull the trigger and the treasure dies too."

Neither man spoke for a moment. Dipp lowered the gun. "The Singer loot is mine."

"Too bad you didn't learn generosity before busting out." Ryder climbed out of the driver's seat and stood. Frog's hood separated the two men.

Ryder continued. "So, tell me ... how's our little cellblock bunch? Still doing each other's laundry? Still drawing names at Christmas?"

"Don't screw with me."

"Then lay the gun on the hood and we'll talk. Pretend we're both free men."

"There's been enough talk. You flapped your worthless jaws every day in that rotten stink hole. And I had to listen."

"Guess you didn't listen hard enough."

"Really?" Dipp formed a sly grin. "Santa Fe's still a good place to hide from the cops."

Ryder froze.

"And that sandwich joint you blabbered about," Dipp waved the pistol. "Figured the old gal running it might still be alive. Still be useful. Cigar smoker. What's her name?"

Silence.

"Don't matter. She's petrified but kicking. When I told her we we'd been roomies—time honored guests of the state of Texas—she spilled her guts. Got a soft spot for cons. Have you tried her fried pies?"

"That's enough of your sleaze." Ryder doubled his fists.

"Seems she's selling the place. Already got a buyer."

"If you touched Merly, I'll—"

Dipp raised the gun. "I ain't no pervert." He cocked it and laughed. "Got my eye on the buyer, though. Some rich, British broad who swears she knows you. Jayne Hansen."

Ryder lunged across the hood, knocking the gun from Dipp's hand.

Boom!

The .357 magnum fired into the dunes as the men tumbled over the hood, punching each other while clawing beach for the gun. Ryder thrust a fist into the convict's face, bloodying his nose.

Whack!

Ryder felt his left knee crack.

Whack!

His jaw.

Reaching the gun first, Ryder hobbled toward the surf and tossed the .357 into the sea. Dipp stood twenty feet away holding a lead-filled blackjack.

"I get the Singer treasure, or the British broad dies. Your choice." He disappeared back into the dunes.

RUNNING DOWNWIND

Ryder knew his knee was damaged. Figured his chin might require stitches. He limped to the water's edge to tend his wounds.

Less than a minute had passed since the gun fired.

Less than a minute since Dipp hit him with the prison made blackjack.

This close to Roughshods, Mick and Julia would arrive at any second. Then Ryder would have to explain everything.

Again.

Exhausted, he stretched out on the sand.

His mind whirled.

Not about his explanation.

Nor images of the Singer treasure.

As he lay there bleeding, Ryder saw …

Jayne Hansen.

CHAPTER 24

Mick and Julia stared at each other in a steely, earsplitting silence, reminding Mick of a silly childhood game. Maybe he'd be lucky, and she'd smile first.

No way.

He swallowed hard.

To ease the tension, he stuck out his hand—a truthful, yet palm-shaped peace offering. "McFarland, Mick McFarland."

Julia frowned. "Not funny." She spun on her heel and marched toward Roughshods.

He raced after her. Catching up, he grabbed her arm.

She jerked it away.

"I'm sorry." Mick heard his trite apology dissipate into the heavy night air.

"Sorry? I don't believe you." Julia kept walking.

"Let me explain."

"Not listening."

He matched her stride. "Look, I can't blame you for—"

"*Can't* blame or *don't* blame? Which is it?"

"Can't?" Mick slowed his pace.

She increased hers.

"Don't?"

She stopped and confronted him. "Life to you is nothing but a spoof, a grand tale to ridicule and later act out."

"Not anymore."

"Really?"

"That's why I'm sorry ... so very sorry."

"Are you?" Julia wheeled around and continued her march. "You've forgotten the definition."

"You're right." Mick caught up with her a second time. "Would you help me remember?"

"Why?"

"I wanted to tell you my real name days ago."

"You didn't."

"I tried several times, but ..." Mick breathed hard. "I'm a pig."

"More like a shirtless swine."

"At least we agree on something."

Ignoring him, she proceeded on to Roughshods and stomped up the stairs.

He followed but stopped on the landing.

She flung open the screen. "You have a sticky mess to clean up."

Mick watched the door bang shut.

The time had come to tell her the truth.

They worked in numbed silence. While Mick attended to the spilled wine, Julia washed the supper dishes, wishing she'd never mentioned the Lady.

Wishing she'd never met Mick McFarland.

"I should've let him drown," she whispered, then with a sideways glance, realized he was standing behind her with an armload of soiled dishtowels.

"Thought I'd pitch these into the washing machine to soak, along with my shirt. Anything else?"

She slammed a fistful of silverware into the hot, soapy water.

RUNNING DOWNWIND

Silence.

Mick trudged toward Ryder's quarters.

Julia knew he hadn't heard her callous words, yet at the same time, hoped he had. Harsh sarcasm was the least of what he deserved. She'd generously exposed a piece of her soul while he'd stood proud and protected atop his stage of deception.

And then she remembered how just prior to supper, he'd gently placed his hand on hers, needing to tell her *something else*, but was interrupted by the oven timer. Perhaps revealing his real name had been his honest intention.

"You still owe me." She slapped sudsy fingers over her mouth before more emotion spilled onto her tongue.

"I know." Mick returned to the sink. "I'd like to begin payback with dessert."

She lowered her hand, allowing bubbles to slide down her chin. "There's nothing here I want anymore."

"I don't mean Ryder's fried pies." Mick inched closer. "This will be my treat. We can go someplace else."

She refused to explain her last reply.

Refused to look at him.

Payback probably included another big lie.

"You've come clean with me," Mick said softly. "Now it's my turn to eat soap."

Julia grabbed a nearby dishtowel, wiped her chin and faced him. "After *you* finish the dishes, I want something cold and chocolate."

"What? Where?"

"The malt shop on the beach road." She headed for the screen. "You drive."

Twenty minutes later, with two large chocolate malts balanced between them, they motored through the dunes toward the sea. Mick paid with change left from his rolled up twenty. If he was to reveal secrets, he didn't want an audience.

Neither spoke.

A mom-and-pop grocery located three miles from Roughshods operated a drive-up soda fountain. Mick downshifted, thinking how lucky he was that Julia agreed to desert. "We're fortunate that place was still open."

She didn't reply.

"I've never seen the beach so beautiful." Mick braked to a stop. "More so now than ... um ... before." He switched off the ignition. "If we were in Frog, we could follow the moon path. Maybe there's a pot of gold at the end."

Julia pushed his cup across the seat and stared out over the water.

"Thanks. I thought we could just sit here in the cab and talk, if that's okay?"

No response.

He took a long sip. Julia hadn't uttered a syllable since leaving Roughshods, not even about the ridiculous shirt he'd borrowed from Ryder's closet. Mick considered making a joke about it being *loud* enough to frighten away Beulah, but Julia was clearly in no mood to laugh.

"I can't believe there's a hurricane coming. There's not a bad breath of breeze, although the waves seem larger than they did—"

"Why weren't you honest with me?"

Her abruptness caught him off guard.

"You mean ... Leonard?"

She glared at him. "Then there're more lies?"

"No. Absolutely not." Mick cleared his throat. "I've told the truth ... except for the borrowed name."

RUNNING DOWNWIND

Silence.

"At least I kept it in the family. Leonard's my first cousin."

"Of course."

"It's the *truth*."

"You've stated that word already."

"I'm sorry."

"That word too."

"Then I'm *sorry* for repeating it." He sighed. If she'd only let him explain.

Julia opened her door.

"Wait. Please don't leave. I've never told you what happened ... the night before you found me."

She paused, still gripping the handle.

"I was sailing solo to Campeche and got caught in a bad storm. The mast broke and my boat flipped upside down. Somehow, I managed to hold on. Then the hull sank just before dawn. I thought I was going to drown."

"You almost did."

"Yeah, but you saved me."

Julia closed the door.

Mick studied her delicate profile, wishing he could rescue *her* from the hurt he'd caused.

She glanced his way. "I almost killed you."

"Not hardly. I was too drunk to drown, remember?" He offered a slight chuckled. "To be *honest*, I'd swallowed a little whisky."

She made no reply.

"Okay, a lot."

Pieces of a smile flit across her face.

"For medicinal purposes."

Silence.

"It's a miracle you survived." She met his gaze. "And didn't die from hypothermia."

"Yep. Seems I emerged from the sea *as pink as a healthy newborn*." He grinned.

Julia gasped. "You did hear everything."

Mick lowered his voice. "Wanna know the details about my scar?"

"No ... I mean ... not as much as Ryder."

"Oh, I suspect he knows already. From the news clipping you found."

"I missed that paragraph."

Mick nodded.

She peered into her cup. "After I saw your picture and the bit about *West Side Story*, I stopped reading."

He realized the moon path was vanishing into an approaching fog bank. "I need to tell you about the day I was shot."

Mick swallowed.

"And a girl who was killed.

"My fiancée, Cherie."

Julia couldn't remember when she'd scooted close to Mick, or if they'd both gradually drifted center.

No matter.

Most important—he'd finally told her the truth, reminiscing about his childhood, Cherie, Broadway career, and what happened on that horrific afternoon in Austin. His voice quavered, followed by an irregular pause and a quick eye swipe. Julia knew he tried not to cry, for she battled her own tears. He recalled something funny, and they both laughed. By the time he chronicled his year in Persimmon, and the journey to Padre in *No Qualms*, the pickup was engulfed in a chilly fog. Raising the windows to a crack, they sat in the dense stillness, wrapped in the comfort of each other's arms.

RUNNING DOWNWIND

Julia could feel the depth of his breathing, knew the lingering emptiness and confusion of having a murdered fiancé. More unsettling, she understood his desperate need to run, and the exhausting effort to remain unnoticed. She no longer blamed Mick for protecting his identity. He'd planned to tell her anyway.

Still, she wondered if he'd shared *everything.*

A restless timbre squeezed the periphery of his voice each time he mentioned Cherie. He'd emphasized how she'd loved him. Much more than a man like him deserved.

Was Mick blaming himself for her death?

Surely not.

He couldn't help the fact he'd been auditioning a grad student on the day of the tower shooter. Had no clue Cherie would arrive on campus to surprise him. Mick hadn't said what the surprise entailed, most likely something to do with a romantic lunch, or the couple's engagement.

Perhaps an upcoming wedding shower.

Julia knew of girls honored by such an event. If the engagement to Dario had been real, perhaps she'd have been fortunate.

The fog cleared, blown inland by a damp breeze. The moon path returned for an instant, then dissolved as fat raindrops spattered against the windshield.

"More foul weather bands," Mick said. "Guess Beulah's on the move."

Julia thought he was going to suggest they head back. Instead, he repositioned his body so she could comfortably lay her head on his shoulder. He was probably waiting for more of her story, but she didn't feel the need to go there.

Not yet.

That moment would come, so why ruin this one. For now, simply being held felt wonderful.

Mick stroked her cheek with the back of his hand. "There's something else I need to say."

An anxious tremor traveled the length of Julia's spine. She'd feared there was more. Always was. "Okay."

"Unlike Ryder, I think we should dig our graves side by side, instead of on opposite ends of the island."

She playfully patted his chest. "Nothing doing. No digging around here, except to plant turtle eggs." Her anxiety melted into a lingering smile.

Mick outlined her smile with his finger. "I wonder when that last group of hatchlings will emerge. Hope the little critters survive the storm."

"Me too."

"However, ghost crabs?"

She giggled. "Remember me telling you about Carmen?"

"Your nanny."

Julia nodded. "If Carmen were here, she'd say, "The turtle eggs are safe in God's hands.""

"Hmm. Means the Almighty must have sand beneath his fingernails."

"You sound like Paco." Julia wriggled out of Mick's embrace and punched open the glove box. The lid fell forward with a loud squeak.

She jumped. "Must be the sticky weather."

"Or you've captured a giant mouse."

"Never. It would terrorize the hatchlings."

They laughed.

Julia produced her mother-of-pearl Bible. "This was Carmen and Paco's gift to me."

Mick raised an eyebrow. "Ryder keeps a pistol hidden in his glove box, and you keep—"

"So?"

"I don't think coyotes can read. Nor mice."

RUNNING DOWNWIND

She considered a smart reply but offered him her Bible. Beulah aside, if the need ever rose to flee, her pickup was the ideal spot for safe keeping.

He opened the cover. "The inscription states *for Maria.*"

"Their special name for me."

"Why?"

"Carmen said I was the blessed daughter she never bore. Maria would've been her name."

"Have you seen them recently?"

"No." Julia swallowed hard. "I wrote them a letter a few months back but haven't received a reply. I hope they're okay."

"Maybe you'll hear something soon." Mick handed back her Bible.

Julia carefully placed it in the glove box and returned to his arms. She'd not shown her precious Bible to a soul since Dallas, nor ever allowed anyone to read the inscription.

"Ma-ri-a," Mick said slowly. "I like that name. It reminds me of a song."

"A song?"

"From *West Side Story*."

"Oh ... that." She frowned. Didn't Mick recall her negative reaction during supper?

He hummed a few bars.

"Begging for me to pour malted milk on your head?"

"Impossible. Mine's all gone, and I heard your final slurp." He continued humming.

"Lovely."

"Thanks."

"Please choose a tune from another show."

"But we're like the leading couple in this one." Mick pivoted his torso and faced her. "Remember Tony and Maria?"

Julia nodded. Until this very instant, she'd chosen to *forget*.

Mick tenderly caressed the back of her neck with his fingertips "They refused to let *anything* pull them apart."

Her knees trembled, voice breathless. "Then sing to me."

Mick stroked her hair. "Can't. I've forgotten the words."

Julia snuggled closer. "Please try."

"With this out of shape voice?" Mick cupped her chin with his hand, lowered his head and brushed both lips against her cheek.

"You're an actor. Fake it."

"Never again." He pressed his mouth against hers.

CHAPTER 25

The next day, Mick awakened to distant banging and what sounded like someone shouting outside his bungalow.

What time was it?

He crossed to the window and cracked the blinds. Probably close to noon, but difficult to tell. Low, dark clouds scudded across the sky. The voice blared from a passing patrol car's loud speaker. A hurricane warning was officially posted, all islanders ordered to evacuate. The mainland causeway would remain open as long as possible. After it closed, residents would be left to their own fate.

"Tell me something new," he grumbled, wondering how last night had gone sour ... again.

You know.

Mick disregarded the thought and scanned the parking lot. Two trash cans had blown over and rolled against each other, drumming their metal overture whenever the wind gusted. He breathed a sigh of relief. Julia's pickup remained parked in its regular spot.

"Ma-ri-a," he whispered, emphasizing each syllable. Julia had asked him to sing the lyrics, but he declined. Instead, caressed her with slow whispers until his lips brushed hers. Though after a few beginning kisses, desire crested more intensely than the waves, demanding he retreat to Roughshods before his willpower crashed. After seeing her safely to her door, they parted with a longer, desperate kiss. So, he lay in bed wide-eyed for hours, considering *why,* and *what* was best. After coming to an arduous conclusion, he'd slipped into a restless sleep, only to dream of racing back to her bungalow to sing.

Just sing.

But she was gone.

Mick rubbed the dream from his eyes. After their final kiss she'd seemed troubled.

Why? You were a complete gentleman.

"Yeah, but ..." Mick knew the truth. He'd respected her physically, not emotionally.

Not completely.

At least he'd not lost his ability to speak, as happened atop the lighthouse. In fact, told her more about himself than ever admitting to anyone.

Wasn't enough.

Mick paced about the room, imprisoned by what remained *unspoken* and *unborn*. His vow to Cherie would forever drive a wedge between himself and Julia. Therefore, he had no choice than to proceed with his plan.

Time was running out.

He needed to act.

Like Beulah, the storm raging inside of him refused to be stopped.

Mickey, never forget your child.

Mick grabbed a pen and tablet, then sat on the edge of his bed.

He knew the words he must write.

And how best to end things.

RUNNING DOWNWIND

By the time Julia exited her bungalow, the wind had increased to a steady whine. Bracing against her pickup, she noticed Ryder's car was gone.

Good.

He wasn't around to give orders, nor ask questions. However, Mick's blinds were open, which meant he might see her and ...

Julia shivered.

She needed to spend time alone where she could think clearly. Due to the gale, Mick wouldn't hear her drive away. She'd be back at Roughshods well before the causeway closed.

Climbing inside the cab, she slid behind the wheel, struggling to close the door. Instead of starting the engine, she sat motionless.

Sat where only hours ago, Mick held her close while emptying his soul.

Sat where he'd tenderly kissed her.

Kissed her.

Until she hated herself.

Julia swiped a tear and started the engine.

She'd demanded honesty.

He'd delivered total truth.

She was nothing but a fraud.

CHAPTER 26

When Mick finished writing, he reread each sentence, then carefully tore the pages from the tablet. Some of the words were much harder to pen than others, their labored syllables dipping into the hollows of his soul. The raw emptiness he felt would eventually subside, but that hadn't made the task easier, hadn't halted the predicted tear-flow. At least he'd developed a plan and was following through. The first step was composing his "goodbye letter."

Delivering it would be the second.

He folded the pages, slipped them into his breast pocket and fastened the pearl snap. It was the same shirt he'd borrowed from Ryder the previous evening. One of these days he'd order the man a new wardrobe so gaudy, he'd threaten to retire his apron. Mick hated to lose the nice shirt he'd purchased, but it was ruined. Indelibly stained with wine and painful memories.

A powerful gust shook the bungalow. He made the bed, then stuffed extra socks, underwear and toiletries into a paper sack. Out of habit, he completed a final walk-through for additional belongings—not that there were any. He'd rinsed and dried both malt cups yet decided against taking them. He couldn't come up with the will to throw them away.

Residents were supposed to be off of the island as soon as possible. Surely Julia was up, packed, and rested. Perhaps the anxiety she'd displayed behind their parting kiss was simple fatigue.

Mick paced about the room.

Yesterday was grueling.

Everything from boarding windows.

To the dreaded news article.

To Ryder lying unconscious on the beach.

The moment Mick thought the chasm separating him from Julia could only grow wider, she'd ended up in his arms.

He returned to the edge of the bed and sat, his voice a bare utterance.

"Am I insane?"

Mick pressed his face against his right sleeve. Delicate traces of her perfume still lingered there, reminding him of the closeness they'd shared.

A bond more poignant than friendship.

An inexplicable connection.

That's why he'd written the letter.

He patted his pocket to make sure his parting words were real.

They were.

Perhaps he should review them one last time, just to make sure he'd covered everything. Unfastening the snap, he retrieved the pages with two trembling fingers, unfolded them, and began reading.

Dear Cherie,

There was so much I wanted to say as you lay dying yet couldn't begin to find the words. And when you said, "Mickey, never forget your child," the phrase struck me more forcefully than any bullet.

RUNNING DOWNWIND

Why?

Because you knew the truth.

Knew I loved you ...

But not as you loved me.

From the moment you grabbed my hand in the fifth grade, until your family moved to Philly at the end of our sophomore year, I tried to match your affection.

I couldn't.

And you knew.

Years later when we reconnected in LA, I thought my feelings changed.

They hadn't, not romantically.

Thinking back, you knew that too.

I asked you to marry me because I detested whom I'd become. Hoped you'd inspire me to reform. Mostly—I'm ashamed to admit—I desired the gift you'd saved for your husband. Once mine, I'd love you without restraint. However, I needed to make sure, so stole the gift before we said, 'I do.'

My sweet Cherie, the wine that night wasn't the reason.

It was my appalling greed.

Even worse, my continued self-centeredness led to what may be unforgivable:

Your death.

We were engaged, yet I allowed myself a final "innocent" flirt on the day of the tower shooter.

You suffered *the consequences.*

Afterward, I wanted to die too.

Instead, I made a vow to uphold your honor by never telling anyone about the pregnancy. In all truthfulness, silence was how I avoided my own fear and guilt. However, the secret was destroying me. Smothered in self-pity, I fled. Thankfully, your memory followed.

"Mickey, never forget your child," I kept hearing you say.

Then early this morning I realized that to "never forget," one must choose to acknowledge the past while living in the present. As I write this letter, I can almost hear your glee at my sudden understanding.

"An epiphany," you'd joyfully announce.

Perhaps I'd agree.

Even though I'm sure you've forgiven me—you'd say Christ would've—I don't know if I can ever forgive myself.

But I do know this:

I will always love you.
Mick

Refolding the pages, he slid them back inside his pocket. He'd watched a play where a man, whose wife had died, penned a note, incorporating it into the wax of a candle. The symbolism was her light lived on. Mick planned to stuff his letter inside an airtight bottle and drop it off the causeway. Cherie's memory kept him alive and afloat when his sailboat flipped, the buoyant bottle implying a similar message. While snooping around Ryder's basement, Mick noticed thick ceramic jugs with rubber corks. Perfect. He just had to slip beneath Roughshods and locate one before grabbing his sack and meeting Julia.

As soon as Mick stepped outside, he noticed the parking lot was empty. Maybe she'd run a last-minute errand and left him a note. The wind off the water had lessened, however ominous thunderheads boiled black across the horizon. He dashed to Julia's bungalow and rattled the door.

Locked.

Gripping the knob with both hands, he twisted hard. No luck.

"Julia!" He knew she wasn't there, though for a split second wondered if she'd escaped without him.

RUNNING DOWNWIND

Impossible.

The woman was too kindhearted.

But Julia *had* seemed troubled. Since her pickup was missing, she'd probably gone somewhere to clear her mind.

The lighthouse.

A cold sweat beaded across his forehead. What if she ventured too far from shore and was swept into the deadly undertow.

Fearing the worst, Mick sprinted to Roughshods and bounded to the top of the stairs. Even from this distance, the waves resembled liquid giants. Hopefully Julia was already on her way back. He peered between the dunes.

Nothing.

Mick spun an about face, almost plowing into Ryder.

"Whoa there, son." Ryder stood on the top step balancing a large box, blocking the path. "One of us 'bout busted up a month's supply of tasty soda."

"Sorry." Mick breathed hard. "I need to go find—"

"Little gal's fine."

"Julia?"

"Unless you're holding another female hostage."

Mick grimaced. Julia was free to do as she pleased.

Ryder set down his load. "Just saw her sitting inside her pickup at the lighthouse. Don't think she saw me."

"But the storm's gonna—"

"Arrive later than predicted. Stalled around three p.m. at 140 miles out. Gave me time to run to the post office, then check on that last bunch of hatchlings. The critters aren't far from breaking out."

Mick leaned against the deck railing. He'd been upset about nothing. At least Julia was able to revisit her favorite spot, though perhaps for the last time. If the hurricane raged as fierce as predicted, the lighthouse could be destroyed.

"I figured you two kids were long gone." Ryder peered out over the water. "Just heard a weather update. Beulah's begun her final lap."

"How soon's landfall?"

"Tonight. In another couple of hours, you'll wish you were raised a fish."

"And you'll meet us on the mainland."

"Ain't that what I said?"

"When?"

"When I get there. After I stash these sodas outta harm's way, plus salvage a few more items from the basement, I'm gonna make a final turtle run."

"Don't wait too long."

Ryder faced Mick. "Ain't my first big blow."

"Let me give you a hand with that box." The gash on Ryder's jaw was still visible.

"Not necessary." He waved away the offer, lifted the sodas and emitted a loud grunt. "You gonna go fetch Julia or get the door?"

"Both." Mick pulled open the screen, wondering if the load of heavy soft drinks came from Ryder's lighthouse stash.

"When you find the gal, tell her she got a letter."

"I'll take it to her."

"Too risky. I'll stash the letter in the pantry for safekeeping. This stout old heap of concrete ain't going nowhere." Ryder sounded irritated, his voice carrying above the rising wind. "Keep an eye on them waves."

Mick scurried down the stairs and headed for the beach.

In case he and Julia weren't back in time to escape over the causeway, Ryder better be right about Roughshods.

CHAPTER 27

Julia stood in ankle-deep surf, struggling whether to tell Mick about her complicated past.

Her stillborn child.

She'd had the chance to share her darkest secrets but chose the comfort of his arms.

The warmth of his lips.

"I should've trusted my instincts." Saying the words aloud reenforced the impossibility of deceiving herself for long. She'd felt guilty before their final kiss grew cold.

Julia trembled.

All Mick did was lie about his name, which wasn't right but understandable. If she could coax the spilled wine back into the bottle, she would. However, dousing him with sticky liquid was *not all she'd done*. Lahoma accused her daughter of insolence, a spoiled child who needed to pay for her bad decisions.

Perhaps her mother was correct.

Julia stared blankly into the dark water. Even at this shallow depth, the powerful undertow yanked her toes, daring to drag her beneath the sea if she ventured out farther. Crushing waves towered and toppled just out of reach, their tonnage reverberating into a series of powerful booms. Like the coyote incident, the sound reminded her of JFK's assassination. She crammed her fingers into her ears.

This time there was no place to run.

The wind stiffened as a terrific updraft sucked her breath away. Lightning crackled overhead like brittle cellophane. Nearby, a huge wave broke, the reactive force slapping her face, blurring her vision. She wobbled, fighting off sudden dizziness, realizing she'd stepped into a knee-deep hole.

After regaining balance, a more powerful breaker crashed on top of her, pressing her head against the gritty bottom. Black brine gushed into her mouth, burned her nose. Panicked, she tried to stand but couldn't. She envisioned the mother dolphin leaping airborne atop the raging sea, her calf—alive and well—swimming beside her. The pair chattered nonstop, as if beckoning Julia to stand and climb out.

Somehow, she managed, coughing up water, barely able to breathe. She staggered backward and dropped onto the beach. A blinding flash plummeted into the dunes exploding into thunder, followed by a wall of wind driven rain. Large drops blew sideways, stinging her skin. Julia covered her face with her hands.

"It's me," she cried. "I'm who's ruined my life."

She wanted to call out to God, though didn't feel worthy, having avoided discussing the same issues with him. *Please forgive me* was all her mind could muster, and then added, *please help me.*

Even though the wind remained constant, the rain slackened, so she raised up on her knees. The water inched closer. Julia needed to drive back to Roughshods before the gale grew too intense. She'd first parked in her usual place in front of the lighthouse, then moved her pickup to a section farther down where the beach was wider and higher.

Turning sideways into the wind, she stood and edged toward her pickup. Her new parking spot had washed away into a large sinkhole, burying the tailgate and rear axle.

"No!"

She pressed on, carefully selecting every footfall until the rain returned with augmented vengeance. Fearing the same fate as her pickup, she headed blindly for Roughshods.

Julia refused to cry, although tears seeped from her eyes, mixing with the downpour. Surely Mick wouldn't come searching for her and risk his own life.

Yet she hoped he would.

"What were you thinking?" he'd later ask, kissing her before she could answer. And then in undiluted whispers she'd reveal everything. But as she fought her way through the rising water, she witnessed only desperation, realizing she might not make it.

A lighthouse shines for the Lady.

Carmen's words flooded into Julia's mind. The lighthouse was her only refuge. Standing less than a hundred yards away, she could barely detect its rusted form through the deluge. Pivoting toward higher ground, she managed to find a winding ribbon of sand that wasn't submerged, yet there was no logical pattern. The path led her up near the dunes, then down near the dangerous sea. Somewhere in the middle of the beach she tripped over a sandy mound and sat down hard.

Struggling to her feet she spied movement.

The final group of hatchlings.

CHAPTER 28

The thunderheads Mick viewed earlier marched closer, dropping angled lightning bolts into the sea like loose pickup sticks. Why Ryder hadn't demanded they both hop in Frog and find Julia was puzzling. By foot, the lighthouse was a good fifteen-minute trek.

Hopefully, there was still enough time.

Hearing heightened thunder, Mick increased his pace. Ryder seemed preoccupied with storm preparations, making him more irascible than normal. Maybe his jaw still hurt. Like the dead coyote, the cherry bomb was another ruse, both stories probably connected to the hidden basement room.

"I'll worry about Ryder's tall tales later," Mick assured himself, "if at all."

Crossing between the dunes, he stepped onto the hem of the beach and stopped. What he'd thought to be thunder was the recoil of crashing waves. He'd never seen them angrier this close to shore. The tire ruts carved into the sand by cars and dune buggies above the tide line would soon be submerged. Beulah must be closing in faster than forecasted. Ryder could forget about a final hatchling run.

"Julia!" Mick yelled, then broke into a jog.

The sand was deeper up near the dunes, requiring more energy to navigate, yet a better choice than getting too close to the dangerous waves. He jogged until he could see the distant lighthouse.

"Julia!"

He'd barely called her name a second time when blinded by a sudden cloudburst. Sheets of rain disoriented his senses, while the wind drove him farther down the beach and toward the sea. The initial bluster on the front side of an approaching hurricane was supposed to come off the water, but wind swirled about him like a muddy cyclone, almost raising him off his feet. Covered in muck, he struggled back toward the dunes when an enormous wave caught him from behind. He tumbled into several feet of water, but managed to stand upright, only to be flattened again. This time the Gulf's foamy tonnage surged over him, pinning him against the bottom. Resisting the vacuum suck of the undertow, he clawed fistfuls of sand, kicking both feet with all of his strength. He surfaced for a quick breath and was again pulled under.

Mick knew he was helplessly being carried out farther.

Deeper.

His mind flashed to the last time he'd been overpowered by the waves.

How Julia saved him.

This time he'd come to save her.

And failed.

He'd never be able to acknowledge *their present* through cleansing *his past*.

Never be able to tell her how much he loved her.

Mick felt himself cry out, even though his lungs would soon burst.

Felt a strong shove against his backside.

Punch-like.

Then another.

Followed by similar forceful blows, propelling him into the shallows.

RUNNING DOWNWIND

Raising his head above the foam, he spit out a mixture of sand and saltwater, then gasped for air while crawling onto the sodden beach, unsure of what had occurred. The heavy rain band passed, the wind still steady. Miraculously he'd not drowned so gripped a partially buried log of driftwood to catch his breath.

Shaky with exhaustion, Mick studied the horizon. The thunderheads he'd encountered were miniscule compared to what was coming. Once again, Ryder proved correct. Atop the distant sea boiled a massive cloud formation depicting photos he'd seen of an atomic explosion.

"Julia!"

The brief lull was swallowed by another passing rain band, this one heavier than the last. Mick realized he was running but couldn't recall leaving the log. Then he saw Julia on hands and knees, gathering something in her arms, her hair and clothes as drenched and muddied as his own. At first, he thought she collected shells, dropping more than she held. The absurdity played comical until he realized the shells moved, crawling toward the churning Gulf.

"Forget the hatchlings!" His shout barely pierced the storm's roar. "They'll be fine. We've got to get off the island."

She replied with a vacant stare, then returned to her work.

"Where's your pickup?" Mick reached Julia and grabbed her arm, causing her to drop the few turtles she'd managed to grasp.

"No!" She pulled away. "I won't lose another baby."

"They'll be fine. Nature has a way of—"

"Take off your shirt. Now. Please."

He remembered her painful story of the dolphin's calf, so complied, forming the shirt into a cloth sack. They worked until rising water covered their feet. Most of the hatchlings swam out of reach, but they were able to save several dozen.

Conversation was impossible. Mick didn't inquire further about the whereabouts of Julia's pickup. With the beach under water, driving back to Roughshods was too dangerous. They'd have to shelter inside the lighthouse.

Mick motioned in that direction, then grasped the makeshift sack in one hand, offered Julia the other. But after a few steps, the wind gusted, her knees buckled. So, he slogged through the rising overflow, carrying Julia and her babies in his arms.

A lighthouse shines for the Lady.

The legend flooded into Mick's tired thoughts. "I hope there's a glimmer for *us*."

His words became lost in the storm.

CHAPTER 29

Ryder stashed his sodas in the pantry, then took stock of what foodstuffs remained. Items he'd not cooked and served, Mick and Julia ate—which was the plan. Those two becoming at odds with one another made matters more complicated.

He rubbed his chin. Some couples treading the fine edge of romance purposely squabbled, a subconscious act meant to test their relationship, make the exhilaration seem more realistic.

"Idiotic," Ryder murmured. Life rustled up enough misery without goading more. But then, romance had a way of confusing reality.

He'd loved once.

Then surrendered a lifetime of bliss at the slammer door 'cause he'd bungled the claim ticket. For all he cared, Mick and Julia could quiz their feelings into infinity as long they were off the island before things got dicey.

Reaching onto the top shelf, Ryder fingered four fried pies, stuffing the first three in his pockets for later. He unwrapped the fourth, chomping down the contents in two bites. Whenever he received his monthly supply from Merly, she included a newsy letter. There'd been no mention of her encounter with Dipp, which meant he'd sullied the café's threshold sometime in the past three weeks.

Memories of Merly filled Ryder's head, then images of Jayne, his thoughts emanating as whispers.

"How long has she been back in Santa Fe?"

The question so consumed him, he almost steered Frog to the Crow's Nest and let his former cellie recover the Singer fortune. But Dipp was interested in more than monetary riches.

Ryder grabbed a grape soda and pried off the cap. He'd debated whether to remove his stash from the lighthouse. Yet after spending the night atop the swaying tower, he wasn't sure the rusty old structure could withstand another hurricane.

"Ain't that a shame." He took a swig and wondered what Jayne would say if he did show. There was bound to be a good reason she'd not attended his trial, nor answered his letters.

Could he accept the truth?

Draining the bottle, he returned to the basement. He'd already removed anything fragile, piling the rest on makeshift tables, or on top of his work bench. According to the old-timers, there'd never been more than a few feet of overflow beneath Roughshods, so he wasn't too concerned. The little brick room he built was more like a watertight safe, which was why he'd *borrowed* the lighthouse door.

Or *rescued* it.

He was out checking on hatchlings one morning and discovered the door partially buried fifty yards down the beach, the top half protruding from the roadway of vehicle tracks. The culprits? Most likely teenage pranksters who had access to brute strength and a cutting torch. Ryder attached a chain to the handle and dragged the heavy iron slab back to Roughshods. Otherwise, some wealthy tourist might drive over it and gut their automatic transmission.

RUNNING DOWNWIND

Lighthouse enthusiasts and local politicians entertained restoring the entire structure. When that day happened, Ryder would gladly return the door. In essence, he'd not only performed a public safety service, but protected a valuable piece of Texas maritime history. Jayne might've said he was a natural-born archivist.

"Which is why I removed the lamp's Fresnel lens ... what was left of it."

He strode to the brick room, released the deadbolt, and opened the door, its perimeter outlined with rubber innertubes which created a dandy, watertight seal. Inside were shelves where he'd arranged the remaining fragments of the giant lens in order of size: smallest to largest. Or since they were mostly circular, *golf ball* to *football*, as his mind preferred to catalogue them. If the lighthouse was ever restored to its former glory, he could sell the crystalline chunks as original souvenirs.

Ryder gazed at the collection. It wasn't as impressive as the treasure he'd soon store alongside, though admiring such intricate glass pieces gave him a feeling of accomplishment. As a boy, he'd seen a similar lens still intact—beehive in shape, three feet across, six feet tall, weighing several tons. The design's abundance of stacked prisms, held together by solid brass, magnified a single flame into a powerful beam. Augustin Fresnel was as much of a genius as the folks who'd engineered Frog, except Ryder figured this man was French. Which meant Fresnel could probably cook.

"Too bad the thieves destroyed beauty for brass." Ryder closed and locked the door. He had no clue what happened to the hundreds of other glass remnants, but vandals desecrated the lighthouse for well over fifty years.

"Lazy scum like Dipp."

As expected, the con entered the lighthouse around 3:00 a.m. but wouldn't climb to the top.

"I know you're up there." Dipp's voice echoed throughout the darkened cylinder.

"Is that you, roomie?"

"Meet me halfway, be a friend for once."

"Friend?" Ryder laughed. "You tried to shoot me the last time we palled around."

"Gun's gone. Got whisky now."

"No thanks. I prefer a grape soda in the rafters."

"What are you, a stinking bat?"

"Now, that comparison ain't very amiable." Far below, Ryder heard the click of Dipp's cigarette lighter, the criminal's head and arms visible from the flame. He held the lighter in one hand, a bottle in the other.

"Why don't you come on down." Dipp raised the whisky to his mouth.

"What? Is my roomie fearful of heights."

"At least I ain't afraid to make a deal ... like you."

"What kind of deal?" Ryder remembered how booze made Dipp more sociable.

"I figure we both have more to gain than lose," Dipp pressed.

"Explain."

"You know exactly where Singer buried his stash. I'd have to hunt."

"At least you're an intelligent drunk."

"Nothin' wrong with a nip now and then. Come on. Let's talk face to face."

Even when mellowed, the man was still a liar, so Ryder stayed put. "I'd rather talk long distance. I'm in my pj's."

Dipp laughed. "We were partners once. Could be again."

RUNNING DOWNWIND

"Cellmates. There's a difference."

"Still the mighty professor." He took another drink.

"Get on with your deal, *friend*. The wee hours are past my bedtime."

Dipp continued. "I imagine a man with your brains wants to protect all the things he could lose. We discussed the ones far away. Others are much closer."

Swallowing hard, Ryder held his tongue. If he didn't appear to cooperate, Mick would end up dead, and Julia ...

"Am I right?" Dipp hollered.

Ryder didn't answer. The crook was intent on having the Singer fortune and whatever else pleased his fancy.

"Am I right?" he yelled again.

"State your deal," Ryder said.

"We hunker down together until opportunity strikes. That way, you can see *my* hands and I can see *yours*. Then we grab the treasure. Split the take as equal partners, fifty-fifty."

The percentage was as bogus as the two men becoming cohorts. But agreeing to the arrangement gave Mick and Julia time to clear out. "Meet me at Roughshods a little before the storm hits. Show up sober or the deal's off."

"I ain't about to drink every drop." Dipp held the bottle next to the flame. "Even you know that." The convict left, leaving only darkness.

Ryder listened to the wind whipping through the tired lighthouse.

And to his own rusty groans.

CHAPTER 30

As Mick carried Julia and the hatchlings into the lighthouse, wind and sea pursued his steps. Remaining edges of daylight eerily outlined the tiny windows, so he allowed his eyes to adjust until water engulfed his ankles. Soon, the doorway would be submerged.

He gripped Julia tightly and located the stairs, climbing to a solid landing about a fifth of the way up. They'd go higher, if need be, but he was exhausted. Hopefully they were located well above the Gulf's dangerous reach. Here, if only the top of the structure collapsed, they might have a chance to survive.

Might.

Depending on where the jagged tonnage fell.

"Are you all right?" He gently lowered Julia to the landing, but she didn't reply nor let go of him. Therefore, he sat, protecting her with the bulk of his body, the hatchling pouch securely pressed against her lap. The thick iron walls muffled Beulah's furious cries outside, while the cavernous inside uttered metallic groans of bygone storms.

Off-key tunes chortling death.

"Are you all right?" Mick repeated, wishing for a towel. Neither of them could claim an inch of dry clothing.

This time she mumbled a reply, but he couldn't distinguish her words. He positioned his ear close to her mouth. "What did you say?"

"The h-hatchlings. Too many to save."

"There's a good chance they'll survive. The little critters are born scuba divers."

Julia frowned.

"Trust me."

"I've heard that line before." She formed a weak smile.

"We're gonna be fine too. I'm—"

A terrific wind blast interrupted his response, shaking the entire structure.

"—not worried."

Another great gust followed, accompanied by a loud thud.

Startled, Julia squealed.

"Probably just driftwood," Mick said.

Julia wanted to reply, but couldn't, as if the gale scattered the remaining bits of her will and emotion. She knew Mick tried to make the best of a dire situation, knew he was frightened too. Yet more than the hurricane, Julia feared what she'd determined to tell him. He'd shared his darkest secrets. She needed to reciprocate. Admitting the painful truth meant she'd not evolved into her mother.

That Julia had scruples.

That she cared about someone else more than herself.

The thought boosted her strength.

"There's a baby," she blurted. "I lost it."

Mick patted the hatchlings. "Focus on the ones you saved."

"No." Julia pulled away from his embrace. "*I had a baby. A little girl. And I killed her.*"

"You what?"

"Please don't make me tell you again."

"Your own daughter?"

She nodded.

"I don't believe you."

"My baby's dead. It's the truth."

"Then you're confused."

Julia buried her face in her hands and sobbed.

Mick stood, no longer hearing the storm, feeling as though his insides were slowly being ripped from his body. Was Julia speaking truth? He took a step, peered over the railing into the darkness below. Her words didn't make sense. She was obviously traumatized, blending fiction with fact. The woman couldn't bear to see a turtle die, much less murder a helpless child.

He faced her. "I'm the actor, not you." Mick wagged his head. "Your story's simply not believable."

She looked up at him and wiped her eyes. "I'm sorry I haven't pleased you."

"You think that's what this is about?"

She turned away.

"Pleasing me has zero meaning."

No reply.

"None."

"Really?" Julia faced him. "Then you're a liar."

He rushed forward and yanked the sack of hatchlings from her grasp.

"Mick, what's wrong with you?"

"*This* is what has meaning." He dangled the sack over the rail.

"Stop!" She leapt to her feet.

"I've no intention of dropping them." He handed back the sack. "And you're no baby killer."

Julia clutched the hatchlings and crumpled to the floor. "My mother would disagree."

"Forget *her* lies. Speak *your* truth."

"It was an accident." Julia cried again, letting the tears flow. "I was nine months pregnant. Rolled the pickup I drove. My baby was stillborn."

Mick wondered if he were dreaming, and this was his mind's cruel way of proving he'd never get past his own pain and loss. However, Beulah still raged, and the lighthouse still stood, which meant the balance of his secretive past finally came due. Until grabbing the soaked shirt full of hatchlings, he'd forgotten about his letter to Cherie, tucked in the pocket and certainly ruined. There wasn't enough light to read it anyway. But as soon as Julia had her say, he'd recite what he'd penned.

Word for word.

He eased down beside her, his voice tender. "Tell me exactly what happened. Please."

As the storm peaked, Julia emptied her soul, confessing about Ray, Lahoma, and even Dario. At times, Beulah's gusty roar made it impossible for Mick to hear every sentence, even with his ear only inches from her mouth. The constant battery of lightening offered him glimpses of her tear-streaked face. He knew she was okay. She finished with dry eyes.

"The dolphin's calf." Mick released a lungful of air. "No wonder you were upset."

Julia nodded.

His arms encircled her again, her head resting securely on his shoulder. "There's more," he said.

RUNNING DOWNWIND

"Nope. I've told all I can remember."

"Not you ... me."

At that moment the tempest increased tenfold, violently shaking the entire structure.

A loud pop.

The lighthouse swayed, seeming to rise and drop at the same instant. Lightning flashed directly above them, resounding into instantaneous thunder. Pungent ozone burned Mick's nose. He was disoriented, yet still gripped Julia's arm with his right hand. "We've been hit."

The landing tilted and they slid downward, the grated metal scraping flesh from his left palm. He felt his feet dangle off the edge, then the same hand bumped a support post. Somehow, he managed to grasp it with only his fingertips. Mick knew he couldn't hold back their weight for long.

Another deafening thunderclap.

Julia jumped.

A finger slipped.

And then another.

"No," he screamed. "Keep still."

Instead, she rolled onto her side and extended a leg over and above him, buttressing his hand against the post with her foot.

Mick's grip held firm, allowing him to reposition his hips enough for his heels to catch.

Julia shifted her weight.

He released his hold.

They inched their way to the landing's apex. Mick spoke with labored breath. "Saved me ... again."

No response.

More rapid-fire lightening bleached the darkness.

He saw her dazed expression.

His ears popped.

Mick felt increasingly heavy, as if something unseen flattened him pancake-like—a cartoon character trapped beneath a steam roller. The tower shuddered violently, followed by a high-pitched whine.

An enormous piece of the outer wall disintegrated with an ear-splitting scrape.

Crash!

Julia's scream reverberated into dead calm.

Moonlight filtered through the silence.

CHAPTER 31

Mick wondered if he were dreaming.
Floating.
Instead of crushing heaviness, he felt weightless.
Woozy.
Surrounded by an abrupt serenity.
"The eye. We're inside of it." Julia still clutched the cloth sack as she huddled beside him, her face suffused with pale moonlight.
He rubbed his sore fingers. "Are you all right?"
"Fine."
"Are the turtles ... active?"
"Asleep."
Instead of asking further questions, Mick gazed upward. The top of the lighthouse seemed intact, yet just beneath the lamp room was a gaping hole. "This place needed another window." He managed a slight chuckle. "Perhaps not such a large one."
She frowned. "Storm's not over."
Mick knew it wouldn't be long before Beulah returned from the opposite direction to finish what she'd started.
When?
Fifteen minutes?
Forty-five?
They needed at least twenty to reach Roughshods, that is, if Julia could walk. While in Persimmon, he'd heard

about folks who'd foolishly ventured outside during Betsy when the eye passed. The furious flipside swept them out to sea with little or no warning.

Mick slowly stood. The tilted landing platform held firm. Hopefully, the stairs would follow suit.

Peering downward, the black water covering the floor looked deep, meaning they'd have to wade, or swim. Once outside they'd be forced to travel atop the dunes, the dense vegetation slowing their pace even more. And then there was the possibility of poisonous snakes, dangerous debris, or sliding into an unexpected sinkhole.

"Let's leave. Now." Julia stood beside him in the eerie stillness. "We can make it." She stroked the hatchlings. "All of us."

"Good thing the little guys can swim." He offered her his hand. "How about you?"

She nodded.

With Mick in the lead, they carefully descended the narrow staircase. At the bottom, the water was only a few feet deep, allowing a luminous glow to penetrate the open doorway.

"Sandals." He pointed at Julia's feet. "You'd better ride piggyback."

"I can walk."

"Better not. I heard glass shatter. Most likely from your teens' empty pickle jars."

Without another word, she climbed on his back.

Outside, pallid light blanched the night. Mick gazed overhead, squinting at the contrast. A full moon hung inside a brilliant halo of starry sky, the intense lunar glow bordered by towering cliffs of massive clouds.

The steeped radiance mesmerized him.

Terrified him.

RUNNING DOWNWIND

He slogged through the overflow to the base of a nearby dune. Here, the water was only ankle deep, so he lowered Julia atop a platform of washed-up lumber.

"Part of someone's deck," he said, wondering if it'd come from Roughshods.

He'd only meant to catch a quick breath and continue on but couldn't help staring at the beach. It reminded him of recent photographs of the pocked lunar surface taken from space. Beulah's powerful winds burrowed out deep craters, then swirled the sand into enormous drifts. Most of the holes overflowed with water, forming a small river flowing into a lengthy, sheer-walled cut resembling a jagged canyon. Mick couldn't see the bottom, yet heard the steady rush far below of ocean redefining shore.

And then something shiny caught his eye, a sliver of reflected moonlight.

Julia stood.

Balanced atop the cut's precipice was a huge debris pile, a tangle of twisted metal, shredded lumber and dark shadows.

"My pickup."

She ran.

He followed.

Farther along the dangerous cut, the rushing sound increased to the volume of wild rapids. Mick tripped, landing hard. He wasn't hurt, but the fall winded him. Regaining his feet, he gulped air. Roughshods was in the opposite direction. There wasn't much time.

Mick continued on.

Moonlit objects were misleading, even more so at a distance. What Julia thought was her pickup might be something else.

Reaching the debris pile, Mick realized he was wrong. Only the truck's front half remained, the bed and rear axle sheared off by the storm. "Julia. We need to go."

She gazed at what was once her vehicle, still clutching the hatchlings tightly to her chest.

"Julia. Did you hear me?"

Instead of answering, she moved closer to the wreckage.

A man stepped out from behind, slapping his hand across her mouth.

"No!" Mick lunged forward, then stopped.

The bald man held a knife at Julia's throat, the stranger dubbed Cue Ball.

"Let her go."

"Not for no midnight comedian." He chuckled gravel. "Be a hero and she dies." Motioning for Mick to follow, Cue Ball dragged Julia around the far side of the debris pile.

The click of Max Darnell's switchblade echoed in Mick's memory, giving him much needed energy. Why Cue Ball grabbed Julia during the eye of a hurricane wasn't clear. Rescuing her before the storm returned, was.

Mick sucked in a slow, deep breath and released it.

Change the madman's focus. Make him angry. He'll release Julia and go after someone else.

"Me," Mick mouthed. He wasn't afraid, knowing the ruse required a mix of quick wit and good acting. Hoped he wasn't too rusty.

The instant Mick rounded the debris pile he saw Frog, the canvas top closed. Ryder stood nearby—his back toward them—in a waist deep hole, holding a shovel. Roughshods's crusty owner had more on his agenda than cooking and watching for hatchlings. The hidden red brick room was proof. Even so, Mick knew Ryder would never harm Julia.

"Pay dirt." Ryder banged the shovel blade on something hard. "Get over here and help me with this trunk."

"Baldy's busy."

"Mick?" Ryder wheeled an astonished about-face. "Let her go, Dipp."

RUNNING DOWNWIND

"Dipp?" Mick scrunched his brow. "That's better than Cue Ball."

Ryder dropped the shovel. "I said let her go."

Mick took a step forward. "Dippy doesn't understand that phrase."

"Stay back!" Dipp squeezed Julia tighter. She still clutched the shirt full of hatchlings, her eyes closed.

"You. Funny-Man. Give my *partner* a hand."

"Partner?" Mick glanced at Ryder. "Is that the same definition as *roomie*?"

Dipp horse laughed. "Guess my *cellie* ain't bragged about his glorious past behind bars."

"Ain't no one's business." Ryder doubled his fists.

"Ain't it?" Dipp pressed the blade against Julia's throat. "Don't they know a con can't be trusted?"

Julia stood firm.

A trickle of blood appeared.

Mick wanted to leap to her rescue but knew he couldn't reach her fast enough.

Knew the tragic result.

Lightening crackled out over the bay.

Dipp eyed Ryder. "The way you flap your gums, they're probably after the treasure too."

"The kids know nothing."

"Don't matter." Dipp squinted at the disappearing moon. "'Cause soon as the loot's loaded into that fancy floating car, the girl's gonna drive me back to your dump for a little celebration." His mouth spread into a sly grin. "We'd wait breakfast, but you two will be swallowing salt water."

More lightening splintered above a sudden, stiff breeze.

Ryder faced Mick. "You gonna admire Beulah's backside or come help?"

"Both." Mick crossed to the hole.

Ryder whispered beneath a drum roll of thunder. "We have less than a minute. I've got Dipp. You hold on to Julia and what's left of her pickup. Frog'll get us out."

The trunk was less weathered, plus much smaller than Mick expected—not that he'd ever dug up treasure—and much lighter. Ryder grunted as though they lifted several hundred pounds.

Dipp scowled. "You're wasting time. Get the loot loaded. Now."

A sudden, mighty wind gust whipped the bright night into cloud covered darkness. Dipp released Julia and lunged for the trunk, fighting with Ryder.

She screamed. "The hatchlings. I've dropped them."

Mick reached for her and missed, as a wall of blinding rain returned.

"No! Julia!"

The blast now pounded from the opposite direction, hurling every syllable out to sea.

He felt helpless.

Lost.

Lightening splintered amidst deafening thunder. Mick glimpsed Julia clinging to the wreckage.

Good girl.

The blow blasted from bayside, meaning the dunes offered protection. However, only feet away, the cut swelled into a raging river of foam and debris. In minutes, the black water would surge, sweeping away everything in its path.

Heading sideways into the wind, Mick managed to climb to higher ground, then inch his way toward Julia. He'd no sooner reached her when he saw Frog's headlights. Hopefully, Ryder was behind the wheel.

Mick pried open the passenger door. Julia scrambled into the front seat. He sandwiched beside her. The door whammed shut.

RUNNING DOWNWIND

"Ahoy." Ryder shouted above the roar.

Mick matched the volume. "Cue Ball?"

"Sleeping with the coyotes." Ryder pumped the clutch, readying Frog. "Hold on. Gonna surf the valley between the dunes 'til Beulah eases her tantrum."

CHAPTER 32

Except for Mick's comforting words, Julia heard nothing but the storm during their tempestuous ride back to Roughshods. Beulah churned with such fury that even Ryder remained silent.

Julia clamped her eyelids shut for most of the way, not so much from fear, but to diminish the constant barrage of thunder and lightning. Twice, she thought they either changed direction or briefly stopped, yet wasn't sure. She fought back tears as images of Dipp and her mangled pickup crowded her mind.

And then she remembered Carmen, Paco, and the little mother-of-pearl Bible.

Julia wept openly.

Mick whispered close, assuring her everything would be okay. The next thing she knew the gale had lessened, and he was helping her out of Frog. Ryder's powerful flashlight revealed a large section of Roughshods's outermost deck area succumbed to ruin, but the stairs remained.

Plus, the cranky screen.

Ryder led them safely inside. "This place was positioned cattycornered on purpose. Blocks whatever bluster threatens the steps from either direction. Protects the bungalows too." He closed and latched the heavy outside door, then lit a couple of kerosene lanterns.

Meanwhile, Mick retrieved some chairs stacked against an inner wall and offered one to Julia. She sat as he fetched an armload of dry towels.

Ignoring the comforts, Ryder continued. "Surviving nature's wrath is part'n parcel to the genius of Roughshods's design. Otherwise, we'd have floated back here for nothing."

"And without a cache of *something*." Mick glared at Ryder. "Hope your trouble was worth it."

He answered with an irritated grunt. "I suggest you two get some shuteye." Ryder grabbed one of the lanterns and disappeared into his quarters.

"Thanks for the chair." Julia hadn't uttered a word since losing the hatchlings. "And the towel."

"I need to see your neck." Mick retrieved the lantern and held it close.

"I'm okay. Nothing but a scratch."

Ignoring her protest, he placed a finger beneath her chin and gently lifted. "The cut looks clean, isn't bleeding. Guess we've both had a proper rain bath."

She hoped he'd wrap his arms around her as firmly as he'd done inside in the lighthouse, and then moments ago in Frog. But he suddenly seemed on edge.

Julia trembled.

Outside, Beulah still billowed copious rain, drenching the night. However, there was something *inside* Mick she didn't want to acknowledge.

Didn't want to accept.

More frightening than any hurricane.

He plopped into an adjacent chair. "I've told you about Cherie," he said slowly, "but not *everything* that happened before she was killed.

And *nothing* about our baby."

CHAPTER 33

The next morning, Mick awakened to the cries of hungry seagulls, signifying Beulah's exit. A moment passed before he realized he'd slept atop Roughshods's plank dining room floor instead of his own mattress.

"Julia?"

He sat up and rubbed his throbbing head. Daylight seeped around the borders of the Gulf-side windows, their plywood coverings still standing sentry. For an instant, he smelled spicy seafood.

Breakfast?

Though the aroma wafted somewhat pungent, his mouth watered. With such scant foodstuffs, one never knew what odd, tasty ingredients Ryder hoarded. Mick wasn't too happy with the man's reckless treasure scheme yet would still eat his cooking.

Was Julia's pleasant voice carrying from the kitchen?

Mick listened carefully but heard only the gulls' distant protests. The steady electric hum of the Jax Beer clock had ceased. *Nine-fifty-two*, the hands read, signifying when the island lost power, declaring when he and Julia clung to life inside the old lighthouse. Afterward—due to Ryder's nonsense—a lunatic held a knife to her throat.

She's a brave woman, as brave as Cherie.

"Julia?"

No answer.

Standing, he peered about the room. The towels she'd used as a makeshift pillow and bedroll were neatly folded and stacked atop her chair. Safety pinned to the pile was a handwritten note. It looked hurriedly written.

Mick,

Watch for the Lady.

Whoever discovers a piece of her precious mirror will find love that very hour. There's a beacon of hope.

Julia

"Why didn't she tell me in person?"

Mick was on the verge of adding *hurt* to the emotional mix, when he realized the odor wasn't seafood, but himself. He reeked of stale ocean and needed a shower. Surely Julia was bathing at her bungalow, meaning the little building survived. Odds were good that his had too.

He started for the door, then stopped.

Wait.

Julia wasn't at her bungalow but doing what she did every morning: sitting on the beach in front of the lighthouse.

Hoping to find a mirror piece.

Hoping to find ...

Love. That very hour.

The concept was obviously the most personal part of the legend, a crucial longing she'd not revealed ...

Until now.

According to Ryder, Julia hadn't missed a sunrise for the past three years.

No wonder.

Didn't she understood her nanny's tale was based upon lore? There *was* no Lady, at least not in a physical sense. Spiritual perhaps, if one believed in that sort of thing.

RUNNING DOWNWIND

Feeling shaky, Mick lowered himself into one of the chairs. Late last night, he'd finally revealed his former relationship struggles and Cherie's surprise pregnancy, the words flowing nonstop. He'd cried when recalling his goodbye letter to Cherie—no surprise. Yet for the first time since his Broadway career skyrocketed, Mick felt free, as if fame's suffocating shackles were finally loosed. Julia was too exhausted to respond, so he'd made her a bedroll with the rest of the towels. By the time he'd claimed his adjacent section of floor, she was asleep.

He'd slept a desperate slumber. Before drifting off, he mentally replayed his entire confession, questioning whether it was more than she could handle. Not only had Julia's past lovers taken every advantage, she'd suffered the loss of a child.

An unborn baby, just like his own.

Would her reaction be scorn or empathy?

"At least I told her the truth," Mick whispered. He'd awakened ready to congratulate himself on his life-cleansing candor.

And now?

Stop second-guessing everything.

"Her note. I don't know what all of it means." He stood and crossed toward the screen door just as Ryder entered.

"Good, you're finally up." The screen slammed shut. "Morning's half over."

"What time is it?"

"Late. Let's talk."

"Not now."

"Julia ain't at the lighthouse."

Mick pushed past Ryder.

"Or at her bungalow. You're wasting your time, son. She's gone."

Still facing the screen, Mick stopped. "Gone?"

"Ain't that what I said? Dropped her off on the mainland several hours ago. A big semi tumbled over and blocked the causeway, so we crossed the bay in Frog."

"Did she give a reason for ... leaving?"

"No. Reckon it's 'cause of the letter that came yesterday. Gal couldn't hightail it outta here fast enough. And don't ask me about the sender. I ain't no mail snoop."

Mick peered out the door and beyond the dunes. The Gulf, blue-green and placid, puddled enormous beneath a translucent sky.

Ryder continued. "All commercial transportation in this part of the state's been crippled, so she hired a crop duster to fly her out."

"Crop duster?"

"Yeah. Entirely her idea. Danged good one."

"How?"

"The Texas Rangers blocked off a cleared section of highway for a landing strip. Some of the duster companies north of here are flying in supplies." Ryder chuckled. "Bunch' a crazy daredevils."

"I can't believe she'd leave without—"

"Suit yourself. I saw her climb aboard and watched the plane take off."

Silence.

"Ease up, son. Good men make honest mistakes. Bad ones force every advantage."

Mick faced him. "Which man are you?"

"One who admires his Maker's handiwork every morning."

"That's not what I asked."

"Yeah, it is. Helps me decide how to approach the day. Ain't complicated, just takes *time* and *dedication*. Which is why I want you to stay on for a while."

Mick shrugged. "I've got the time. Dedication's in short supply."

RUNNING DOWNWIND

Ryder strode to the pantry, fingered four grape sodas and a box of fried pies. "Lunch."

They sat in the kitchen at the same prep table where Mick watched Julia prepare supper. After downing three pies apiece, both men were on their second soda before either spoke.

"I need to take an extended leave of absence." Ryder unwrapped his fourth.

Mick peered toward the sink. His and Julia's playful water fight was a lifetime ago.

Ryder chomped a healthy bite and swallowed. "Gonna ask me?"

"What?"

"Where I'm headed."

"You've never asked me."

"Ain't 'cause I wasn't interested."

"The Yucatan." Mick eyed Ryder. "You?"

"Santa Fe."

"Nice town. I performed there once. Bet you've already figured that out."

"Didn't take no Einstein."

"Most things don't." Mick paused. "Others are more complicated."

Ryder nodded. "Wanna stay around for a while and watch over the place?"

"Might as well."

"Good. I've lined up a jeep for you. Also drinking water and groceries. Fellow I know from the doughnut shop will deliver everything when the causeway opens. 'Til then, I reckon you can survive on fried pies and grape sodas."

"A feast for the sweet-toothed gods."

"Exactly. Emergency gasoline's in the basement, five-gallon cans, along with extra kerosene. I'll pay you in advance for your trouble."

"What makes you think I'll still be here when you return?"

Ryder rubbed his chin. "When a man decides what's important, dedication ain't that sparse."

CHAPTER 34

Ryder gathered his belongings, packed Frog and splashed across the bay toward Port Isabel. As on his earlier run with Julia, the water was littered with floating debris.

"Slow and easy," he stated aloud.

The caution wasn't a call against aquatic carelessness, but more of a vocal pat on the back. A reason to break out a fresh carton of grape sodas and toast his good fortune.

He grabbed the first bottle, pried off the top and took a satisfied sip. Roughshods—including both bungalows—survived another major hurricane with only cosmetic damage. As expected, several feet of water flooded the basement, which was why he'd raised anything of value off the floor.

Value.

The word played hopscotch in his head all morning. After hearing Jayne was back in Santa Fe, he questioned why he'd collected so much "stuff." All a man really needed was what easily fit into a small suitcase. Anything more tended to dilute what was of genuine worth. And too many possessions strangled his freedom.

Freedom.

Another hopscotch participant, the *bedrock* of folks' natural yearnings. Fueled by passion, freedom was gradually chiseled into the shape of each individual's hopes and dreams. As a young man, the term meant righting a few of the wrongs forced on hardworking families during the Dust Bowl. The righteous act landed him in prison. After his release, freedom meant finding the Singer treasure, which he'd done ... well, almost.

Ryder chuckled.

Planting a false sea chest near his predicted site of the real one was creative brilliance. The toughest challenge entailed slipping the fake down into the hole when Dipp wasn't looking. That's why he'd *pocketed* a plan.

They'd ridden out the first half of the storm at Roughshods. When the eye passed overhead, the men jumped into Frog and raced to the treasure site. Fortunately, Beulah drug her heels once she'd made landfall, meaning they had a fair amount of time before the backside wallop.

At first, the unexpected wreckage of Julia's pickup unnerved him, slowing his progress. When Ryder saw no one inside, he relaxed his frazzle. Common sense kicked in, indicating another failed battery. The kids must've hitched a ride to the mainland. So, while Ryder made an animated show of looking at his notes and pacing the area, he secretly dropped a handful of counterfeit doubloons on the far side of an enormous sand dune. After bragging where he'd noticed "a tidy scattering of washed-up Spanish coins," Dipp quickly disappeared in that direction, giving Ryder time to dig a hole, then plant the decoy.

The last person he expected to see was Julia.

With a knife at her throat.

Which changed everything.

Ryder pounded his palm against the steering wheel. He'd researched the Singer treasure for years, eventually locating the massive fortune others hadn't.

RUNNING DOWNWIND

Others *couldn't*.

His endless, patient study and countless calculations—combined with last minute creativity, plus an honest gambler's luck—*would've* unearthed the find of a lifetime. The best he figured, the odds of his success were imminent because Mother Nature stacked the deck. As anticipated, Beulah accomplished most of the digging.

Swigging his grape soda, he let the fizz dissipate before commenting. "'Cept life tends to get in the way of life, sometimes colliding with death."

When Dipp barged into Ryder's plans, he was forced to engineer a feint. Bury a weathered, wooden box filled with fake doubloons and handfuls of ornate costume jewelry. His former cellie wouldn't realize the scam until afterward. By then, Ryder would've returned and claimed the actual prize. Before Dipp caused another stink, an anonymous phone call to the cops would immediately end the con's vacation from incarceration.

Ryder followed his next swig with a sigh.

Like the predicted tumble of well-positioned dominoes, the ruse would've worked. But due to Mick and Julia's surprise visit, Ryder's *treasured* efforts were no longer secret, possibly resulting in negative consequences. His private life was nobody's business. Therefore, he'd returned to the site at first light to see if anything useful survived.

Or anyone *useless*.

Nothing.

During the backside of the storm, the cut eroded even more, then suffered a massive cave-in. Tons of beach swallowed Dipp and the phony box, along with John Singer's fortune. Events beyond human control were best left alone, though they still possessed value.

Ryder rubbed his chin, picturing Julia's half-buried pickup—a sad monument to the past twenty-four hours.

He drained the final inch of his soda, then tossed the bottle into the back seat. Instead of reaching for another, he slid two fingers inside his shirt pocket and retrieved a large diamond ring.

Value.

He'd admired the stone umpteen times that morning, the brilliant sea-sky facets set in white gold. Ryder wasn't sure how Julia came across such finery, but she'd almost bargained it away to some hotshot crop duster. However, Mr. Hotshot was fonder of cash than jewelry.

And Ryder?

Happy to oblige the green.

He dropped the ring back into his pocket and grinned.

In hopscotch, freedom won every time.

CHAPTER 35

Later that afternoon, Mick walked around the immediate area for a looksee. Many of the beach homes and businesses were badly damaged or destroyed. Folks who'd not fled to higher ground attended to their properties, some extending a brief wave. Mick mimicked the gesture, though was too weary to stop and visit.

He spoke into a gentle gulf breeze. "Guess I should get a pry bar from the basement and begin removing plywood." He heaved a sigh, wishing someone were there who cared about his intentions.

Someone?

"Yes."

Who appreciates your carpentry talents?

"Why not. A lovely someone to laugh with. Hold. Perhaps kiss."

Too bad Ryder's already gone.

"Badum-tish." Mick imitated a drum roll followed by a rimshot. "Nothing like a vaudevillian punchline." He felt ridiculous talking to himself. Even more so, responding to his own tired jokes. But absurd humor was his shield.

His impenetrable fortress.

Mick knew the deep pain of Julia's absence would eventually breech all barriers. At first, owning up to the truth seemed the right move. In retrospect, she probably couldn't bear *his* troubled past alongside *hers*.

He released another sigh. The tragic elements of their life stories were mirror images. Worst of all, Mick represented the villain in both scenarios, which was why—on a subconscious level—she could probably never forgive him.

Which was a feasible explanation.

Except for her note.

The distant banging of hammers peppered into Mick's thoughts, followed by the buzzing of chainsaws. The sounds reminded him of the sweaty job at hand, so he trudged back to Roughshods. His skin itched, increasing his desire to bathe as the day grew hotter. Saltwater would be better than nothing. Plus, jeep-guy wouldn't be along for a while. Before retrieving the pry bar, Mick headed for the Gulf.

He'd not walked five steps when he a thought surfaced— pools of fresh rainwater might still dot the beach.

Guess we've both had a proper rain bath.

His own prior statements now haunted him, meaning Julia's responses would follow. Mick increased his pace.

If staying on the island dredged up too many memories, he'd walk away, leaving Ryder's advance payment in the red brick room. Just before the old cook left, he'd gunned the engine and handed Mick a large roll of bills.

"You won't have to rob no banks." Ryder punctuated the remark with a belly laugh while urging Frog out of the parking lot.

The sandy footpath between the dunes had vanished. Mick followed a series of washed out, crustacean-covered avenues, detouring around tangled piles of shredded insulation, building materials, and drift wood. His sneakers offered some protection from nails and decaying sea life, but he'd torn gaping holes above both big toes.

RUNNING DOWNWIND

"Great. These shoes aren't much better than Ryder's flip-flops." Mick envisioned Julia's smile about his hand-me-down wardrobe, then recalled her reaction about him losing his big toenails while snow skiing. Her initial delicate laugh made him wonder if he were falling in love.

That very hour.

The phrase was the most confusing line in Julia's note, though an instantly grand romance was what most couples desired.

The makeshift path disappeared, so he backtracked a short distance and located another, this one more treacherous than the first. Pieces of razor-sharp shells amplified the marine stench.

Beulah must've crunched conchs for a midnight snack.

Mick considered climbing over the dunes, however, the underbrush attracted snakes in droves. When visiting the shore as a kid, he'd nearly stepped on a poisonous sidewinder. No shoreside restroom facilities existed, and the sodas he'd chugged weren't particular. So, he'd headed behind the nearest privacy mound. Afterward, Mick was glad his bathing suit was already wet.

Reaching the hem of the beach, he spied the lighthouse. The hole in the top remained the only significant damage.

He shivered.

They could've died.

There's a beacon of hope.

"Hope for what?"

Julia was gone, leaving *hopelessness* in her wake. Ryder believed she left because of a letter. She'd mentioned writing her nanny. Perhaps the message was from Carmen. Hopefully, she and Paco were okay. Or maybe Julia's mother was involved.

The horde of possible reasons mattered least.

Because Mick lost the woman who mattered most.

He studied the lighthouse.

Somehow, they'd survived.

The next thing he knew, he was running. Not back to Roughshods, but to the treasure site. When Mick arrived, the deep cut was gone, but not the crumpled ruins of Julia's pickup.

He squeezed headfirst into the wreckage, ripping away tangles of fishing line, seaweed and hunks of driftwood. When he reached what resembled the cab, only half the windshield remained, so he shoved his upper body through into the driver's side, scooping out a mixture of sand and broken glass. The steering wheel—now blob shaped—wasn't connected, the seat cushion battered into foam rubber shreds, its innersprings bunched into wadded wire coils.

Mick tediously removed more sand and glass, then managed to balance on the dashboard, turn sideways and draw his legs inside. He raked most of the cushion debris clear with his feet. Bracing a foot against the jagged steering stump, he flipped onto his stomach. Reaching down with his right hand, he located the knob of the stick shift, unscrewed it, and stuffed it into his short's pocket.

Inching forward, he extended an arm into the passenger's side. No more glass, but at least a foot of sand.

Mick dug until his fingers bled.

Reached again.

Not yet.

Dig deeper.

Almost there.

Stretching with all his strength, he uttered a loud grunt. Then sucking in a huge breath, brushed away the remaining grit and located the latch button.

A hard index-finger-punch.

A soft click.

He released his breath and waited.

The glove box dropped open with a familiar squeak.

CHAPTER 36

After bathing in a clear, rain filled pool, Mick hiked back to Roughshods. Jeep-guy had come and gone. Parked in the shade was exactly what Ryder promised. The vehicle wasn't new—Army surplus. During a trial run, the engine only backfired once, the clutch less cantankerous than the one in Julia's pickup.

With your left foot, push the pedal all the way to the floor.

Mick stepped out of the jeep.

"If only I could push *her* from my thoughts."

His utterance followed him inside, where he changed clothes before hauling the groceries and drinking water to the pantry. Mick prepared two peanut butter & mayonnaise sandwiches, swallowing them in hurried bites, along with potato chips and a fried pie. After mixing a pitcher of instant iced tea, he stirred in a pouch of presweetened lemonade—his mom's recipe—then spent the remainder of the day removing plywood. As before, physical labor agreed with him. He hoped the task would occupy his muscles more than his mind.

This tea's not as satisfying as Julia's.

"Nothing is."

Mick dropped the pry bar and refilled his cup ... which was *her* cup ... the malt container he'd washed and saved.

Sallye would examine your motives.

"And Babin would wag his head and grin."

Mick's plan was to call them, as well as his parents, when the telephone lines were restored, but that could take weeks.

As dusk deepened over the island, he removed the final sheet of plywood, carried it down to ground level and stacked it with the others. Mick wasn't hungry, though knew he needed to eat something. The last time he'd been too depressed to eat was sailing solo in *No Qualms*, turning to whisky for nourishment.

Nourishment? More like self-induced amnesia.

"Because there was much to forget."

Mick plopped down on Roughshods's steps.

The paradox—the more he'd tried to forget Cherie, the more he'd clung to her memory. And now?

The same held true for Julia.

Except *she* was alive, which in a way hurt worse.

Throughout the afternoon, he'd sensed his emotions gradually freefall. During iced tea breaks he'd close *his* eyes and immediately picture *hers*.

Slate-colored beneath tears.

Silver above a smile.

After the hammers and chainsaws stopped, the cadence of her voice echoed through the dusk, while a steady Gulf breeze wafted sweet scents of her laughter.

Standing, Mick gazed skyward. Moisture laden clouds covered the moon. With no electricity on the island, night would quickly conquer day. In another ten minutes, he'd no longer be able to distinguish the stairs. And what good would he be to Ryder with broken limbs.

That's why you're a house-SITTER.

Mick ignored himself. He'd told Ryder he'd stay but now wasn't sure. Wasn't certain of anything ... except

RUNNING DOWNWIND

what was stashed in the pantry. Besides the current food supply, the pantry was where Ryder secured the wine.

For safe keeping.

A man of such varied background most likely squirrelled a few bottles of something harder close by.

When things got complicated.

When he needed to simplify his troubles.

Heading up the stairs, Mick swore he'd only have a few sips. Nothing like *No Qualms*. Just enough refreshment to relax and refocus.

He dug the stick-shift ball from his pocket, the object upon which he and Julia—accidently—first held hands, a reminder to stay sober and avoid future complications.

Remember what else is stored in the pantry?

Mick returned the ball to his pocket. From the glovebox, he'd rescued Julia's little mother-of-pearl Bible, placing it on the topmost shelf next to the fried pies.

In case she returned.

In case she'd consider forgiving him.

He didn't believe in miracles, but the Bible was untouched by the storm.

Guess Beulah was a God-fearing gal.

"Gal?" he laughed. Ryder's hand-me-downs must ultimately have a vocal effect on the wearer. Next, Mick would be trading bawdy stories with fishermen's wives.

Inside Roughshods, Mick lit a lantern. If Ryder had a flashlight, he'd taken it with him. Mick glanced over to where he'd last seen Julia, to the stack of towels where she'd pinned her note. He'd pondered her words all day, yet none of them corroborated her leaving, especially after what they'd been through. Therefore, his earlier conclusion about *him* representing the villains in her life must be correct. For whatever reason, she couldn't separate Mick from the two men who'd betrayed her.

That's why Mick needed the booze.

He entered the pantry, setting the lantern on the floor across from the wine, the shelves now stuffed with groceries. If there *were* whisky, it was most likely hidden on the top shelf behind the pies.

He reached up with his right arm.

"Ouch."

He'd strained a tricep in the pickup's wreckage and was forced to use his left. "I should've been born a lefty. Might've helped me in baseball, a much less caustic career." Mick decided not to return to Broadway. Earning a living would eventually loom large, making carpentry an interesting option.

Standing on his tiptoes, he felt a bottle behind the pies, yet couldn't reach it. Even though the lantern glowed faintly into the kitchen, dimness prevailed. Retrieving the step stool required a lot of hunting.

Mick jumped, still missing his mark. On the second attempt, he leapt harder, hooked a finger around a bottle and drug it off the shelf. And then a dozen more followed, along with a tumble of fried pies ... and the Bible. Several bottles crashed into the kerosene lantern, spilling fuel and fire.

Mick scurried to the sink.

No water.

He ran back to the pantry and grabbed a large bag of flour. It broke prematurely, dumping onto the wrong spot. Dropping to the floor, he scooped with his hands. There wasn't enough and the flames continued. Kerosene doused the little Bible. Mick stood and tried to kick it away from the fire, but the Bible *was* the fire.

Carmen and Paco's gift to me.

"Save Julia's Bible. Now." Mick ran for the stack of towels but tripped and fell in the darkness. He struggled to stand, unable to push with his strained right arm. He immediately repositioned himself, then tried with his left. The fall injured his ankle, which refused to bear weight.

"God. Help me."

Mick made another failed attempt to stand, returning to the pantry on hands and knees. Out of desperation he raked what groceries he could reach onto the fire. The blaze smothered.

Slumping lower in the pitch darkness, Mick knew Julia's Bible was ruined.

Knew it was his fault.

His last chance to earn her forgiveness failed.

Miserably.

"Thanks for the Almighty leg-up." Mick scowled. "That's what I get for asking."

There *had* been two positives during the fiasco. Since he'd removed the plywood and every window was open, smoke wasn't an issue. As far as he could tell, none of the falling whisky bottles broke.

Mick continued his downward spiral in the black stillness, sitting cross-legged in the soot. A cool gust of wind drafted around him, igniting a small flame from the ashes. He watched light penetrate darkness.

Mick scoffed. "The beacon of hope. Just enough glow to open a little whisky." He'd figured on finding a small amount, not enough for a miniature distillery.

When a man decides what's important, dedication ain't that sparse.

"I've decided." Mick's words bounced off the pantry walls. "I'm dedicated to the hard stuff until God show's me something softer."

Mick reached behind his back and grabbed one of the bottles.

It wasn't whisky.

But a grape soda.

CHAPTER 37

By the time the hammers and chainsaws resumed their eight a.m. blue-collar symphony, Mick ate breakfast and took inventory of what the fire ruined—mostly dry food products, along with the bulk of the fried pies. Badly singed, the lower pantry shelves needed to be replaced. Minor smoke damage darkened the kitchen walls, none smudging the dining room nor Ryder's quarters. Fortunately, his door was shut.

A large kettle whistled time to brew more coffee. Mick filled an aluminum drip pot with fresh grounds, poured in boiling water and waited. His ankle hurt, though wasn't discolored or swollen. What he'd feared to be a sprain was a minor twist.

He double checked the cooktop, making sure the burner was off. Most beach homes and businesses stored their own supply of liquid propane. Numerous tanks broke loose during the storm, but not Roughshods's. Since the fridge and stove ran on gas, Mick was able to store and fry bacon and eggs. Someone smelling the smoky aroma might bang on the screen in hopes the restaurant was open. No one had, nor even dared. Before Ryder left, he'd mounted a large, spray-painted sign out front:

AIN'T OPEN! DON'T ASK!

If nothing else, the man was blunt.

After the fire, Mick experienced more than just altered thinking. He'd suffered a humbled Great Awakening, realizing—among other revelations—that Ryder possessed a unique "gruff wisdom."

Mick poured another cup and sat atop the prep table. He was exhausted, yet energized, convinced of Julia's return.

When?

He wasn't sure.

Why?

A combination of fear and logic.

Yesterday he'd run a panicked marathon, every step pitting Julia's note against her leaving. When he couldn't solve the mystery, he blamed himself. Mick felt like a skydiver with a torn parachute, too depressed to mend the tear. In the past, he'd remedied perplexing situations with the contents of a whisky bottle.

Which now scared him.

Standing, he walked over to a window and peered outside. Beulah passed less than thirty-six hours ago, but the island was already crawling with activity. The little drive-up malt shop was rumored to reopen in a day or two. If Julia were back, they'd be two of the first customers.

Julia.

An intelligent, reasonable woman who possessed a deep relationship with God, just like Cherie.

The problem—much about Christianity wasn't realistic. Cherie argued if God were so easily explained, there'd be no need for faith.

True.

Her argument was also ... reasonable.

Most Christians also believed in miracles, which weren't logical. Some would expound that Julia's Bible surviving the storm was miraculous. However, a glove box is a small, enclosed area offering excellent protection.

RUNNING DOWNWIND

Mick sighed.

He wasn't sure if faith played a part, but something unexplainable happened to him inside the pantry. Yes, he thought he'd grabbed a whisky bottle. No, a grape soda wasn't a miracle. Why? Because he'd known—just momentarily forgotten—that Ryder parked his lighthouse stash there. In fact, Mick had offered to help Ryder with his bulky box of soft drinks, then fled in search of Julia, finding her with the hatchlings as the storm began to rage.

He still felt terrible about her Bible, which wasn't as charred as he'd first believed. What convinced him of Julia's imminent return was the flame's reappearance after the fire was out. He'd scoffed about the flicker being *a beacon of hope* because deep down, he fought truth. That's why he'd challenged God to produce something *softer*.

God had.

By awakening Mick to his own self-destruction, he'd experienced a glimmer of heavenly light. A true *beacon of hope* he'd never believed existed. More than mere feeling was a deep and gentle knowing.

Mick rinsed out his coffee cup and retreated outside to Roughshods's deck. A stiff, southeasterly breeze cooled the busy morning. Facing the sea, he propped a foot atop the railing. Julia's forgiveness wasn't a sure thing, but he'd do all she'd suggested in her note. In addition, he'd somehow recreate the lighthouse lamp, shinning a bold beam for the Lady.

He focused upon the distant horizon.

Perhaps he'd discover a mirror piece.

And then ...

Find love that very hour.

CHAPTER 38

Mick worked tirelessly, expecting everything and nothing ... at the same time. He restored the pantry first, locating all needed materials in the basement, including paint. Realizing his version of a better design might not fit Ryder's definition, Mick refrained from major improvements.

Because of the fire, he was leery of using the kerosene lanterns in case of another accident. So, he kept the windows fully uncovered, working when there was natural light. At night, he lit a few wax tapers from the hundreds hoarded down in the basement. A toppled candlestick wouldn't spill ignitable liquid.

On day fourteen, the electricity suddenly returned. No gleeful shout shook the island, but after breakfast Mick heard a comforting hum. The Jax Beer clock was back in business.

Another week passed before anyone ignored Ryder's sign and inquired about the restaurant. On the next day around noon, two men wearing western suits with Stetsons tromped up the stairs. The shorter man banged on the screen.

Mick had just fried a hamburger steak for lunch, presuming the men smelled the aroma. He'd barely reached the door when they flashed their badges, introducing themselves as Texas Rangers.

"Come on in." Mick had recently phoned his parents, agent, and Babin—Sallye wasn't home. Unless she was in one of her "moods" and wanted Mick hauled in for deeper analysis, he had no clue why the authorities squeezed their hats inside Roughshods's dining room.

The taller ranger spoke. "We need to visit with Hugh Ryder."

"I'm sorry, he's not here."

"Know where he went?"

"New Mexico."

"Know when Mr. Ryder will return?"

"He didn't say." Mick might've admitted, Santa Fe, if the Ranger had pressed.

The shorter handed over a photograph.

Dipp.

The taller continued. "This dangerous convict escaped from the state penitentiary in Huntsville a few weeks back. We just dredged his stolen pickup out of the bay. Have you seen him?"

Mick nodded and returned the photo. "He was here."

"When?"

"A couple of days before Beulah hit."

"Did he mention why?"

"He was looking for Ryder. Said they'd been roommates in college. There's some big class reunion scheduled. This guy claimed to be the social chairman."

The Rangers traded glances, though remained stone faced.

"I see." The taller dug a business card from his coat pocket. "Please, have Mr. Ryder call when he returns."

As soon as they drove away, Mick dropped the card into the cash register, glad he wasn't interrogated more fully. He should've offered additional information but didn't want to get Ryder into trouble. The man wasn't perfect yet took Mick in, provided for his needs, and hid his identity.

RUNNING DOWNWIND

Or tried to.

Dippy simply earned his due. He'd not only threatened Julia's life, but her dignity.

Her privacy.

Mick spoke to the Jax Beer clock. "Good thing the Rangers didn't press for clues about Cue Ball's current location."

Mick chuckled.

Sleeping with the coyotes was the most truthful answer.

A few days after the Rangers' visit, Mick decided how he'd recreate the powerful lighthouse beam. He'd been down in the basement enjoying the overhead fluorescent, when he realized the door to the red brick room was no longer locked. Instead of *true treasure*, he discovered blobs of yellow glass. Close to classifying Ryder a certifiable lunatic, Mick noticed a newspaper article beneath of one of the pieces about a Fresnel lens.

"Of course." Mick couldn't help but shout. "Anyone in showbiz should've recognized it." Even though theatrical stardom was his past life, he had an idea. Build a pyramid of shelf-like, wooden platforms in the lighthouse's vacant lamp room. Atop the platforms, mount candles stuck in empty grape soda bottles, magnified by the larger lens pieces.

"Why not," he reassured himself. "The concept's doable."

Mick hauled tools and lumber up the winding staircase. First, he constructed an improvised landing over the one that nearly fell. The task proved challenging. More difficult were the memories associated with what could've occurred. Still, he awakened each morning with renewed energy.

At dusk, three days after he'd initiated the plan, the job was complete. His makeshift Fresnel lens resembled a modern Christmas tree, more than a rounded glass beehive. Upon lighting the candles and repositioning the glass hunks ...

The lamp worked.

Sort of.

Instead of forming a single powerful beam, brilliant light shot in every direction.

Mick's eyes watered.

"A lighthouse shines for the Lady," he whispered, picturing the *real lady* he so desperately sought.

CHAPTER 39

For days afterward, Mick climbed the lighthouse steps before sunup to light the lamp's candles and watch for the Lady. Yesterday, he'd viewed something ghost-like hovering out beyond the breakers. Probably a low flying pelican, or wisp of thick fog. He'd expected to glimpse dolphins, particularly the mother and her new calf.

But hadn't.

Maybe Beulah drove them into deeper water, and they'd not yet returned.

Julia hadn't either.

Since completing the homemade Fresnel, keeping his hopes alive was harder. Where his appetite soared for three weeks, he now existed on saltines, spoons of peanut butter and endless cups of coffee. Once, he drove the jeep over to the mainland to see if there was a letter from Julia. The postmaster found nothing with Mick's name attached, so he'd motored back across the causeway in a sour mood.

Today, instead of rising early, he considered sleeping in. But as always, awakened long before the dawn.

Mick sat up on the side of his bed. All the self-imposed projects were complete.

He yawned.

After more than a month he'd heard nothing from Ryder. Mick didn't want to leave Roughshods unattended yet needed to move on before losing the desire. If he stayed, the ever-increasing emptiness would inhabit all that was left of him.

After dressing, Mick exited his bungalow and headed for the lighthouse. The sky never boasted as many brilliant stars. Instead of climbing the stairs to light the lamp, he walked to the water's edge and gazed heavenward until the last glittering remnant faded. What Ryder said about admiring his Maker's handiwork held true. Mick wished he'd learned the maxim earlier in life, perhaps making a difference in his relationships.

He sighed.

Too bad his *time* and *dedication* hadn't brought Julia back.

Mick stepped into the sea, just as the sun's first rays reached over the edge of the earth. Turning to leave, something caught his eye.

Reflective.

Shiny.

Tumbling in the surf.

A mirror piece?

Could it be?

He bent down and retrieved the egg-sized object before it disappeared beneath the sand. Mick had never glimpsed anything like it, the tiny mosaic bits of polished pyrite too numerous to count. It reminded him of a geode turned inside out. And as he watched new daylight spread pink and orange above the watery horizon, the entire piece glowed. He held it at eye level, steadily staring until he saw himself.

Until he grasped the scope and reflection of all which lay about him.

At first, Mick thought he was trapped in a delayed night dream, the idyllic scene vanishing into guilt-ridden insomnia. Or perhaps a vision. Didn't those who balanced the frayed tightrope connecting grief with disappointment sometimes see things?

But there, right there, inside the mirror's concave boundaries appeared a woman walking barefoot in the surf, holding hands with a child. Mick watched, fully entranced until the image stepped into focus.

"Mick?"

He turned, and there stood Julia, smiling.

Mick couldn't speak.

"This is Maria. My child."

He swallowed hard. "Your ... baby?"

"Yes."

She was the most striking little girl he'd ever seen, a replica of her mother. Mick couldn't move. A slow tear slid down his cheek, trailed by another.

Releasing her daughter's hand, Julia pointed toward a nearby group of small, colorful seashells. "Look, Maria, over there. Aren't they beautiful? They're not rocks, but you can add them to your collection."

"Ocean pebbles," the girl whispered.

As soon as the child scampered away, Julia stepped toward Mick, speaking in a low voice. "Those are the first words she's said all day. As you can imagine, we're still getting to know each other."

More than anything, Mick wanted to hold Julia in his arms, but somehow couldn't.

Not yet.

"Julia ... when—"

"Please. I need to finish."

His stomach cartwheeled.

Julia took a deep breath, then released it. "On the morning after the storm—while you slept—I entered the kitchen to brew coffee. Propped against the pot was a letter from my nanny."

"Carmen?"

"Yes."

"And Paco?"

"Please."

Mick nodded.

Julia glanced at Maria. "Mother lied about the stillbirth, ordering "the godless child" delivered to an orphanage in Mexico. Instead, Carmen and Paco raised Maria themselves, hiding her amongst their closest friends."

Mick nodded again, unsure how to respond.

"If only I'd known my baby was alive." Julia's eyes filled with tears. "She was two weeks old when I ran away to Dallas."

"Why didn't Carmen and Paco tell you?"

"They couldn't. Lahoma threatened great harm to anyone who uttered a word. Plus, finding me was impossible."

Julia swallowed. "Two years ago, Mother suffered a heart attack ... and ...."

Silence.

"The hard part wasn't her death, but the fact I didn't know."

Mick nodded.

"I can only imagine your questions when I left the island. Your pain. That's why I penned the note. The Lady's search for the mirror represented my own deepest longings. I shared the rest of the legend in case I didn't—"

"Come back?"

"Yes." She turned to watch her daughter. "The moment Mother died, Carmen and Paco told Maria about me. A month later they received my letter."

"And Carmen wrote back a reply."

Julia gazed out over the water. "I wasn't sure if Maria would agree to travel here, or even accept ... me." She faced him, her eyes once again brimmed with tears.

RUNNING DOWNWIND

"No tissues allowed on the beach." Mick grinned. "You'll have to use my shirt."

They laughed.

He took a step toward Julia, recalling the feel and fragrance of holding her close. "I love you."

Before she could respond, Maria returned, tugging on Julia's arm, handing her a brightly colored shell. Another one to Mick.

"Thank you." Mick took a knee, recalling the song, *Maria*, the melodic strains mixing with soft breeze. He faced the child and whispered.

"Ma-ri-a."

The natural rise and fall of the syllables resonated within his soul's deepest chambers. Mick opened his fingers, revealing the brilliant mirror piece.

Julia gasped.

"A Lady, who was a very brave princess, lost this long ago." Mick handed Maria the mirror piece. "She'd want you to have it.

"This very hour."

Standing, he reached a hand toward Julia, her eyes wide and silver.

Their fingers interlocked.

Mick pulled Julia into his firm embrace.

Her deep kiss filled his heart-shaped cavern.

THE END

ABOUT THE AUTHOR

Timothy Lewis is author of the bestselling novel, *Forever Friday*, which was translated into multiple languages and featured in *Reader's Digest Select Editions*. He's only the second *Reader's Digest* author of an inspirational crossover title in over twenty-five years. Reviewers on BookBub, Goodreads, Barnes & Noble, and Amazon compared his poetic prose to Nicholas Sparks. In an article for *USA Today*, a literary editor likened Tim to Garrison Keillor.

As a published playwright, Tim's penned more than twenty plays/musicals and over a hundred songs. His article, *Freighting on the XIT Ranch of Texas*, was published in the *Panhandle-Plains Historical Review*. Committed to help fellow writers, he cofounded the West Texas Writers' Academy, held annually at West Texas A&M University.

Mr. Lewis holds a bachelor's degree of Music Education (BMED) from Sam Houston State University, and studied master's level playwrighting at The University of Texas. Moreover, he's a graduate of The Institute of Children's Literature and a cowboy poet.

Tim and his wife, Dinah, live "happily ever after" atop the beautiful high plains of Texas.

If you've enjoyed *Running Downwind*, Tim would appreciate you writing a short review and posting on Amazon, Goodreads, and/or Barnes & Noble. To contact Tim, check his website, https://https://timothylewisbooks.com/

ANOTHER TIM LEWIS BOOK

Made in the USA
Middletown, DE
08 November 2022